LIGHT SEEKER

VOLUME 7

THE GREAT FORGET FANTASY SERIES

TERRY IRONWOOD

All rights reserved. No part of this publication may be reproduced, stored or transmitted in any form or by any means, electronic, mechanical, photocopying, recording, scanning, or otherwise without written permission from the publisher. It is illegal to copy this book, post it to a website, or distribute it by any other means without permission.

Copyright © 2025 by Terry Ironwood

This novel is entirely a work of fiction. The names, characters and incidents portrayed in it are the work of the author's imagination. Any resemblance to actual persons, living or dead, events or localities is entirely coincidental.

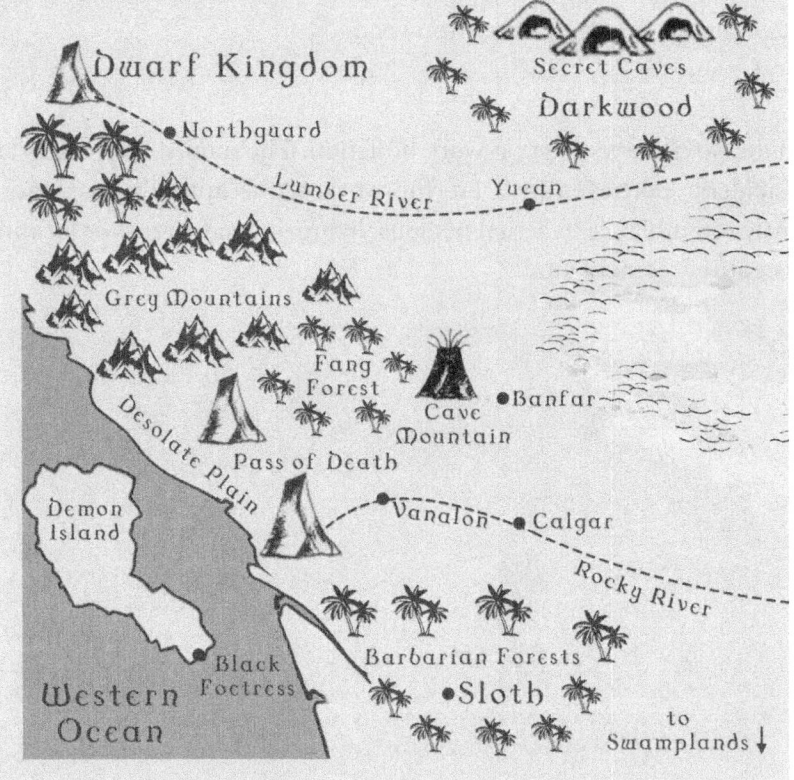

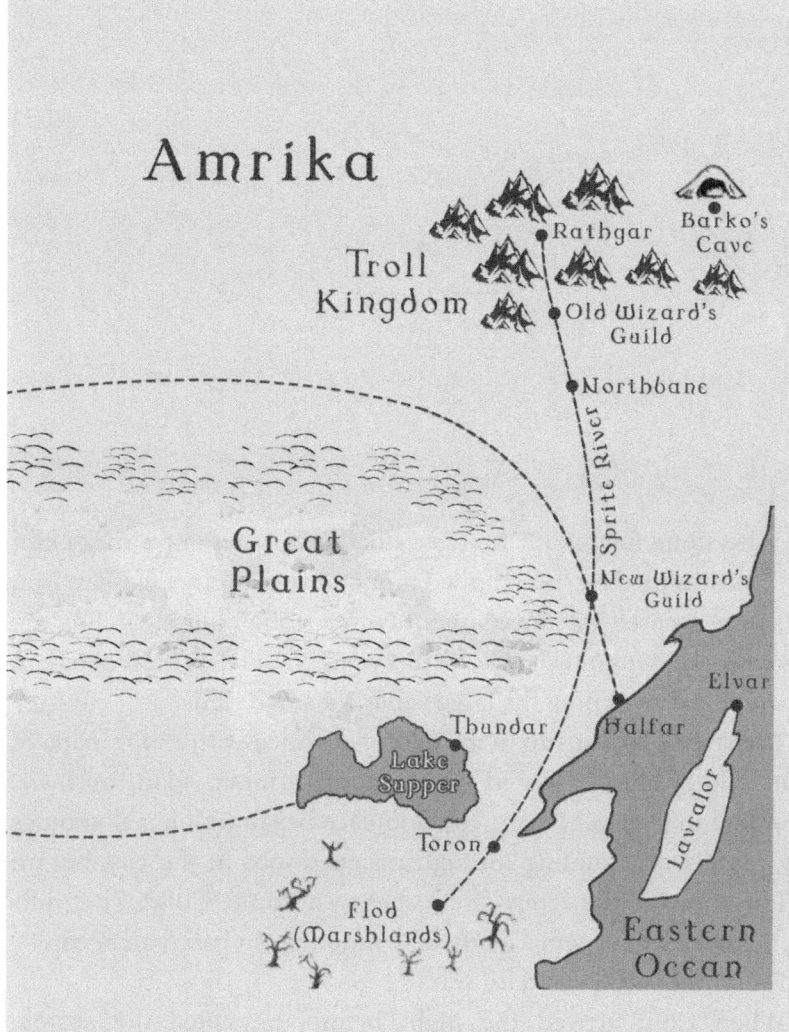

1

The stone fortress in Rathgar stood at the base of a rocky cliff surrounded by snowcapped mountains. The city's massive iron gates were securely anchored into fifty-foot stone walls encircling the troll capital. Mountain hawks with keen eyes circled high above in the wintry air, searching the large valley for small game.

The streets leading up to the keep were lined with shops made of stone. The wares consisted of weapons, armour, food, and ale. According to Queen Miriam, the populace began training as soon as they could walk, rotating through assigned jobs in the city, but all held positions in the army. The mages went to the Guild. The trolls had no monetary system. Goods were rationed out based on need.

Everything was geared for war.

When Chip arrived the night before, he noted the austere surroundings. It was a minimalist environment with unadorned stone walls and few embellishments beyond the occasional statue of King Jaggar. Queen Miriam had casually destroyed them with her Power as she walked up to the keep, taking her rightful place on the throne of the Troll Kingdom.

They had spent five days trekking to the capital from Barko's cave. The companions received the royal treatment, which in troll terms meant tents with braziers, food, and water. It was most welcome after the harrowing journey of the previous days.

The unicorn herd had patiently waited for them several leagues west of the frozen lake, weathering the elements until they caught sight of each other. The horses began prancing about excitedly as the boy ran across the tundra to embrace Redmane. The unicorn had trembled with excitement, nuzzling him affectionately while sending images of them running wild over the frozen landscape.

The small party rode the rest of the way on the magnificent animals, keeping pace with the trolls. The soldiers gave the horses a wide berth, respecting the Guardian's instructions not to eat them. After pledging their allegiance on the plateau before Barko's cave, the mages and soldiers treated the humans with newfound respect.

Upon arrival at the capital, the unicorns chose to graze in the valley while the companions stayed in the keep. The herd would not enter any city, especially one run by trolls.

The fortress itself backed onto a cliff. It was a monstrous structure with two stone towers connected by a walkway midway up that gave a clear view of the valley over the high walls. After a good night's sleep in a sparse but serviceable guest suite, they gathered in the throne room to discuss the path forward.

A huge stone table laden with what appeared to be various breakfast foods greeted them as they all took seats around the Troll Queen, who sat in the center with a warm smile. Miriam wore a plain but beautiful white dress and a diamond necklace. Her crown rested on the seat of the giant rock throne at the end of the room. The gesture clarified that she welcomed them as friends and did not need to flaunt her power or station. Her brother Striker, now the general, sat wearing a clean uniform to her right. Despite their threatening size and bark-like skin, the siblings gave off an air of respect.

"Good morning," she began in a high but clear voice. "I trust you all had a much-deserved rest." They nodded as one. "Good. Please sample any of the delicacies as we discuss the next steps."

Chip watched the different expressions play across his companions' faces with mild amusement as they looked at the breakfast fare with barely concealed apprehension. Mary, to her credit, even tried to smile.

"We thank you for your hospitality," Xander began, reaching for a slice of bread, which likely contained deer lice. "I am afraid our stay will be a short one. We must head west to continue our journey."

"West," Striker mused in a deep voice. "I didn't expect the Light Elves to be in that direction." Xander looked at Chip. The boy knew the wizard debated whether to disclose their findings in the archives room. He shrugged and nodded to the old man.

Xander sighed. "You have earned our trust, a leap of faith that all newfound friends must eventually take to move forward. The truth is we do not know the exact location of the Light Elves." Queen Miriam's eyes widened, and Striker released a low whistle. Chip was surprised he could manage it with fangs.

"You certainly had the trolls fooled, foremost my father." The prince leaned back. "So why head west?"

The wizard paused for a moment longer. "We seek a talisman that will guide us to the Light Elves. It is called a Seeing Stone."

"Interesting. And where might you find such a thing?"

Xander glanced around as if the walls might have ears. "In the Secret Caves within Darkwood Forest." The Troll Queen gasped. Striker's eyes widened, and Chip detected a hint of fear.

"That forest is cursed."

"I know. My father, Arkan, was the last to make it through and tell the tale. This was before he united the humans against the trolls and elves. Since then, reports of strange creatures have only increased. Darkness festers there and grows more malignant by the millennia. My brother Balor created the Ancient Forest near the new Wizard's Guild as a refuge for the gentle creatures of the land. Darkwood is the opposite. Tales abound of fanged and clawed creatures, wraiths, and strange lights roaming the fringes. The few who dared enter would run out screaming, claiming ghostly apparitions and terrifying sounds that make blood run cold. Knowing that witches inhabit the Secret Caves leads me to conclude that they had a hand in creating these heinous denizens. I fear dark magic created unspeakable things."

"What did your father find in the caves?" Miriam asked, still wide-eyed.

"Nothing. Only a residue of what he described as dark magic. I suspect the witches fled upon his arrival or burrowed deeper into the cave system until he departed. Arkan was the most powerful magic wielder of all the races at the time, and the young witch cult likely feared him. The passage Chip read from the book in the archives spoke of a nearly naked elf picking up a stone in the ice desert millennia ago and bringing it to a woman named Morgeth on the outskirts of Darkwood. This was five hundred years after the Great Forget, a couple of centuries before my father entered. She knew a way through the forest and led the elf into the Secret Caves. He described seeing old women with white eyes surrounding an altar. This is where he placed what they called the "Seeing Stone." Their sacred text, The Book of Seeing, ordained that someone in need would bring the stone to them. The elf was told it could show what a person was doing and lead you to them. You only had to say their name."

Miriam and Striker looked at the wizard without moving, apparently waiting to see if he jested. Xander remained silent.

The queen finally turned to her brother. "Goodness me. This is not what I expected." She looked back at the wizard. "We will help in any way we can, of course, but Darkwood is a place even the trolls fear to enter. The frozen desert is dangerously cold and nigh impassable in winter, but that forest is..." She looked down.

Striker put his hand on hers and surveyed the group. "Let's remember, there is always hope. The Guardian of the Races and six powerful wizards accompanied by seven skilled Protectors sit before us. If anyone can make it, they can." The prince smiled as best he could.

Chip wondered what stories the trolls had heard to make them so afraid of Darkwood. The stirrings of doubt entered his mind.

"You will need assistance," Miriam decided. "I will send a healing mage and a dozen warriors."

Xander looked like he would object but then nodded. "I will not refuse aid. I do not know what awaits us in those cursed woods, let alone the Secret Caves, so I gladly accept."

He looked at the others, who all agreed. Chip noticed trepidation on most of their faces. Striker was not one to show fear lightly.

"Do we march across the frozen desert straight to Darkwood?" the boy asked. "And follow the elf's path from long ago?"

"You would not survive," Striker warned. "Winter is underway. It would take at least ten days in the coldest temperatures you will ever feel. The wind can knock you off your feet, and storms descend out of nowhere. The sound itself can make you go deaf unless you stuff your ears. Even with the best furs, trolls have frozen to death. They traversed it millennia ago, but the ice desert has only gotten colder. If you use magic to generate warmth, it will eventually run out, leaving you defenceless."

"The unicorns would also freeze to death," Chip added. "They were never meant to live in such cold climates. The horses would have already struggled in these mountains if their magic hadn't ignited through the bond to keep them warm.

"What's the alternative?" Eleanor asked. She sat between him and Mary. The two women looked at the troll general.

"Skirt the edge of the ice desert, heading southwest. You will only experience the intense cold for a couple of days. I would head straight to the Lumber River and follow it to Yucan. It lies a day's ride south of Darkwood. You will need to resupply there anyway."

"What's in Yucan?" Chase asked from several seats over.

Eleanor looked at Mary, and they both hid smiles. Chip knew that his best friend had not been the most attentive student in their history class. The mischievous boy used the time to irritate Miss Owl, who loved the subject. Even Chip had dozed off on occasion after listening to her hour-long lectures.

"Yucan is the town where the lands of humans, trolls, and dwarves meet," Queen Miriam explained. "A Triumvirate rules it.

One dwarf, one human, and one troll form the governing body. It's the only city in Amrika where such a thing exists. Yucan is neutral. The soldiers keeping the town's peace comprise all three races."

"Yucan is proof that the races can coexist," Xander said. "Even thrive. It's a trading town."

Miriam nodded. "Our people barter furs in exchange for a range of items. The troll governor is Birch. I will send a mountain hawk to inform him of the change in leadership at Rathgar and urge him to prepare for your arrival. He will know the safest spot to enter Darkwood and give you provisions."

"Isn't it easier taking a boat up the river?" Ethrang asked as he broke a giant egg into his bowl and slurped it up. The skinny blond boy made a funny face and smiled.

"The Lumber River flows down the mountains from the Dwarf Kingdom," Mary said without looking at him. "To go upriver against the current, you would need a rowboat, which would be slower than riding."

"Especially on unicorns," Eleanor added.

"Makes sense." The orphan from Banfar shrugged and grabbed another egg. Mary watched with thinly veiled disgust.

"Queen Miriam? What are those white things?" Kristan pointed at a bowl with what looked to be small potatoes. His twin brother Thomas picked one up and held it between two fingers. It appeared to be moving.

"Oh, those are hard to find," Miriam gushed. "They are the giant fly larvae from our cave homes behind the fortress. It is late in the season to find any that have not pupated."

"Aren't they just big maggots?" Thomas asked, staring at the wiggly specimens.

"Yes, that's right!" The Troll Queen nodded vigorously, pleased with the interest.

"Pupate?" Ethrang whispered to Chase, who shrugged.

"Can't hurt to try it, brother," Kristan elbowed his twin, indicating that everyone was watching. Miriam leaned forward, excited to see his reaction.

Thomas turned abruptly to Kristan, then to the queen and back again with a pleading look.

"We don't have all day," Ethrang piped up, covering his smile.

The blond twin gulped. "Oh, alright. It's a delicacy, yes?"

Miriam nodded with a broad smile, her fangs gleaming. Thomas put half of it in his mouth and pressed his teeth together.

"Don't bite them—" The queen warned as the twin bit the larvae in half, causing a pus-like substance to spray sideways into Kristan's eye. The stronger twin shrieked, almost falling over before his eyes blazed bright blue to remove the foul substance. He sat back down, trying to pretend nothing had happened.

"You aren't supposed to bite them," the Troll Queen finished. "You swallow them whole. The pus has a rancid taste if you break them apart. Did you like it?"

Thomas stared at her for a long moment then swallowed. His lips twitched, and his eyes began to water. "Delicious," he managed.

Miriam beamed. "Take as many as you want. I can even have the caves searched for more before you go." Ethrang laughed out loud and then covered his mouth. The blond twin appeared unable to speak. Garth Stone watched the whole thing with an arched eyebrow.

Xander cleared his throat. "Queen Miriam, there are a few more items I would like to discuss before we conclude today." She nodded, giving him her full attention. "Can I pen a message to General Gunnar in Northbane instructing him to evacuate the city? I trust you will allow him a week to clear out?"

"Of course. It would take that long to get there anyway. I am happy you offered it in our negotiations. My trolls need to feel victorious after a millennium of war."

The weapons master let out a rare chuckle. "I do not wish to be Gunnar when he arrives back in Toron to explain that he has given up the High King's northernmost city. Dominor tends to look at things differently. We will likely have to smooth things over when we arrive at the capital with the Orb of Power, the Creator willing."

"Do you think the elves will give it up?" Miriam turned to Xander.

The wizard sighed. "No, I learned a long time ago that nothing is ever easy. However, difficult challenges can be the most rewarding. We must focus on one thing at a time."

"Well said," Striker added. "When things look impossible, focus on one task at a time."

"Any news on those two Dark Elves we spotted across the frozen lake several days ago?" Xander asked the general.

The troll's face took on a dark demeanour, and he squeezed a massive fist. "No, but we found two mages and a dozen trolls dead after they went missing near Barko's cave. The search party said the mages had been burnt to a crisp and the soldiers dismembered. They were sliced apart. We launched more patrols to scout the area but couldn't find anything. Then another storm hit, and we withdrew. Hopefully the culprits froze to death."

Xander's face hardened. "I only caught a glimpse of them, but the one with white hair may be an ancient Inner Circle member named Hagatha. She almost rivalled Arkan in Power and dealt death with impunity. She is ruthless and extremely dangerous. I do not know who the Dark Elf in green is, perhaps a Protector of sorts. If one man can cut apart that many trolls, he is a force to be reckoned with."

Garth Stone raised his eyes but said nothing.

"I cannot imagine that two Dark Elves could do such a thing," Striker muttered. "A dozen trolls...that's hard to imagine. There may be others."

"Continue sending out patrols," Xander said. "Make them larger, accompanied by your stronger mages. If this is who I think it is, then the Creator help us. Hagatha was notorious in the Elf Wars, killing many Light Mages. She is the mother to Bashan, the Depraved Elf." Chip looked over, startled. "She had a hand in guiding the Demon King to power."

"Should we try to find her?" Chip asked.

"No, she is cunning. We would waste time and energy. Hagatha knows we are looking for her and will remain well hidden. She may even have left the area. We will keep a vigilant watch during our travels. If we spy her, then we can attack as one. We need to find the Seeing Stone. Winter is underway, and I suspect our journey is far from over. Time is our greatest enemy. I want to leave at dawn and make for the Lumber River."

"I will handpick the soldiers and make preparations," Striker said. "I would join you but must remain to prepare our troops for the Last Battle. Unless you object, I recommend One Eye accompany you and direct the soldiers."

Garth shrugged. "I take no issue."

Striker nodded. "He is crude but cunning. His loyalty, once pledged, is solid. The captain is fearless and an excellent fighter. He also understands not to eat the horses."

"Fearless and cunning is what we need," the weapons master agreed. "I can assist you with preparations. I would like to look at your armoury, if I may. I'm running a little low on weapons."

"As you wish."

"Queen Miriam, may I ask you something?" Chip said.

"Of course. The Guardian of the Races does not require permission."

The boy smiled. "We are all on the same side. Courtesy helps to achieve that end. I wanted to ask you about your father's crown. May I see it?"

Miriam's eyes flashed a dazzling blue, and she reached out to the stone throne. The crown flew across the room into her hand. She placed it before him.

Chip stared at the slightly red circular stone—twelve identical points formed around the top like upside-down fangs. For a moment, he marvelled at the history the crown had witnessed over millennia. Jaggar's father, King Malkor, had worn it long ago before falling to Luminor's hand.

The boy picked it up and immediately felt a deep-rooted magic. There was something else too. A...darkness. He looked closer at the inside and saw tiny runes carved along the perimeter.

"It holds great Power," he said. "The runes contain the magic, likely inscribed by Barko as one of their bargains. The material is strange. It does not feel like a normal rock."

"It isn't," the queen stated. "We call it painite. It is an apt name for the pain required to unearth it. Only one stone was ever found in our deepest mines to the north. Malkor linked with his High Mages to carve it, such was its hardness. It was then he realized the stone could store Power. Since my grandfather's death, Jaggar has fed the crown magic for four millennia. Students must funnel their Power into it daily for a month to pass our endurance test."

"It seems certain materials on Earth can store magic, especially with runes." Chip placed it back on the table. "I sense a risk to wearing it, though. The runes can let something else in, creating dark intent. I would wear it sparingly and only in battle. It has more than magic stored in it."

The queen looked surprised.

"Very astute, young man." Xander looked at the queen. "The Guardian is right. Objects or talismans with runes are dangerous. The witches in Banfar used to sell the citizens charms for good luck, but the runes on them eventually brought the wearer ill fortune. Be wary of its Power. Save it for the Last Battle."

Miriam nodded. "Sage advice. Barko would be the one who inscribed those runes. The wearers of this crown have committed evil deeds." She seized her magic again and levitated it back to the throne. The Troll Queen then surveyed the table with a broad smile.

"Now, who wants dessert?"

2

The companions gathered at the gates of Rathgar at dawn. A cold wind blew in from the north, cascading down the valley to blanket the city in frigid air. Dark clouds formed in the west, daring them to enter its dark embrace. The sun looked small and cold, spilling weak light over the eastern horizon. The brooding stone mountains withdrew their shadows grudgingly, allowing the wan light to glisten off the snow.

Redmane was already leading the herd across the massive valley towards the boy, neighing musically. Chip smiled as their minds connected. The horses were excited to be off. Seventeen beautiful unicorns ran in spearhead formation, the tip a red blur.

"They are elegant and proud," Striker said, coming to stand with him. The troll general was a massive man, well over seven feet tall. "And loyal to you."

Chip looked up and nodded. "I am grateful for them." Redmane slowed to a canter and stopped before the boy, nuzzling his shoulder. He rubbed the magnificent animal's neck then turned to the others.

The group before him consisted of six wizards, seven Protectors, one healing mage named Daria, and a dozen massive, mean-looking trolls led by One Eye. The captain displayed a fiendish grin. For once, Chip welcomed his ferocity. They would need it in the days ahead.

Queen Miriam stood behind them all, a sad look on her face. The boy knew she would miss the companionship. Eleanor and Mary had become her friends, likely the only ones she ever had. Growing up under her father's shadow, restricted and controlled all those years, must have been terrible. But now she had broken free like a small bird opening its wings to fly.

The Guardian leapt atop Redmane and addressed the group. "We thank you, Queen Miriam, for your hospitality, kindness, and strength. Without you, I would not be sitting astride this beautiful animal."

The queen beamed. One Eye stared hungrily at the unicorn then looked up. The boy noticed his reaction.

"The unicorns are not food. Let me make that very clear. I bind you, Captain One Eye, to your pledge of allegiance. Your mage and soldiers are most welcome to assist us in this crucial journey. The fact that trolls and humans can work together after millennia of war is a testament to the power of forgiveness and a turning point in our history. When we defeat the Demon King in the Last Battle, the Creator willing, I want to usher in a permanent peace between our races. This journey is the first step. Once we find the Light Elves, the races will convene in Toron for a meeting of the High Council. We will send word through pigeon. Please instruct the mountain hawks not to eat them anymore."

"Already done," Striker assured.

"Good." The boy looked at them all in the rising sun. His red cloak billowed in the cold wind. "So begins our journey to seek the light in the darkness. A great evil amasses in the west, casting a long shadow. We must stand against it. We must fight it until we have nothing left. We carry the hope of the world." He paused, sitting tall, watching them nod in agreement. "In essence, we are light seekers. It is an honour to ride with you."

The trolls thumped their chests, and the humans cheered.

They began loading the unicorns with food and gear. Queen

Miriam approached as he dismounted to help. The boy looked up at the towering troll. She cupped his head with two massive, gnarled hands.

"May the Creator shine on you, Guardian of the Races. You have freed the trolls from bondage. We will stand proudly with you until the end."

She could snuff out his life with one squeeze, yet Chip felt no fear. The queen's eyes became wet. He saw her unimaginable suffering over countless years, yet she had emerged through it with unbreakable determination. He had no doubt she would be a great queen. A lump formed in his throat as she cradled his cheeks with her thick skin.

"You freed your people," he said. "We only showed you it was possible. May the Creator shine on you."

Miriam released her grip and covered her mouth as more tears formed. The boy impulsively hugged the Troll Queen. Cheers sounded, and he saw trolls lining the battlements, bellowing as they thumped their chests. Striker stood to the side and bowed his head. Chip was unsure if a human had ever embraced a troll, let alone their leader. Mary and Eleanor came over and hugged Miriam as well. To the right, One Eye had a strange look on his face. The lines around his eye softened, and his shoulders relaxed. The troll captain stared at them with a look a child would give a doting parent. He stepped back and looked down, unused to the emotion.

Eleanor released Miriam and clasped her hand. "We will see you again soon." The Troll Queen wiped her eyes.

"I will be waiting."

The others said their farewells, and in short order, the companions were riding away at a light canter. The trolls jogged beside them, led by One Eye. The towering snow-capped mountains ringing the valley funnelled them west towards a broad opening leading to the frozen desert. They followed a thin trail over hard-packed snow for the better part of the morning before the mountains fell away.

Chip stared in awe at the vista before him. As far as the eye could see, there was only white emptiness. The clouds had moved closer, roiling and dark, hovering over the ice desert like a dark spider. The wind picked up immediately, emitting a forlorn mourn, a lonely sound matching the landscape. Patches of brown sand appeared and disappeared as the snow swirled into piles, then quickly vanished. It was a moving landscape, forever changing yet remaining the same. Nothing could grow here.

The boy felt something in his bones and instinctively sent his presence out. The others stopped to watch as his eyes blazed a bright red. It was faint at first, but then he sensed something in the ground. It was massive, extending out as far as his presence would allow. He knew it was not a lifeform but rather a...residue. Someone or something had released unimaginable magic, so powerful that it had impregnated the land. There was something else that startled him...a familiarity. The type of magic seemed like his but was so faint he could barely sense it.

"What is it?" Xander called over the wind, his cloak whipping sideways.

Chip turned, eyes still blazing. "Great magic has been used here, like mine, but I can't be sure." Xander's eyes suddenly shone bright blue as he probed with his mind.

"Yes. It is so subtle that you would assume it is simply energy from the land itself. Yet this land carries no life forms. The energy is in the ground. It is vast. I do believe this is the source of the Great Forget."

The boy nodded. "I have never felt anything like it. Perhaps the Seeing Stone will provide more answers." The wizard agreed, and they both released their Power.

Chip turned Redmane south, hugging the mountains to their left, which had ended in jagged cliffs. There would be no reprieve from the wind or shelter in this inhospitable place. Chip shivered, pulling his cloak tighter. They continued for the remainder of the afternoon, the temperature steadily dropping. The wind grew bolder as the sun disappeared behind the dark clouds now spreading south.

"A storm is coming," One Eye shouted above the rushing air as he jogged alongside the Guardian. At least the trolls didn't have to slog through mounds of snow, for the wind swept it away as quickly as it formed. "We should continue into the night until it forces us to stop. The tents won't hold in this. We can camp against the cliff wall, wrapped in blankets, for a few hours. Increase the pace. We can keep up. Running keeps us warm."

Chip nodded, urging Redmane forward. He knew if the unicorns had their way they would gallop until the ice desert was far behind them, yet the boy restrained the animals. They needed to keep pace with the trolls.

Things began to go from bad to worse. Thunder erupted overhead as the sun set in the west. The wind increased in intensity, swirling snow around them until their eyes crusted. Chip felt a deep-seated cold, worse than he had ever experienced from the elements. The boy realized that going straight across the ice desert would not be survivable. Even the trolls, with their bark-like skin, could not withstand such an environment. The heat from the great magic released five millennia ago had disappeared, leaving a cold, dead land. He began to feel concerned, especially for the unicorns.

Chip was about to enter Redmane's mind to soothe him when the clouds opened. Jagged lightning danced across the heavens, lighting the landscape for a moment in stunning clarity. Snow started pouring down in huge sheets, buffeting them without mercy. The sound of the wind increased to a frenzied whine. One Eye was shouting something, but the boy couldn't hear. The huge troll produced bits of cloth and pointed at his ears.

Another peal of thunder sounded, shaking the ground. The unicorns neighed in alarm. The whine of the wind turned into a high-pitched shriek, and then all his senses were afire. He was in a maelstrom of sound, light, and freezing cold. With the sun gone, the temperature plummeted until he began to have difficulty breathing. The air burned his lungs, and he started losing feeling in his extremities. Chip looked down and realized One Eye was pressing bits of cloth in his hand.

He couldn't feel it.

The unicorns formed a spearhead, and a dull hum sounded.

Their magic flared to life, forming a protective shield. Heat entered his body, and he could breathe again. The sound of the wind muted. He looked at the others and saw relief on their faces. Everyone stuffed cloth in their ears and pulled their cloaks tighter. They had no choice but to carry on.

The black stone wall of the cliffs added to the darkness, but above him, he could see a narrow strip of stars between the clouds and the cliff top. More lightning flashed, followed by bone-jarring peals of thunder.

They pushed on. The trolls ran beside them, faces grim. Chip knew Striker had hand-picked them, and they would not complain. Their skin was a natural barrier to the cold but could only withstand so much. The boy bent his head, using the dark cliffs for guidance, and continued south.

The unicorns maintained the shield for several hours before it failed.

Chip sensed it as his body temperature dropped and the wind shrieks increased. Then it fell away completely. Like a hammer striking an anvil, the storm's full force struck them. The wind knocked him sideways like a battering ram. Redmane tried to stay upright but couldn't hold his footing. They both went down.

Chip pushed off to avoid getting crushed and landed on hard-packed sand. The air left his lungs as he rolled and scrambled to his feet. He turned in time to see a troll flying sideways as it slammed into his chest, sending them both tumbling towards the cliff. He couldn't breathe for a long moment, and a memory of his rib sticking out after a huge white ape charged into him flashed across his mind.

Hands grabbed his shoulders and lifted him to his feet. He managed to look up, still trying to breathe, as a flash of lightning illuminated a horror scene. The unicorns and riders were lying on their sides in a tangled mess. The trolls were trying to reach them, but a gust of wind picked them up and threw them back towards the cliffs. Chip tried to seize his magic as the hands holding his shoulders disappeared. Before he could, a wall of air picked him up like a rag doll and carried him away.

The boy flew towards something huge and dark. He needed his Power. The Wall appeared in his mind, and he desperately tried to subdue his fear. Despite being in the open, there was a terrible claustrophobic feeling to the wind as it enveloped him in a cocoon he couldn't escape.

A jagged stream of lightning erupted across the clouds as he flew headfirst towards the cliffs, outlined for a moment in jagged clarity. A dark figure to his left struck the stone wall before him, and he watched the troll's head explode like a ripe melon. He put his hands out but knew they would do no good. Before he struck the cliffs, the boy screamed one word.

One word that could save him.

"Eleanor!"

The Wall in his mind shattered with rage. Chip flung his Power out in a cushion of air along the cliff wall on both sides, trying to protect everybody. He was a fraction too late. His hands struck the cliff wall before the air solidified, breaking on impact. Intense pain ran up both arms, and he watched in slow motion as his body came to a halt in the compressed air, but not before a sharp point of rock pierced the center of his forehead.

Blood ran down his face, but he ignored it. The boy landed on his feet and turned around. Red coils of Power ran around his body as he gave into his rage.

The others were being flung about like bits of straw, with several bodies flying into the cliff wall. Thankfully, his cushion of air held. The unicorns were a tangled mess, several with broken legs. Xander, Eleanor, Ethrang, and the twins had seized their Power to bring the flying bodies down to the ground. Chip walked forward, eyes blazing in his blood-covered face, and extended his broken hands to form a massive shield around them all. The wail of the wind abruptly disappeared, and the screams of pain from the humans and horses became audible. He pulled the writhing bodies apart with his magic, disengaging twisted limbs and resetting broken bones. The others joined in, including the powerful Yellow Level troll mage, Daria. She ran to the most grievously injured, repairing wounds with incredible precision and speed.

Mary was in rough shape. Her unicorn had landed on the small woman, crushing her ribs. Blood sprayed out of her mouth as she took her last breaths. Before Chip could react, Daria was there, filling her with intense yellow magic. The Blue Wing Leader's halted breathing slowed then became regular, and her ribcage expanded as the bones knitted together. The boy breathed a sigh of relief and turned to the cliffs. Two bodies were on the ground. The troll whose head got crushed was beyond saving. A dark-skinned Protector named Ward was on his side. He had survived all the trials of the Stone Kingdom, and Chip was not about to let him die here. The boy turned him over and gasped. He had struck the cliff wall face-first, knocking out all his teeth and cracking his orbital bone. One of his eyes hung out of its socket by a thick cord. Incredibly, he still lived.

Chip controlled his nausea as he worked to repair the man's face. His skull had also been fractured, and the boy knew there was little time. He could feel Ward's heart beating erratically as he worked. Chip struggled with the eyeball and then left it to mend his skull. It was not working.

Then the troll mage was there, and he watched her reopen the skull to release pressure and soothe the man's brain. She expertly melded the bones, then deftly reinserted the eyeball into its socket, tying it with many minuscule muscles. Daria whimpered as she worked, absorbing the pain. Chip watched in fascination, memorizing her technique. She reformed Ward's teeth and restored his collarbone. The Protector took a deep breath and bowed low.

"Thank you."

"It is my duty and privilege to help those in need," Daria said.

"You are the best I've ever seen, though a woman named Miss Owl might protest," Chip said with a smile before wincing from the pain in his hands.

The troll mage nodded. "I am the best in Rathgar. I cannot speak for other places." She took his hands without asking and infused them with soothing magic. The mage mended his bones, realigned his knuckles, then repaired his forehead. A wave of weariness and pain crossed her features, but she forced a smile. Chip put a hand on her shoulder.

"Thank you. It is good to have you with us."

The boy looked around to ensure nobody else needed assistance, relieved that all had regained their feet. He continued reinforcing the shield, surprised at how much Power it took to hold the wind back. For a moment, Chip thought he sensed someone using magic far to the north, but then it was gone. It could have been his imagination.

The Guardian turned to look at his companions. The unlucky troll thrown headfirst into the cliff wall was the only one who had not survived. The others were shaken but whole. He turned to the cliff while maintaining the shield and raised his hands.

"No, let me." Eleanor stepped forward, eyes blazing a ferocious brown with red chips.

He nodded and linked with her. "Take as much as you want."

The queen smiled and faced the cliff wall. Chip watched as she inserted their combined magic into the stone's base in a wide semicircle. Their power went through the rock like butter. She cut deep lines using their brown-red magic like a scythe. Far into the cliff she went, becoming one with the rock. Then a vibration sounded, and Eleanor stepped back, pulling a monstrous single piece of stone with her. The opening was the size of a house.

The boy felt her use more magic as the massive block of rock detached itself from the wall. The cliff shuddered as if losing its footing, but the sounds ceased. Everyone stepped around the rock and gasped. A fifty-foot-long rectangular cavern extended into the cliff wall. The huge piece of rock blocked most of the entrance, forming a natural barrier.

"Everyone in, unicorns included," the queen ordered. Redmane seemed to balk at being confined, but Chip sent him a series of images, and the horse neighed in understanding. The options were to go in the cavern or die outside. It was an easy choice. The companions picked up their belongings that hadn't blown away, ushered the unicorns in, and followed. There was more than enough room.

Once inside, the boy released the shrinking shield. The screaming of the wind returned, and lightning raced among the black clouds. Frigid air rushed around the corner like groping hands trying to pull them back out. Eleanor raised her arms and pulled the massive stone closer until only a tiny slit remained to allow airflow. The sound of the storm diminished to a faint rush. Xander released a blue ball of light, providing illumination.

"That was fun," Chase said to no one in particular. "I now know what an autumn leaf feels like."

Ethrang giggled. "It didn't matter which shape I chose. The wind still picked me up like a feather."

Chip turned to One Eye. "I'm sorry for your loss. I couldn't save him."

The captain waved it off. "There was no dishonour in his death. The Creator decided it was time."

The Protector, Ward, grunted. "I almost joined him. I wouldn't be here without the Guardian and Mage Daria."

One Eye shrugged. "It wasn't your time."

"Indeed." The dark-skinned Protector set his cloak on the ground. He was in superb physical condition, muscles rippling as he settled down like a cat.

Xander stepped forward. "We should take advantage of this respite and get some rest. The Creator willing, this nasty storm will blow over by morning."

"It is large but fast-moving," Garth added. "Sometime overnight, it should travel east over the cliffs."

"Is it normal to have such heavy storms on the fringes of the ice desert?" Mary asked the troll mage.

"Not normally," Daria said, "But the weather started acting odd a few weeks ago." The wizards shared a knowing look. "Few brave the fringes anymore, and the hardiest troll will not cross the frozen sands in winter. The good news is that by tomorrow evening, we should be out of the desert."

Everyone nodded, setting down their cloaks. Some pulled out

blankets if they were lucky enough to save their packs. Eleanor pulled out hers and came up to the Guardian.

"Is this spot taken?" she whispered with a smile.

"Yes, by both of us," the boy said quietly, grinning. They stretched out, and she snuggled close, resting her head on his shoulder. Chip closed his eyes, breathing in her scent of flowers and soap.

The wind coming through the crack became a soothing sound. Despite being trapped in a stone tomb, he felt safe and warm. He was about to ask her a question, but her slow, rhythmic breathing indicated she was already asleep. He followed her soon after.

3

A sliver of light shone through the rock entrance into the large rectangular cavern. Chip peered at it with fascination from half-lidded eyes. It looked like a ray of hope in a world of darkness. The sound of the wind had diminished, indicating the storm had finally moved on. He stretched his arms and then realized Eleanor was not beside him.

"It's about time," Chase said from across the room. "We thought you would sleep through the whole day."

Chip pushed himself onto his elbows. Everyone was up, huddled in different areas and talking in hushed voices. The unicorns were gathered at the far end. They all turned to stare at him.

"Awkward," he muttered, feeling a wave of guilt. "I'm ready when you are." The trolls chuckled.

"I guess humans like to sleep a lot," One Eye said, grinning. "Then again, you are the Guardian. Maybe that requires more rest. Would you like some larvae?" The big troll pulled out a wriggly white oblong thing from a bag. "They didn't freeze because I held them under my armpit."

Chip stared at him. "Uh, no thank you." He looked around. Ethrang was holding his mouth, letting out tiny squeaks of laughter.

The twins grinned from ear to ear. "However, I know Thomas likes them. He told Queen Miriam that, which made her really happy. He likes delicacies."

"Oh, nice. Most humans can't appreciate good food." The hairy, scarred troll walked over and deposited the wriggling specimen in Thomas's hand. The blond twin stood with a frozen smile on his face. One Eye waited in front of him. The young wizard took a breath and popped it in his mouth, swallowing it whole. His eyes bugged out and began to water, but he put on a brave face. Ethrang moved to the side and doubled over.

"Some of them got squished when the wind tossed me around. They released their pus on the others, so they aren't as good as normal." He popped a few from the bag into his mouth. "Still better than human food." The big troll offered Kristan some.

"Already full, I'm afraid," the stronger twin said, stroking his belly. One Eye shrugged and wandered away.

Chase tossed Chip a strip of cured meat. He took it gratefully.

Xander stepped forward with an amused expression. "Alright, if everyone is ready, let's pack up and be off. It will be a long, cold day, but we should be out of this cursed desert by nightfall."

The boy wolfed down his food as everyone gathered their belongings. When they were ready, Eleanor walked towards the cave entrance. Her eyes flared to life, and the massive stone began to vibrate. It slid to the left. A strong, cold wind rushed in to greet them. They moved out in single file.

A brown and white landscape greeted them as far as the eye could see. The tail end of the dark clouds was disappearing east over the cliffs towering above. The sun would not make an appearance until it crested the mountains. Everyone tied their packs back on the unicorns and saddled up. Chip urged Redmane south, hugging the cliffs. The wind had abated, but strong gusts still struck them, chilling them to the bone.

The boy turned to Xander as they rode. "I thought I sensed someone using magic far to the north last night, but it could have been my imagination, or effects of the storm."

The wizard's eyes immediately blazed to life as the old man sent his presence out behind them. After a few moments, his eyes returned to normal.

"I am limited by distance but do not sense any life forms behind us. You can trust your instincts and not chalk it up to imagination. A couple of Dark Elves may be following us. Stay alert."

The trolls ran easily alongside the horses as the morning progressed, eating up the leagues. Twice, the boy felt the bond ignite as the unicorns formed a triangle and used their magic to generate heat. It was short-lived, for they knew not to expend all their energy. The companions stopped briefly at midday to eat whatever was available. Half their belongings and supplies had been ripped away in the storm. Incredibly, Chase spied a burlap sack against the cliff wall and broke off to retrieve it.

"Ha. It's one of our bags of food!" He looked inside and pulled out the frozen contents. The tall boy's face drooped when he realized it was lice bread and unrecognizable meat with small bones.

"Ah, snake and bread. Wonderful." One Eye rubbed his hands together. Chase looked at him dubiously and handed it off. The fact that it had travelled this distance showed the incredible power of the storm.

They continued riding throughout the afternoon, huddled over their mounts, saying little. The sun moved west, providing almost no warmth. The wind picked up again, refusing to give them any reprieve. It was not strong enough to force them to insert cloth in their ears, but the constant whine was difficult to bear.

It wasn't until the sun began to set that Chip finally noticed the air getting warmer. The cliffs ended to their left, revealing small mountains that continued to dwindle in size. They pushed on, eager to escape the desert. Stars appeared in the night sky, and the wind finally abated, but not before a final blast of shrieking cold air hit their backs. The boy could swear it was intentional.

"Let's go a little farther, then set up our tents," the wizard called out.

"Turn southwest," One Eye said, running up beside him. "We can cut the corner until we reach the river."

Chip nodded, veering off to his right. The air continued to warm. Patches of grass appeared between the snow, and Redmane whinnied with delight. The boy could tell the magnificent animal wanted to run at full speed with reckless abandon, but the trolls could not keep up. They did maintain a solid pace.

Late into the evening, the companions made camp. Everyone had to share the few tents that remained. The trolls hunkered down in the open, claiming the air was mild. The Protectors and soldiers took watch at either end of their encampment, rotating through the night. Chip felt safe with the added protection. The long, cold day had sapped their strength, and everyone took advantage of the rest. He shared a small tent with Chase, Ethrang, and Eleanor, and they went to sleep in moments.

It took two more days to reach the Lumber River. The land held a mix of grass and snow, giving way to rolling hills and meadows with sporadic clusters of trees. The unicorns enjoyed the terrain, spirits lifting after their harrowing journey through the Stone Kingdom. Chip felt their happiness through the bond, making him smile.

The Lumber River was much wider than he imagined. The swift current sparkled in the late afternoon sun. He knew it began high up in the mountains of the Dwarf Kingdom, running east along the northern edge of the Great Plains. He could see endless fields of long grass on the other side of the river, but much was already snow-covered. A gravel road ran parallel to the river.

"This is the Peace Road," Xander said. "It is a bit of a misnomer, as this section is plagued by ruffians who cause strife unless you hire them to guard your goods. They are a mix of Northbane deserters, Banfar derelicts, and devious locals. Rumours are they are very closely related. The traders call them the Hill People. Most caravans are heavily guarded against these bandits. They've built up a lucrative business over the centuries. Nobody wants to solve the problem, as it's considered a no-man's land. Yucan is still a week's ride west, so they rarely send patrols this far out. The drug Wack, which originated in Banfar, is quite prevalent here. Most people prefer to ride by boat to avoid this section. Even then, guards are necessary to avoid piracy."

One Eye grinned. "Let these bandits try to take something from us. My trolls are itching for a fight."

"I think we are quite safe with seven wizards, an equal number of Protectors, a mage, and almost a dozen trolls," Ethrang noted.

The huge captain looked down at the skinny blond boy. "You don't look like much, but not even I would want to fight Furiosa."

Ethrang grinned. "I don't think she'll be necessary here. I will save her for Darkwood." One Eye grunted and clapped him on the shoulder, nearly knocking the boy over.

"The Hill People's village is up ahead," Xander said. "The inn is a bit rowdy if memory serves, but there will be ale and a warm meal."

"Ale is good," One Eye responded. "Running is thirsty work."

Chip led the way west on Peace Road. Houses started appearing on the banks of the river, with some on the northern side set far back. Most were dilapidated, with people lounging on the porches. Many were smoking something through a pipe. They did not look friendly.

The number of homes increased as the evening progressed until they arrived at a large village. A massive inn made of wood sat on the south side of the road, backing onto the river. The sounds of revelry reached their ears well before they arrived. A long verandah ran the entire length of the front and sides. Redmane stopped, making it clear the herd would go no further. The people drinking on the porch in front of the inn started pointing, and one ran inside.

"We will leave the unicorns here. They can graze in nearby fields." Chip sent his presence into Redman's mind, making it clear the herd should stay away from any homes or people. The unicorn whinnied in understanding. The companions removed their packs, and the beautiful horses galloped away, running down the road before turning into a wooded field.

The travellers trudged up to the inn, which had two batwing doors that swung both ways. Several unkept people holding drinks and pipes gave them suspicious looks but said nothing.

The common room was more like a giant hall. A loud group of musicians stood at the far end on a makeshift stage, playing fiddles while they sang out of tune. At least one hundred people filled the room, sitting in chairs around tables full of drinks. A line up of patrons clamoured for beverages at a sidebar. Chip noticed several hooded figures nursing a drink along the walls. For a moment, he thought they were Dark Elves, but they seemed too small.

"My goodness," Xander said loudly enough to carry over the din. "This place is worse than I remember." The music suddenly stopped, and all eyes turned to them.

"No trolls," a huge man barked from the other side of the room. He had a long black beard and would have been considered muscular if not for his immense pot belly. "You can stay in the stable with the other animals."

One Eye grabbed the handle of his axe.

"No weapons," Garth Stone said.

The troll gave him a look and shrugged. "Even better." He cracked his knuckles.

"Are you deaf, beast?" the man shouted. The fifty-odd men gathered around him bellowed with laughter. The musicians gave each other a knowing look and began putting their instruments in their cases.

"I didn't say you could leave, minstrels," the large man said gruffly. "Play for your king. The King of the Hill People." He let out a boisterous laugh, and the others joined in. The weapons master touched One Eye's shoulder, and the troll turned away.

"Hey, I wasn't finished with you yet, dog." The man stood up and slowly walked across the room, flexing his hands. The others got up to follow. Garth Stone paused and looked again at the troll then shrugged. One Eye turned around with a grin.

"You think it's funny, beast. You think those silly-robed wizards are going to help you. We aren't afraid of them. The Hill People aren't afraid of anyone." The big man stopped in front of the troll captain and, despite his size, had to look up. Bulch moved forward to stand beside the troll. The man's eyes widened at the size of the Protector, then he sneered. "There's a lot more of us than you. In fact, it's all of us against you."

The entire room started chuckling.

The bearded man held up his hand. "However, the King of the Hill People is a generous man, and I will give you a chance to save your dignity and not get beaten to a pulp. Pay us ten gold coins, and we will let you be. Heck, we can even protect you on your journey." One Eye turned to Garth. Before the weapons master could respond, he added, "I meant ten gold coins, and this ugly dog has to grovel on the ground at my feet like the animal he is." The troll captain continued to stare at Garth.

The weapons master gave One Eye a slight nod.

The huge troll slammed his fist so hard into the man's beard that the sound of his jaw cracking caused people outside the inn to peer inside. At least a dozen teeth flew out of his mouth. He landed in a starfish pattern on the wood floor and didn't move.

"Don't use your magic," Xander whispered in Chip's ear.

The room exploded into action. The man's followers charged the group from all sides.

Garth Stone dodged a sloppy roundhouse punch from a large villager before executing a devastating overhand elbow to the bridge of the man's nose. Blood sprayed the oncoming crowd. He then slipped into the fray, throwing kicks and punches with blistering speed. More popping noises erupted.

Chase let out a whoop of joy as his eyes shone with bits of red and sent a flurry of strikes at anyone close. The other eleven troll soldiers took positions around One Eye and hammer-fisted anyone foolish enough to get close. Daria stood to the side, rolling her eyes. Ethrang hit a muscular man in the face three times in quick succession, but the villager licked the blood off his lips and charged the skinny blond boy.

Quick as a thought, the Banfar orphan ducked the man's hands and squeezed between the trolls, only to reemerge a moment later as Furiosa. The look on the villager's face turned from gloating to abject fear. The female troll came in with a massive uppercut, sending the heavily muscled man clear off his feet to land on his back.

Two hill people tried to reach for Eleanor with leering expressions, which was all Chip needed to react. The boy came in at an angle with a straight shot extending through one man's jaw, then pulled back to block two weak punches from his companion. He went inside the man's guard as trained and delivered two uppercuts to his sternum, then drove his knee upwards into his chin as he doubled over.

A man lifted a chair to smash it on the weapons master, but Garth knife-chopped him on one side of his neck. The villager's hands went limp, and the chair came down on his own head.

A woman with stringy hair and a flimsy dress ran shrieking at Eleanor, who reached back and punched her square in the chin. She wobbled away dazed. Chip acknowledged the queen with a grin as more people came in swinging. He unleashed his repertoire of front kicks, knees, elbows, and punches while trying to keep an eye on the women.

The boy knew they could use magic but did not wish to reveal themselves if they could help it. Mary came up behind a man who Chip had spun around with a right hook and planted a solid kick to his groin. The sound made the orphan cringe, but he gave her an approving nod.

The Hill People fell in droves until a circle of bodies surrounded them, the conscious ones crying in pain. Chip noticed three hooded figures stand up and move towards the door. One turned for a last look, and he saw a woman's face covered with tattoos featuring strange symbols.

He moved to follow, but a fresh set of men burst through the common room doors to throw themselves into the fray. Chairs flew through the air, and tables overturned, but in the end the remaining Hill People waved their hands in defeat. They grabbed drinks from tables still upright before moving off to the corners of the room.

The companions looked at each other and laughed. Ethrang

appeared as himself and slapped Chip on the back. "Nice moves, Guardian. It's about time you fought fisticuffs again."

The trolls thumped their chests, paying special homage to Garth and Chase, who had taken out a sizable portion of villagers. Bulch, Carvor, Ward, and Sheldor nodded with respect.

"Nothing like a good bar fight," One Eye said with a broad smile. "I am a little disappointed it ended so fast."

Groans and cries sounded throughout the room.

"Bring him outside," Xander said, pointing at the bearded leader on the ground. He was still out cold. Bulch and One Eye grabbed his legs and dragged him onto the porch, which was now empty. The wizard pulled his hood up, covering the blaze of his blue eyes. He levitated the man upright, healed his jaw and regrew the leader's teeth. The man looked at him in shock.

"Don't kill me, please!"

The wizard gave him a hard look. "If I wanted to kill you, you would already be dead," he said in a low voice. Some patrons tried to come out the door, but Garth and One Eye blocked the entrance. "Listen to me very carefully." Xander waited for the man to nod. "I will let you live, but I want you to do me a favour in return." He pulled out a clinking purse and deposited ten gold coins in the man's hands. The leader's eyes widened. "Two people might be following us. One is a woman with white hair dressed in black, and the other is a man dressed in green. I want you and your followers to kill them. Come at them with everything you have. The gold they carry is yours. Do you understand?"

The man nodded, excitement returning to his voice. "No problem, Wizard. I would have done a lot more for this amount of money."

"One more thing." Xander leaned close, full of Power. "Look into my eyes." The man did and shrank from his gaze. "If I find out you did not do this or took the money and ran, nothing in the world will stop me from finding you."

The self-proclaimed King of the Hill People gulped and nodded.

"Wait," Chip said. "Who are the hooded women with tattoos on their faces?" A look of fear crossed the man's face, and he spat.

"Witches. Many came here recently after being driven out of Banfar. They want a cut of the action, and since they have magic, I have no choice but to agree. They hold meetings here once a week, trying to get everyone to join their cult. They preach something about a Demon King, but no one really believes them." He looked at the boy's robes. "They said a...Guardian or something in red robes cleaned up Banfar and forced them to leave."

Chip leaned closer. "Do not tell them we made this deal. Do what the wizard says. Trust me when I say he will know if you don't. Oh, and don't listen to these witches. It's all lies."

Xander's eyes returned to normal, and he released the man.

The leader of the Hill People looked at them and chuckled. "If I knew you could fight like that, I never would have started anything." He disappeared into the inn.

"Let's go back the way we came and call the unicorns," Xander whispered. "We will go around the town and carry on to the next village. If memory serves, it is not that far."

They all nodded and followed the old man back east down Peace Road, leaving the village behind.

Once they were far enough away, Chip turned to the wizard. "Do you think he will do as you ask?"

"Yes, especially since I added that he could have their gold. These people are desperate to earn money to support their habits. They have been accosting and robbing people for many years. Even if they don't succeed, I have achieved a different objective."

"Which is?" The boy gave him a perplexed look.

"If Hagatha and her green-clothed friend are as dangerous as I think they are, then we solved the ruffian problem." The old man winked at him.

Chip thought about it and nodded. "Either way, we win."

The herd of unicorns met them in a large field, and they gave the town a wide berth before continuing west. The trolls ran beside them, still grinning at each other after clobbering a room full of humans. No one had sustained any significant injuries besides bruised knuckles and minor scratches.

It took them two more hours to reach the next village, which had no inn. They carried on and pitched their tents a short while later in a farmer's field. Chip had to admit he was disappointed. He remembered staying in inns along the One Road to the Wizard's Guild and enjoyed the experience. His favourite memory was the evening they spent at Ulrich and Anna's house on their farm outside Banfar.

As Eleanor snuggled beside him, he relived the memories of the soldiers eating, laughing, and dancing the night away in the farmer's barn.

Then, with a cold start, he realized that, other than Captain Melvin, those soldiers were all dead.

How many more were going to die before the end? Chip Oathbinder shuddered, and the importance of their mission took over his thoughts. He would not let all those men die for nothing.

They needed to find the Light Elves.

4

The companions rode west along Peace Road for the rest of the week. The days began to grow colder, and snow fell at times. Winter was in full swing this far north. Still, compared to the Stone Kingdom, it was relatively mild. The trolls, with their thick skin, considered it downright warm.

They stopped at several inns along the way, finally able to eat human food again. Chase was in his glory, downing steaming bowls of lamb stew or roast pig. Breakfast consisted of normal eggs, bacon, and toast. The trolls called the food slop.

The townspeople mostly ignored them. Only a few asked whether they needed protection on their way to Yucan. One Eye would grasp the handle of his axe or cudgel and ask if they needed protection instead. That ended any further conversation. It was clear that most ruffians and bandits lived in the Hill People's village back east. Here, the citizens looked like real farmers or tradespeople, with only a few vagrants. The inns usually had rooms available. If not, they opted for the barn.

Chip knew they could have made better time on the unicorns without the trolls, but he welcomed their protection and was starting to like One Eye. It was amazing how people could change when they had a common goal or when you showed them you were not the enemy. New experiences shared with others, especially exciting ones, created friendships.

He hoped the trolls felt the same way about them. After a thousand years of war, it was good to know people could change.

On the morning of the seventh day, a group of riders appeared on the road ahead. Chip slowed Redmane, and everyone halted. By the dust cloud from the gravel road, it looked like a sizable force was coming their way. The Protectors fanned out to the sides, creating a human shield around the wizards. The trolls rested their hands on the ends of various weapons.

About twenty riders approached them, slowing their mounts to a trot before reining to a halt on Peace Road. Chip's eyes widened. The group consisted of an equal number of dwarves, trolls, and humans. Several were female.

"Captain One Eye, you are still alive?" A small troll with white tufts of hair leapt off his horse with a wheeze.

"Silver, you rascal. Always trying to make money." One Eye clasped the shorter troll's extended hand. "Too old for the front lines, eh?"

"Money doesn't do me any good in the Stone Kingdom. Jaggar posted me here a long time ago to manage trade. If I make a little extra on top, so what? Money talks in Yucan." He leaned in conspiratorially. "Birch told me our king is dead. Is it true?"

"Saw it myself. Miriam threw him in the air and burnt him to a crisp. Sorry, I meant Queen Miriam." One Eye grinned.

Silver shook his wrinkled head. "I thought I would never see the day. He's ruled us for many millennia. Most of us don't know anything else. Can't say I will miss him."

"Ha, a couple of weeks ago, that would have got you skinned." The troll captain chuckled. "Truth is, I don't miss him much either. These silly humans are growing on me." The men and women on the horses gave him a mild look of disapproval. He noticed the reaction. "And who might these people be?"

"How rude of me." Silver pointed to his comrades. "This is the

Peace Road Patrol. There are seven dwarves, seven humans, and seven trolls. We always assign people equitably in Yucan. It's the only town like it. I replaced one of the trolls because I'm the only one who would recognize you, besides Birch, but he's busy with his Triumvirate duties. We were heading east to intercept you and provide an escort. I'm surprised you got this far so quickly." He looked at the others. "My job is to accompany you to the governing chambers. You can introduce your friends there."

One Eye looked at Chip, who nodded. "Lead the way." A thought seemed to strike the captain. "Do you always ride horses?"

Silver laughed. "It beats running, especially at my age. Horse meat is not allowed in Yucan. They are noble beasts that carry goods, help farm, and provide fast transport. If you live in Yucan long enough, you will change." He smiled and climbed onto his mount. One Eye stared after him then shrugged.

They followed the Peace Road Patrol for the remainder of the morning. Clouds began to move in, obscuring the midday sun, and light snow fell. The group crested a rise, and a large valley appeared before them, cradling a sizable town.

Massive warehouses lined the banks of the Lumber River, which was wide and straight, cutting across the valley in a blue line. Boats of different sizes were moored to the docks behind the buildings. A short stone wall surrounded the town, with guards spaced evenly atop the walls, carrying bows.

"Welcome to Yucan," Silver announced. "The river here runs wide and straight, making it an ideal location. It will freeze over in a couple of weeks, and then goods must be transported over Peace Road. Many traders will go home until next season. The large stone building in the middle is the governing chamber."

The troll led the patrol down the hill. At the bottom, they turned left off the road and approached the main gates. There was a long line. Redmane and the unicorns halted as one. The companions dismounted, and Chip sent images to the horse to graze in fields until the following day. Redmane whinnied his understanding, and the herd sped off with fluid grace.

"Those beasts are magnificent," Silver said with a look of approval. He turned and signalled a guard in a blue uniform, who waved them forward to avoid the line. One of the metal doors opened to allow them passage. The patrol dismounted and held their mounts' reins to walk alongside the group.

People bustled about the town in a frenzy. Dwarves, trolls and humans moved about with horse-drawn wagons full of goods, haggling over prices at street corners, or selling wares from makeshift stands. Everyone seemed to be buying, selling, and working. Peace Patrol guards stood at every corner, observing the traders.

A large white sign stood inside the gates with three rules printed in black letters. "Treat Everyone With Respect, No Violence, and No Stealing." To the bottom right, it was signed, "The Triumvirate."

"You must abide by the town rules," Silver explained as they made their way through the main square. "Everyone pays a tithe to fund the governing body and the Peace Patrols. Anyone who breaks the rules is severely punished. Depending on the severity of the crime, they may pay a heavy fine, have their goods confiscated, go to prison, or outright banishment. Anyone banished who tries to reenter is shot on sight. The guards on the wall are superb bowmen. It may seem extreme to some people, but the measures provide a safe city where everyone treats others with respect. It is common and expected to address everyone as a sir or a madam. Courtesy goes a long way to fostering mutual respect. Squabbles regarding contracts or negotiations are brought before the Triumvirate, which issue binding judgments."

"You are telling me no fights occur in the ale houses?" One Eye asked.

"Public intoxication is prohibited. There are no ale houses." The troll captain stared at him in shock. "But there are coffee houses! Would you like one?" He grinned.

One Eye could only shake his head.

"Come. It's not as bad as you think. In the north part of town, there are stately apartments with a lovely central park. The Peace Patrol and year-round workers live there. Everything is manicured, and they enforce a no littering policy. Most traders though are in and out within a matter of days. A multitude of inns provide them with lodging and meals. In the center, we have the bustling market and governing body, and to the south are the factories and loading docks. The Triumvirate is expecting you, Sir." He emphasized the last word, which caused Ethrang to giggle. One Eye continued to stare at him as if he was a stranger.

Chip found the city quite interesting. It amazed him that three different races could get along, conduct business, and live together.

"Don't the trolls and humans have animosity towards each other?" he asked as the patrol turned south down a wide cross street.

"Did you not read the sign at the front gate, Sir?" the troll said, giving him a strange look. Chip heard muffled laughs from the twins behind him. He ignored them.

"I simply meant all that hatred over a thousand years..."

Silver let out a wheezy laugh. "Trolls can change too. It's proven here. That's why all races make up the Peace Patrols. Same with the governing body. It's much harder to hate yourself. The trolls in the Stone Kingdom need a new enemy. They may hate you for now, but give it time. There's an old saying that a former enemy can make the best of friends. One Eye has only known you for a short time, yet you are already changing him. The trolls are trained to fight since birth, it's true, yet it doesn't mean we cannot change, Sir."

One Eye stepped forward. "Agreed, but coffee houses...Sir?"

Silver let out a hoarse chuckle. "See, it's happening already, Sir."

They arrived at the center of the town in front of a square stone building with large columns. The rest of the patrol bade farewell, their mission complete, and led the horses away. Silver waved them forward as he mounted the stone steps to double wooden doors.

The companions entered a huge wood-panelled room with a high ceiling. There was a long line to an old dwarven woman sitting at a wooden desk. Silver ushered them forward. The sounds of their footsteps echoed off the walls. Everyone spoke in whispers, but their voices carried. The people in the line gave them mildly disapproving looks but said nothing.

The old woman at the desk held up her hand. "Stop there, Sir."

Silver nodded. "Yes, Madam." She rose, knocked on a set of doors behind her, and quietly slipped in. The dwarven woman came out and waved them forward.

"They are finishing a case, but you can go in and take a seat, Sirs and Madams."

"Thank you kindly, Madam." Silver held the door open, and they entered a large room with rows of benches.

At the far end was a long oak table with only three seats. A large troll, a dwarf with a long white beard, and an older woman with glasses sat in the chairs. They were all wearing black robes. Silver put a finger to his lips, and they took seats behind the first row.

A dwarf and a troll stood in front of the table, facing the Triumvirate.

"The agreed-upon trade was three hand made axes for a snow ape pelt, Sir," the dwarf said as he smoothed out his long brown beard.

"The axes are too short, Sir," the troll said, shaking his head.

The dwarf looked over at him. "Those axes will never break. They are of the finest craftsmanship, Sir," he said, keeping his voice level.

"I wanted long-handle axes for battle, Sir," the troll growled.

The black-robed troll at the table gestured. "Bring me the contract, Sir." His voice was deep and strong.

The dwarf produced a parchment and reached up to place it on the large table. The troll studied it for several moments then leaned over to the other two members of the Triumvirate. They whispered back and forth.

Finally, the black-robed troll turned back. "We have come to a judgment. The contract does not stipulate the length of the axes, so it remains valid. You will hand over the snow ape pelt and fulfill the agreement. In the future, please make it clear exactly what goods you are trading for, Sir."

The troll looked displeased but bowed his head. "Thank you. I will be more accurate next time, Sirs and Madam of the Triumvirate."

Both parties turned around and exited the room. When the doors shut, the black-robed troll looked at those gathered.

"Welcome to Yucan. I have been expecting you. I trust Silver provided a suitable escort into the city." They all nodded. "I am Birch. This is Treed, and Martha sits to his left. We form the Triumvirate. I received a message recently from the newly crowned Queen Miriam that you seek supplies and a tracker. May I ask your names, Sirs and Madams?"

Xander cleared his throat. "Our mission is secretive, but I suspect the Triumvirate already knows who we are. I know you are a neutral city. In the world of trade, knowledge is power, and your eyes and ears throughout the lands keep you well informed of events about crop yields, the price of commodities, changes in nobility, and a hundred other things. I should know since I created the first Triumvirate a thousand years ago. Your neutrality was part of the treaty I negotiated between the trolls and humans to ensure the flow of trade."

Birch smiled and nodded.

The wizard continued. "I have been away for many years, so I have never met you, Sirs and Madam. I am Xandrostika, Grand Wizard of the new Guild. My Protector, Garth Stone, Honourary High Commander of Toron, and Chase Longfellow, the Invincible Protector, are with me. Behind them sit hand picked Protectors Carvor, Sheldor, Bulch, Ward, and Shimko. Queen Eleanor of Vanalon sits with Mary, the Blue Wing Leader, beside Blue Level twins Kristan and Thomas. To their right is Ethrang, our young green-robed wizard. Captain One Eye commands a contingent of trolls. Daria, the healing mage, sits to their right. To my left is Chip Oathbinder, Guardian of the Races and the one true hope, Sirs and Madams."

The panel's eyes rested on Chip.

The woman pushed her glasses higher. "Your work in Banfar is commendable. It still stands. We have not determined why the Demon King has not attacked it. Cave Mountain is only a two-day journey away. His demons would freeze, but a score of Dark Elves could lay waste to the town, Sir."

"Banfar needed a good cleanup," the dwarf to her right, Treed, added, stroking his long white beard. "Unfortunately, some of the...

undesirables made their way up here. Cult members, Wack users, and vagabonds fled northeast to the Hill People's village and surrounding lands. If some genuinely want to change, we take them in. They agree to a stringent program where we limit their freedom while they learn a trade. We have a high success rate. The problem now is that the cultists are rounding up new followers. Witches have become increasingly prevalent. I'm sure you saw them during your bar fight in the village of the Hill People, Sir."

"What do you know of the witches in the Secret Caves?" Chip asked, not showing surprise that they already knew what had transpired in the village. "Sirs and Madam," he added.

The boy noticed a fleeting look of guilt on Treed's face. Birch shifted slightly, and Martha looked down, lips pursed.

The troll cleared his throat. "They are real. The caves are protected by Darkwood Forest, which is impassable." He leaned forward. "Though we do not know what you seek in the caves, I urge you to abandon this quest. It will only lead to your deaths, Sirs and Madams."

"What do you know of the forest, Sir?" the boy asked.

Birch sighed. It was too drawn out for Chip's liking. "Not much, I'm afraid. No one has entered it and returned." Treed's eyes flicked to his right. "Those who go close report wraith-like figures, strange lights, and non-human sounds, Sir."

"Have you ever met any of the witches from the Secret Caves?" he asked. He purposefully left out "Sirs and Madams."

"No," Martha said a little too quickly. None of them noticed his breach of etiquette, which he found odd. "How could we? No one goes in or out...Sir." She looked a touch flustered but hid it with a shrug.

Birch nodded, spreading his hands. "We wish we could help more..."

Chip stood up, striding forward, and seized his Power. Red coils of fire swirled around his body as he faced the Triumvirate.

"You lie!"

Suddenly, all their eyes blazed a bright blue, and they stood up.

"You dare challenge the Triumvirate!" Birch lifted his hands, and Chip felt all three of them link. The doors to the back of the room opened, and Peace Patrol soldiers began flooding in. He felt his companions seize their Power, but he held up a hand.

The boy raised his other hand and put a shield around the Triumvirate and his companions. The patrols recoiled from the shimmering red energy, unable to move forward.

Birch threw the Triumvirate's Power at the shield, trying to break it.

He withstood it easily, filled with rage.

The boy walked forward, picked up the desk with his magic, and moved it to the side. The Triumvirate stood exposed, faces straining. He lifted them off the ground, drawing them close, surrounded with red Power. They struggled, pushing against his magic with everything they had. The bearded dwarf looked at the panel and then back at the Guardian. The fire began to dim in his eyes.

"Enough," shouted Treed. "We will tell you."

Birch and Martha glanced over in shock, and then a look of resignation covered their faces. They both nodded and lowered their hands.

Chip set them down but maintained his shield. The blue fire went out of their eyes.

Birch turned to the patrols. "Leave us, now...Sirs and Madams."

The soldiers looked at each other in surprise and then filed out.

Chip pulled the heavy oak table back and released his Power. "Tell me everything. You can leave out the formalities. Those forms of address are suitable only for those who deserve it."

The Triumvirate slowly sat back down.

"She will kill us..." the dwarf began.

"Who?"

"Morgeth."

Chip shared a look with Xander. "She still lives?"

"Not only does she live," Martha said, "she does not age. She is young and beautiful."

"Are you in league with her?"

"No," the woman said with a haunted look. "It may look that way but we have no choice. Morgeth is incredibly powerful and has a large following. The witches are behind the cults in Banfar and the Hill People. It's why we allow the bandits and ruffians to take their share. Morgeth has a hand in it all."

"What deal has she made with you?"

"We provide her with goods and information."

"And what does she provide you in return?"

Martha's face became filled with fear. "She allows us to live. Morgeth says if we cross her, she will release the creatures of Darkwood upon the town. They will enslaved any survivors, including the Triumvirate."

Chip stared at her. "How long has this been going on?"

Martha looked down in shame.

Birch cleared his throat, trying to hide his embarrassment. "Since the first Triumvirate a thousand years ago." There was a long silence. The dwarf hung his head.

"My goodness," Xander muttered.

"The witches know everything," Birch said. "We are not proud of it. The Triumvirate receives information from across the land financed by the profits of trade. We are the wealthiest entity in Amrika. Our eyes and ears spread out to every town, city, guild, and royal court. Information is power. We believe in the ideals of this city. It models what can occur if the races work together. Yet we have failed in our mandate."

"You are corrupt," Chip stated. "You promote peaceful unity within these walls, yet your actions have devastating effects on the races at large. The witches seek to prepare the world for the arrival of the Demon King. When he comes, you will be nothing better than slaves if you survive at all."

Treed looked at him with wet eyes. "The dwarves are a noble race who only seek peace. I have betrayed them. We have betrayed everyone. Please understand that Morgeth is powerful beyond measure. She has existed since the Great Forget. Her followers are vast and growing. We felt we had no choice. What would you have us do?"

Chip's face grew hard. "What everyone should do. Fight the darkness with every breath you have. Don't let evil control you. Even when it seems impossible, there is always a way. The greatest institutions must be vigilant against greed and corruption. We all have an inherent selfishness. It's the great paradox. Without our selfishness, we wouldn't be here today. We needed it to survive and evolve, but it is the one thing we must conquer. It is our great struggle."

The Triumvirate stared at him.

"How do you know all this?" Treed said softly.

Chip looked at the wizards, Protectors, and trolls behind him. He saw hope in their eyes. "I learned it from these fine people here." The boy turned back to the panel. "We are a group like no other. We need to go through Darkwood and enter the Secret Caves."

"And then what will you do?" Martha asked with wide eyes.

The Guardian of the Races stared at the Triumvirate.

"I am going to kill all the witches."

The panel looked at him for a long moment, and Chip finally saw a yearning for hope and redemption. Yet also fear.

The boy stared at each in turn. "We believe in forgiveness. Your help will be vital in the days to come. Share the information you collect with the Wizard's Guild, for Balor's ears only. We need to keep tabs on the demons and Dark Elves. When the Unnamed One marches at the end of winter, we need to know when and how many. Root out the cults out in all towns and cities. When the Demon King marches, send all Peace Patrols to Toron. We need everyone to stand with us in the Last Battle."

The Triumvirate turned to each other. They whispered briefly and then nodded.

"You have our allegiance," Birch said.

"Good. Now, where do you meet Morgeth?"

"On the outskirts of Darkwood, a day's ride north. There is a black stone a short distance from the forest. We meet to share our information and provide goods. The tracker can take you there."

"How often do you meet her?" Chip asked.

"Once a month. She brings a group of witches and always carries a dark wood staff."

The boy nodded. "I know of these staffs. They shield a person from magic, at least temporarily. When was the last time you met her?"

"Three days ago."

Xander cursed behind him. The weapons master arched an eyebrow.

"We cannot wait that long," the wizard said. "What did you tell her when you met three days ago."

"We informed her of the events that transpired in the Stone Kingdom. I'm sorry, but she knows you are coming to Darkwood."

The wizard grunted. "Do you know which path she takes to enter or leave the forest?"

"No, she waits until we are gone. We have theorized that the creatures do not attack the witches. They must have some control over them."

"She uses the Dark Arts," Chip said. "Same as Barko. Controlling animals is possible, but I cannot imagine they could control an entire forest. I saw symbols on a witch's face in the Hill People's village. Perhaps they keep the animals at bay."

Treed nodded. "There are runes and symbols on the trees at the forest's perimeter. It would explain why the animals do not wander out."

"Like a ward," Xander mused.

"The runes and symbols are part of the Dark Arts," Chip said. "Barko used them to sustain his transformation over the millennia. They draw in magic from a dark Force. This Force has developed an... awareness. It seeks to gain a foothold in the world of life. It is Death itself." The Guardian sighed. "We are fighting on many fronts, yet all tie together."

"So, to summarize," Chase piped up from the back, "we are trying to find the witches in the Secret Caves who seek an alliance with the Demon King, including his Dark Elves and demons, who control a creature that isn't alive called the Dim, who is trying to eat all the

Paths and erase existence itself, and we just have to kill them all to restore the Balance." He took a breath.

Everyone stared at him. Ethrang giggled.

"When you put it like that..." Kristan said with a weak smile.

"It could always be worse, right?" Thomas added, trying to sound reassuring.

The Triumvirate looked at each other, mirroring doubt.

"It is more important than ever that we stand strong and fight evil on all fronts," Chip said earnestly. "We now have the backing of the Troll Kingdom and Yucan. Banfar is mobilizing. The Guild and Toron are preparing. We must all unite to fight this."

"We stand with you," Martha reasserted, pushing her glasses higher, reminding him of Miss Owl. "A tracker named Rake is waiting for you at the Trader's Inn down the street. Silver can take you there. He will gather what supplies you need. Get a good night's rest and leave in the morning. It will take you all day to reach Darkwood, even on your unicorns. I would camp outside the forest and enter at dawn the following day. We do not know how long it will take to reach the Secret Caves. Remember, informants have seen you riding into Yucan, so the witches know your every move. Be wary."

"Is there anything else you require?" asked Treed.

Chip looked back. Everyone shook their heads.

The Triumvirate glanced at each other and turned as one.

"May the Creator shine on you, Sirs and Madams." They all stood up and bowed.

"Thank you," Chip Oathbinder said, nodding. "Sirs and Madam."

5

Silver escorted the party of travellers to the Trader's Inn. It was a sizable structure with a large common room. A mixture of dwarves, trolls, and humans sat at various tables, talking amicably. A thin fellow with several scars running down his cheeks stood at the side of the room and waved them over. Three empty tables were pushed together, and he gestured for them to sit.

"Greetings, Sirs and Madams. I am Rake, a Yucan tracker. I have been assigned to take you to a certain location. This is the largest inn in the city. Much business is conducted here. Most traders stay for a day or two to negotiate contracts." He lowered his voice. "I have ordered supplies for your journey, which should last you a week. They will arrive in the morning. Do you have any questions, Sirs and Madams?"

"Yes," Garth Stone said, keeping his voice low. "How long does it take to travel through Darkwood to our destination, Sir."

Rake glanced around and leaned forward. "No outsiders have made it through in several thousand years, at least that we know of. I've seen a score of men enter and never return. Based on the perimeter that extends to the frozen desert in the east and the Dwarf Kingdom in the west, I'm guessing it will take two days to reach the middle. Sleep will not be an option for you, so start at dawn and go through the night on foot. Your mounts would be an added safety risk. I have entered the fringes of the forest at various points and seen things that haunt my dreams. Most people don't believe me. The nighttime is by far the worst. Strange lights, shiny eyes, and screams that would make your blood cold. These scars on my face were caused by a white thing that fell from the trees and wrapped around my head. I ran full force into a tree to dislodge it, and the creature ran up the trunk to disappear into the canopy. It...laughed at me, Sirs and Madams."

"Why did you go there in the first place, Sir?" Eleanor asked.

"The Triumvirate sent me to gather information. The more we know about something, the more we can prepare. I am afraid most of the forest is a mystery. It is too dangerous for anyone. If I could advise you, it would be not to go in, Sirs and Madams."

"I have a way to tell how long it would take," Ethrang said. Rake stared at him. "Sir."

"No time for jokes," Xander admonished.

A short, black-haired woman appeared beside One Eye with a broad smile. "Hi, I'm your lunch server today at the Trader's Inn. It appears your meal has already been paid for, so please feel free to order anything you want. Today's main courses are freshwater catfish, baby goat in rosemary butter, rib-eye steaks, seafood pasta, and roast chicken with truffle sauce. Steamed asparagus and buttered fingerling potatoes complete the sides." She looked at One Eye. "What would you like, Sir?"

The troll captain did not hesitate. "Steak and ale for me...Madam."

She gave him a look one would typically reserve for a mischievous child. "Oh, that's precious, Sir. You know public intoxication is illegal. There's no ale in Yucan. Would you prefer coffee or water, Sir?"

One Eye stared at her while some of his soldiers snickered.

"Water," he said shortly.

"Good choice, Sir. And no offence, but please remember to add the salutation 'Madam' when you speak. We foster an atmosphere of courtesy in Yucan, and manners go a long way, Sir." She gave him another rich smile. One Eye looked dumbfounded then nodded. His soldiers grinned.

Everyone ordered their meal, and Chip returned to the tracker. "Why haven't you followed some witches from the Hill People's village to see how they enter Darkwood, Sir?"

"That's just it—they don't. Twice, I saw Morgeth meet some local witches at the black rock, but they returned to the village. I don't think lesser witches are allowed access. Their job is to establish cults on the outside. Once, I saw the local witches escorting hooded figures to Morgeth. They left, but the figures stayed. I waited to see where she would take them, and then a powerful presence filled my mind, and I flew high in the air. Morgeth's eyes turned bright blue, and she screamed at me in a terrible voice. The High Witch told me if I ever spied on her again, she would kill me and the Triumvirate. I don't follow people anymore. I only keep an eye on the forest to make sure the creatures stay there." He looked at them with wide eyes. "That place is evil, Sir."

Chip sat back. "So I've heard." He glanced at the others. "Enough talk of doom and gloom. After lunch, why don't we walk around town and check out the city? We could go to one of their famous coffee houses." He looked at One Eye, who barked a laugh.

"It can't be worse than your human food."

"That's the spirit," Chip said. "I for one would like to enjoy everyone's company."

"Can we get up to some mischief?" asked Ethrang. The twins nodded vigorously.

Mary looked at Eleanor. "Why don't we let the boys cause trouble on their own? I don't feel like babysitting. We should be able to find a spa and relax."

The queen's eyes lit up. "Oh dear, that would be lovely!" She patted Chip on the cheek. "You understand, right? He could not help but nod.

The food arrived, and they all ate heartily. Everyone raved over the fine cuisine except One Eye, who grunted. Chip did notice that he finished his plate.

Silver stood up, walked over to the front desk, and returned a short while later with their room keys. "My work is done here," the troll said. "I bid you farewell, and may the Creator shine on you."

"Go back to making money," One Eye said with a grin.

"Indeed, that is the plan. Keep one eye on them, Captain." He laughed and left the inn.

Rake told the group he needed to check on their supplies and would meet them again in the common room at dawn.

They nodded and climbed the stairs to the second level to deposit their belongings. To almost everyone's delight, hot baths awaited the guests. The trolls did not seem to care much for hygiene and returned downstairs. Chip and Eleanor shared a room. They looked at each other at the same time.

"Uh, I will see you guys downstairs in a little while. Just washing up." He glanced at Eleanor, who was turning red.

Kristan elbowed his brother. "You do that. Take your time."

Ethrang giggled while Chase rolled his eyes.

"What?" said Chip. "It's true." He decided he was not getting anywhere, so he went inside the room and shut the door.

Eleanor squealed and immediately disrobed then slid into the steaming wooden tub. He followed suit, almost tripping over his clothes. Two brushes with a mint-smelling herbal mixture sat on the ledge, and they each started brushing their teeth, trying not to laugh. When finished, Eleanor pulled him close and kissed him deeply.

A thrill went through him as he savoured the moment, feeling the heat of the water, her warm touch, and the smell of mint. Moments like these were precious, and he let the tremendous weight of his responsibilities go, floating in a sea of warmth and pleasure. She was the most cherished part of his life, and he loved her with every fibre of his being. The boy held her close, not wanting to ever let go. He looked into her eyes, feeling their souls connect as they did in his spirit essence in the Wizard's Guild.

A feeling of gratefulness overcame him, and he thanked the

Creator for allowing him to be with her. All the darkness, struggle, and pain seemed such a small price to pay for their love. The possibility that it could end abruptly made it that much more precious. He remembered the man with the silver hair describing an eternal moment.

Chip Oathbinder was in an eternal moment.

He let the feelings of love wash over him as he drew her close. Chip kissed her softly, bodies and spirits fused as one. Their presences touched, and they rode a wave of love and completeness together, soaring in peace and harmony. In a distant part of his mind that cared to think, he realized that love was the ultimate happiness. It must be cherished, protected, and nurtured. It came in various forms, but the foundation was caring, joy, and giving. It was a verb, an action. Its enemies were hate and indifference. It was a struggle worth fighting for. It was the light and the meaning.

He flew through time with her, riding waves of joy and oneness. The world fell away, and only utter bliss remained.

A knock sounded.

The world came crashing back down.

"Everyone's waiting for you," Ethrang called through the door.

"Uh, oh, yes, we are coming. Time flies," Chip called.

He heard a giggle. "See you downstairs."

They looked at each other and burst out laughing.

"Alright, grab the soap," Eleanor instructed. "Hurry. You go first."

They washed quickly, dried off with the towels provided, and pulled on fresh clothes from their packs. The two hurried out the door and arrived in the common room, only then realizing their hair was in disarray.

Everyone stared at them.

Chip hastily patted down his locks. Mary took one look at the pair, walked over to Eleanor, grabbed her hand, and pulled her up the stairs to the rooms. They started whispering excitedly.

Xander coughed delicately. The twins covered their mouths. Chase folded his arms, but his lips twitched in a smile. The trolls appeared clueless, looking bewildered in the silence.

Chip clapped his hands together, desperate to move the moment along. "Alright, who wants to go for a walk?" he tried to smile.

"Ahem, yes, we have been waiting." Xander gestured for him to take the lead. Chip walked out of the inn and went left. Ethrang sidled up beside him with a grin. "They made me knock," he whispered. "Sorry."

"Oh my goodness," Chip said, borrowing the wizard's favourite phrase, "No trouble. Now, find us somewhere to go."

The companions found one of the numerous coffee houses and tried several varieties. The trolls took a sip, and some spit it out. One Eye drank his coffee with a stoic face, feigning a smile that, for a troll, looked eerily similar to a grimace.

Ethrang and the twins used the "Sirs" and "Madams" to absurd levels, saying them after every sentence and sometimes in between. The servers avoided talking to them, displaying frozen smiles that did not reach their eyes. This, of course, made them laugh harder. The trolls stared at them all as if they were mad.

Chip felt strangely jumpy after drinking so many cups, so they decided to walk through the main park to burn off energy. He looked around at his companions, in good spirits, then realized that not all would survive the road ahead. He made it a point to talk to each of them. The two Protectors he did not know well were Ward and Shimko. They were fierce fighters and showed tremendous courage to make it this far. They rarely spoke, which was the nature of most in that line of work.

"How's your eye working?" he asked Ward.

The man smiled. "Good as new. It would have been fine though. I have a spare one. The Creator gave me two." Chip laughed and looked at Shimko. He was stocky with dark-brown hair framing a good-natured face.

"Still wish Maxim had selected you for this journey?" the boy asked.

Shimko's face took on a look of pride. "It has been the greatest honour of my life. I have only ever known training. Now, I get to see the world. It is not easy, which makes it worthwhile."

Ward echoed the thought. "It is an honour to assist you."

Carvor and Bulch both looked over and nodded. Garth Stone smiled.

Chip sighed. "There is still a long road ahead. May the Creator shine on all of us."

"Hear, hear."

As the afternoon wore on, the companions swapped stories with the trolls and pointed out interesting sights and people. Their camaraderie strengthened, which made the boy feel good. They were going to need each other in the days ahead.

The group returned to the inn and had a fantastic dinner. The staff lit a fire in the huge hearth, and they gathered around, drinking hot chocolate while making small talk. Nobody wanted to drink more coffee, knowing its effects on their sleep, except Ethrang. He drank three more cups, but it seemed to have the opposite effect on him.

As late evening approached, the skinny orphan began to nod off. That was the cue to bid each other good night, and they retired to their rooms. He snuggled with Eleanor, holding her tight, and drifted off.

The morning brought bustling activity as they washed, dressed, and assembled in the common room. To the trolls' chagrin, breakfast consisted of bacon, eggs, toast, potato wedges, waffles, and pancakes. One Eye made a face while eating the pancakes and complained the eggs tasted off. The others looked at each other. Ethrang tried not to laugh.

Rake approached the troll captain. "I brought fourteen mounts for your soldiers and mage, plus three packhorses, Sir."

One Eye gave him a strange look. "It's only a one-day run, Sir."

"I've already tied the packs to the horses, Sir."

Ethrang looked at One Eye with a straight face. "If Silver can ride a horse, so can you, Sir."

The troll captain squinted at the green-robed boy. "You think I'm scared? I've been cooped up for a day and want to run." He looked at his soldiers, who chortled. "What? I'm not scared. Very well, let's ride the beasts, but if it throws me off, I will eat it."

The weapons master arched an eyebrow.

"It was a joke. You humans make lots of jokes." He bellowed a short laugh, causing him to pass wind. The other trolls joined in at the apparent joke, making embarrassing noises. The odour in the common room became unbearable. Rake stared at it all in shock then rubbed his nose.

"Let's be off then, Sirs and Madams," the tracker said in a strangled voice. Ethrang doubled over.

The common room emptied quickly. Even people not part of their group poured out onto the street. The trolls mounted and waved at the townsfolk, apparently thinking they were seeing them off. Some of the soldiers appeared apprehensive if not downright afraid of the horses. The animals whinnied, eyes bulging, but the Protectors grabbed their harnesses, soothing them.

"I was told your mounts are outside the city, Sir," Rake said to Chip, taking the lead.

"Yes, we will walk alongside until we are out of Yucan, Sir." The tracker nodded.

"Follow me, Sirs and Madams."

They moved through Yucan's main square. Already, the town was bustling with morning hawkers and bickering traders. Wagons and goods were moving to their destinations or changing hands on the spot. They made their way to the gates, and the guards waved them through.

It was a cold, blustery day. Low gray clouds blotted out the rising sun, casting an eerie shadow over the landscape. Chip sent his presence out and found Redmane over a low hill to the north. The herd started galloping towards them. A few moments later, the unicorns appeared over the hill's crest, whinnying in excitement at being reunited. The sound brought a smile to the boy's ears.

Redmane nuzzled him, and he patted the horse's elegant neck. The wizards and Protectors tied their packs to the saddles and mounted up. Rake looked on, slack-jawed.

"They are magnificent, Sir," he breathed.

"Yes, they are. By the way, since we are out of Yucan, can we lose the Sirs and Madams...please," Chip asked.

"Of course, Sir, I mean...of course." The man regained his composure. "We ride straight north. The black stone borders the southwest portion of the forest." They nodded and followed the tracker.

Chip pulled his cloak tight against the wind. After two days of comfort, he was not used to the cold.

The boy smiled. The weapons master always said comfort was the enemy of humans. It could stunt growth potential and sap motivation to do better. It was helpful in small doses as a reward but should not be the primary objective. Goals should always be related to reaching one's full potential, such as milestones of growth, not comfort.

It was not the achievement that mattered so much as who you became in the process.

The company rode north over low hills, passing farms and dirt roads. Many were deeply rutted with wagon tracks. Snow had accumulated in the lower elevations.

The morning went by slowly. The number of farms dwindled and then disappeared as nature took over. Chip suspected that few wanted to live near Darkwood. They stopped for lunch in a wide meadow, watching the grey clouds spread. To the west, a dark smudge on the horizon meant bad weather was heading their way.

"A storm is coming. Likely by tomorrow," Rake said. "Pretty common this time of year."

They finished eating and continued riding. It was late afternoon when they crested a final rise, and the tracker pointed ahead. "That's Darkwood."

To Chip, it looked like a black line on the horizon, but as they rode closer, it grew taller and spread across their whole field of vision. Its size surprised him.

The sun was beginning to set when Rake reigned up behind a cluster of trees. "I recommend you go no closer."

"I can take a bird's eye view of things if you want?" Ethrang suggested. The tracker looked at him funny.

"No, they may sense you," Xander cautioned. "We do not know

their strength." The blond boy nodded glumly. "Let's set up our tents and eat a cold meal. No fire tonight. We get up before dawn. A triple watch is called for."

They set to the task. After a cold dinner of cured meat and bread, Chip, Chase, and Ethrang retired to their tent. Eleanor shared hers with Mary.

"What do you think it will be like?" the skinny orphan asked when they were settled inside.

"What will what be like?" Chase said.

"Darkwood."

"Oh, I think it will be dark, and there will be woods." Chase yawned.

"No, seriously," the blond boy pressed. "All those stories can't be true."

"I'm thinking it will be worse than those stories. You see, the ones we don't hear are the stories of people dying. We don't hear them because they're dead. So that means the real stories are much worse. And since no one has made it out in thousands of years, I think it will be really bad."

"I thought you said once that nothing is as bad as it seems." Ethrang looked at the Guardian.

"Well, everything has exceptions." Chip gave the orphan a light punch in the arm. "Get to bed. We are going to need all the rest we can."

"Alright, Guardian."

Chip dozed off soon after but woke in the middle of the night. He was not sure what had awakened him. Ethrang was sitting upright. The skinny boy put a finger to his lips. Then, a distant scream sounded. Chip's heart quickened, and they both silently crept to the tent flap and peered out. Ward and two trolls were on watch, pointing off in the distance.

Another faint shriek sounded, and he could make out flashes of light along the black smudge of Darkwood. Then there was dead silence. The two orphans looked at each other.

Suddenly, something powerful seized both their arms.

"What's going on," Chase asked, bleary-eyed. He released his grip.

"You almost gave me a heart attack," Chip whispered, holding his chest. Ethrang stifled a laugh. They all peered out.

More screams sounded, followed by a deep, evil laugh that chilled Chip to the bone. Different-coloured lights flashed again, followed by a final high-pitched cry, and then it stopped.

The watch had not moved, so there was no immediate threat. Everything was distant. They waited a while longer then crawled back under their blankets.

"What could make such terrible noises?" Chip said.

"The real question is what made that laugh. It was not a witch," Ethrang said with wide eyes.

"Oh, we will find out tomorrow." Chase turned over and started snoring immediately.

"Really?" Ethrang said. Then he started laughing under his blankets.

"Yup, that's Chase. Alright, nite."

"Nite, Guardian."

It took Chip a while to fall asleep, and his dreams were dark.

A head poked through their tent flaps.

"It's almost dawn," Xander said. "Let's get packed up."

The boys looked at each other, groaned, and rolled out of bed.

Everyone packed up and was ready to go a short while later. A wicked wind had whipped up, and the dark clouds to the west were almost upon them. Another system was moving in from the north.

"Oh, this is going to be a bad one," Rake said, craning his neck upward. Two storms meeting over Darkwood." He glanced around. "I wouldn't want to be you."

"Take us to the black rock, please. It's quite chilly." Xander smiled.

"Of course, my apologies."

"No need."

Everyone mounted, and they road north. The sun crested the horizon, providing a dim, otherworldly light through the low clouds. An eerie fog blanketed the ground.

"We couldn't have picked a better day for it," Chase muttered to no one in particular.

A black stone appeared ahead, emerging from the fog like a misshapen head. The trees of Darkwood appeared in greater detail, twisted and bent. Chip immediately sensed a growing malevolence. The tracker reigned up at the stone. Redmane neighed shrilly. He did not like the rock or the forest. They dismounted, removed their packs, and surrounded the black object. It was strange and shiny. He had never seen anything like it.

Chip looked closer and saw runes etched over its surface. It emitted a brooding darkness, and he shuddered from more than the cold.

A sudden streak of lightning appeared in the sky as the clouds collided, followed by a jarring rumble of thunder.

"Here we are," Rake said with a weak smile. "It's half a league to the forest. I will camp a couple of leagues south. If...when you make it out, that's where you will find me."

"The horses are all yours," Xander said. "Give us five days. If we don't return by then, expect the worst...Sir." The tracker smiled and nodded.

"Yes, Sir."

Chip approached Redmane. He would understand if the horses left and rode south. The red unicorn shook his magnificent head before he could even ask. They would wait. He rested his forehead against the horse's muzzle, then stepped back. The unicorns dipped their horns and then galloped away in spearhead formation.

The group shouldered their packs, bade farewell to Rake, and continued on foot to the forest. More lightning and thunder erupted, and the light dimmed further. The fog had also thickened, giving the world a hazy, mystical look. The trees ahead were black and twisted, beckoning them forward with grotesque limbs.

Chip shared a look with his companions, took a deep breath, and entered Darkwood Forest.

6

Hagatha walked with purpose along a road parallel to a wide river. She knew not the names of either, nor did she care. Humans had named them, and they were beneath her. Her long white hair shone bright in the late afternoon sun. Blade kept pace, his movements measured and graceful, green cloak swirling behind in the cold winter wind. The two approached a sizable village with a large inn. A filthy, wretched boy playing on the road noticed them and ran off. They could finally get horses and make up for lost time.

The Inner Circle Dark Elf was in a foul mood. It was a tolerable state of being, not quite bordering on outright emotion, which she despised. The frozen desert had been an unexpected challenge. After witnessing the end of King Jaggar by his ungrateful daughter's hand, the pair had to reassess their situation. Even now, thinking of the daughter's betrayal of her flesh and blood almost evoked unprecedented emotion. Such a display of disloyalty was unfathomable. She pressed her teeth together, letting the nausea subside. Such a betrayal was almost unheard of. Hagatha caught herself. Killian had killed his father, Elf King Galal.

Yet that was acceptable. Galal had tried to disown and banish him, which was unforgivable. She and Morgo had counselled him on the only appropriate course of action. Comparing that scenario to Jaggar was ludicrous. What could the Troll King have possibly done to his daughter? Jaggar had even put his crown on her head! And her first act was to turn on him. Disgusting.

King Jaggar deserved retribution for his disloyalty millennia ago, no question, but not from her. Hagatha made a mental note to kill the new Troll Queen personally. No act of disloyalty was forgivable. Ever. The new queen's Power did surprise her. Even from a distance, she could tell it rivalled her own, which was a rarity. She could count on the fingers of one hand who had ever been as strong as her. With Blade at her side, the outcome would not be in doubt.

She recalled the rest of that bizarre event. Watching the entire troll nation bow to a pathetic human boy almost caused her to misstep. Bile rose in her throat, but she ignored it. They had killed a scouting party of a dozen trolls and two mages the day after. They left one mage alive long enough for him to describe the events in detail. She shook her head at how long Blade had to skin him before the mage's tongue loosened.

The trolls claimed they would never submit or break, but that was a lie. Everyone broke with enough encouragement. Nobody heard his screams deep in the mountains, but inwardly she admitted the sound was gratifying. Getting pleasure from another's pain was a lesser form of transgression. It could also lead to benefits such as information.

After the mage broke, they discovered that the red-eyed boy wizard had killed Barko, the only noble troll in the Stone Kingdom. Morgo had revered Barko for giving him nearly unmatched Power and embracing narcissism. The troll-turned-man was also loyal to a fault. He never broke a bargain.

For a moment, Hagatha speculated whether a broken bargain was the reason for the boy's vengeance, but the implications were too disturbing. She would not sully Barko's esteemed reputation based on conjecture. The troll mage had said Barko died at the boy's hand, knowing no further details. It was simply another reason the child would suffer.

She recalled the events leading up to her foul mood. They had stolen some supplies from the dead trolls near Barko's cave and followed the main army to Rathgar. Their speed demons had died long ago, freezing once they encountered snow on the trail leading up to the lake where the boy wizard and his horse fell in. She paused, trying to stem the revulsion from the thought of a red unicorn bonding with a human.

Hagatha subdued it by reliving the memory of her murdering the white unicorn all those years ago. Killian had foolishly grown so attached to it. She almost smiled but caught herself, knowing such a breach of emotion would create a period of self-loathing.

Despite wanting to kill all the unicorns in the valley before Rathgar, Hagatha and Blade had instead waited patiently. They watched the humans leave the city from a pass high up in the mountains. Trolls were too barbaric and ignorant to ride horses, so they could not steal any. They had to follow the unicorns on foot.

Hagatha did not run.

She had never run to or from anything. She was patient and would hunt them down at her own pace. It was only a matter of time, and the outcome was not in doubt.

That brought her to the frozen waste and the source of her foul mood. The weather conditions had shocked her—the Dark Elf immediately scolded herself for using such an emotionally charged word. The conditions had mildly surprised her. Yes, much better. The wind's strength and the cold were unexpected.

Then a nasty storm came, and even with her formidable Power, they had no choice but to seek refuge. The pair were far enough behind the red-eyed boy that her magic's use would likely be undetected. Regardless, it was a necessary expenditure. She had carved a small hole in the cliffs and slid a rock in front of the entrance, weathering the storm. She sensed the immense Power used millennia ago in the ice desert. It was the source of the Great Forget. What else could it be?

Now, there was only a residue of magic left in the ground, its heat nearly gone. Only a strong magic wielder would even be able to detect it. Once her Master killed the boy and the red-eyed king, he would have all the answers to the Great Forget. Depending on how long he wanted to keep the boy alive to torture, of course. He would likely take his time.

After the storm had passed over the frozen desert, they continued following their quarry. When they started finding items of food and clothing strewn about the snow, she suspected they might have perished in the storm. Then they came upon the huge cavern carved out of the cliff. The amount of Power required for such a feat was impressive. A dead troll with his head caved in was the only resident. The humans were long gone.

The journey took many days on foot, and they were a week behind by the time they reached the river. The Dark Elves needed horses and food.

With a full belly and transportation, she wouldn't be in a foul mood any longer.

Hagatha and Blade pulled their cloaks tight as they entered the village. There was no need for anyone to see their eyes. They passed houses set back from the road with unkept humans lounging on the porches. Some were inhaling smoke from glass pipes. She ignored them.

In the middle of the village stood a huge inn backing onto the river. A tall, bearded man with a large potbelly sauntered out.

"Hey folks, how are you?" he said in a loud voice, raising his hand in greeting.

"Mistress!" Blade warned.

Hagatha seized her Power, but it was too late. An arrow struck her in the right breast, puncturing her lung. As she fell to one knee, the elf woman saw Blade snatch two arrows out of the air before they hit his chest. His eyes blazed yellow, and the weapons expert sent intense healing energy into her body, pulling out the arrow and repairing her wound. She wrapped herself in a blue shield.

Blade was the greatest Yellow Level in the world, with unmatched healing powers. She was completely whole again. More arrows struck their shields but burned into ash.

Hagatha stood up and for the first time in three thousand years could not control her rage. How dare they attack an Inner Circle member? Pathetic human scum. Archers were positioned in open windows on the second level of the inn and other buildings beside her. They continued firing.

She raised both hands and screamed. The archers flew through the windows at odd angles, breaking legs, arms, and even their necks. She levitated their bent bodies before her, twenty feet off the ground. Usually, she would kill an enemy instantly, not believing in gratification by delaying another's death.

But today was different.

She ripped off a limb at a time from each of them. Blood sprayed in fountains over the road. More villagers began pouring out of the inn and houses.

"Tommy, no!"

"Charlie, I will save you!"

"Nobody touches my husband!"

A woman ran at her, face constricted in madness, clawing at the shield even as her hands melted. More villagers charged at them, holding farmer's tools and other weapons. Normally, people would run away when she displayed her Power, but these villagers were raving lunatics. She realized many were on some drug by the expressions on their hollow faces.

Hagatha burst the archers' hearts and let them fall in broken heaps. She turned to the oncoming villagers and unleashed thick ropes of blazing blue magic into their bodies and faces. Whole groups fell at a time, their bodies melting together. She turned to see Blade release his shield and take the citizens on in hand-to-hand combat. His eyes gleamed with a feral excitement as he pulled both swords from his back.

Then he turned into a blur of destruction.

A good thirty villagers came at him at once, swinging cudgels, pickaxes, sickles, shovels, and pitchforks. He moved so fast that many struck each other, swinging wildly. Then he was outside the circle, working his way back in. Decapitated heads flew in quick succession, necks spraying geysers of blood. The weapons expert parried and blocked, using human bodies as shields. Once, a knife got through, appearing between two villagers. It pierced his neck, but only the tip went in due to his toughened skin. His eyes flared yellow, and the wound was gone.

The scene became one of gore and mayhem, with body parts flying everywhere. Many only had time to raise their weapons before being disembowelled.

Hagatha sprayed blue fire to the front and sides, cutting shrieks short as their vocal cords melted. Eventually, the noise died down, and the pair of them picked off the remaining survivors with ease.

Over one hundred bodies littered the ground.

The man with the pot belly stood white-faced on the porch, shaking.

Hagatha pointed her finger, and he flew towards her, stopping inches from her face. The man's crotch became wet as he begged for his life.

"I'm so sorry. Please, forgive me."

"Forgiveness?" Hagatha stared at him but didn't lash out. Her emotions were once again well under control. The Dark Elf would analyze the situation later to see why she became weak and emotional. "Forgiveness is not an option. Why did you attack us? Tell me the truth, or I will hand you over to my weapons expert. He has ways to encourage you to speak."

"It was a group of wizards, Protectors, and trolls. The old wizard gave me ten gold coins to kill you."

"Is ten a lot?" she asked. "I care not for money but am curious what price a human puts on my life."

"Yes, it's a fortune."

"So your greed for money made you do this?"

The pot-bellied man nodded.

"Typical. Where did they go?"

"They walked east back the way they came, then north into a meadow. I don't know after that." He gave her a pleading look.

"Anything else?"

"The wizard said not to tell the witches."

"Where are the witches?"

The pot-bellied man gestured towards the inn with a shaky hand.

"Good, then your usefulness is at an end." She squeezed her fist, bursting his heart, then tossed the body to the side.

Hagatha stepped over multiple corpses before climbing the stairs to the inn. She pushed open the batwing doors to reveal an empty common room except for three women sitting at a table. They had tattoos on their faces. She recognized the symbols from the ones Morgo used to draw.

The Dark Elf calmly pulled out a chair across from them and took a seat. Blade stood to the side. They stared at her blazing blue eyes.

"Why did you allow this?" she asked without preamble.

"We did not know. The leader of the Hill People did not tell us," said the witch sitting in the center. She was young with short black hair.

"I believe you. If I didn't, you'd be dead. Where are the group of wizards that were in here about a week ago?"

"They left the inn and returned the way they came, mounted unicorns in a field and headed west out to Yucan."

"Yucan?"

"It's the largest trader's town. They stayed a night and headed north. That's all I know." The witch stared at her calmly.

Hagatha respected the woman's control over her emotions. "What is north of Yucan?"

"The only thing directly north is Darkwood Forest."

"What's in the forest?"

The witch paused.

Hagatha leaned forward. "Careful," she said in a whisper.

The witch looked at the two beside her. They both nodded. "The Secret Caves."

"And what's in these Secret Caves?" the white-haired woman asked softly.

"Morgeth, the High Witch and her coven."

"I want to meet her. Take me there."

"We cannot enter. We are lesser witches, but we can tell you where to go if she agrees to meet you."

"She will meet me."

"Can I ask your name?"

The white-haired woman rose. "I am Hagatha, Inner Circle member and advisor to Killian, the Demon King."

The lesser witch finally showed a crack in her composure but quickly recovered. "We will give you horses and supplies. Ride west to Yucan. Be there in seven days. Someone will meet you on the city's north side and take you to Darkwood. There is a black rock on the south side of the forest. Morgeth will meet you there. I will send a message now heralding your arrival." She paused. "Is it true? Is he coming to save us?"

Morgeth smiled, not out of emotion but for their benefit. "Yes. You will be saved."

All three witches stood up and bowed low.

7

Darkwood enveloped them in a shroud of darkness. The trees were tall, but their limbs twisted and intertwined into a canopy resembling a cage. The leaves had fallen, leaving a spiderweb of limbs, creating a latticework that blocked out the warmth and light of the sun. The weight of the forest seemed to press on them, like a malevolent mother cradling them in a deadly embrace.

"There are symbols on the trees around the perimeter," Mary noted, pointing at trunks with odd markings.

Chip moved closer and saw runes and symbols of strange letters, upside-down stars, hypnotic spirals, waning moons, and, most disturbing, an open eye. A sense of dread and despair permeated everything like an evil blanket. The cold air was still, and he could see his breath in vapour clouds. The fog was the most disturbing, moving in slow swirls along the ground by a wind he could not feel. The light brightened as lightning raced across the dark clouds overhead, and then a deep, booming thunder broke the unnatural silence. He could feel it in his bones.

"Weapons out," Garth ordered. "Let's move together." The Protectors and trolls formed a ring around the wizards, and the party moved forward, senses alert. They went deeper into the forest until the black, twisted trees looked the same in every direction.

"Use magic only if you must," Xander warned. "They can pinpoint where we are every time we use it."

"The fact that they have a Seeing Stone also doesn't help," Chase pointed out. "Can't they see us anyway?"

"We are basing everything off a story written over four millennia ago," the wizard replied. "We don't know how this supposed stone works, assuming it even exists. What we do know is magic reveals our location. We also need to save our energy for later. Stay sharp."

The fog rolled in thicker, making everything from the knees down invisible. Chip had never seen anything like it. Normally, fog appeared at a distance, but this was like a living soup, obscuring the bottom half of his legs. A flash of light lit the tree limbs in stark relief. He saw a white head far to his left between a fork in two branches, and then it vanished.

"I think I saw a face in the trees," he warned.

Thunder erupted again, jarring his senses.

"Something grabbed my leg," shouted Chase. He swung down with his sword, but there was nothing there.

The sounds of everyone breathing seemed abnormally loud in the silence. The Protectors waded forward in a crouch, coiled to spring.

"A shape moved in the trees over there," Ethrang said, pointing to his right. A branch snapped in two from the same direction. Lightning flashed again.

This time, Chip saw multiple white faces with gleaming fangs around them.

"Watch out!"

High-pitched screams erupted from sharp-toothed mouths, and small monkey-like creatures began dropping from the trees to disappear into the fog. A moment later, Chip felt a terrible pain in his left leg as something bit him. Shouts and cries erupted from the group as the creatures savagely attacked their lower bodies. Everyone started swinging wildly through the fog. Then, the white things started leaping on them. They had long claws on their hands and feet, driving them like small daggers into their flesh.

"Ow!" yelled Chase as he switched from sword to dagger, driving the point straight into the head of one of the beasts. The others tried frantically to keep the creatures from reaching their necks as they crawled up their bodies. Mary held her arm out to stop one, and it bit her forearm to the bone. She screamed. The Protector Shimko, moving with whip-like speed, impaled it in the neck, and it fell off dead.

The twins stood back-to-back, slashing furiously. Ward allowed a creature to bite his arm and then stabbed it through the heart.

Three of the things shimmied up Bulch. The massive Protector grabbed them with his bare hands and smashed their heads open on tree trunks. One troll had six on him and went down. Garth and Chase moved from person to person, driving daggers into the creature's temples.

Two were on Ethrang, fangs sunk into each shoulder. He looked straight at Chip, pain and fury in his eyes. "Sorry." The blond boy disappeared into the fog.

Chip felt the peculiar crackle of magic, and a wasp demon emerged from the mist. Six creatures covered it, but none could pierce its thick armour. The wasp ripped them to shreds with its massive talons in a flurry of motion. Then it dropped on all fours through the fog, and wails rang out as creatures flew through the air in pieces. Scraping sounded as the remaining creatures scampered up the trees, leaping from branch to branch, before disappearing.

The companions looked at each other in disbelief. Blood covered everyone except Chase and Garth. Ethrang reappeared as himself, arms bleeding. The trolls picked up the one who fell, but his throat had been torn open. They thumped their chests and released him. Daria started healing her comrades, eyes blazing yellow. Mary and the twins rested a hand on her arm, then linked with the Yellow Level troll mage, easing the burden.

"I had to shift," Ethrang said. "They were on my shoulders, and I couldn't raise my arms. When I changed, they fell off. My armour protected me."

"That's alright," Xander said. "They know where we are now anyway. The goal is to conserve magic for the caves. We lost one already, and it is not even mid-morning. Stay alert."

Even as he said it, a high-pitched laugh sounded in the distance. It was eerie and child-like. Then the forest went silent again.

Everyone stared at each other. Chip felt a chill run up his spine.

"Let's move," Garth said. "Staying in one spot is not wise."

A flash of light and another peal of thunder increased the tension. Then snow began to fall, filtering through the interlocking canopy above. The beautiful shimmering flakes seemed out of place amidst the dark ugliness around them. The fog persisted, moving in slow swirls.

Up ahead, a large tree with a hole stood by itself in a clearing. In spots where they could see through the mist, bones of different lengths, most unrecognizable, littered the ground. Above the gaping hollow in the tree were symbols and runes. The most prominent symbol was an open eye.

Chip felt an evil presence emanate from the hole.

None of the trees were comparable to the behemoths in Fang Forest, but this one was the largest so far, easily thirty feet around. The hollow was disturbingly large. Inside was inky blackness.

No one spoke lest they wake whatever lurked inside. The mist swirled around the tree in concentric rings, giving the impression it was an island. The trunk shot upwards but abruptly stopped near the canopy, the top half long gone, a vestige of time past. He got a sense it was a long-dead parent of its lesser offspring. The eye symbol carved into the black trunk above the hole stared at them balefully.

Garth put a finger to his lips as they entered the clearing and drew his sword. The others followed suit. Everyone faced the hollow and began sidestepping in a circle, careful not to step on bones.

A deep growl sounded from within the tree, echoing off the interior. A rare look of alarm crossed the weapons master's face, followed by recognition.

Suddenly, huge yellow eyes appeared in the hole.

"Swords forward. Stand—" Garth yelled but couldn't finish.

Out of the darkness charged a massive black cat, bulging muscles carrying it forward with astonishing speed. A terrifying fifteen-foot-long body followed. The cat's head alone was the size of half of Chip's body. The creature screamed as it sprang forward, revealing two-foot-long fangs. In one bound, the cat reached the Protectors in the front. Only Carvor had time to raise his sword before the feline monstrosity crashed into him, Ward, and Shimko. All three flew backwards, taking out half a dozen trolls, including Daria. None of them got up. The cat skidded to a halt with Carvor's sword impaled in its right shoulder.

It snarled at the stuck blade, bit the hilt, and tossed it aside. The beast turned its yellow, bloodshot eyes on the rest of them. In those eyes, Chip saw a fury and primal madness like no other.

Fear ran through his body as he stared at a perfect killing machine. Its back height was higher than his head. He knew one swipe of its paw would kill a grown man. The beast stared straight at him, exposing a maw that could bite him in half. It sprang at the boy with one push of its massive hind legs.

Chip Oathbinder saw death coming for him in a blinding rush of speed.

He had no choice but to use his magic.

Seizing his Power despite the fear, the boy tried to wrap himself in a red shield but couldn't form it in time. The beast struck the orphan full force, sending him hurtling backwards thirty feet into a tree trunk. The wavering shield absorbed some of the impact, but the back of his head struck hard. A round knot on the deformed tree went deep into his back, and he heard his spine snap. The world fragmented as he slid down the trunk. Waves of dizziness washed over him, and the shield vanished. He knew his back was broken and screamed involuntarily then vomited. The monstrous cat skidded to a stop, shaking its head. His red magic had burnt its lips off, and now all its teeth gleamed in the dim light. It lowered its body to finish him off. He cried out in helplessness, writhing in agony.

"Protect the Chosen One!" Garth screamed, and Chip heard fear in his voice for the first time. Their eyes met briefly, and the boy knew from the look on his teacher's face that he was dying.

Everyone left standing charged the cat at once, no longer concerned with their own lives. The wizards seized their Power as one, but the trolls were there first, hindering their ability to use magic. The cat turned and swiped the first troll's arm clean off at the shoulder.

It sprang into several others, sending them crashing backwards into the wizards in a tangled heap. It turned to Xander, the only one still standing, and launched its body like a projectile. The Grand Wizard managed to spray blue fire before it bowled him over, barely shielding himself in time, such was the cat's speed. Chase and Garth leapt to the side, but a swipe of the beast's paw raked his best friend on the hip, sending him slamming into the weapons master. They flew backwards, landing hard.

Xander's fire ravaged the side of the cat's face, melting one of its eyes and smoking its fur. If anything, the pain made it angrier. The troll captain ran forward, swinging his sword, but the beast swiped viciously at his legs, sending him somersaulting into Bulch. They both went down. With everyone flat on their backs, the monstrosity spun around and locked its remaining eye on Chip.

Nothing would stop its charge now.

The Guardian of the Races leaned with his blood-soaked head against the tree. His spine was broken, and the boy could feel his last breaths rattle in his throat. Dizziness and nausea washed over him, but the pain was diminishing as he succumbed to Death's cold embrace. He felt a last surge of pride that his friends had given everything to protect him.

They had recklessly thrown themselves on the beast, worried more about him than themselves.

They had done everything they could do.

He knew none would get up in time to stop the monstrosity from catapulting into him. He stared at the cat's remaining eye and saw a primordial madness. This creature only knew how to kill and was the best at it. It lowered its body, coiling its muscles to spring. He had been its target all along.

Their quest had failed.

Darkwood had won.

It sprang forward, all fangs and claws.

As the boy's sight dimmed, he hallucinated a massive silver wolf launching at the beast from the side.

It was Silvermane. Chip's mind couldn't grasp how. His thoughts began to fragment. His vision reduced to an ever smaller ring, but he saw the massive mountain wolf latch its jaws around the cat's neck, smashing into it with incredible force. Even so, the black monster skidded and whipped its head furiously, shaking the wolf loose. Silvermane landed hard on his side, trying to scramble to his feet.

That was all the time the massive cat needed.

Chip watched it spring at him out of the diminishing corner of his eye. The great cat launched through the air, and time slowed.

Then a blaze of red and white arced across the clearing. It moved impossibly fast. As the cat opened its mouth wide to cover his face, he saw a sword slide into its side up to the hilt, followed by a hand and a face.

It was Chase.

The red flecks in his eyes blazed brighter than the orphan had ever seen. As the cat's fangs touched Chip's forehead, his best friend slammed into the beast with such force that he could hear its bones break. Chase bowled the cat over onto its back. The orphan's head lolled to the side as he watched the tall boy wrench out his sword and stab the massive beast through the heart.

The cat stilled in death.

Then he heard screams and many people surrounded him, blocking the dim light.

"Hurry! Link with me," someone cried.

Chip felt his last breath rattle in his throat.

His vision shrunk, and the last sight before he died was the face of Eleanor looking at him with overwhelming concern and love.

A single tear formed in the corner of his eye, and then he could not hold on anymore.

"We are losing him!"

"I'm afraid he's gone."

"Keep trying!"

Chip felt his spirit essence leave his body. He went with it.

He was it.

The Divide appeared across the vast expanse of the void. He began picking up speed, hurtling towards it.

Then he saw it.

Death.

Through the Divide, a blackness formed, coalescing into an entity.

It laughed, a sound of tombstones rubbing together.

A sound only Death could make.

Even so, Chip felt a calm and peace he could only dream about. His burden was finally lifted.

He was free.

"Come back to me."

The boy paused.

"Come back to me."

Eleanor!

He turned to see a beautiful white essence approach him, trailed by a long white tether.

"Don't go any further."

He willed himself to stop and waited.

Something screamed behind him and began reaching out.

Death was coming.

Her tether suddenly ended, having no more give. She was so close.

She reached out with a white hand, an extension of her spirit essence. He did the same. They were just out of reach. He pushed his hardest, straining against the Laws. She did the same.

Their spirit essences touched. She pulled him into her, and they hurtled back across the void. A terrible scream sounded behind him.

His love melded with hers, and for a glorious eternal moment they were one.

"Breathe."

Chip Oathbinder breathed in life. And then he felt pain.

It wasn't the pain of injury but the pain of life.

The pain of living.

It slowly subsided, and he opened his eyes. Someone was lying beside him. A ring of faces filled his vision. Expressions of relief washed over them.

The person beside him lifted their head.

Eleanor smiled. "This makes us even."

Before he could respond, she kissed him deeply, and he did not resist.

The Queen of Vanalon let go and stroked his hair. He shifted higher on the tree trunk, fully expecting his back to protest.

"My wounds? They were…irreparable."

The troll mage Daria looked at him with dark rings under her eyes. "It took all of my skill and everyone's Power. Even then, it was not enough." She looked at the queen. "Eleanor went after you."

He turned to the love of his life and smiled. "I know. I taught her how to do it."

The Queen of Vanalon laughed. "It only worked because you had just passed. Your spirit essence had not made the full journey. I brought you back. Any longer, you would have been out of reach. I guess I have a shorter tether than you."

Chip shook his head. "No, I suspect the Balance shortened tethers after I pulled you back through the Divide. It is not allowed anymore, remember?"

Everyone was looking at them like they had three heads.

Chip laughed. "Nevermind. Thank you for saving me."

Xander smiled. His eyes were wet, and he looked tired. "Dear boy, you have saved us many times over. No need to thank us. We are only returning the favour and still owing." He turned his gaze to Eleanor. "I see why you needed to be saved. Without you, he would be lost."

Chip nodded. "I can't argue with that. So, what was that thing?"

"It is called a Yagr," Garth Stone said. "Smaller ones grow in the barbarian forests to the south. This was by far the biggest I have ever seen."

"You've seen them before?" Chip asked, a little surprised.

"A long time ago," Garth said but didn't elaborate.

Ethrang appeared. "It shook Silvermane off like he was a rag doll."

Chip laughed. "In my state, I thought Silvermane had come back to life." Then he remembered Chase and saw him standing to the side. His best friend had a strange look on his face, like the few times he had cried as a kid. "I've never seen you move that fast."

"I was mad," Chase said. "Really mad."

The boys gave each other a knowing look as only best friends could.

"Indeed, we were all mad and scared," Xander said. "That cat nearly wiped us out. It seemed particularly intent on killing you, lad."

"Maybe it likes the colour red?" Chip said innocently.

"Which cat? This one?" Ethrang moved back, and suddenly the massive black Yagr stood beside the tree with muscles rippling. The trolls stepped back, hands on their weapons.

A moment later, Ethrang reappeared, laughing. "Good luck to anyone who challenges that thing."

"My goodness, something good can come out of something bad," Xander observed. "It usually does. We have destroyed their weapon and created one ourselves."

"Did anyone...not make it?" Chip asked.

"The troll whose arm got torn off bled out."

The boy sighed. One Eye and the others thumped their chests.

Xander looked around. "We have used some Power already. Stay alert and try to conserve."

"We need to move again," Garth said. He held out a hand to Chip, who took it. The weapons master pulled the boy to his feet and gripped his shoulder. They shared a look, both knowing no more needed to be said.

They re-entered the clearing, at the ready for anything else.

Ethrang couldn't help peer into the hole in the tree trunk. He wrinkled his nose and turned to the others. "Half-eaten things. I can't even tell what they are."

"This place reeks of evil and death," Xander said. "Those symbols are a gateway to darkness."

Chip stared at the large eye carved into the tree above the hole and shuddered. His ordeal with Death again made him realize the tremendous preciousness of life. The Yagr had taken him by surprise. He couldn't shake the feeling that it singled him out as if instructed to do so. The boy would now assume he was the prime target for whatever waited within Darkwood. Chip vowed to react sooner.

The forest resumed its silence. The thick fog moved about their legs in eerie swirls, controlled by something unknown. The snow began to fall thicker amidst the twisted trunks.

On the other side of the clearing, the ground rose steadily, and the fog began to thin. The overhead trees were less intertwined here, allowing more dim light to shine in. Dark, angry clouds revealed themselves, and lightning lit the trees in garish light as if they were wading into a sea of macabre skeletons. Then the sound started, low at first but increasing in volume as the ground rose. It was the mournful sound of the wind, lamenting like a lost soul forever doomed to wander a dead land.

A low ridge materialized before them, its hulking shape taking form as they climbed. Pine trees covered the side, but their forms were bent and unnatural, and some needles looked sickly and yellow. Strange rocks dotted the base of the slope, marked with runes.

They entered the pine forest with trepidation, knowing anything could lurk behind the large, bushy trees. The canopy above disappeared, and the fog vanished, unable to maintain its tenuous hold on the slope. Dead pine needles littered the ground, mixing with the snow to create a soft carpet. Once the unnatural pine forest enveloped them, the wind died down again. Snowflakes floated everywhere.

A growl sounded to their left. Everyone froze with weapons at the ready. Another growl came from up ahead and then to the right. The familiarity of the sound struck Chip. Hungry whines erupted all around, moving steadily closer.

The boy seized his magic.

Suddenly, white, mottled, two-headed bodies hurtled into the small group from all directions. They were mutant wolves, attacking as a pack.

"Form a ring," shouted Garth

Chip had time to register the terrible condition of the animals. Chunks of white fur were missing from their bodies, revealing grotesque, pink lesions dripping with pus. They were smaller than mountain wolves, but each sported two heads with long fangs and otherworldly white eyes. The creatures snarled as they struck. The trolls and Protectors hacked and bludgeoned the wild beasts with ferocity. More slunk through the trees, gnashing their teeth, waiting for their moment to spring. Others circled them with cunning eyes, demonstrating the wolves' patience.

Chase fought three of the beasts at once. He moved with breathtaking speed, but one of the six heads latched onto his thigh, fastening its jaws in a death grip.

"Ow!" he cried, and the red chips in his eyes flashed brighter. The tall boy sliced off several other heads and then brought the pommel of his sword down hard on the wolf's skull. Its eyes rolled up, and it slid down his leg. The wound closed immediately, and he continued his grisly work.

"Take off both heads," Garth instructed as he swung his sword in a horizontal arc, decapitating the animal in front of him. Two heads fell to the ground at his feet.

The wizards stayed in the middle, eyes blazing. Everyone conserved their magic but watched intently in case they needed to lend aid.

Ward and Shimko fought side by side, shoring off heads with precision. A pile began to grow around them. Their arms were bleeding from the grazing fangs, but they did not relent. The trolls bludgeoned whatever came close with their massive clubs. Many wolves had only one live head while the other hung down with its skull caved in. Still, the beasts fought on, growling and snarling.

"Enough of this," Ethrang said and disappeared from the middle of the group. A moment later, a monstrous black cat appeared amid the wolves at the back. The dog's snarls turned into frightened whines as they took in the massive Yagr. The wolves finally showed fear.

Ethrang sprang into action, shredding the beasts like paper with his long claws. He moved in a circle, scattering the wolves in his wake. Any that stood their ground were bowled over as he charged straight into them. Howls of pain erupted, and with a seemingly hidden signal, the animals bolted back into the trees.

"Let's move!" Garth ordered. "We need to get out of their territory."

The wizards healed any serious wounds and then ushered everyone forward. They moved quickly, weaving between the sickly trees. As the storm above them intensified, the snow came down harder, obscuring the dead pine needles with a white carpet.

The growls started again, and Chip saw slinking white shapes between the trees. The wolves did not attack but kept pace. Ethrang remained in Yagr form, bringing up the rear. The black cat glided gracefully, a thing of deadly beauty.

The group approached the top of the ridge, which was devoid of trees. The storm's full force struck them, wind whipping the snow sideways. Thunder and lightning exploded in the dark clouds above, a show of light and sound.

A massive white wolf with two oversized heads sat on its haunches at the top of the ridge between two rune-covered stones, staring at them with hateful, milky eyes. The great beast raised its head to the sky and emitted a long, deep howl.

The pine trees on both sides shook as dozens of wolves poured out from all directions. The two-headed beasts streaked across the clearing and attacked.

"Shield!" The twins said as one, and a wall of blue fire surrounded everyone. A few wolves catapulted into the flames and caught fire. The others skidded to a halt. More poured out of the trees until scores of two-headed wolves surrounded them.

They all sat on their haunches.

"The beasts are waiting until we run out of magic," Mary said in disbelief.

Ethrang reappeared. "They are listening to their leader," he said, pointing at the oversized wolf that had not moved. The skinny blond boy walked to the front of the shield, flexing his hands. "Shoot fire into the others, and I will take him out."

Xander nodded. "Trolls and Protectors, crouch down. Magic wielders, get ready." He looked at the orphan from Banfar who gave him a signal. "Drop the shield!"

The twins released the blue wall, and the two-headed wolves stood up, hackles raised. The wizards and troll mages shot out deadly streams of multi-coloured fire, striking the animals in a broad ring. Ethrang leapt forward, shape-shifting into the massive Yagr. The wolf leader crouched at the ready, both fanged mouths opening wide. The great cat rushed it, but the wolf dove to the side at the last instant and then leapt back in, one huge mouth trying to close around Ethrang's neck. The Yagr hissed and swiped with blinding speed at the great head, ripping half its face off. With one more vicious slash, the wolf's jaws fell away, its face wholly shredded.

The monstrous white wolf pulled away, one head hanging limp, and then leapt in to tear at the cat's hamstring. Ethrang spun around, avoiding the gnashing teeth, and the two huge beasts circled. Blood leaked from the cat's neck. The one head hung uselessly from the wolf's shoulder, unrecognizable. The leader emitted another howl, and more wolves spilled out of the forest.

"You might want to hurry!" Chase called.

The Yagr stood on the top of the ridge facing the massive two-headed wolf and launched itself in a streak of black. The white wolf leapt to the side again, but this time Ethrang turned with it, swiping its shoulder. The beast rolled over onto its back, and the Yagr pounced on it, huge jaws fastening on the white neck. He tore at the wolf's stomach in windmill fashion with his forelegs, shredding its belly. Red blood sprayed over the snow and fur.

The white beast shook once, and then the alpha wolf went limp.

The other wolves racing across the ridge stopped as one. They all turned to their leader with heads bowed. The wizards and mages paused to watch the spectacle, hands still outstretched.

At the same time, the beasts raised their heads and howled. The sound drowned out the storm's fury and spoke of loss and defeat. They turned at the same time and trotted back into the pine trees.

The Yagr roared in victory then padded back to the group. Ethrang reappeared, holding his neck. "It's not deep. That cat has thick skin."

Daria reached over and touched him lightly, repairing the wound.

Kristan put his hand on the orphan's shoulder. "Epic fight. You defeated a mighty foe."

"Yes," Thomas added. "It was a sight to behold. A little sloppy at first, but let's not get picky."

"I didn't think it could get out of the way that fast." Ethrang grinned. "When I'm the Yagr, nothing seems faster than me. The world moves in slow motion. My arms feel like the fastest weapons in the world. It's...exhilarating."

"Well, don't feel invincible," Chase said. "I already killed you once."

"Ha!" the green-robed boy laughed. "It took all of you last time. Don't forget I can choose to shield myself. Be happy we are on the same side."

"Yes, you are quite lucky," Chase said smugly.

"Let's not tarry here," Xander urged. "The wind will die down once we get off this hill."

Everyone nodded, and they hurried past the great two-headed body of the white wolf, setting a brisk pace down the other side of the ridge.

8

The wolves did not follow or keep pace. Chip let out a sigh of relief. He had expended little magic throughout the ordeal, knowing he would need more for what was ahead.

They reached the bottom of the ridge and emerged from the pines, which only grew on the slopes. Once more, a wall of twisted limbs greeted them. At the lower elevation, swirling snow blanketed the ground.

"Let's get under the canopy and eat lunch," Xander suggested.

Good, I'm famished," Chase responded. "After a morning like that, who wouldn't be?" The trolls nodded wholeheartedly.

"The tales are true," One Eye said. "Few could have made it this far, and we still have a long way to go."

"Yes," Chase agreed once inside the shelter of the forest. He rested both hands on his hips and looked around. "A morning in Darkwood starts with a greeting by killer monkeys, followed by a mid-morning attack by the most ferocious cat that ever lived, and then before lunch, it sends a hundred two-headed diseased wolves at you. I'm looking forward to a fun-filled afternoon. How about you?"

Mary gave him a scathing look, causing One Eye to grin.

"If it were easy, everyone would do it," the troll captain remarked. "Even a small army would have trouble in this place."

"I'm more worried about the night," Mary said quietly. "There's a reason it's called Darkwood."

Everyone stared somberly at her. Chip could tell different scenarios were playing through their minds. The weapons master's voice came through in his, "Nothing is as bad as it seems."

Surely, some things were worse, weren't they? Then again, he conceded that the mind could create fearful thoughts not based on reality. He refused to let his imagination run wild and instead prepared for the worst. Few realized how powerful the mind was, sometimes turning into one's worst enemy. When it craved something or nurtured an irrational belief, the mind was clever at focusing on evidence that supported itself.

Many lived their whole lives with irrational beliefs and self-justified desires. Few looked at all the evidence to change that belief into a rational one. Yet that was how change could occur. He wondered what the beliefs the witches of the Secret Caves held and how they justified them for millennia. He would have the answers soon enough.

They ate cured meats and cheese standing up, listening to the storm rage above. At least the wind had died down, its force lessened by the trees. Stopping in one place was not advisable, so Garth urged them on once they finished.

The land levelled out, and they made good time. The fog had not settled as much here, but the lazy snowflakes grew larger, creating an ethereal landscape. Nobody noticed it at first, but the trees grew closer together. Soon after, Chip could reach out and touch the trunks on either side. Then the sounds started, seeming like voices.

"What was that?" Kristan said, "Did you say something?" He turned to his twin.

"No, I thought you were muttering." Thomas looked around fearfully.

"Shhh." Eleanor held a finger to her lips. "I hear whispers."

Everyone stopped and strained their ears.

"Ssssss."

"I heard it!" Ethrang exclaimed. "It's coming from my right."

They looked around but saw nothing.

"Weapons out," Garth ordered. "Keep moving."

Chip reached for his Wall, ready to break through in an instant. He brushed the snowflakes out of his eyes. A growing sense of dread filled him.

The party moved forward in the dim light. The trees grew closer together, forcing them to move in single file. The canopy overhead tightened until the dark sky was barely visible.

"Ssssss."

"I heard it again."

"It came from your left."

"No, it came from my right."

"Ssssss."

"It's blocked up ahead," Ward warned from the front. The trees had now closed in. Dark, twisted limbs draped over them like some demented mother, soothing them before they were smothered. The trees had become much smaller, lowering the canopy as they moved forward.

"Ssssss."

Chip pushed towards Bulch. "Can you lift me?" he asked the giant Protector.

Bulch grunted and grabbed him under his shoulders. The boy flew up and saw that the trees ahead of Ward and Shimko had intertwined, making it almost impossible to get through. His heart sped up, and he took a deep breath. The space they were in felt like a black wooden tomb or coffin.

"We have to go back," Chip urged. "I don't feel good." He looked at the canopy that had somehow lowered. They were in a dark cocoon.

"Ssssss."

"It's louder."

"It's right next to us!"

"I can barely see anything!"

"Ssssss."

Chip stared at the canopy, letting his eyes adjust.

And then it moved.

The tree limb he was staring at suddenly untwisted, and a large triangular head with beady eyes appeared before him.

"Sssssss!"

"Snakes!" he screamed, seizing his Power. The head struck forward with blinding speed, but his shield held. He forgot Bulch was holding him, and the big man let go as his hands began to melt.

"Ssssss."

Magic flared to life as the wizards tried to shield themselves, but everyone was crammed together.

"You're burning me!"

"Ow!"

"Ssssss."

What they thought were tree limbs came to life as dozens of snakes unwrapped themselves and struck out. Most were over fifteen feet long. The forest became alive with writhing movement.

Screams of pain erupted. Everyone frantically tried to stab the quick-moving serpents, but the others hampered them. Sharp fangs sank into shoulders and thighs before the snakes looped around their victims. Then, the real screams began. Chip watched a massive snake drop its coils over a troll's body and squeeze with immense strength.

The sounds of bones breaking became audible. Bodies fell into him as they scrambled backwards, and he had to release his shield. He desperately sought a way to use his magic without hurting the others. Several of his companions went down with snakes wrapped tight around their bodies. Fangs sank deep into his calf, and he screamed in pain. A large snake shimmied up him so fast he scarcely believed it.

"Ssssss."

The serpent squeezed, and he couldn't breathe. He ignited his shield, and the thing's entire body melted off him. He released it immediately as Eleanor stumbled back into him. The queen's eyes blazed reddish-brown, and the tree limbs began moving on their own. The branches became her wooden hands, and she snatched snakes off people with deft precision then flung them hard into the trees. The sounds of serpent spines breaking joined the human ones. Chip dashed about, touching any snake he saw and sending red fire throughout its body, killing it from the inside.

"Ssssss."

Ethrang turned around with a snake around his neck. A green flare ignited in his eyes, and then he was gone, the snake dropping harmlessly to the ground. A giant eagle appeared with folded wings. Its giant beak began stabbing at the bodies of any snake in sight, ripping them in half with one bite. He spotted Shimko on the ground, a massive serpent wrapped around his body. Even so, the stocky Protector stabbed it repeatedly with a small dagger in the neck with his one free arm. Its eyes rolled back, and the death grip loosened.

Bulch used his melted hands to unwind a snake from his body with sheer strength, and it worked. He flung the writhing beast hard against a tree. Mary shot coordinated bits of fire into the serpents' faces, blinding them. The twins were completely wrapped by the biggest snake Chip had ever seen, their noses touching.

"Link with me," Kristan gasped as their ribs broke. Chip reached out to kill the snake, but their bodies shimmered with blazing blue fire, and the massive serpent melted into a gooey mess. The twins both clutched their broken ribs, healing each other at the same time.

Eleanor continued using the trees themselves to snatch and stab the snakes. Some of the trolls had gone down, but Daria and Mary were sending fire up and down their scaly bodies. One troll had two massive snakes around him. With a snap, his body bent in half, and the soldier's feet touched his face. The troll stared with vacant eyes. One Eye killed the snakes by chopping their heads off with his axe.

Light flashed everywhere as the magic users fought valiantly, creating a strong smell of cooked snake flesh. Chip surveyed the whole group and sent a red shield around everyone. The last few snakes tried to attack but melted upon contact.

Then it was over, and the healing began. Other than the one troll bent in half, the rest only sustained broken ribs or fang bites. Chip sent his presence out to find a half-dozen snakes still in the trees. He reached out with a red hand and ended their lives.

The boy released his shield. "Is everyone alright?" The others nodded.

"We have lost another brother, but he died well." One Eye and the rest of the trolls thumped their chests, standing over their fallen comrade. The fourteen trolls who had set out were down to ten.

"There is a way forward now," Garth called out. "It's still tight, but we can slip through."

The canopy now showed large openings. The snakes had used this trap to ensnare travellers or other animals, creating the illusion of a dead end. He shook his head at the variety of life in Darkwood, realizing that these were the strongest, cleverest creatures evolved over millennia. It was a very dangerous place.

The trees began to spread apart again, and the boy sighed in relief. By now, the snow had blanketed the ground, and they walked on a white carpet through a twisted maze. Chip looked up to see the storm had finally moved east to wreak havoc over the ice desert. He could see his breath in the late afternoon air, but the chill paled compared to the bone-deep cold of the frozen waste.

His training taught him that one of the best ways to enjoy the present was to experience something worse. The weapons master told him as a young boy that if he felt ungrateful about his current life situation, then he needed to experience worse conditions. Training intensely, taking away life's wants, restricting freedoms, and immersing oneself in extreme environments all served to improve the realization that life should never be taken for granted. Garth would remind him that life could always be worse.

Chip would fall back on memories of his first three weeks of training, which were unbearable. Similarly, he remembered the extreme cold of the ice desert and used it to appreciate the relatively mild temperature of Darkwood. All the lessons played through his mind. All the years of training, failure, and challenges.

Ultimately, his goal was to love, learn, help others, be grateful, and reach his full potential.

It was a journey, not a destination. And sometimes the journey was not fun, but that was where the most growth occurred.

As the sun began to fall westward, he shivered at the thought of being in the forest at night. That particular shiver had nothing to do with the cold.

They plodded on in the dimming light until Thomas stopped, pointing.

"Oh no," Chase whispered. "Dear Creator."

Chip followed the blond wizard's arm to see what his best friend was afraid of and with relief saw that it was just a spiderweb between two tree branches. Granted, it was a large web, but the most it could trap was a large rodent or perhaps a medium-sized bird.

"It's not that big," Chip reassured. "Likely a leftover from the summertime. In winter, spiders hibernate or lay eggs. Don't worry."

Chase thought about it. "That's true. When we were in Fang Forest, it was early autumn. Spiders don't go out in winter."

He began to smile, and his shoulders relaxed.

"In normal places, they don't." Ethrang slapped him on the back. "But this is Darkwood."

Chase blanched. "I hate spiders," he muttered, glancing around.

"Keep moving," Xander called back. "If we only encounter spiders from here on in, we should count ourselves lucky."

They plodded on as the light began to fade. Disturbingly, more spiderwebs appeared between branches and then the tree trunks themselves. They also grew in size. Now, a full-grown troll could get caught in one. Chip felt a nervous flutter and tried to give Chase a smile of encouragement, but he failed. His friend turned white.

"It's alright," Kristan called from the front. "The trees are ending. Even spiders can't make webs out of thin air." Thomas nodded in agreement.

Ahead of them was a strip of land extending a good league in both directions. It was only a couple of hundred feet across before the forest resumed.

"I wonder what caused this," Eleanor said.

"The logical explanation is a forest fire that burned itself out," Mary answered but seemed doubtful.

"It's only a dirt strip," Kristan noted, stepping forward. A gust whipped up his hair. "The wind must have cleared the snow off earlier today."

"Some event occurred here to kill the trees," Xander conjectured. "I sense a residue of magic in the ground."

"Do you think it had something to do with the Great Forget?" Chip asked.

"No, I don't think so. It's very localized." The wizard squinted ahead. To their left, the sun was right on the edge of the western horizon. "Let's get across before it gets dark."

They moved forward. A cold wind sprang up, shrieking at them. Chip should have experienced relief after being in the confines of the forest, but he felt too exposed in the open. The earth absorbed their footsteps as they reached the halfway point. It felt...springy. The only sound was the wind.

A sharp laugh abruptly rang out from the trees on the other side. Chip thought he could make out a hooded figure.

"Something is not right..." Xander began.

Bulch stamped his foot down. "The ground is not right." Chip heard a strange clicking noise around them in a wide circle.

Suddenly, the earth below fell away.

The boy felt weightless as he watched everyone fall with him. He seized his Power and desperately formed a cushion of air below him as something struck hard into his back. Visions of his spine breaking earlier in the day caused his shield to falter, but he asserted his rage by thinking of Eleanor.

Then spiders were all over him.

He was on his back in a giant hole twenty feet deep and twice as wide. The light from his magic showed spiders over two feet long with bulbous bodies trying to pierce his shield with long fangs. They had two smaller front forelegs ending in pincers that appeared to be used for cutting. The creatures snipped at his shield and tried to bite it then hissed as their legs and fangs melted.

In horror, the boy looked to the side to see hundreds more crawling out of small holes in the walls of the giant pit. He realized the ground above them had been a massive spiderweb with dirt pushed over it.

Chip sat up, eyes blazing. Pain ratcheted through his body, but nothing felt broken. He looked upon a scene of nightmare. No one had seized their magic in the fall. The spiders bit his companion's bodies in a frenzy and immediately began wrapping them in a thick web casing. Dozens surrounded each victim, using their forelegs to turn the bodies over.

He was the only one to stay conscious after the fall.

At least twenty bodies were immobile before him. He knew the spiders would carry them away and then slowly ingest their living fluids over the next few weeks until they were fat and plump. His bile rose, yet his rage was greater.

Chip Oathbinder stood up in the massive pit, red coils of Power snaking across his body. Hundreds of large spiders turned to him and hissed.

The boy lifted his hands.

They charged at him, unafraid of his magic.

He unleashed his fury, sending out wide swaths of red Power. Dozens died in each stream. His only constraint was not to hit his companions.

More spiders came at him until he wiped most of them out. Even as he did, distant hisses sounded, and another wave erupted from the holes, giving him pause. He realized that eventually he would run out of magic. He needed another solution. A vision of Eleanor shaking the cliffs and bringing down rock walls in the Stone Kingdom surfaced. He remembered her technique.

Ignoring the spiders that leapt on him from all directions to die on his shield, the boy focused on the earth around the holes in the pit. He infused his magic into the dirt then shook his hands. Immediately, the holes sealed themselves, but he did the job too well. The pit's walls caved in all around him, an unstoppable tidal wave of dirt.

It covered all his friends' bodies and went over his head. He couldn't move, and a wave of panic rushed through him.

He lost the shield. Then he lost his magic. His fear had reasserted the Wall.

Something bit his hand.

Immobilized by the dirt, a wave of nausea and dizziness rushed through him, intensifying his fear. Everyone Chip cared about had been bitten by poisonous spiders, about to suffocate in their silk wrappings. He was on his last breath, trying to hold on. Panic ratcheted his body. He felt another bite on his leg. His mind exploded with dizziness and fear. He couldn't breathe.

But neither could she.

Eleanor!

Chip Oathbinder latched onto that last thought and gave into his rage.

His Wall exploded, and he drew in a massive amount of Power. The boy shot his magic up and outwards, sending a fountain of dirt into the sky. He melted everything around him even as more dirt rushed in, then seized it all and levitated it out of the pit, tossing the mound of earth to the side.

Taking ragged breaths, the boy stumbled from dizziness, knowing the poison was taking over his body. Brushing the nausea aside, he pulled in more magic and levitated his friend's bodies out of the dirt to the open ground above. Some of the spiders had survived and were coming at him.

He tried to climb out of the hole, but the side walls kept falling away, and he slid back down. He tried again but could make no progress. The boy knew he couldn't levitate himself. It didn't work that way.

Another wave of nausea and dizziness struck him, and this time he fell to one knee. More spiders were shaking themselves out of the dirt and lurching towards him. His breathing began to slow, and he felt his hold on his Power weaken.

Chip screamed in frustration, staring up from the bottom of the giant pit. His shield flickered, and the spiders hissed in anticipation.

He shot weak fire at them, staggering. His aim was off, and his vision blurred. His arms began to grow numb. He wanted to sleep.

Forever.

Two more painful bites sank into his shoulders as the shield disappeared, and he knew it was over.

Suddenly, he was airborne, flying over the rim of the pit and tossed onto the ground like a rag doll. A giant eagle landed hard beside him, stumbling as it tried to stay upright. He realized the bird's talons had sunk into his shoulders, not spider fangs. Yet still the damage was done. He felt the poison from the first two bites working through him.

The eagle shifted into Ethrang, who grabbed his head and looked into his eyes. The blond boy's face blurred in and out. He did not look good.

"Heal me," the Banfar orphan croaked. "Get the poison...out." With a start, Chip realized the shapeshifter had also been bitten.

Ethrang toppled over beside him. "Use your magic...Guardian." The boy threw one arm over his body and remained still.

Chip felt his Wall ripple as it appeared and disappeared from his mind. He stared with blurred vision at the blond orphan beside him and gave into his rage. He shattered the flickering Wall long enough to send a stream of healing magic into his friend. Even as his vision faltered, Chip located the poison in the boy's blood and pulled it out. A wave of darkness washed over him.

In the dim light of dusk, Chip dizzily saw Ethrang open his eyes, which suddenly blazed a bright green with a hint of silver. Something bit him in the back, and his last sight was of a skinny wizard spraying green fire over his body. The spiders were crawling out of the pit.

Ethrang rested one hand on his chest while spraying shards of green magic with the other, sending healing energy into his body. Chip gasped as Ethrang pulled out the poison. His vision cleared, and the nausea disappeared.

The Guardian of the Races leapt to his feet and spun around, seizing his Power.

The blond boy stood with splayed hands, incinerating the spiders as they crawled out. Holes had appeared on the opposite dirt wall of the pit as more spiders dug through. Chip sent his magic into both sides of the pit using giant red hands and clapped his hands together. The ground shook as the walls caved in, burying the spiders in an earthen tomb.

He blasted the last few from the lip, then sat down wearily, taking deep breaths. It had been too close for comfort. He understood now why Chase hated spiders.

Ethrang dropped his hands, breathing hard. "Took you long enough, Guardian."

"Sorry, I wasn't feeling well." He grinned and put his arm around the skinny boy. "Thanks. Couldn't have done it without you. Now, help me heal our friends."

The orphans ran over to the inert bodies, pulling apart the silk wrappings one at a time. They sent healing magic into each body, pulling the poison out and increasing their slowed heart rates. Some of them had broken bones from the fall. As more wizards revived, they lent their assistance. Ward had fractured his skull again, but Chip used Daria's technique to release the pressure and then reform the bone. A short while later, they were all revived.

Ethrang and Chip sat down, exhausted.

"Nice work, Guardian."

"You too."

Chip looked at the blond orphan. "How did you survive the fall?"

"I landed hard, but nothing broke. A spider bit me as I flew away, and then the dizziness took over. I crashed into the ground above the pit and threw up. I staggered back to the lip of the hole and saw you were in deep trouble. I didn't know if I could fly, but I knew I had to try anyway. Sorry if I squeezed your shoulders too hard with my talons." Ethrang grinned. "After I pulled you out, I couldn't shapeshift or stand anymore. I did my best."

Chip put a hand on his shoulder. "Your best was enough, even though only one spider took you down. It took two spiders to bring me down. Well, three. Though I admit the last one was overkill."

"It's not my fault that I'm skinny," Ethrang countered. "Poison hits me faster."

They laughed and stood up.

"Can we please get out of here?" Chase begged. "I never want to be near spiders again."

"I second that," kristan said.

"I third it," Thomas added.

Even Garth Stone nodded. The companions began moving into the trees on the far side.

"Keep your eyes open for whatever laughed earlier," Chip warned. "It looked like a hooded figure."

He turned to see the sun disappear behind the horizon and followed them into the forest.

It was night in Darkwood.

9

If the forest was eerie before, now it was downright frightening.
As a consolation, the moon appeared, and the stars began to shine through the last remnants of the storm, providing weak light that trickled through the canopy and reflected off the snow on the ground. The sound of everyone's feet crunching the white carpet was amplified in the night. Due to their heightened senses, the creaks of the misshapen trees were also more pronounced.

They moved deeper into the woods.

Nobody spoke as they concentrated on listening for any sign of danger.

Garth held up his hand. "I smell smoke."

Chip sniffed the air and also detected the telltale odour.

"All we need is the bloody forest to catch fire," muttered Chase.

Ethrang giggled. "At least we would be warm." The twins stared at him. "Well, at first, anyway."

"We have no choice but to keep moving north," Xander said. "Carry on."

The companions trudged forward for the better part of an hour. The smell increased until they could make out a glow of light up ahead. Garth slowed and crept forward.

They all stopped at the edge of a large valley. Chip could not believe his eyes. Giant bonfires were spaced out evenly along the valley floor. There were three of them. In between were triangular stones with arcane symbols etched onto their surface.

"What the heck is this place?" Chase asked.

"Maybe the witches practice strange magic here," Kristan said.

"Or make sacrifices," Thomas added, smiling weakly.

"It looks like the valley ends over there in the distance. Maybe we should go around it," Mary said, pointing.

One Eye pushed forward. "I may only have one eye, but I see some large structures or something on the other side."

Suddenly, Chip heard running feet on the snow behind them.

Then maniacal laughter.

Everyone turned to see dozens of dark, hooded shapes charging at them through the trees.

"Head for the fires," Garth ordered. "We will make a stand there."

They all tore down the hill, dodging trees, desperate to get to the light and see what was attacking them. Chip ran beside Eleanor and Mary, making sure they were safe. He turned to see that the hooded shapes were already at the valley's edge. He could almost make out faces. The Protectors and trolls surrounded the wizards as they sprinted for the fires.

The companions reached the snow-covered valley floor, which was devoid of trees. They raced across the flat ground to the nearest fire. Only then did Chip realize how huge it was. Giant logs had been placed in a pyramid formation and then set ablaze, releasing intense heat and light. He could only guess at what could move logs that big.

When the heat was unbearable, they all turned with weapons drawn. No one had seized their magic yet, but everyone was at the ready. The boy knew he would have no choice once they were attacked, yet the instructions were clear. He would conserve until offered no choice. The Guardian braced himself, hands poised.

Yet no attack came.

He peered at the valley's slope, expecting dozens of hooded

figures to appear through the trees. No one was there. He searched the valley rim, but it was empty as well.

"Something is not right," Mary said, still breathing heavily.

"It could be a trap," Elayne responded. "Let's see what's behind us."

They moved around the fire and approached the stone between it and the subsequent fire. Near the top of the large triangular stone, an evil eye symbol stared at them.

"What's that over there?" Chip said, pointing to the other side of the valley. They all moved closer and peered at the slope. It looked like small fires or lights shone from several locations. As his eyes adjusted to the dark, the boy saw huge trees bundled together in square formations.

"Good grief, those are houses," Kristan said in awe.

"They are huge," Thomas added.

"They have windows. That's where the light is coming from." Eleanor pointed, and Chip could now make out massive log homes.

"They even have porches," Chase looked confused. "What are huge houses doing in Darkwood?"

A giant log door to one of the structures suddenly opened, and a figure emerged. It was man-like in shape with tree-trunk-sized arms and legs. It wore fur pants and no shirt. Black hair covered its chest, and it gripped an enormous club—no, a log. The thing had a bald head.

Chip stared in amazement. "What is that?"

"That, my boy, is an ogre," Xander said. "I was hoping not to meet them."

"There are such things as ogres!" Chip exclaimed.

"My goodness, yes."

"You never told me that," he protested.

"You never asked. My father Arkan told me about them once. He said he saw a few in Darkwood. I frankly didn't remember until now." Xander shrugged innocently. Everyone stared at him.

An enormous bellow sounded throughout the valley. Doors in the other houses clanged open, revealing more hairy ogres.

"Oh dear," Eleanor murmured.

"I think they can be reasoned with," Xander said weakly.

A half-dozen ogres started shouting simultaneously and charged down the slope to the valley floor. They ate up the ground in insanely long strides. Each was at least twenty feet tall.

"Oh look, they only have one eye, like me," One Eye said. "Well, I originally had two eyes, but you understand."

The ogres' features became more apparent. They had blunt noses, tufts of hair at the sides of their oblong faces, and a single eye high up on their bald heads.

Chip looked around. Even the trolls seemed afraid. "Chase?" He glanced at his best friend.

"What? Are you crazy? Those things could eat me in one bite."

Xander stepped forward. "Here, let me." His eyes blazed a bright blue, and he amplified his voice to emit strength. "I command you to stop!"

The ogres did not slow. They had reached the valley floor and continued their charge.

"My goodness, that didn't work," he admitted then stepped back.

Chip stared at him with wide eyes.

The boy sighed and turned to the ogres. He seized his Power, eyes blazing. Red coils of magic swirled around his body as he walked forward.

The ogres paused briefly, pointing, and then ran straight at him with roars of glee. Chip had the distinct impression he was being targeted.

And he was out of time.

The Guardian latched on to the only thing everyone was afraid of.

Fire.

Seizing two long flaming logs from the bonfires with his Power, Chip whipped them forward before him, holding them in the air at the ready. The ogres skidded to a halt.

The tallest one stepped forward and slammed his log on the valley floor, causing the ground to shake. His face twisted in a snarl.

"We only eat boy with red eyes. Others can go." His deep voice was slow and halting.

"Why do you want to eat me?" Chip asked.

"She told us to," the ogre said.

"Who told you to?" he responded politely.

The ogres looked at each other and let out deep laughs, holding their bellies. "The one we must listen to. Morgeth."

"Why must you listen to her?"

The ogre looked around the valley and then pointed to the stones. "She keeps bad things out. Hooded people. And Darkwood King."

Chip was about to ask who he was talking about, but the ogre's face changed.

"No more talk. We eat you."

The huge ogre swung his log with incredible speed and knocked both of Chip's fiery logs to the ground.

Then they attacked.

The Guardian raised his hands and froze their motion, surrounding them with concentrated air. He grimaced at the Power required to hold six twenty-foot-tall ogres in place. The twins came up, one on either side of him.

"Amazing." Kristan nodded in approval.

"Well done," Thomas agreed.

Chip gritted his teeth and looked at one and then the other. "Do you mind linking with me?"

"Oh, sure."

"No problem."

The twins' formidable Power became one with his. He reached back to form six massive, condensed balls of air and flung them at the ogres' chests. They flew backwards to land hard on their behinds. Several passed wind. The immense beings slowly got to their feet, groaning. Some rubbed their behinds, while others felt their hairy chests to see if anything was broken.

The tall one slammed his log on the ground again. "You make us mad."

"I don't want to fight you," Chip said calmly. "I don't want to hurt you. Let us go, and we will kill Morgeth, so you no longer have to be afraid."

"Ogre not afraid for himself. Only for baby. Morgeth help baby. Baby very sick." A sad look passed across the ogre's face, but then it changed to one of rage. "We eat you, then Morgeth help baby."

"Oh, enough of this already," Ethrang said from behind him. Suddenly, the Yagr leapt forward, baring its fangs. The monstrous cat, a fifteen-foot killer, crouched low, roaring at the ogres.

The leader stepped back, nearly dropping his log. "Darkwood King." The others looked horrified.

Chip knew that despite their size, an ogre would likely lose to a cat that big. "We killed the Darkwood King and made another. I control him now," the boy said, stepping forward. The Yagr looked at him, eyes widening. "Well, he controls himself, of course, but he listens to me...generally."

The tall ogre looked taken aback. "You are very strong to kill king." He looked at the others. They were still eyeing the Yagr. "But we still must eat you. Morgeth help baby."

"Wait. We can help your baby and make it healthy. Then we will kill Morgeth. We already killed the Darkwood King and made another." Chip held his breath.

The tall ogre turned to the others and conferred. Their faces contorted in consternation as they reasoned through the ramifications, casting fearful glances at the cat. After a while of heated discussion, the tall ogre turned around.

"You heal baby. We don't eat you."

"That sounds fair," Chip agreed. "Take us to your baby."

The tall ogre grunted and waved them forward with his large hand.

"Stay in that form," Chip whispered to Ethrang. "Their fear gives us a better bargaining position." The black cat nodded slightly.

The companions followed the ogres across the dark valley until they reached the slope on the other side. An enormous house with lit windows loomed before them.

"What is your name?" Chip asked the tallest ogre who had been speaking.

"Me Gruk." He pointed to his hairy chest.

"I'm Chip. Nice to meet you." He introduced his companions.

"Too many names. I can't fit in head. I call you Redeye. Come."

They followed the giant up the slope to the porch of the huge log house. It looked like full-sized trees had been tied together with rope. The side of the hill had been dug out, so the structure was level. Gruk opened the door, and they followed him into a living area the size of the throne room in Vanalon. The other ogres stayed on the porch.

"This is wife Grima," Gruk said.

A female ogre nearly twenty feet tall with long hair was bending over a large cradle on the opposite side of the room. She wore fur pants and no shirt. Grima turned around and screamed then grabbed a giant broom leaning against the wall and ran at Ethrang, her naked breasts swinging wildly.

The Yagr crouched low and bared his fangs.

Gruk grabbed the broom on its downswing. "Grima no, it different Darkwood King. They come to help baby."

Grima stood panting heavily, her ample chest moving up and down. "Oh, sorry. You scare me."

Chase's face turned red at the sight of the half-naked ogre. Mary had a look of disbelief then disgust. The Yagr started making a wheezing noise, which Chip realized was the cat's way of laughing.

Grima looked them up and down until she saw One Eye. "Oh," she said in delight, "Ogre baby!" She stepped forward and picked him up with two giant hands.

"Put me down at once," One Eye bellowed. He looked like a small doll in her hands.

"Don't talk back, baby," she cooed then started shaking him. Grima's face broke into a lopsided grin. The troll captain was for once speechless and tried to squirm his way out, but she held him tight. Finally, he found his voice.

"This is... How dare you... I am not a..." One Eye protested, but then the motion finally caused him to smile, and he began laughing then passed gas.

Grima nodded in appreciation, her one eye blinking. "See, ogre baby. Different but same." The other trolls pointed and, unable to contain themselves, joined in the laughter until the room was full of bellows and the sounds of flatulence.

Mary looked too shocked to speak, and then her nose wrinkled involuntarily. Xander turned with amusement to Garth, who arched an eyebrow. Chip and Chase glanced at each other, grinning.

The female ogre finally put One Eye down and waved them forward. A pig was roasting on a spit in a massive hearth on the side of the room. The furniture consisted of a rough-hewn table with chairs. Chip's head barely reached the top of the chair. She drew them to the giant cradle, and her face grew sad.

"Please help baby. He very sick," Grima said, her one eye wet.

Chip peered over the edge of the cradle to see a baby larger than himself resting under a wool blanket. Unlike his parents, the baby's skin was gray, and he drew short, wheezing breaths. His one eye remained closed, and a light sheen of sweat covered his bald head.

The troll healer Daria looked exhausted, so Chip broke through his Wall. His eyes blazed bright, causing Grima's one eye to widen. He sent his Power into the baby, probing for any abnormalities. There was nothing wrong with the small ogre physically, but he sensed something off that was very familiar. In the baby's blood was the same poison that he had withdrawn from Ethrang.

He turned to Grima and Gruk. "Your baby has been poisoned. Does he play near the spiders?"

Both parents shook their heads. "Spiders in ground in winter. They put webs over holes then cut them with pincers when anything walks on ground. We do not go there."

"Then someone has fed him poison."

The ogres' eyes widened. "The witches give medicine for baby. They say it helps him. Keeps him alive." Grima's face showed understanding. Gruk was still trying to process the implications.

"The witches are poisoning your baby so that you follow their orders. They are evil." Chip waited until the ogres both understood.

Gruk's face turned redder. "We will kill all of them," he growled. Grima nodded, her eye taking on a dangerous glint.

"I will heal him, and then we'll talk." Chip turned back to the ogre baby. He spread his magic throughout the child's body then wrapped it around the poison, drawing it out. There was much more poison than Ethrang had, suggesting the witches had been feeding him their medicine for a long time. He drew all the poison out and vaporized it. The child's skin turned back to white.

The ogre baby immediately went into a seizure. Gruk and Grima gasped.

Daria stepped forward. "Let me." Chip nodded, always eager to watch how she used her considerable skills. The troll healer sent yellow magic into the baby, soothing the distressed ogre.

He watched as she removed toxins from the child's liver, surely due to the build-up of poison over a long period, then expanded the blood vessels to the baby's brain. She cooled the inflamed areas. The seizures slowed and then stopped completely.

The small ogre opened his one eye and smiled at his parents.

The love and joy on Gruk and Grima's faces were difficult to describe. Chip watched as they picked up the sizable infant and hugged him fiercely. Tears formed in each of their eye. Watching such huge, terrifying creatures display such love made Chip emotional.

He realized the ogres were capable of being so much more than monsters. They had lived in Darkwood their whole lives and knew nothing but danger and survival. The witches had likely used them for their ends, causing the ogres to do terrible things to anyone who entered the valley. The capacity for love and feelings of joy they now expressed showed him they were redeemable. The boy released his magic.

The ogres turned to him and Daria. Gruk patted Chip's shoulder with one finger, almost sending him to his knees. Grima grasped Daria's hand between two fingers. "Thank you, small ones. You healed baby. His name is Gorky."

"It is my pleasure," Chip said, smiling. The baby looked at him in wonder, and he watched as they placed him on his feet. The little ogre wobbled then stood looking at him with curiosity. Gorky's one eye was level with his two. The baby reached up and touched his hair with a hand already double the size of his.

"Baba," he babbled then poked the Guardian of the Races in the cheek. Chip laughed and looked up at Daria.

"He thinks you baby," Grima explained with pride.

"He is healthy now," the troll healer told the ogre's parents. "No more medicine."

Gruk looked at her, and his huge face turned angry. "Witches bad. Make us mad. Next time, we hit them with log."

"Can I make a suggestion?" Chip said. The ogre gave him a confused look. He rephrased it. "Can I talk with all the ogres at the same time? It's important."

Gruk nodded. "Yes. Some sleeping. I can wake."

"How many are you?"

Gruk began counting on his huge fingers. Grima stepped in. "Twenty ogres plus two babies."

"How old is your baby?"

"Sixteen years," Grima answered.

Chip blinked. "Huh. I'm sixteen. He's still a baby."

"Yes, you both babies."

"But I'm not... How long do ogres live?" he asked.

"Oldest is five hundred seasons. We are about two hundred. See, so sixteen seasons still baby. Only few ogres born every hundred seasons. They very special. Gorky and Greta only babies in village."

"Oh, that makes sense." Chip looked around. The Yagr was wheezing again. Eleanor smiled at him. "Alright, well, can I talk to all of you?"

"Yes, you help baby and tell us about bad witches," Gruk said. "Come."

They followed him back outside. Grima grabbed Gorky's hand and led him on wobbly feet to the porch. The other five ogres were still waiting. When they saw the baby trying to walk, they cheered and broke into crooked smiles.

"Gather ogres," Gruk boomed. "We make council at fire."

The others nodded and dashed off with long strides. Soon, they could hear loud knocks on the front doors of the other houses.

The companions descended the slope and crossed the valley floor to stand before one of the raging bonfires. A short while later, they heard the heavy pounding of feet and ogres filled the valley before them. Gruk and Grima stood in front. Chip stared at the twenty-foot giants in awe. All of them were shirtless with fur pants. There was roughly an even split of males and females. The only babies were Gorky and Greta. He looked over at Chase, who was turning red again.

Some of the ogres pointed at Ethrang, showing a mixture of fear and respect. The cat sat next to Chip, towering over the boy.

Gruk lifted his hand, and the ogres quieted. "We make council. Redeye want to say something. He and small girl heal baby. We listen."

Chip cleared his throat. "We have come to Darkwood to reach the Secret Caves. On the way, we have killed countless monkeys, spiders, the white wolf leader and his pack, and even the Darkwood King." The ogre's eyes widened, and their mouths dropped open. "We seek to kill the High Witch Morgeth and her followers. They have created cults in the lands that worship the worst enemy of all, the Demon King."

They looked at him blankly.

"Who is Demon King?" Gruk asked.

"He is a Dark Elf lord who has been trapped behind a magic barrier on an island far to the west for three thousand years. He commands a demon army that seeks to wipe out every living thing in this world, including you and your babies." Looks of anger crossed many faces. "The magic barrier has now fallen, and upon winter's end the Demon King will release his hordes of demons across the lands to kill everything in their path. Morgeth is trying to join him, but she does not realize he will enslave and kill the witches too. The

High Witch is evil and has been poisoning Gorky for a long time. I believe she has controlled the ogres for thousands of seasons. You protect her because you are afraid of her. If you stay here, you will all die. I am here to warn you that the Demon King is coming. You can do nothing and wait for death, or you can do something about it now. It is up to you."

The ogres looked at each other then began gesturing as they conversed in their halted speech. Chip waited patiently.

Gruk finally turned to him. "They say you too weak and small to defeat Morgeth."

Chip strode forward, seizing his Power. His eyes blazed bright red as coils of crimson fire wrapped around his body. Several ogres stepped back, shielding their eyes. He amplified his voice.

"I am Chip Oathbinder, Guardian of the Races, which includes ogres. I have slain the demon general, Morgo, the black dragon, Fang, buried a creature that can destroy us all, called the Dim, killed countless demons and Dark Elves, looked upon the face of Death and returned, and united the entire troll nation to join the armies of humans to fight against the demons in the Last Battle. I am the only Red-eyed human magic wielder in the world. I may look small and weak, but I am not."

Chip turned and lifted both hands. The stones set between the fires all along the valley floor shook, raised, and levitated higher than the giant's heads. He drew in more Power and then squeezed both fists. The stones burst apart in a shower of dust and debris.

The ogres stood slack-jawed. None of their one eyes blinked.

Gruk finally recovered. "Those stones protect valley."

Chip grimaced. "Sorry, I forgot about that. The point is that those stones had runes and symbols on them that are evil. The witches use those dark forces to control everything that lives in Darkwood. Morgeth has been deceiving you for thousands of seasons. You should be free, and you should be mad. How can you stay loyal to someone who poisons your baby? I am asking you to join us in the Last Battle and fight the Demon King. Will you do this?"

The boy waited. The ogres still stared at the crushed stones, trying to process his words. They turned and began conferring again. A long time passed, and then Gruk turned back.

"Some of them don't believe you."

Chip's eyes blazed brighter, and he sent his presence into Gruk's mind. "I will show you." He revealed his memories to the ogre leader, showing him the demons attacking Vanalon, the Dim, Death, and the trolls. He watched the ogre's reactions. Some of it Gruk did not understand, but he knew the memories were true.

The ogre went back to the others, white-faced. Chip waited again.

This time it did not take long. Gruk turned back. "What do you want us to do? We cannot fit in Secret Caves."

Chip nodded. "Leave the witches to us. I want you to leave this place immediately. Pack your things and head south to the river. On your way, you will meet a human named Rake, who will be camping with a bunch of horses. He will be terrified, but we can write a message to give him. You will likely have to run him down, but don't hurt him. He stays a few leagues south of the black stone on the forest's southern edge. Rake will take you to the leaders of a city called Yucan. It is ruled by the Triumvirate, who will help get you to the New Wizard's Guild. That will be the safest place for you until the Last Battle. The High Wizard there is named Balor. He will provide you with food and shelter. His living room alone can hold all of you. The Triumvirate will notify him that you are coming. My best guess is they will send you in pairs by ship."

It took them even longer to digest this new information. Chip had to repeat it several times, waiting patiently. He looked back at Xander, who gave him a nod of encouragement.

Gruk looked at him. "If we help, what we get?"

"You get to save your babies and live. Beyond that, once we win the Last Battle, I will make sure you get nice big houses in your own valley where you will be safe. I warn you that not all of you will survive the battle. All I know is that if you stay here, you will die. Of that, I am certain."

They conferred again. After a while, Gruk turned. "Can we eat people when hungry?"

"No, you cannot eat humans, trolls, or dwarves."

"Oh," Gruk nodded. "So just children."

"No, you especially cannot eat children. Would you like your babies eaten?" The ogres shook their heads, mollified. "I didn't think so. We protect our babies the same as you. You can eat livestock like cows, pigs, and chickens."

"Bears?"

"Yes."

"Wolves."

"Only the bad ones."

"Horses?"

"No, especially not the ones with horns. They are called unicorns. Do not ever try to eat them. Oh, and you must wear shirts." The Yagr wheezed.

Gruk grunted. "We fight Last Battle with you, Redeye."

Chip smiled. "Thank you. I must ask you to swear an oath of allegiance." The ogres looked at each other in bewilderment. "You show your loyalty to me by going down on one knee and saying the words 'I swear allegiance to Chip Oathbinder, Guardian of the Races.' I do not ask this to feel special or powerful. I do ask it so you are bound to your oath by word and deed."

The ogres conferred briefly this time, and then Gruk shrugged. "Ogre keep word, so we do this."

The leader of the ogres bent down on one knee, and the others followed. Twenty giants knelt on the valley floor and raised their heads. The words boomed out loud and clear. The others looked on in awe.

"I swear fealty to Chip Oathbinder, Guardian of the Races."

Gruk stood up with a grin. "Now. Can baby pet Darkwood King?"

Chip laughed. "Of course."

The Yagr stared at him in a cat's version of shock then bowed. Gorky waddled over and reached up to pat his head. Soon, the other ogres came over, and everyone took turns petting the giant cat, even Gruk. Ethrang cast Chip a withering look, but he bore it well.

"Who are the hooded figures?" Chip asked, releasing his Power.

"We do not know. They avoid ogres. Not allowed in valley. We never see faces. Sometimes lights. We do not know."

"Alright. We will meet again at the Last Battle." Chip extended his hand, but the leader of the ogres instead patted him on the shoulder. He staggered but remained upright. Grima suddenly picked him up and gave the boy a tight hug. He closed his eyes as his face buried in the center of her chest.

"Thank you for saving baby."

Chip held his breath, trying not to make a face. Finally, she set him back down on his feet. It was his turn to blush. His companions looked at him with covered mouths. The Yagr started wheezing again.

"All right, that will do it. Let's head off," Xander said with a smile. They waved at the other ogres and then made their way up the northern slope of the valley. Gruk told them to follow a trail between two houses, which they found quickly.

At the top of the valley, everyone turned to see the ogres gathering supplies and items for their journey. Chip took in the roaring bonfires and the lights shining out of the houses. He had not expected to make friends in Darkwood. Then again, he was building an army to fight the demons, and all were welcome. He smiled and headed north with his companions to the Secret Caves.

10

Ethrang reappeared by his side, putting his arm around Chip's shoulders. "Did you enjoy getting hugged by Grima?" The blond boy stifled a laugh.

"Did you enjoy getting petted by twenty ogres?"

The Banfar orphan made a face. "I have to admit I almost bit them. Being in the shape that long makes it difficult to control an animal's instincts. It was amazing though to feel that powerful. The Yagr is truly the most vicious killer I've ever turned into. I see why the ogres are afraid of the Darkwood King."

"Yes, I know firsthand, remember? I couldn't even react in time, and when I did, my fear got the better of me. I suspect we will need the Yagr again before this is done."

"No problem, Guardian. I got your back." The skinny, green-robed boy flexed his fingers with a look of disappointment. "I feel so weak now."

Chip gave him a sideways look. "You do look kind of weak." Ethrang lightheartedly threw him a roundhouse punch, but he dodged it easily, laughing.

"I would hit you back, but I'm afraid you will turn into the Darkwood King."

"Don't tempt me."

"I heard something," Xander called back. "If you two don't mind, I'd like to remind everyone we are still in Darkwood. We have a long way yet to go."

The orphans nodded, trying to keep straight faces.

The twisted trees had returned, lit weakly by the starlight. They trudged forward through the snow, senses alert.

"Something is walking alongside us," Gurth murmured. "It is keeping its distance."

The Protectors and trolls had resumed their positions around the wizards, hands resting casually on their weapons. They continued heading north, making good time as the evening progressed, despite hearing odd noises or spying distant movement. Twice, they heard a branch break, and everyone froze. The sound did not repeat itself, so they continued.

It was drawing near the middle of the night when the attack came. Shimko screamed, clutching his face. Blood spurted out between his fingers. At first, Chip couldn't tell what was happening but saw a large gray thing hovering above the wounded Protector.

It took him only a moment to realize it was a giant bat, beating its wings almost soundlessly. They spanned seven feet, ending in talons. The face was gargoyle-like with white almond eyes and fuzzy brown hair. Razor-sharp teeth ran the perimeter of its oversized mouth. The claws at the end of its wings dripped blood. It emitted a piercing scream that chilled the bone, and more swooped in, pulling up at the last instant to use their foot talons to shred faces. Sickening thuds sounded as the winged creatures slammed into the trolls and Protectors. The one above Shimko spun upside down and tore his ear off with its sharp teeth.

The wizards seized their Power, and lights flashed. Chip sent a thick stream of red Power into the bat harrying Shimko, sending it sailing fifty feet back to slam into a tree. It slid down with a hole in its chest. More dove at the trolls in the back. Chip turned to them, bringing two more down, but another pair latched on to a troll soldier and carried him away. The boy sent his Power out to seize them, but they darted between the trees and disappeared. The bats' swiftness shocked him. Eleanor screamed as more dropped down from the trees above, opening their wings at the last second to stop their descent. They sought to latch onto the head or neck of their victim. One tried to pick her up, but her shield melted its claws.

Then a giant eagle appeared covered in a green shield, even larger than the hovering bats. It darted forward with its beak to peck gargoyle-like faces and shred the membrane-like bat wings with its massive talons.

"There's more hanging in the trees," Xander warned.

Chip looked up to see dozens of six-foot-long bats hanging upside down from the canopy with large wings folded over their furry, man-sized bodies. Even as he watched, more dropped straight down, opening their wings at the last second then slamming their talons into unprotected faces. Blue fire arced upwards from the twins as they stood back-to-back with arms raised. Several hanging bats burst into flames as their magic found its mark.

Chip was about to unleash red fire into the canopy when he noticed a motion to his side. An injured bat walked unsteadily towards him with teeth bared and wings extended. Its resemblance to a demon was striking. It screamed and struck forward with its hideous head, trying to bite at his face. He sent a stream of fire down its mouth, burning it alive from the inside. More came in from the sides.

"Foul beast!" yelled a gruff voice from the back. Chip spun around to lend aid and gasped to see One Eye with an empty eye socket where his good eye should have been. The troll captain was swinging blindly at a hovering bat above him while another raked his head from the back. Blood streamed down his face. Chip seized both creatures and slammed them into each other with a sickening crunch. He was about to wrap everyone in a shield, but Ethrang was still in the air, wreaking havoc. His green magic withstood the bats' teeth and talons, and he continued ripping into them in a frenzy. An unending number of man-sized bats dropped in, and the wizards threw concentrated balls of fire at multiple targets

Chase's eyes glinted dangerously red. He disposed of two bats and leapt into the air to shear off footlong talons, moving with stunning speed. He then jumped higher than any human should be able to and sliced off wings or slit throats.

"They are slowing down," Ward said as he hacked at another coming in through the trees.

"Bulch thinks so." The giant Protector stood with a bloody club amidst a pile of dead bat bodies. Another one swooped in behind him, and the surprised looks on everyone's faces caused him to swing his club without turning, caving in the bat's head. It landed in a twisted heap on the pile.

The wizards disposed of the remaining creatures with short bursts of fire, and then Ethrang landed beside Chip, covered in bat blood.

The green-robed boy wiped his face. "I killed ten myself."

"One Eye!" Chip shouted with alarm and ran to the back, but Daria was already tending to the troll captain. Chip watched as she regrew the eye and attached newly formed muscles. Her dexterity was a sight to behold. She stood up with a light sheen of sweat on her brow and staggered slightly. The use of their magic was taking its toll.

One Eye stood up, blinking. "That's better," he said, squinting. "I can finally see you again."

"Why don't you heal your other eye?" Ethrang asked, voicing the question that had also sprung up in Chip's mind.

The troll captain opened his new eye with shock. "Trolls carry their scars with pride. We are not like humans. It is not a mortal wound. It also makes me look scarier, evoking fear in my enemy's heart." He grinned wolfishly, fangs gleaming.

Ethrang was about to retort, but Chip elbowed him.

"What about the troll that was carried away?" he asked. "Let's look for him."

Everyone nodded and backtracked to where Chip said he saw the bats turn into the trees. They did not have to walk far to find the troll's remains. The soldiers and mages thumped their chests. Garth said a brief prayer to the Creator, and they returned to the site of the attack.

Bat bodies were everywhere.

"Darkwood is full of surprises. This has used up much of our magic," Xander said. "I do not want to contemplate what happens if we run out. Let's keep moving."

The others nodded, avoiding bodies as they moved forward. Mary looked with particular distaste at the corpses, shuddering as she stepped over gargoyle-like faces.

They continued into the later hours of the night. The moon arced across the sky, following the same path as the sun, then began its westward descent. Chip felt weary after a full day of fighting and using magic. He hoped that the forest would hold no more surprises but, as trained, expected the worst.

He did not have to wait long.

A bone-chilling laugh rang out to their right. He had heard that laugh once before. Could it have been following them the whole time? Even as the thought entered his mind, a voice whispered something to their left. For a moment, he thought it was the hiss of a snake again, but he could almost make out words.

Then he heard it again.

"Come."

"Did you hear that?" Chase said, pointing to the left.

"We are waiting."

Everyone froze. Chip felt a tingle go up his spine. A slight wind had arisen, carrying the voice through the dark, twisted trees. The carpet of snow shone as the moon appeared through holes in the canopy.

A high-pitched cackle rang out, a little closer this time. He thought he saw a dark thing between the trees to his right, but it wasn't moving. Then, a maniacal laugh pierced the night on the other side. The sound of it seemed human, but how was that possible? Were the witches here? Chip looked back between the trees to discover the dark thing gone.

"Come."

Chip shuddered.

"We will drink your blood."

He looked at Ethrang. "Do you want to check where that's coming from?"

The skinny boy looked at him with wide eyes. "Are you crazy? I'm not going in there!"

"There's something up ahead," Garth said. "I think it's a clearing. Stay alert."

They all moved closer, weapons drawn. Chip kept the Wall clear in his mind, ready to break through in an instant. He struggled to subdue his mounting fear, knowing it would hamper his ability to seize his magic. Something about the voices unnerved him, coupled with the fact that they were walking in the middle of the night through the center of Darkwood. He decided to add haunted forests to the list of things he did not like. He remembered the tracker Rake mentioning wraiths and lights.

A deep chuckle sounded behind them.

Then child-like giggles erupted on both sides, causing the hairs on his neck to rise.

Everyone pushed forward, seeing the break in the trees. Despite what might be waiting in the clearing, it was better to be out in the open so they could at least see what was around them. Even the trolls and Protectors appeared skittish.

"Hurry up," Chase whispered. "I hear things all around us."

"Dear Creator," Elayne gasped.

The companions had spilled out of the forest.

Before them, in the center of the clearing, a small, hooded figure knelt on the ground with folded knees, its head bowed.

Strange rock formations with runes and symbols formed a semicircle along the edge of the clearing.

Everything was silent. The moon lit up the landscape with an eerie light. The boy walked forward, taking the lead.

The thing lifted its head.

The face of a little girl revealed itself. She was grinning from ear to ear.

Chip stopped. Something about her expression sent a wave of fear through his body. It was the teeth. They were filed to points. And her eyes held an evil aspect. She could not be more than twelve summers old.

"The red-eyed boy," she said in a high voice. "We have waited for you."

"Are you a witch?" he asked, glancing around the clearing.

"A witch?" she screamed and spat on the ground. "We hate them. We hate them. We hate them. But we hate you more." She leered at him and growled.

Chip tried to maintain his composure. She was a small girl, so he shouldn't be afraid, but she was...off. "Why do you hate us?" he asked.

She struggled for words. "Why? Why? Why?" The girl rose to her full height, facing him. She barely came up to his chest, but he involuntarily stepped back. She clenched her small hands. "You dare ask why!"

"Yes, why?" he said, trying to remain calm.

"Because you are wizards!" she screamed. "That's why!" She took a step forward. "You hurt us more than all of them. You took what was ours. Ours!" She shook with anger, and then her screams turned into laughter. "But now you are ours! All ours!"

"Who are you?" he said, his anger beginning to mount.

"Me? Us?" she said, pointing at her chest. She gave him a mischievous grin. We are the Lost Ones." She took another step. "Do you want to hear us sing? Of course you do!" She raised her hands to the sky. "Sing!" she cried. Sing!"

At first, Chip could only hear whispers.

Come, come,
We are the Lost Ones,
Forsaken by all,
We stand before you
To make sure you fall,
Give us your flesh,
Give us your bone.
We drink your blood,

And hear you moan,
Come, come,
We are the Lost Ones.

The chant became louder and repeated itself. More voices joined in, coming from behind the stones.

Chills ran up his spine. The girl in front of him joined in, screaming the words.

Come, come...

"I ask you again," Chip shouted. "Who are you?"

The little girl raised her hand, and the chant died out.

"You should know," she hissed menacingly. "You walled us from our Power!"

Chip looked at her in shock. "Do you mean the Guild?"

"Yes!" she screamed. "The cursed Guild." She wrung her hands. "Oh, how we suffered. Then the witches came. They took our Walls down. We thought we were free, but this didn't work right." She tapped her head. "For some, it did, but not the Lost Ones. The witches abandoned us too. Cast us out. But my brother, our leader, says now we are truly free. I will bring you to him." She giggled. "He especially wants to drink your blood."

Understanding began to flood his mind. "You had Permanent Walls put up so you could not access your magic," he said softly. "Then the witches took you to the Secret Caves?" The girl nodded with a leer, happy he understood. "But you must understand that we didn't wall you off. We wouldn't do that."

The little girl waggled a finger at him. "Liar," she said, then her voice increased. "Liar, liar, liar!" she screamed. "Balor's brother is right there!" She pointed at Xander, and her brown eyes suddenly blazed bright green. "Kill them all!" she cried. "Drink their blood!" She started laughing hysterically.

Chip felt the peculiar crackle of magic. Dozens of hooded figures spilled out from behind the stones, screaming and laughing. Their eyes blazed with Power of all colours, including the Blue Level.

"Behind us!" Carvor shouted. The forest lit up with shining eyes. Hooded figures began emerging from the woods.

"Shield!" yelled Chip. "Link with me!"

He threw his Power around everyone as magic fire shot at them from all directions. The link formed, and he strengthened the shield. Most of the magic users were at the lower level, but the combined force was still substantial. He gritted his teeth and raised his arms to incinerate them. Then he realized how young they were. Most were around his age, walled off from their Power because they couldn't pass the tests. Some were older, but many had not aged much. At least one hundred hooded figures surrounded them in the clearing.

He could see by their faces they had lost their minds to madness caused by the Permanent Wall Balor insisted was necessary for those who could not pass the Tests. The High Wizard believed that any magic wielder who could not show constraint or control their Power must be walled off to protect society. Chip remembered the Cleric telling him that those who refused were imprisoned until they agreed, and once released they went mad.

Chip didn't want to hurt them. It wasn't their fault. He lowered his arms.

"What are you doing?" Mary said in a strained voice. "Kill them."

Even as she said it, several of the former students of the Guild ran straight into the shield, laughing hysterically. Others were so overcome with rage that they threw themselves on it, trying to break through. All of them died instantly.

Chip stared at the madness in horror. He raised his hands. He needed to try something else. And he needed to do it fast. Digging deep, he seized handfuls of students and slammed them into each other, grimacing at the sound of broken bones. Most were knocked out or groaning in pain. He continued with the grisly work, trying his best not to give them mortal injuries. The strain on the shield lessened. Moaning Lost Ones littered the whole clearing. Only the little girl remained standing.

She looked around in disbelief then screamed and ran straight at the shield. He stopped her in place with his magic.

"Take me to your brother, leader of the Lost Ones," Chip commanded.

She stopped screaming and eyed him shrewdly. "You will kill him."

"No, I will not. I have not tried to kill anyone." Two hooded figures got up and raised their hands. He casually slammed them together, and they went down, groaning. "See, I'm not trying to kill them. I only want to talk to your brother. If we can't come to an agreement, we will be on our way."

She cocked her head and giggled. "My brother is very strong. He will kill all of you anyway. Deal." He released her. "Follow me."

The young girl moved quickly between the moaning bodies, not even glancing at them. She slipped between two large rune-covered stones at the edge of the clearing. Behind was a set of rough-hewn stairs leading down. She urged them on before disappearing into the darkness.

Chip released the link but maintained a shield around himself. The other magic wielders did the same. The twins moved closer to him.

"We have seen that girl before, about seven years ago," Kristan whispered. "She couldn't complete the Tests, and neither could her brother, so Balor sent them to the dungeons. We do not know how long it took for them to agree to put up their Permanent Walls. We never saw them again."

"If I recall, the brother showed great promise but failed everything," Thomas said. "He also couldn't control his emotions. Balor doesn't tell anyone what happens after they go to the dungeons."

"Are you coming?" the little girl called from the darkness.

Chip sighed. The whole situation was very sad. "Yes, we are coming." The boy shot a red ball of light forward and followed the girl down the stairs.

11

The steps went down for quite some time before emerging into a tunnel. The smell wafting up spoke of unwashed bodies and urine. The little girl danced along, waving for them to hurry while grinning mischievously. He could see a light at the end of the tunnel, making the girl's silhouette look macabre. He covered his nose.

They entered a huge cavern lit by torches. A hooded figure sat on a large stone in the middle.

"Why did you bring them here? You were supposed to kill them!"

Chip was surprised to see he was a teenager, not much older than himself. He had brown hair and eyes. The boy stood up, shaking his head.

"They had a shield, Kylo!" his sister protested. "It burnt some Lost Ones. I failed you!" she wailed, pulling her hair out.

"Stop doing that. It's too late now. I will take care of them." He looked at her sadly. "I love you."

The boy's eyes suddenly blazed an insane brown, and he lifted his hands straight up, sending his Power into the cavern's stone ceiling. He vibrated his energy, as Eleanor had done in the Stone Kingdom to bring down the cliff walls. He was going to collapse the roof down on all of them.

"No!" Chip shouted, surrounding the figure with a red shield. The boy's stream of brown magic stopped, but dust and debris fell from the stone ceiling. Cracks began to form, and a loud rumble reverberated. The roof began to shift.

"I will fix it," Eleanor said, pushing forward as more loose stones rained down. She raised her hands and sent brown magic laced with hints of red into the collapsing roof. The little girl ran at her, sending streams of yellow fire into the queen's body.

Eleanor gasped as her robes caught fire. She dropped her hands, and the roof shifted. More rocks fell. The hooded boy named Kylo laughed inside the red shield. Mary froze the little girl with her Power while the twins extinguished the flames.

Then the roof came down.

Chip released the shield around the Leader of the Lost Ones and threw it over his companions as the tunnel collapsed, protecting them in a bubble of Power. At the same time, he directed the rest of his magic into the falling roof. The cavern was massive, and the Power required was immense. He held up the stone ceiling, stopping it above their heads. The weight of the earth above pressed down. The little girl, released from Mary's magic, began dancing excitedly.

The Guardian of the Races gasped, shaking from the effort.

Kylo walked up to him smiling, eyes blazing ferociously. Other than Eleanor, he had never seen a Brown with such strength. The boy pulled his hood off and came right up to Chip's straining face. The Leader of the Lost Ones stared into his eyes.

"You are going to die. I am going to shoot all my Power straight into your heart. You are the strongest magic wielder I have ever seen, but Darkwood has drained you. Your Power is running out. You are not strong enough anymore to stop me."

"But you will die too," Chip said through gritted teeth.

"I died a long time ago," Kylo said sadly, "when my sister went mad. Now, I will have my vengeance."

Chip's magic began to waver, and he felt the others link with him. They could do nothing else while trapped in his red shield. He began to panic, and the Wall flickered in his mind. The Leader of the Lost

Ones raised his hands, pointing at Chip's heart, almost touching him. There was nothing he could do about it.

"Kylo, stop!" Chip urged. "Look at your sister. She deserves to live. Do you want to be the one who kills her?"

The leader looked at the little girl, jumping up and down madly, trying to touch the low ceiling. Tears formed in his eyes. "We will die together."

"I never gave you Permanent Walls," Chip groaned. "I fought Balor on it. He would not listen."

Kylo's head whipped around. "His brother Xander knew about it. He is behind your shield. We've been watching you for quite some time. He allowed it." The boy raised his hands again.

"He fought Balor on it too. That's one of the reasons he left the Guild. Release us, and we will kill Morgeth, and then you can return to a normal life. I will cure your sister of her madness."

This gave the dark-haired boy pause. "Madness cannot be cured. I am the only one here who never went mad. I made the witches think I was, as I did in the Guild, so they cast me out with my sister. Yet that's what makes it so hard. I have watched her suffer enough. I have suffered enough."

"We will try."

"It is too late for that. I do this for all the Lost Ones."

With tears in his eyes, Kylo raised his hands and unleashed his full magic into Chip's chest.

The Guardian staggered from the onslaught. The red coils of Power around his body resisted, but slowly the brown magic worked its way through. Holding up the roof while shielding everyone in the tunnel was all he could do. Almost all.

Kylo's magic began to get through, and Chip felt his skin melt over his heart. He screamed in pain and frustration. Tears filled his eyes as he stared into the face of the Leader of the Lost Ones.

"You've made your decision, Kylo, but I won't let your sister die."

Chip strained with all his might and lifted the bottom of his shield, pulling the little girl to safety. His chest began to smoke, and he knew his heart would incinerate in moments. He was about to release the cavern's roof and strengthen the shield around his companions, knowing it would kill the boy in front of him.

Then Kylo released his magic with a look of shock. Confusion and something else played across his young face.

"Why are you trying to save her?"

Chip looked at the lost boy with the last of his strength, a tear sliding down his cheek. "Because all life is precious. We must fight for it with everything we've got."

The Leader of the Lost Ones stared into the Guardian's red eyes. Chip recognized the expression that materialized on the boy's face.

It was hope.

Kylo's eyes blazed back to life, and he raised his hands, sending a thick stream of brown magic into the roof. Chip felt the boy's considerable Power meld with his and watched in awe as he expertly strengthened the stone, sealing the cracks and fissures. Eleanor had been good at it, but Kylo was something to behold. He wove the stone into an intricate latticework down to its tiniest particle then buttressed the sides to withstand the weight above. When finished, the boy reformed the tunnel over Chip's companions, making an arch stronger than the previous flat ceiling. Granted, the cavern's roof had now lowered to a short distance above their heads, but it was solid.

Kylo lowered his arms, his eyes returning to normal. "You can release your magic."

Chip let go of his Power and collapsed. His chest burned terribly, and he felt overwhelmed by utter exhaustion. Garth Stone picked him up as the others entered the cavern, setting him on the stone in the center of the room. The wizards and mages staggered with weariness. Everyone eyed Kylo with suspicion, yet the twins showed signs of recognition. The little girl ran up to her brother, dancing in place. He stared at his sister sadly and hugged her.

The twins looked tired but placed their hands on Chip's chest and used their remaining Power to heal him. Everyone was nearly spent.

"You are safe here for now," Kylo said. "I must see to the Lost Ones above, and then I will return. If I find that you killed them, I will drop the cavern on you from above. This time, you cannot stop me. Your magic is spent. I have studied earth and stone for many years, honing my skills. It is an extension of me...as if we are one. I have allowed you to live because you showed kindness, and I saw something I had not seen in a long time. I saw...hope." He paused. "I may be a while. I suggest you use the time to rest."

Kylo turned, waving his sister over, and disappeared into the tunnel.

"Well, that was fun," Chase said, trying to smile but failing.

"I could have taken him out," Ethrang said, "but the shield stopped me."

"We made a mistake staying in the tunnel," Garth added. "It was a death trap."

Chip sat up, rubbing his chest. "It was my fault. I didn't expect such skill at the Brown Level. Other than Eleanor, he is the strongest I have ever seen, and his dexterity with stone is unmatched."

"Indeed," Xander mused. "He is more adept than Elohan was. My goodness, so much for conserving our magic."

"It was worth it," Chip said. "Killing him would not have solved anything. He leads the Lost Ones, and they need our help. Balor caused this pain and suffering. When I make it out of this, I will have strong words with him. The practice of installing Permanent Walls on failing students must stop."

"Yes," Xander said with a sigh, "my brother has much to answer for, starting with the bargain he made with Barko." Chip nodded.

"Uh, is no one concerned with this Leader of the Lost Ones dropping the roof on us from above?" Chase asked, staring at the low ceiling. "I don't want to die in a stone tomb."

"A gifted magic wielder leads an army of Lost Ones above us," Chip responded. "I'm afraid we must ride the tides of fate. I am going to surrender the outcome. A nap would also be most welcome."

He rested his back on the stone and closed his eyes. Chip heard his best friend mumble something about people sleeping at a time like this then opened his eyes to see Eleanor snuggling up beside him. She gave him a weary smile and closed her eyes. He drifted off.

"Wake up," Chase said. "They are coming."

Chip opened his eyes. He did not know how long he had dozed but felt better. Eleanor stirred beside him. The Protectors and trolls had formed a semi-circle around the tunnel opening, hands resting on their weapons.

"No need for that," Kylo said, striding in. "I have healed the Yellows and instructed them to heal the others. The Lost Ones are unpredictable, given their mental illness, but they generally listen to me. I have learned each of their idiosyncrasies and can usually bring them back to lucidity. I also know when to avoid them when they suffer episodes."

Chip listened to him, realizing he spoke more maturely than his young face implied. "When did Balor wall you and your sister off?" he asked, sitting up.

"Seven years ago. Clare's magic appeared when she was eleven, which is unusual. She was not strong enough to pass the Tests, so I failed mine to be with her. She refused to be walled off, so Balor threw her into the dungeons. I joined her shortly after. For a year, she held out under horrible conditions. I offered her support through the bars, trying to lift her spirits. She is very stubborn, but I convinced her to let him perform the procedure. Within three weeks of being walled off, she went mad. I have felt guilty about it ever since."

Kylo looked hauntingly at his sister, who was dancing around, clutching at things in the air only she could see. "Most people have a connection or need for the Power that is so strong they feel dead without it. Their minds eventually fragment or create alternate realities to escape. I am truly the leader of a lost people, abandoned by those who should have nurtured and protected them."

"I feel your pain and am sorry," Xander said compassionately.

Kylo turned to him with menace. "You come from the same bloodline, Grand Wizard. I should burn you alive!" His eyes blazed a bright brown. Garth Stone and Chase stepped forward, ready to spring into action.

Xander's eyes narrowed, and his voice took on an edge. "The failings of a sibling should not be passed on to their kin. My brother made some terrible choices, but he is the High Wizard. By your reasoning, should I not then take on the successes of my father, Arkan, who saved the world? Should people worship me because I'm related to him? Balor made his own decisions. Many were right and made the world a better place. He has trained wizards for three millennia to advise royalty, stop wars, and educate magic wielders.

"I am the Peacemaker of the Races, stopping many conflicts and preventing others from occurring. I stole the Orb of Power three millennia ago to turn the tide of the Great Battle and help banish the Demon King. I spent thousands of years searching for the Chosen One that could lead us into the Last Battle and give the races a chance to stave off certain death. If you want to judge me, do it fairly, not based on my brother's failings."

His voice softened. "I am truly sorry for the plight of the Lost Ones. I should have fought my brother harder on this issue. Instead, I left and pretended it wasn't happening. That is my burden to bear. So now we can spend the rest of our lives seeking vengeance for past wrongs or try to solve this problem. One day we can even forgive. I for one believe in solutions."

Kylo stood there, eyes blazing, staring at the Grand Wizard, who returned his gaze without flinching. A multitude of emotions played across the boy's face. The Leader of the Lost Ones finally unclenched his hands and released his magic. "I must dispel this hate in my heart," he said wretchedly. "Vengeance has motivated me for so long that I know little else. It eats at me from the inside. I only want things to be back to the way they were, before all this happened."

Xander looked at him with sympathy, and his eyes became wet. "That, dear boy, is something nobody can get. Don't chase the past. It is gone. Everything changes, and it must. But even though the past is gone, we can still create a future equal or better. Sometimes, we cannot see it because we dwell on the past. It holds us prisoner. Let it go, Kylo. Remember, we can use the lessons of the past, no matter how painful, to make a better tomorrow. Now, let's focus on solutions."

Kylo smiled bitterly. "The solution is to make the Lost Ones sane again. It cannot be done."

"There may be a way," Daria said, stepping forward. "In the Stone Kingdom, trolls learn to fight as soon as they can walk. Some develop a bloodlust that cannot be satiated, no matter how many enemies they kill. Former King Jaggar looked favourably on this. But a few go truly mad and begin killing their comrades. They become uncontrollable and must be put down. I have studied the art of healing for many years, perfecting my craft. All ailments have a source. Over the years, I've healed countless soldiers, likely more than anyone alive today, and learned many things about the brain and mind. Mental illness is a profound condition that can arise in anyone under the right conditions. For the trolls on the front lines who develop what we call the Bloodlust, I found a way to heal them. I would like to try it on your sister. I want to caution you that it does not work for everyone. My experience is that the longer someone is ill, the less likely they will heal. Your sister is young, so it may work."

Kylo stared in disbelief, expressions of hope and doubt vying for control on his young face. He turned to his sister.

"Clare, come here, sweetie. Let's play a game."

The little girl squealed and jumped up and down.

"I want to play!"

Daria came forward and kneeled in front of the girl.

"She looks strange," the girl whispered to her brother, half covering her mouth.

"She is a troll healer who may be able to help you. Listen to her, and then we can play a game."

"Oh, goody." Claire clapped her hands, growled menacingly like a dog, then giggled.

Daria sent yellow magic into her head and closed her eyes. "Watch what I do. I have little magic left, but if this works, you can help the others."

Kylo leaned close. Chip stared in fascination as the troll healer dove deep into the girl's skull, probing each section.

"There are four areas that I have found control emotion and rational thinking. The front, the base of the brain, and the two sides. Here," she finally said. "The blood vessels are compromised in the front of her brain. Link with me, and it will become clearer."

Kylo looked at her suspiciously for a moment then sighed and linked. "Yes, I see," he breathed in wonder. "Her brain reminds me of a rock with minerals. It is very difficult to see the stress points unless you know what you are looking for. This is fascinating."

"This is dangerous work," Daria said. "Only someone highly skilled should even attempt this. And success is never guaranteed."

Kylo nodded. "I understand." Chip watched as Daria created new blood vessels with her magic in the front of the brain.

"There is also heat within her brain that is unnatural. She is inflamed in the side tissue. That can also damage the vessels." Chip watched as the troll healer pulled the heat out of each side with magic and then healed the damaged veins. The level of complexity was remarkable, but he thought he understood.

"I'm going to add more vessels to the base of her brain where habits form. I know this because a troll was missing a large part of his brain after a human cleaved part of his head off, and I kept him alive. I could not regrow his brain, but he could still perform rudimentary habits like dressing, washing, and making food. Granted, he couldn't speak or fight anymore, but the soldier lived to be one hundred." She added extra minuscule blood vessels to the base of the girl's brain. "There, that should do it."

Clare stood stock still, then her eyes seemed to refocus, and she stared at her hands in wonder. The little girl looked around the room wide-eyed and turned back to her brother.

"Kylo, I feel different. I feel...normal." She reached for him, and he hugged his little sister.

"Is it you, Clare?" he cried in her cloak, squeezing her tight.

"Yes, it's me," she sobbed into his chest. "I felt like a puppet for so long. I couldn't control things." They separated, and she stared into his eyes and cupped his face. "I don't understand what happened, but I've missed you." She embraced him again.

Tears poured out of Kylo's eyes as he sobbed into her shoulder. Eleanor began to cry, and even Mary wiped at the corner of her eye.

Chip felt a lump form in his throat. He stared at the two of them and thought what it would be like to hug his real mother and father. Or a brother or sister. He wondered what it would feel like to have a real family. Tears formed in the corners of his eyes. He was eternally grateful for his friends, but to be held once by his real parents, to look into their eyes and see their love for him, to feel their embrace, would mean the world.

A great sadness engulfed the orphan, long buried. Memories surfaced of him crying to sleep at night as a little boy. The walls of the cold, dark storage room surrounded him again, a prison he thought he would never escape. Abandoned, scorned, and bullied, he was desperate for love.

He had been so terribly lonely, wondering what he had done to be discarded by his parents. Only the occasional visit by Auntie Clare kept him going. He lived for the brief joy of seeing her smiling face. Sometimes, he would dare to daydream of living a normal life, removed from the darkness, escaping to a world where he was loved. But the darkness would always come back. He was called worthless and stupid too many times to count. The orphan's loneliness became a certainty.

He knew he would never be like the other children. He was forsaken. And it was his fault. Why did he have to be born with red eyes?

And then he saw the face of Death. It had touched him. It had changed him. He saw the preciousness of life and the importance of self-love. And now, he would fight for it with everything he had. Even so, for once, he wanted to experience the love of his real parents.

The boy sighed.

Eleanor put her arms around him, holding him close. She didn't say anything, intuitively knowing what he was thinking. He smiled, grateful beyond words that he could know love through her. He knew she had been orphaned as well, and his heart went out to her. They rested their heads together as they watched Kylo reunite with his long-lost sister.

Chip smiled, happy that the Leader of the Lost Ones was experiencing the daydream he had dreamt for many years. It filled him with hope despite the sadness. He knew fulfilling someone else's dreams was the next best thing when yours was impossible. It was a joy all its own.

"Keep in mind she will have gaps in her memories and likely nightmares for a while, but it is the real Clare," Daria said. "I can tell it worked. I am happy for you."

They both included the troll healer in their embrace.

"Thank you," Kylo said, his voice breaking up. "I have wanted this for so long."

"I think you are one of the few who can heal like this," Daria said. "I have never seen dexterity in magic like yours. You will likely even surpass me. There is an army of Lost Ones waiting to be healed. You cannot heal them all, especially the older ones, but this work can bring you much joy." The troll healer wiped away a tear from the side of her face. "May the Creator shine on you."

Chip looked around the room. Many others wept, and even the troll captain's eye looked shiny. Garth Stone remained stoic, but Chip detected a smile of approval. Xander looked like a young man again, his face filled with wonder.

"We can help many people with this technique," the wizard said. "Perhaps one day we can eliminate mental illness. It has always been a fantasy, but now I see it's possible."

Kylo turned with his arm around his little sister. "I want to thank you for this. I also want to apologize for trying to drop the roof on your heads...and trying to incinerate your heart," he added, smiling at Chip. "I offer these humble accommodations tonight for you to rest. The cavern is yours. I have another one like this in a clearing nearby. I will take the Lost Ones to it and begin the healing process."

"What will you do after?" Chip asked.

Kylo thought about it. "To be honest, I never thought that far ahead. What would you have us do?"

"I ask that you swear allegiance to me, Chip Oathbinder, Guardian of the Races, and stand with us in the Last Battle."

Kylo and Clare raised their eyebrows. "Is he serious?" she whispered to her brother.

"I think he is," he whispered back.

The Leader of the Lost Ones smiled. "It would be an honour. I swear allegiance to you, Chip Oathbinder."

Clare shrugged. "I swear allegiance to you, Chip Oathbinder."

Chip smiled. "I am glad to hear it. We all need to stand together to fight the coming darkness. One hundred extra wizards would be most welcome. I understand you will not return to the Guild while Balor remains in power, so I recommend that you travel to Yucan once the Lost Ones are healed. See the Triumvirate. They can provide you with money and supplies for your journey to Toron. Xander will write you a note to present to them. We convinced the ogres to join our cause as well."

Kylo's mouth dropped open.

"How?" he gasped.

"I healed their baby," Chip said. "I also showed Gruk, their leader, my memories. He knows if he stays here that demons will kill them all. The same fate awaits your people if you remain. I cannot stress the importance of leaving this place. It is not good for the mind. Evil permeates this forest through symbols and runes carved by the witches. They worship a dark force that seeks to gain a foothold on Earth."

The Leader of the Lost Ones nodded. "I know of what you speak. The witches are somehow able to detect those with Permanent Walls. They seek them throughout the lands and bring them to the Secret Caves. Morgeth can remove their walls, and the witches try to convert them to their cause. Many join willingly. Some have gone mad and cannot be saved. These she releases into Darkwood. I have gathered many and made shelter for them. There is strength in numbers. Some I cannot control, and they wander alone or in small groups throughout the forest. A few congregate on the fringes, for it is safest there. Many do not survive the journey. I know most of the denizens in Darkwood, but I have not explored it everywhere. The ogres are her pets, and we are told to avoid their valley on pain of death. Wards, runes, and symbols keep most creatures in their zones, but some cross. Without these boundaries, it would be a free-for-all, and the inhabitants would end up killing each other. She aims to make the forest as deadly as possible to protect the caves."

"What is so special about the caves?" Eleanor asked. "Besides the witches trying to protect themselves."

"I have heard the witches speak of a stone. I have not seen it. Morgeth's mother, Zara, is the only one she listens to. They call her the High Seer. Her eyes are milky white, and when she looks at you, it feels like she is staring into your soul. They follow *The Book of Seeing* and perform arcane rites. The whole place reeks of evil. I feigned madness so I could be released with Clare into the forest. We were only in the caves a few months." Kylo looked at them and for the first time displayed fear. "Even if you make it through Darkwood, you will not survive the Secret Caves. Morgeth is very powerful and commands dozens of black-robed witches. The grey-robed acolytes who have had their Permanent Walls removed constitute scores more. If she deems them fit to join her cause, they swear an oath and become a witch or servant. The males are assigned cooking, chores, and other tasks or are sent out to recruit members for their cults. She says a male's energy differs, and *The Book of Seeing* forbids their membership. If an acolyte is sane but refuses the oath, she makes a public blood sacrifice to appease the darkness." A look of horror crossed his features. "I have witnessed it several times. The screams..."

"Why do the Lost Ones sing their chant?" Chip asked. "It is morbid."

"They created it themselves." Kylo struggled with the words. "You have to understand, Darkwood...changes you. The evil that emanates from the Secret Caves plays with your mind. It causes one to twist...to desire blood and killing. The chant reflects this and unifies them, so I allow it. I have withstood the madness, the witches, and the forest, but not wholly. The evil has changed me, giving me dark, murderous thoughts of vengeance and retribution. Only today, through your actions, have I allowed myself a glimmer of hope. Now that my sister is healed, I remember the old thoughts of love and kindness. I was a good person before Balor and the witches imprisoned us. I have seen kind, loving people converted into monsters through the cult's false beliefs and evil control. Even in the so-called greatest institutions, such as the Wizard's Guild, corruption exists based on false beliefs or greed. I believe that when one person holds absolute power, their idiosyncrasies magnify. Power corrupts. False views and justifications can pass down the generations through draconian means. The best leader is the one who doesn't want it in the first place."

Chip nodded, thinking of his incredible magic and its potential for misuse. "It is the human condition, I'm afraid. The hallmarks of corruption are greed, the desire for ever more power, and the deliberate avoidance of the truth. I have seen it many times. Yet hope remains. I will always believe that. Negative beliefs are always based on the need for acceptance or the desire for control. Once identified, we can change them. You have already started on the path of redemption." His face hardened. "These witches and their cults have allowed much evil into this world. My understanding is they formed right after The Great Forget. A Force, which is Death, used them to gain a foothold. They must be destroyed."

"I hope you are strong enough," Kylo said. "For all our sakes."

"Why have you never tried to leave the forest?" Chip asked.

"The witches told us if we ever tried that they would kill us. Even if we managed to get out, they would hunt us down, so we stayed."

"What lies between us and the Secret Caves?" Xander asked.

"There are wild boars that come to your shoulders with tusks as long as your legs. They usually only attack in herds. We pick the weaker ones off with our magic and eat them. My advice is to climb the trees and wait until they lose interest. The witches have little control over them due to their low intelligence. The real threat are the green-eyed Rakshas, a four-armed apelike creature of high intelligence. They are the last line of defence for anyone who makes it that far. The witches created them over the millennia through the Dark Arts. Their skin is tough, almost armour-like, and they are capable of using weapons such as rocks or sticks. Their fangs are poisonous, so even the smallest bite will kill you in under a minute. Otherwise, you should be fine."

Everyone was dead silent except Ethrang, who burst out laughing. Garth raised an eyebrow. One Eye grinned.

"So to clarify," Chase observed, "we only have to avoid being gored by massive boars, then conquer an army of four-armed poisonous apes, then destroy a cult of powerful ancient witches, then backtrack through Darkwood and do it all over again?"

"The witches blindfolded us when we arrived. There is a secret way to enter and exit the caves. I suggest you keep one alive so she can show you how they do it. Otherwise, you should be fine." Kylo tried to hide the doubt on his face.

"Oh dear," Eleanor said.

"Nothing is ever easy," Xander muttered.

"Spend the remainder of the night here and replenish your magic," Kylo advised. "If you leave mid-morning, you should arrive late in the afternoon. I would offer help, but it will take some time to heal the Lost Ones, and I do not believe any would risk returning. We are moving east to another cavern, so we will not meet again until the Last Battle, fortune willing." He paused, shaking his head. "I thought the Creator had forsaken us, so I have not said this in many years." He looked up, holding his sister tight. "May the Creator shine on you."

"May the Creator shine on you," they echoed. Clare waved at them, and then the Leader of the Lost Ones left the cavern holding his sister's hand.

The others looked at each other, digesting the information. They had overcome insurmountable odds, but even greater challenges were ahead. Chip sighed, drained of energy.

"Get some rest," Xander said, finding a spot along the wall. "We are going to need it."

"I will take the first watch," the weapons master said, moving to the tunnel entrance. "One is sufficient." Several other Protectors and trolls volunteered for subsequent watches.

Chip rested close to Eleanor, covering them in his red cloak. The challenges ahead would be many, but for once he was too exhausted to worry. He set it aside for the morning.

The boy closed his eyes once and remembered no more.

12

Chip woke with a start.
"He's awake!"
"Well, it's about time."
"You won the bet. It's still before lunchtime. I was so close," Chase complained. Ethrang laughed.

The boy pushed himself up on his elbows to see his companions all staring at him. "Awkward," he mumbled. "Are you saying it's already midmorning?"

"No, it's almost lunchtime. The morning is gone," Chase explained, hands on hips, pretending to be Miss Owl. He failed miserably.

"I'm so sorry," Chip said. "You should have woken me."

"I was about to," Xander confessed. "Our goal is to reach the Secret Caves before the sun sets. None of us wish to spend another night in Darkwood."

Chip instinctively thought about washing, changing, and dressing but realized he could do none of that. He swung his legs off the stone. "I'm ready." Ethrang laughed again.

The small party exited the cavern through the long tunnel and ascended the stairs. They emerged behind the stones and entered the clearing. The day was cold and windy, with snow blanketing the ground.

They immediately noticed the bodies. Several large black birds were picking at the corpses with long, sharp beaks. The ravens cocked their heads at them then crowed loudly, angry at the interruption. White, dead faces showed from the cowls of the bodies, some disturbingly young. Many had their eyes pecked out.

Chip shook his head. They were the ones who had thrown themselves on his shield. He felt a wave of guilt for a moment, but it was not his fault. That way of thinking would paralyze him and serve no useful purpose. Still, he experienced a pang of sympathy for the dead and made a silent prayer to the Creator.

"Let's get moving," Garth said softly. "We have much ground to cover." They nodded and trudged after him, heading north.

The dark, twisted trees enveloped them again, but at least it was daylight. They did not hear any whispers, chants, or laughter. The Lost Ones had moved east and would leave the dreaded forest when healed. Chip could not imagine living there for any length of time, even with one hundred magic wielders.

As the afternoon progressed, low shrubs grew in size between the trees. They became wary, hands resting on their weapons. One troll stopped and peered into a large bush. He pulled out his sword, letting out a guttural yell, but it was too late.

A monstrous, black body exploded out of the foliage, impaling him with six-foot-long tusks. It was a massive boar, grunting as it hefted him high, twisting its head so its tusks could do more damage. Both pierced the troll in the abdomen, above his groin. The screams coming out of the soldier were difficult to hear.

Chip lifted his hands to lend aid, but loud grunts and the sound of hooves grew in volume.

"Get in the trees," Garth shouted. "It's a herd."

Everyone ran for the nearest tree, but some were too slow. A huge boar blasted through another bush to strike Bulch in the legs, sending him flying through the air to land hard on the open ground. Chip seized his Power and levitated the giant Protector into the high branches of a nearby tree. One of his legs hung at an odd angle to his knee.

Ethrang appeared as a giant eagle, trying to pull the troll off the boar's tusks, but it was too late. His innards had spilled out onto the forest floor, and his body had deflated like a torn rag doll. The eagle flew into a tree and landed on a branch, surveying the scene.

Chip lifted Eleanor and Mary into the branches. More boars appeared, charging at anything moving on the ground. They seemed to notice his red cloak and changed their course to target him. Chip picked up three of the beasts hurtling towards him and sent them high in the air.

Others appeared through the bushes and lunged at him. For once, the timing couldn't have worked out better. As they neared him, the airborne bodies returned to Earth with a vengeance, slamming into the others with bone-crushing force. A pile of writhing boar bodies formed before him.

"We are safe, climb," Eleanor called. He turned and leapt at the lowest branch, swinging himself up. The boy jumped from branch to branch, ignoring his fear of heights. More boars ran through the bushes to mill around at the base of the trees. They snorted and tried to stand on their hind legs but weren't built for that. The distinct smell of pork infused the air.

Bulch was hanging between two branches, groaning.

"Daria! I'm going to levitate you to him for healing." She nodded, and Chip sent her floating over the male pigs to land on the tree limb beside the huge Protector. She immediately put her hands on his broken leg and went to work.

The companions had to wait several minutes, trying to ignore the animals tearing at the dead troll on the ground, feasting on his remains. They jostled each other to rend his flesh, making obscene crunching noises as they chewed on his bones. Eleanor turned away, closing her eyes while Mary looked like she would vomit. The trolls in the trees thumped their chest, paying homage to a fallen comrade.

Finally, when nothing remained of the troll, including his bones, they moved off. Two stayed to nibble on the bushes, but Ethrang tossed a broken branch at them, and they stalked off, following the herd.

The companions quietly climbed down and followed Garth north. They continued through the snow, occasionally seeing boar tracks.

A short while later, they heard a snort nearby and took to the trees. A herd passed below them a few moments later, stopping to graze on the bushes before moving off. One looked up and noticed them, but the beast flicked its tail dismissively and plodded on.

The group had to take refuge in the trees twice more before the bushes began shrinking. By mid-afternoon, the shrubbery disappeared, and only the stunted trees remained. Dark clouds began to move in from the west, blotting out the weak sun.

"Not another storm," Chase complained as the light dimmed.

"Did you expect any less?" Chip smiled, patting him on the back. "Be thankful you got to see the sun. We may not see it for a while. I've heard caves are dark…and full of spiders." Chase groaned.

"We shouldn't be too far from the meadow in the middle of Darkwood," Garth said, stopping to turn around. "Keep your eyes open for Rakshas." They nodded grimly. The idea of encountering four-armed poisonous apes was daunting.

They continued, their only company the silent, twisted limbs creaking in the mounting wind. Chip didn't notice it initially, but the trees were growing taller and wider. The low-hanging branches disappeared.

The trend continued as the afternoon wore on until Darkwood resembled Fang Forest. Yet none of the trees were straight, and the black bark looked sickly. The crooked trunks were massive, with knots and holes running up the bark. The canopy interlaced far above, creating shadows on the ground. An eerie stillness blanketed the woods as the wind had no choice but to surrender to the towering boles.

"I don't like this," Chase muttered. "Brings back memories of giant spiders."

"I would be happy if that's all we had to face," Chip retorted, growing more apprehensive. He sensed a growing darkness in the woods, infusing the trees. As if on cue, runes and symbols appeared on the giant trunks. Carved eyes stared at them, daring them to continue.

"This is the heart of Darkwood," Xander said softly. "These are the original trees. The rest of the forest is their lesser progeny, much younger and smaller than their ancestors, stunted by evil. These were here since the Great Forget."

Though Chip could not see it through the trees, he knew the sun was beginning to set. They were almost out of time.

A distant bark sounded up ahead. Everyone froze.

"Sounds like a dog," Chase commented.

"How do you know apes don't bark?" Mary asked, turning her nose up.

"Well, I…"

"Shhh," Garth whispered. "They know we are here."

He drew his weapon, and they followed suit, creeping forward, eyes alert. Chip knew that anything could be hiding behind each massive trunk. Garth pointed to the ground ahead, and the boy's eyes widened. Huge prints with five toes appeared in the snow, leading to a giant trunk. The big toe was more sideways, which allowed for grasping and climbing. There were random holes in the tree and knotty projections. It wasn't easy to see the top, such was the height. They moved on, glancing up fearfully. More prints appeared, leading to different trunks.

Another bark sounded, much closer this time.

Garth moved stealthily, a weapon in each hand, body coiled and ready to strike. The others took similar stances. The air was thick with tension.

A third bark sounded, coming from behind the vast trunk before them. There were no low-level branches to climb to safety anymore. It wouldn't do any good anyway. Chip stared at the holes dotting the crooked trunks like gaping eye sockets, sensing that many eyes were watching them.

The weapons master stopped and pointed at the ground,

revealing dozens of large five-toed prints. Chip looked up and caught sight of a bald head with green eyes peering at him halfway up the trunk. The others noticed as well.

The Raksha opened its mouth, displaying sharp fangs and emitted an ear-piercing roar. Grey creatures with green eyes began pouring out of the holes in the trees then shimmying down with terrifying speed. They used four muscled arms and two legs to grip the bark, effortlessly descending to the ground.

The ape-like creatures were hairless with thick grey skin that looked tough. Their eyes glowed green in the fading light, deep set in flat, blunted faces. They landed on the ground and roared, beating their chests with four large-knuckled fists. Some had rocks or short sticks in one of their hands. They were as tall as the trolls and more muscled.

"Don't let them bite you," Garth warned. "They are poisonous."

Dozens of Rakshas surrounded them. The one who had let out the initial roar dropped onto the snow. He was a head taller than the others, reminding Chip of Furiosa. The thing grinned at them evilly, causing a saliva-like fluid to drip from its fangs. The drops hissed on the snow. The other apes stood in a half crouch, heads slightly bowed. He was clearly their leader.

The huge ape looked at them, his naked body crisscrossed with scars. He settled his glowing green eyes on Chip and pointed. The boy felt a chill run up his spine.

The thing's mouth worked, trying to form a sound. Even though it was guttural and garbled, the single word was unmistakable.

"Die!"

He had rarely seen a more menacing creature, but the boy was tired of everything trying to kill him.

The Guardian of the Races stepped forward and seized his magic.

"I will not die!" Chip responded and sent a ball of red fire at the creature's center. The ape leader managed to leap sideways, but the flaming ball struck his upper arm, tearing it clean off. The impact sent the thing hurtling backwards into the tree trunk. There was a stunned look on its face, and the three-armed green-eyed beast straightened and roared. The sound echoed off the trees.

All the apes attacked at once.

Grunts and hollers came from all directions. Chip knew it would be disastrous if he allowed the Rakshas to get close. He remembered the strength of the white apes in the Stone Kingdom, but these looked stronger.

He threw up a thick red shield surrounding his companions. Several apes ran into it and began melting. Two made it through, but their armour-like skin couldn't withstand his red magic. They staggered into the circle and fell facedown, smoking. Other apes stopped and poked their hands through the shield, watching in fascination as their skin smoked.

The four-armed creatures learned quickly and stepped away, looking at their leader. The giant ape stood back, watching them. His severed arm was cauterized so it did not bleed. The tall ape grinned, exposing sharp fangs, and made a lifting motion to his minions. A dozen apes took the cue and leapt into the air with shocking agility, landing in a single bound on top of the shield, which was much weaker.

Chip tried to strengthen it but it was too late.

The Rakshas slid through his magic, bodies smoking, but they did not melt. Suddenly, they were in their midst, swinging with multiple arms. One picked up a troll and threw him into the shield. Chip watched in horror as his red Power destroyed the soldier.

The wizards used magic to shield their bodies, but the Protectors and trolls had no defence. The sound of loud thumps and breaking bones erupted. The giant Protector Bulch used his club to smash an ape in the head, but it grinned at him and started pummeling the big man with its four fists.

The twins combined their magic to good effect. Thomas froze the Raksha in front of him by surrounding it with compressed air, and Kristan shot his full Power straight into the ape's heart. Surprisingly, even his considerable magic took its time getting through the dense skin.

Two of the beasts ran at Eleanor and Mary. Chip raised his hand despite the strain of maintaining the shield, but before he could unleash a stream of red fire, the Darkwood King appeared. The apes paused, expressions turning to ones of fear, then snarled and ran at the giant cat. One had a rock, and the other a stick.

The Yagr slashed the first Raksha with blinding speed, leaving huge rents in its chest. The ape stumbled, dropping the rock. The second one swung hard at the cat's head with its stick, but the feline was quicker. Ethrang ducked low, then swung his talons upward, ripping the ape open from groin to chest. The creature barked weakly and sank to its knees, insides spilling onto the ground. The Yagr turned and went to finish off the first ape.

Then, out of nowhere, a Raksha landed on the cat's back, green eyes glowing. Chip called out in warning, but it was too late. The four-armed creature sank its fangs deep into the Darkwood King's neck. Ethrang shook the thing off with a snarl and tore out its throat before it landed on the ground.

Yet the damage was done.

The Yagr staggered, eyes bulging as the poison went to work.

"Daria!" Chip screamed. "Get the poison out." He wanted to help, but the shield required his strength and concentration. Healing needed skill and extreme focus. Daria tried to reach the dying cat, but two apes blocked her, fighting furiously in the middle. The wizards shot multiple shards of fire into their bodies, but it took repeated blows to pierce the thick skin.

The giant Yagr disappeared as Ethrang took on his true form. The boy was gasping on his back, his blond face contorted in pain. Blood leaked down his neck.

Chip looked at the orphan, knowing he would be dead soon. In frustration, he made a bold decision. The Guardian seized the shield, adding even more Power, and exploded it outwards with all his strength. A wall of pure-red fire struck the apes with tremendous force, sending all in the vicinity hurtling backwards with ferocious speed. The creatures slammed into the trees and slid down the trunks in jumbled heaps. Chip seized the apes still alive in the middle and tossed them sideways.

Ethrang made a terrible choking sound, and blood began to pour out of his nose.

"Daria!" Chip called, but she was already running to him. Yellow magic went into the orphan's convulsing body. He watched as she pulled the deadly poison out of his veins and threw it on the ground, where it hissed in the snow. The boy's lungs were severely damaged, and he took his last breath.

The Banfar orphan's eyes rolled into the back of his head, and his chest stopped moving. Chip watched in disbelief.

"No, no, no," he repeated, willing his friend to survive. Chip closed his eyes and drew in more Power, sending it to Daria while reforming the shield. The apes that could still get up stumbled back towards them. She repaired Ethrang's heart and lungs, strengthening the damaged blood vessels, and healed his neck. The troll healer forced air into his lungs and used her Power to make his heart beat.

The skinny blond boy's eyes remained closed.

Daria turned to Chip with great sorrow and began to shake her head.

Then a gasp sounded, and the blond orphan sucked in air, breathing on his own. Ethrang opened his eyes.

The boy groaned. "That's twice I've been poisoned. I can tell you ape poison is much worse than spider poison." He flexed his hands and looked at his body. Ethrang's eyes held a haunted look. "I wanted to die. The pain was so bad. It's like all your veins are on fire. But I knew you needed me, Guardian." He stood up slowly.

"Good to have you back," Kristan said. Thomas patted him on the shoulder.

The others gathered around.

Chip moved to embrace his friend then stumbled. A wave of dizziness washed over him. Eleanor looked at him with concern.

"I can't maintain this shield much longer," he gasped. "We have to move." The others immediately linked with him, but their Power was also waning. After two days of fighting, they were again running out.

Garth took the lead. The remaining apes gathered around the shield. Chip watched with dismay as more dropped to the ground. Their leader had been thrown against the tree when the shield exploded, causing one of his three remaining arms to hang uselessly by his side. Yet he still gave them a lecherous grin, pacing back and forth, seeming to know their magic would ultimately fail.

They hustled forward between the massive trees, watching with chagrin as the ape ranks swelled. None of the creatures touched the shield anymore. The Rakshas simply waited.

"We need to reach the meadow and escape into the caves," Xander said, moving briskly though his face showed exhaustion. The wizard closed his eyes, sending out his presence, and opened them in fear moments later. "We are off course, somewhat. Head northeast. I'm afraid there are many more apes ahead. The witches took no chances when they created these creatures through the Dark Arts. The Secret Caves are well protected. I hope our magic can sustain us."

"Even if we make it, we will have little Power left for the witches," Kristan noted.

"One problem at a time," Xander responded. "Sometimes, you must go forward knowing it's impossible."

The blond twin nodded in agreement, his face turning resolute. "We will go down fighting until our last breath." Thomas looked over at his brother and nodded, grim but determined.

The light began to fail as they veered northeast. Even with their combined magic, the shield was becoming difficult to maintain. The apes kept pace in silence, ambling with ease, being frustratingly patient. Chip knew if he dropped the shield for a moment, they would attack as one, ripping them to shreds with their muscled arms or biting them with poisonous fangs. He felt a growing sense of dread. The idea of facing them with no Power was terrifying. Even the Protectors could not long defend against such brute force.

Chip made a vow to at least take out their leader. The creature seemed particularly intent on killing him. He thought through his options. It would be easy to drop the shield and send out arcing streams of wizard fire, but in his current state, the boy knew he could not kill them all. The amount of wizard fire and pain the Rakshas could sustain was disturbing. The others needed repeated, concentrated bursts of Power to pierce their armour. The next option was to hurl them through the air, but most seemed to get up and still come forward despite their injuries. He had never met a foe quite like this. The boy knew they would already be dead if they had not slept the night before and renewed some of their magic.

Darkwood was indeed a formidable place.

Yet they were so close to making it through. He reduced the shield slightly to sustain it longer, gritting his teeth. "We should run. I cannot hold it much longer." His weary companions nodded, and everyone increased their pace to a jog. They zigzagged through the enormous trees, watching more apes descend. Barks sounded up ahead, and roars followed. The creatures were primitive but organized.

Agonizing minutes passed. The Rakshas that joined the others followed their lead, keeping them company. The only sounds became one of panting breaths. At least one hundred four-armed apes were now surrounding them, keeping pace.

Chip felt his magic sputter. He staggered again.

"The meadow is still a league away," Xander said with difficulty. The blazing blue fire in his eyes started to diminish. Daria faltered, and her yellow eyes returned to normal.

She missed a few steps but maintained the pace, giving him a shameful look. "I'm sorry. That is all I have left."

He nodded.

Their best healer was out of magic.

Ethrang breathed heavily beside him. "If I keep this up, I won't be able to shift."

"Release your link," he responded. The boy let go. Chip immediately felt the burden increase on the others.

That was when he knew they were not going to make it.

He looked through the shield at the multitude of apes around them. Their green eyes glowed brighter as the sun descended below the horizon. Many were grinning, their fangs gleaming.

A wave of fear washed over him, and the shield rippled. Eleanor turned to him.

"You have to drop it, or we all die," she warned. "I have enough to sustain us for a little while and provide a distraction." There were tears in her eyes. "Chip, you have to let it go."

"Half a league left," Xander gasped.

"We will protect you," Garth Stone said. "It is our duty. The most important thing is that you make it. Release us."

"Let us do what we were created for," Chase said. His eyes glinted dangerously as he allowed his anger to flare. The boys shared a look.

Chip nodded in anguish, knowing they spoke true.

"Fine," he said through clenched teeth. "But we are taking a lot of them with us."

13

The boy waited until they were in the open between a circle of trees. He disconnected the link, pulling in more of his diminishing Power.

Chip Oathbinder released his magic.

The shield exploded as before, but he turned it into red daggers this time.

Crimson shards shot outwards in a burst of colour, lighting up the growing darkness and ripping apart the apes in a blinding display of Power. Holes appeared in dozens of them, and they sank to the ground. The ones running closer to the shield blew apart, arms and heads flying off into the forest. Such was the devastation that, for a moment, all the apes were down.

"Run!" shouted Xander, and the group followed the spry wizard at a torrid pace. For a moment, it looked like they would make it to the meadow, but more apes appeared in front of them, shimmying down the tree trunks. These looked even larger, the last line of defence. Chip looked back to see the ones furthest from the exploding shield get up. Some had wounds on their arms, legs, or chest, but they shook their bald grey heads and sprang forward with a vengeance.

"Trolls to the back!" yelled Garth Stone. "Protectors, to me!"

The weapons master moved to the front, attacking the new apes without slowing. A steely determination lit his grey eyes, and he moved like a man possessed, tearing into the creatures. Chase moved to his side, face full of fury, charging full force into the enemy.

The two of them cleared a path, chopping off limbs and stabbing faces.

"Aim for the eyes!" Garth shouted, using the tip of his sword to wreak havoc. Several large apes tried to swing at him with their multiple arms, but he dodged out of range. Then he leapt forward and impaled them in their glowing green eyes, causing the beasts to drop lifelessly to the ground.

The group ran through the hole, but by now the wounded apes had caught up, harrying the trolls in the back. Chip watched as the leader materialized with a maniacal look on his blunt face. Two bleeding holes in his chest and leg did not seem to slow him down.

The Raksha leader leapt on a fleeing troll and buried his fangs in the soldier's neck. The others turned to help, but the overwhelming numbers forced them to retreat. Only six trolls remained.

Everyone ran through the gap, and Chip could see the meadow in the distance. His sight became blocked as more apes appeared. They were forced into a tight circle and stopped, surrounded.

"Stay back," Eleanor said and lifted her arms, eyes blazing brown with flecks of red. The ground ahead shook as great mounds of earth flew into the air, carrying the apes with them. They soared halfway up the trees before hurtling back to land in the holes she had dug. The dirt rained down on top of the creatures, burying them alive. Chip turned to the apes in the back and sprayed red fire in a wide swath. The ape leader anticipated his move and hid behind a group of his brethren. The boy grunted in dismay.

Kristan and Thomas turned to one side while Xander and Mary faced the other. Blue magic burst forth from their splayed hands, ravaging those trying to attack their flanks. The whole area became a bloodbath as arms flew and bodies melted.

And then their magic began to run out.

Mary's eyes returned to normal, and she stumbled. Kristan and

Thomas, who had linked, ran out of Power. They looked back in consternation. Eleanor cried out as her magic disappeared. Yet the devastation to the ape population was significant. For a moment, the way was open.

"Run!" the weapons master shouted.

Everyone turned and bolted. Chip saw the opening again through the trees. Even in the fading sun, he could see a white meadow with a cluster of rocks in the middle on a low hill.

They were so close.

A few hundred feet remained to the edge of Darkwood before the remaining Rakshas converged again. Several dozen had survived, and the companions had to turn. A knot of five ran from the side towards Chip. A troll soldier leapt in their path, but one of the creatures held a rock and cracked the troll's head open with a devastating downward strike. The boy raised his hands and released a stream of red fire that arced across their chests. The Rakshas flew backwards, catching fire.

Another two glowing-eyed beasts leapt across their flaming bodies, intent on destroying him. The Darkwood King suddenly appeared, a fifteen-foot-long behemoth of pure savagery. Ethrang launched himself into them, tearing with his monstrous claws. Pieces of the two apes flew off in sprays of blood.

Yet more replaced them.

"Fall back," Garth ordered. They retreated in a coordinated fashion, swiping at anything in range. Chip turned to see Chase and the weapons master cleaving a way forward. The twins had pulled their swords, standing before Eleanor and Mary. Carvor and Sheldor took the left flank, with Ward and Shimko on the right. Bulch went where needed, swinging his massive club.

Then the Rakshas attacked simultaneously.

A dozen charged the trolls in the back while several bounded high into the air to land on top of them. One Eye went berserk, swinging a short sword in his left hand and a cudgel in the other. The sound of breaking bones rang loud and clear. For several moments, the trolls held, and then two went down. The apes pummeled them with huge fists before sinking fangs deep into their bark-like skin.

Bellows of pain rang out, but they went silent quickly. Chip moved to lend aid, but three more demented creatures came at him. He sent out two daggers of red magic while the Jagr tore out the throat of the third with his massive jaws.

Xander moved to the back. "Duck!"

One Eye, Daria, and the two remaining trolls crouched as the wizard sprayed blue fire into the throng. The apes in the front began to melt as they fell backward, giving the companions a brief reprieve.

"Keep moving," ordered Garth, and everyone ran towards the meadow, now only a hundred paces away.

The respite was short-lived.

The two dozen remaining Rakshas swarmed again. Half of them leapt high in the air with their powerful legs to land in the middle of the small group.

Pandemonium ensued.

One crashed into Chase, bowling him over, but the tall boy rolled to his feet and disembowelled the creature with a backhand slice. Unlike the others, he could easily cut through the ape's tough skin due to his enhanced strength. The red chips in his eyes glowed with a primal fury.

A large Raksha sailed through the air to land on Sheldor's back, wrapping four huge gray arms around his body. Carvor cried out as the creature sunk its fangs deep into the Protector's neck. The Silver Sword Champion chopped at the thing until it let go, but the damage was done. Blood leaked out of the two puncture holes in the stout Protector's neck.

Sheldor stood in shock, then a look of acceptance crossed his square face, and the Protector's eyes rolled back as he fell to the ground.

Chip tried to lend aid, but two apes blocked him, landing in front of Eleanor and Mary. One backhanded the Blue Wing Leader off her feet, and the woman went down without moving. The Queen of Vanalon cried out as the other ape grabbed her throat, lifting her off the ground. Chip pointed at the back of the ape's head and sent all his remaining Power into its skull, but it was only a tendril. The Raksha's skin merely smoked.

He was out of magic.

Chip frantically tried to pull his sword out as the creature squeezed Eleanor's neck. The twins got there before him, leaping in with faces full of cold determination. They both stabbed at the same time, each puncturing the green eyes of the four-armed monstrosity. It let go of the queen.

Eleanor choked as she sucked in air and landed on her feet.

Chip went to steady her when something huge knocked him sideways. He landed hard but sprang to his feet, sword in hand.

A massive shape rose before him. It was the Raksha leader.

The twins tried to help, but another blocked their progress. Chip looked around for Ethrang, but the Yagr had leapt into the fray, trying to save Sheldor. The giant cat was too far away to lend aid.

Chip stared into the face of pure evil.

The massive ape grinned at him, fangs shining in the dying light. The beast had wounds all over his body, but two of his four arms still worked. The creature swung at him viciously. The boy dodged the first blow, but the second glanced across his arm, breaking it and spinning him around. The Raksha leader seized his shoulders and pulled him close, opening its jaws wide.

Despite his terror, the boy waited until it was within range, holding his sword parallel to his body. He took the hilt with both hands and shoved it upwards with all his strength, leaning backwards. The thing's fetid breath surrounded his face, and he felt the broken bone shift in his left arm. As he screamed in pain, the tip of his sword came up into the roof of the ape leader's mouth, stopping his jaw from closing. The hands loosened on his shoulders, so he jumped up with all his strength, hitting the hilt with his right knee. The sword tip went up through the ape's mouth and out one eye.

The leader made a choking sound before sinking to its knees. The Raksha's remaining glowing green eye widened.

"Die," Chip grunted, kicking the creature in the chest and freeing his sword at the same time. A fountain of blood came with it. The four-armed abomination fell on its back, blood fountaining out of its eye.

The Raksha leader seized up and then let out its last breath.

There was dead silence. Chip looked around to see that the other apes had stopped fighting to stare at their fallen leader.

"Run," Garth whispered, taking advantage of the lull. Chip staggered towards Eleanor while Bulch grabbed Mary and carried her easily in his arms.

The silence did not last long. Barks and bellows erupted with new intensity. Chip looked back to see the other apes pointing at him with murderous looks. Their roars turned to screams of rage, and they all converged on him.

The orphan ran for his life.

The Protectors and trolls fell back to slow the charge.

"Keep running," Ward said as he passed him to intercept the oncoming Rakshas.

The wizards sprinted for the meadow as one, breath ragged, accompanied by Garth and Chase. Chip saw a final group of three apes appear behind the last tree to bar their way. He gritted his teeth in frustration. Then Xander's eyes lit up, and his hands raised.

The old wizard had saved some magic after all.

Bolts of blue fire shot directly into the Rakshas' faces. They screamed, clutching their melting features. Xander tried to send more to finish them off, but his eyes returned to normal.

The Grand Wizard had used the last of his Power.

Yet, it was enough to create an opening. They danced around the wounded apes and suddenly emerged from the trees. A large meadow opened before them.

Fighting erupted behind them, and everyone turned back.

Chip saw that the trees ringing the clearing had large runes and symbols carved into them. He wondered if the apes could cross.

"I think they only need to get into the meadow," Chip told Garth, clutching his broken arm.

The weapons master eyed the runes and nodded. "You all stay here. That is an order." He looked at Chase, who nodded. The pair reentered the forest. Bulch handed Mary off to Kristan and followed. The giant Protector did not hesitate.

The sounds of fighting intensified. Chip looked at the twins, and an unspoken message passed between them. Kristan set Mary on her feet. She had regained consciousness but looked around in confusion. Eleanor steadied her. The three set off back into the forest.

"They are doing this for you, Chip. Get back in one piece," Xander called out. The boy respected that the old man didn't try to stop him. He would not let his friends die while he was still breathing, orders or not.

When they arrived, the Rakshas had encircled the Protectors and trolls. Ethrang kept the ones on the side at bay with vicious swipes of his claws. The trolls at the back hacked furiously, but it was only a matter of time before they were overrun.

Two creatures were trying to sneak up on Chase and the weapons master. Chip and the blonde twins ran forward, throwing caution to the wind. Only at the last moment did the two apes hear them and spin around as swords stabbed deep into their eyes. Both Rakshas dropped.

Roars rang out as the beasts noticed their main quarry had returned. The pause gave the others a chance to break through toward the meadow. Everyone ran, but the trolls in the back weren't fast enough. The apes dragged down the last of the soldiers, knocking Daria over. One Eye turned around, trying to free them, but a large Raksha sailed through the air, wrapping him in its arms. The troll captain, covered in blood, finally stopped fighting, knowing it was over. Instead, he grinned in the face of his enemy and bit the creature's neck. There was a moment of surprise on the ape's face, and then it reared its head back to tear One Eye's throat out.

Quick as a thought, Garth Stone stopped and turned, pulling a dagger from his boot. He whipped it across the clearing as the large ape tried to bite down on the troll captain's neck.

The beast's head snapped back, the hilt of Garth's dagger jutting out of its right eye, letting go.

One Eye stared in wonder then leapt up and kicked the dying ape into the others, knocking several over. He pulled Daria from the fray and was about to continue trying to save his fallen comrade, but the remaining troll had multiple bite marks.

The troll captain pulled Daria away and ran back to the others. Ward, Shimko, Carvor and Bulch valiantly formed a line while they retreated, slowing the apes in the lead. Once everyone was past, they turned to dash away. It became a footrace to freedom. The apes reached out as they cleared the last of the trees then stopped.

They were through to the meadow.

The Protectors whirled, swords at the ready. A dozen apes remained, and everyone spread out to take them on.

The Rakshas stopped, snarling savagely. The Protectors backed up warily until the group was a safe distance from the trees.

They watched the glowing green eyes of the apes standing in a line motionless at the edge of the forest. A dozen remained.

The sun had set.

A shiver ran up Chip's spine. "They cannot cross the tree line. The runes or symbols must stop them."

"Likely to protect the witches themselves," Xander mused.

"Looks like we made it through Darkwood," Chase said as he sheathed his sword.

"Indeed, we have," Xander said softly.

"May the Creator protect the fallen," the weapons master intoned, putting a hand over his heart. The others did the same. All the trolls except for One Eye and Daria had perished.

"I almost saved Sheldor, but there were too many," Ethrang said sadly, reappearing as himself.

"Not everyone can be saved," Garth said, and his face softened. "You did well."

"Good knife throw," One Eye grunted to the weapons master. Chip knew that was as close as the troll captain would come to saying thank you as they would likely ever hear.

Garth nodded then turned to Chip. "I gave you an order to stay here."

The boy looked at his trainer. "You know I couldn't do that. Blame it on the twins." Kristan and Thomas feigned indignation. "Besides, I outrank you," Chip said with a grin. The weapons master arched an eyebrow and then gave him a small smile.

"It worked out. We didn't see those two apes behind us."

"Now what?" Mary said, trying to fix her hair, which had become dishevelled when the ape knocked her unconscious. "We are out of Power."

Everyone looked around. A strange rock formation rested on the top of a low hill in the middle of the massive meadow. Chip looked up to see stars appearing. He allowed himself a long, deep breath. The boy absently realized he was clutching his left arm. A dull pain emanated from above his elbow.

Ethrang noticed his reaction. "Does it require healing? I have enough."

"Only if you can spare some," Chip said.

"I can, Guardian." The blond orphan rested a hand on Chip's elbow, and soothing green energy infused his arms. He felt the bones reconnect and the muscles mend. A pained look passed across the boy's face, but he smiled. "There, good as new."

Chip flexed his arm. It hurt slightly, but he understood Ethrang was not the best healer. "Thanks, it's great. How does it feel being the only one with magic?"

"I have enough to shift a couple of times, but that's it. Still, it's better than nothing."

"Uh, those apes are still staring at us," Chase gestured. "Those green eyes are a little scary. Not like spiders...but you know what I mean." He looked around to see if they agreed. One Eye chuckled.

"I think it prudent to make our way to the middle of the meadow," Xander said.

"And then what do we do?" Kristan asked.

"One problem at a time, remember?" the wizard gave him a small smile. "You and Thomas are quite the swordsmen. I didn't know."

"It's what happens when you play fight with wooden swords for many years," Thomas laughed. "We picked up pointers along the way, watching the Protectors."

"I'm happy it came in handy," Kristan added.

"Yes, it did. Good show." Xander started moving toward the rock formation in the middle of the meadow.

Chip noticed the eerie silence as they progressed. The meadow was round, surrounded by towering ancient trees. There were no clouds in the sky, revealing a multitude of brilliant stars. He breathed in the cold night air deeply, relieved to be out of the confines of the forest. With a start, he realized the caves would be the opposite.

The boy sighed. At least they had made it through Darkwood, a feat on its own. A wave of sadness passed over him when he realized how many lives were lost. The wizard's saying ran through his mind. "Nothing is ever easy." Even as the thought entered his mind, the boy felt vulnerable. He was still in the heart of Darkwood, walking across a meadow in the open with no magic. It unnerved him. He turned back to see the glowing green eyes still staring at them from a distance. Who else was watching?

They approached the low hill with three rocks near the top, standing silhouetted against the sky like dark spectres. Immediately, he sensed a malevolence emanating from the formation. He could make out symbols engraved in the stones as they drew closer.

The place reeked of evil.

Xander stopped a short distance away, stroking his white beard. "A great darkness resides here. Its stench is foul indeed. What is that?" The wizard suddenly turned to them, the stars illuminating his white face.

"They are coming."

A light appeared behind one of the rocks, casting flickering shadows. Ethrang immediately turned to Chip. "I will hide as a fly in your cloak," he whispered. "Don't squish me!" The boy disappeared.

Chip felt a buzz in his sleeve, and something landed on his forearm.

Then a torch appeared as if floating on its own, followed by many more. Shapes in black cloaks detached themselves from the rocks' black background.

"Oh dear," Eleanor muttered.

"Do not fight unless I tell you to," Xander cautioned, but that was all he could say.

"Quiet, old man," a woman commanded from the front. She wore a long black dress and carried a wooden staff.

Chip's breath caught in his throat. He heard Chase gasp. She was stunningly beautiful. Rich midnight-black hair flowed down her shoulders, framing a perfectly proportioned face with cream-coloured skin. Her eyes were dark brown surrounded by long eyelashes. The black dress rippled across her curvy form. Yet great darkness radiated from her, one that spoke of evil deeds and heinous acts. Yet there was an undeniable lure to her, a sexual energy that would make men weak in the knees.

"Ah, Morgeth," Xander said politely.

"You will address me as High Witch, Orb Stealer." She walked down the hill and stood before him while a ring of twenty dark-cloaked figures surrounded the group with torches. The light revealed female faces.

"My mistake, High Witch." Xander dipped his head apologetically.

"That's better," she said, eyeing him up and down. "You do look like your brother, but not as strong. Balor and I could have been something if things were different. He caught me in an awkward moment long ago, but I got my way. I always do." She ran a finger along the old man's cheek. "One day soon, I will get my staff back. It has served its purpose. The darkness in it has corrupted him."

Xander's eyes narrowed slightly. "How so, High Witch?"

"He allowed me to turn many magic wielders to my cause for one. Did you think it was his idea to wall them off for failing a test?" She let out a laugh, throaty and deep, almost sensual. "The true Force controls everything. It has shaped history, moulded powerful rulers, and set an unstoppable chain of events. The truth is we are pawns of prophecy. Your only real choice is to choose which side you're on. A long time ago, I chose the winning side."

"I believe in free will," Xander countered. "We always have a choice. I choose to fight for good."

She shrieked in delight and nodded to a female hooded figure to her left who stepped forward and struck the wizard across the face. "You forgot 'High Witch.'" Garth and Chase stepped forward, but her eyes blazed a stunning blue, freezing them in place. The rest of the cloaked figures seized their magic, ranging from Yellow to Blue, but remained motionless.

Morgeth turned back to the Grand Wizard. "Oh my, how precious. Fight for good? Please. Who decides what's good? You? The rulers of a people? The Creator?" She laughed again and then her face grew serious. "You dare enter my forest, kill my beloved pets, and think you can push me aside and take my stone?"

Xander straightened, his face red on one side. "My goodness, that was the idea...High Witch."

Her eyes narrowed, and her face turned menacing but still beautiful. "You're a foolish old man. You fell right into the trap, as my mother said you would. Now, you will all suffer, begging to die until your voices run out, and then your silent screams will last for eternity. The Demon King will be quite pleased." Her face brightened. "Now, who do we have here."

Morgeth turned to Garth and Chase, eyes blazing. "If you ever move towards me again without permission, I will chop off a piece of you each day until you are on the brink of death, and then I will heal you so we can start over. I am saving you all for Killian, but we can start early if you wish. Torture does not satisfy me. I prefer other pleasures." She smiled and ran a finger along Garth's cheek. "My, what a handsome one."

The High Witch then cocked her head at Chase. "You are different. Dangerous." She held both sides of his head for several moments and gasped. "I did not think it possible. A Protector with traces of red magic. How fascinating. I heard it was done through love and sacrifice." She made a face. "It is not for me, but the Demon King can study you. This is the Balance's way of making this fight appear fair even though the outcome is now assured."

She glanced at the other Protectors, One Eye and Daria, then turned away with a dismissive hand wave. She looked at Eleanor and

Mary. "You two could have been so much more." She paused, studying the Queen of Vanalon. "I have heard about how unique you are. It is another fascinating study. I will ask him if I can keep you as a pet." She lifted Eleanor's chin. "Is his love worth it?"

The queen nodded, eyes filling with tears. "Yes...High Witch."

Morgeth gave her a sad look. "I thought so too, long ago. So long it is now a dim memory." Her face turned cold. "Love is a fool's dream. It will only cause you pain and death. But you will have all the time in the world to learn that."

The High Witch finally turned her blazing gaze to Chip. "Ah, the best for last. The Chosen One. The Red-Eyed Boy. The Defender of Hope." She stared into his eyes.

He saw a darkness in her, a malevolence that looked familiar. Her midnight black hair reminded him of someone else. He shivered involuntarily.

"Do I frighten you?" she asked softly, cupping his chin. He shook his head, trying to pull away, but her grip was strong. She leaned closer, their faces almost touching. "You lie. When I ask a question, I expect the truth." She took a black nail and dragged it across his cheek, drawing blood, then released him. "I have waited a long time for you. My mother, Zara, has ordained your coming. Many Paths showed your death. In one, you were stillborn. In many more branches of prophecy, you died in Vanalon, Banfar, the Wizard's Guild, the Stone Kingdom, and by Barko's hand. Even the fork to Darkwood showed your death. Yet you came back." His eyes widened.

She let out a melodious laugh. "That one came to pass. My mother Sees like no other. Now, how did you return from the dead?" Chip glanced at Eleanor. Morgeth smiled. "She saved you? The false hope of love. The Balance indeed has a sense of humour."

The witch dropped her gaze, searching him. "Where is it? Ah, there it is." Her eyes gleamed in awe. "Give it to me." Chip's heart sank. She had found Ethrang. "To possess an Original dragon egg. It is more than I could have dreamed. My Master will be so pleased. Give it now!"

He hid his surprise and reached under his cloak to undo the strings tied around his belt. Reluctantly, he handed her the pouch containing the egg. She looked inside, and her face showed wonder.

Morgeth suddenly looked at his arm. "You have a residue of magic on you." Chip could feel Ethrang on his elbow, not moving. A pang of fear raced through him.

"Yes, I just healed his broken arm. It was the last of my magic," Xander interceded smoothly. Then his face turned menacing. "Or else I would have used it on you."

The High Witch spun around. She lifted him high in the air and tossed him on the side of the hill. He struck hard then went limp. Garth Stone's face turned to granite, but he didn't move.

"Bring them inside," Morgeth called to the cloaked figures as she walked up the hill carrying the egg. She did not even look at Xander. "Make sure he's not dead. Heal him if necessary. They must be alive when we present them to the Demon King."

The other witches moved in and pushed them forward, eyes blazing. They had no choice but to follow. Chip let out a sigh of relief that Ethrang was not discovered. He wondered if the boy would leave now or risk going inside. He would not blame him if he used the opportunity to escape.

Chip watched as two witches picked up Xander, who groaned in protest. The wizard's intervention was timely, providing an intentional distraction to take Morgeth's focus off his arm and the discovery of Ethrang. It had cost the old man.

Xander stumbled forward to join the others as they ascended the hill. Chip tried to move closer to Eleanor, but someone pushed him roughly from behind. He followed the witches around one of the large black rocks. It contained many symbols and runes, the most prominent being a single eye. They went between two bushes with no leaves and stood before a black circular opening on the side of the hill. He took one last breath of the cold night air and entered the Secret Caves.

The fly stayed put on his arm.

14

Flickering torches lit the rock tunnel, which descended deep into the bowels of the hill. Chip sensed a dark, malevolent presence below them, like a large spider waiting in the center of her web. The eerie silence was only punctuated by their echoing footsteps. No one spoke.

He felt the fly crawl forward to his wrist, observing the surroundings. Ethrang needed to see where they were being taken. Despite the sliver of hope the shapeshifter provided, Chip could not shake the feeling that they were hopelessly trapped. What could the orphan from Banfar do against a lair of witches? Yet he clung to that last shred of hope. It was all he had.

Their journey through Darkwood had been taxing, to say the least. He was exhausted, emptied of energy and magic. He couldn't dispel the nagging thought that this might be the end of their quest and the beginning of a life of slavery and torture. He was in the clutches of pure evil, the heart of darkness. He sensed it in every fibre of his being.

A growing fear infused him —not only for himself but for the others. What if they hurt Eleanor? What if she never again saw the light of day? What if this was the end? He stopped himself, falling back on his lessons. The "what if" scenarios were anxiety's weapons. It was an anticipatory emotion fueled by uncertainty, creating a slew of negative thoughts that might not be based on reality. They could be dispelled if the facts did not support them.

Yet sometimes the facts did support them. Sometimes the thoughts were correct. What did one do then? He remembered asking this of the weapons master a long time ago. What if your anxieties and fears were correct, supported by facts? Garth was quick to answer. "Then accept it. Full acceptance will dispel the fear."

The boy sighed. He would not accept his fate yet. He would focus on the present, not the what ifs. Right now, he did not know what he was up against. He took several deep, calming breaths.

He would fight to the end.

The tunnel suddenly stopped at a stone wall. Morgeth drew an intricate pattern with her finger, and the wall slid into a recessed alcove. A witch stood inside the tunnel at attention. She bowed to the High Witch, but Morgeth walked past without acknowledging her. His heart skipped a beat. If Ethrang didn't leave now, he would be trapped in the Secret Caves.

Chip was unsure the blond orphan's green magic could penetrate a wall of that thickness. He shook his hand to signal for the shapeshifter to leave. The fly moved but remained on his wrist.

When everyone walked through, Chip turned to see the cloaked witch on guard tracing the same symbol on the wall. The heavy stone door slid back into place, and the witch resumed her position. A sense of finality struck as if a gong had signalled his death.

They were now in a stone tomb.

He shook his head, hoping Ethrang knew what he was doing. They dared not link presences or use any form of magic. The boy was stuck in the fly shape until he could escape. Or they found him out.

The tunnel continued downward before reaching a fork. Without slowing, Morgeth turned right. They turned left and right several more times until the ground levelled off. When they turned left the final time, the tunnel widened, and metal doors began appearing on either side of them. Chip's jaw dropped as they emerged into a cavern of immense proportions.

It was in the shape of an upside-down five-pointed star. Each arm of the star radiated from the central chamber, lined with metal doors. In the center was a large stone altar with a giant eye painted on the front, surrounded by wooden tables and chairs. Clumps of a strange green substance that looked like fungus covered the walls up to the stalactites a great height above. They gave off a bright green glow, bathing the room in enough light that torches were unnecessary.

Scores of grey figures sat poring over books. He remembered the leader of the Lost Ones, Kylo, describing the grey-robed ones as acolytes who had not yet sworn the oath. They were supervised by dozens of black-robed female witches looking over their shoulders.

Thirteen chairs faced the altar. The largest looked like a throne, with six smaller ones on either side. Thirteen ancient-looking women wearing black dresses with an eye stitched on the front stared at them. They had white eyes and nearly bald heads. Wart-like lesions covered their faces. Chip shrank back at their gaze, his skin crawling. The hunched one on the throne held a wooden staff. She stared at him.

They all stood upon the High Witch's arrival.

"Acolytes, out," barked Morgeth. "Back to your rooms. Take *The Book of Seeing*." The grey-robed figures picked up their books and filed out quietly, heads down. Chip realized they all held identical copies of the book. The fly buzzed and then left his arm.

Morgeth approached the one holding the staff and kissed both her warty cheeks. "Mother, a gift." She held out the pouch with the dragon egg.

The old woman's white eyes bulged, then she threw her head back and cackled. "At last. I have waited five millennia. Put it on the altar." She turned her head and stared at Chip. "Bring him to me."

Morgeth beckoned, and a witch pushed him forward. He walked to the ancient woman. Up close, she was even more repugnant. A few wisps of white hair still held on tenaciously to her bald head. Warty lesions covered her cheeks and long, hooked nose. The milky eyes seemed to see through him. She reeked of evil.

"This is my mother, High Seer Zara. Bow."

Chip did the slightest bow he could. Morgeth was about to rebuke him, but Zara leaned forward.

"His Power grows as we speak." Her voice was high and drawn out. She placed the staff between them. "Once we fix him, you will enter his mind, daughter. He is dangerous…" She paused, looking about, sniffing the air. "I sense something hidden. The boy is capable of creating his own Path. Be watchful. For him to be here is against the odds. We are fortunate."

A clawed hand reached out and scratched his forehead. She wiped her thumb across the cut then stuck it in her mouth.

"Ahhh, the taste of the Red Level. So pure, so…powerful. It is a shame we cannot sacrifice him. He will guarantee our protection for millennia to come. The true Force will enter Killian, and you, my daughter, will stand by his side betrothed in glory forever." She began to chuckle grotesquely, bits of phlegm dribbling out of her cracked lips.

Zara wiped her mouth. "Don't look at me like that, boy. I was pretty once, and I will be again. You will make it so. Our sacrifices will be rewarded. The Tellings ravage our bodies, yet the fungi sustain us." She gestured at the walls of the cavern. "The Force provides."

"The Force is Death, and he only provides for himself," Chip said calmly.

Gasps erupted amongst the other old women, likely Seers. Morgeth almost dropped her staff. The High Witch raised her hand to strike him, but Zara held an arm out. "This is not one you can strike like a dog and expect obedience. We will break him the slow way once he is fixed. I want him meek when we present him to Killian. Isolate the boy the old way. He will break. They all do." She grinned, showing black teeth.

"What about the others, Mother?" Morgeth asked.

The High Seer waved. "Fix them. Use whatever means necessary. Keep them alive until the emissaries arrive. Hagatha can decide which ones to keep." The old woman craned her neck. "Do not kill the Orb Stealer. He must pay for his crimes. Killian will be most pleased."

She let out a final high-pitched cackle and dismissed them.

Morgeth signalled, and two witches came forward to grab the boy's arms, leading him away. Chip glanced at Eleanor and the others. She put on a brave face, but her eyes were wet. He tried to give her a reassuring look. They led him down the star's left arm to a solid metal door at the very end. One of the witches produced a key and opened it. It was dark inside but empty. They pushed him in. Rough-hewn stone walls surrounded him. The metal door clanged shut, and he was in pitch blackness.

He did not like it.

The boy was trapped deep inside the caves under the hill in the middle of Darkwood Forest. Worse, a brood of witches who worshipped Death and called the Demon King their master surrounded him. No, he did not like it at all.

Chip shook his head. All his struggles and suffering from the Pass of Death to the present had led him to a dark hole. It was so unfair. The Secret caves were a prison. They were foolish even to come here.

It was all for nothing.

He caught himself, realizing where that train of thought led. Chip gave himself some slack, realizing that the last two days of fighting in Darkwood had sapped him of physical, mental, and emotional strength. He was completely exhausted. The only thing he did not understand was why they were leaving him alone. He could already feel glimmers of his Power returning. Something did not feel right. What did they mean by "fixing" him? His greater fear was for Eleanor and the others.

Chip sat on the stone floor. He could not even see his hand in front of his face. There was also complete and utter silence, as if the doors had been designed to shut out all light and sound. It was unnerving. He needed to figure out how to escape.

There was always a way.

He clung to that thought, repeating it over and over. Despite their dire predicament, his eyes grew heavy, and he rested his back on the ground. In moments, despite trying to stay awake, the Guardian of the Races fell asleep.

A key clicked, and the metal door opened, causing a vertical beam of light to shoot into the room. Chip opened his eyes, disoriented. He put his hand up to shield his vision. He had no idea how long he had slept. Instinctively, he broke through his Wall and, with a rush of joy, realized his Power had built up.

The boy's eyes blazed bright red, and raging energy filled him. Red coils of magic wrapped around his body. He stood up, waiting for the witches to come inside so he could incinerate them. A powerful linked magic flared to his right in the Secret Caves.

No one entered. The door remained ajar.

Chip peered out, expecting a trap. He strengthened his shield. No one was in front of the door. He opened it fully and looked down the hall to the altar.

At least one hundred witches surrounded the wizards and Daria. Their rigid stances told him his companions were all frozen in place. Morgeth and Zara stood beside Eleanor and Mary, their staffs before them.

"Come forward, red-eyed one," the High Witch called. She slipped behind Mary and put a knife to her throat. The High Seer did the same with Eleanor. All the witches' eyes blazed the level of their colour. Several were Blues, including Morgeth and her mother.

"Despite your Power," Zara said in a high voice, "We are stronger. You are not at full strength yet. Come closer, but do not use your magic, or they all die."

The Guardian of the Races strode forward, consumed by rage. He did not understand why his companions had not seized their Power. He decided to wait until they did before unleashing. Combined, they were nearly unstoppable.

"That's far enough," Morgeth said, holding the knife tight to Mary's neck. "All your magic-wielding companions have been walled off from their Power. They cannot help you. If you attack us, we will unleash our combined magic on you. The Demon King will be disappointed but understanding. We have other gifts for him."

Chip looked at Xander. The wizard stared back with sad eyes. He looked different, much older than before. Eleanor had tears in her eyes, while Mary's expression was resignation. The twins looked defeated.

"Only you can build a Permanent Wall in your mind," Morgeth said. "All you must do is pull in all your Power and then use it to build your wall from the outside. It's that simple." The High Witch smiled.

"Is it true, Xander?" Chip asked in disbelief, his voice full of raw Power. "Why would you do that?"

"They walled us off individually while you slept," he answered in a tired, weak voice. "They can be very persuasive, using torture and threats. They waited until we had replenished some of our magic, for it cannot be done without a seed of Power. As our magic continues to build, it will strengthen our Wall from the inside. We are cut off. They overpowered all of us one at a time. With you, they wish to take no chances. I'm sorry, Chip, we had no choice."

The boy reeled from the implications. Without magic, they would have no chance to escape. This was his last chance to use his Power, likely for the rest of his life. His mind raced. He looked to the arm of the star leading out of the caves, deciding if he should wrap himself in his Power and get help."

Morgeth let out a rich laugh. "If you try to escape, we will kill them anyway. Let me demonstrate how serious we are." She pressed the knife tighter against Mary's throat until blood leaked out.

Mary sighed and then turned to the High Witch, causing the knife to cut deeper. "I have counselled royalty, including the High King of Amrika. I know how most of those in power think. I know you are going to use me as an example, so get it over with, cave bitch."

Morgeth grinned evilly and slit her throat.

Blood sprayed outward, and Mary slumped to the ground.

"No!" cried Eleanor.

Chip stepped forward, lifting both hands.

Morgeth moved quickly, putting the knife to the queen's throat, under Zara's. "Don't!"

The Guardian reeled, trying to withhold his magic but unable to. Red Power flew randomly off his body, knocking pieces out of the stone walls and melting metal doors. He rode a wave of rage, trying desperately to reign it in. His vision shrunk until all he could focus on was Eleanor. She stood with two knives at her throat, powerless to resist.

He wanted to help her with every fibre of his being, yet any move on his part would ensure her death. He shook with frustration, face contorting. His Power went into the floor of the caves, and the earth shook. Several stalactites dropped from the ceiling, and bits of debris shook loose.

Zara looked at him in wonder. "Such Power," she breathed. Then her face turned hard. "Control yourself, boy. If you bring this place down, she dies anyway."

"Release her," he said through clenched teeth.

"No. Wall yourself off. This is your last chance." Morgeth pressed her knife harder, and blood began to seep down Eleanor's neck.

Chip walked along the edge of madness.

He frantically sought his lessons, trying to recite them. One stood out above them all. He learned it in the Wizard's Guild, when he went through the Divide and felt the icy embrace of Death. Chip had realized that he could not give up everything because of his own selfish desires. At the time, he was willing to risk all to save her. He didn't value himself enough to believe it was possible to live without her. He did not have enough self-love.

Yet now he did. He didn't need to sacrifice the world to save her. He had to be willing to let her go. He began to raise his hands. Morgeth's eyes widened.

But this was different.

He paused and lowered them. Another lesson surfaced.

Look for the solution.

He breathed deeply and exerted immense effort to assume the Calm. He needed to think; otherwise, he would make a rash decision in anger. If he built a Permanent Wall, it wasn't really permanent. Kylo said the witches had found a way to take it down, giving their acolytes a chance to join them or be sacrificed. He almost walled himself off in the Wizard's Guild when he thought Eleanor was dead. He was down to the last brick of Power before he remembered that he had given his word to keep fighting.

And his word was everything.

When he was twirling that last brick of Power in his fingers, ready to seal his Wall, he had sensed a weak spot. He felt at the time that a Wall could break if one knew the weakest brick. The witches had found a way to find that spot, proving there was hope.

There was a way.

And if there was a way, he was a fool to sacrifice them or himself.

He breathed again then stared at Morgeth. "I will do as you say, but mark my words. If you hurt her, nothing in this world or the next will stop me from destroying you."

The other witches gasped, looking around in shock. Zara's eyes narrowed.

Morgeth, for the briefest of moments, showed fear, and then her face hardened. "I take curses seriously. I will not harm her. You have my word. I want her as a pet anyway. Now wall yourself."

Chip nodded. He paused, savouring the feeling of his magic for perhaps the last time, and then drew in all his Power, every last drop. The boy sent it into his mind, building a wall, brick by brick. It grew quickly, and a feeling of separation filled him as if he was splitting himself in half. He used all his magic except for the tiniest bit.

The boy made sure to use the least amount in the bottom left corner. Again, he paused, realizing the enormity of what he was about to do. He was reminded of someone trying to choke themselves out or bite their own hand off. A part of his mind was screaming at him to stop, not to go through with it, but deep down he knew he must.

Chip sent his last bit of magic into the corner of his Wall, and then, his Power was gone.

Completely.

He stood again as a young boy before Miss Stern, helpless and defenceless. Despite all his physical training, he felt frail, like all his strength was gone. The ramifications of what he had done sunk in.

He had given everything away.

Morgeth let out a deep laugh. "It is done!" She went over and danced grotesquely with her mother. "After all these millennia, we have won!"

Zara's face was one of rapture. Her milky eyes stared at the altar. "The Force has delivered. *The Book of Seeing* is validated. The Balance has spoken."

The other witches began chanting.

For sacrifice of blood on stone,
We seek to rend the flesh from bone.
Water and wind, to Earth and fire,
Give us power, our hearts' desire.
Enemies fall before our will,
We seek to maim, we seek to kill.
The Force is all, the only one,
We worship you, your thoughts be done.
Book of Seeing, the truthful lore,
We will not break the oath we swore.
Master will rise, bringer of death,
He conquers all and gives us breath.

Chip Oathbinder watched the macabre proceedings in horror. They repeated the chant over and over, dancing with glee. Zara let out a high cackle while Morgeth raised her arms, grinning wickedly. He felt sick to his stomach, regretting his decision. Yet he knew he could not have overpowered them all. He looked at Mary's body, surrounded by a pool of blood. The witches danced in it, mocking her. Eleanor stood in shock, staring at her dead friend, looking lost and alone.

A fly landed on the back of Chip's neck.

"Go get help," he whispered to the insect. "I think I know a way you can break through my Wall. I can then release the others. I should be at the end of this hall behind me on the left. If you cannot find me, seek me with your presence. You must leave now before they read our minds or see you. Get help. Good luck, my friend."

He looked up to see Zara staring at him. A chill went through his body.

The fly left his neck.

"How is there magic still in you, boy?" Her high voice sliced through the air like a knife. The chant stopped. Everyone turned to stare at him. Morgeth looked puzzled. Chip realized no one had seized their Power.

Zara's eyes narrowed then widened.

"A shapeshifter!" she screamed, her eyes flaring blue as the Darkwood King materialized to crash into her and Morgeth. The impact sent Zara into the other Seers with a sickening crunch, snapping their bones and burning them with her shield. Morgeth received a glancing blow, careening into the other witches, making a score of them fall backwards in a tangled mess.

"It's the Darkwood King!" a witch shouted in terror.

The Yagr continued without slowing, running straight through the entire throng of chanters, bowling them over like a horse through tall grass.

Then he vanished.

"Get him!" Zara screamed, still maintaining her shield. It was the only reason she was not dead. The other Seers had cushioned the impact, and a half dozen were bent and twisted, several with bones sticking out of their bodies.

Chip saw a sparrow arcing down the arm of the star that led to the tunnel. A group of witches, still upright, seized their magic and flung fireballs at the fleeing bird. One seemed to strike the sparrow as it turned the corner, but he couldn't be sure. Dozens of them gave chase, eyes blazing.

Screams erupted from injured women writhing on the ground. Morgeth was unmoving, surrounded by a huddle of witches. Yellow healers pushed forward to lend aid. Chip held his breath, hopeful that the High Witch was dead, but healing magic infused her body, and she sat up.

Her head swivelled to stare at him with unbridled hatred. She picked up her staff and ran at him, screaming incoherently, eyes bulging.

Chip stood there as the High Witch of the Secret Caves barreled towards him. Her eyes blazed a bright blue, and she lifted her staff on high to smite him. As she swung, the boy rolled to the right at the last moment, returning to his feet. The force of the swing caused her to fall forward, and she landed hard on her face. She slid on the stone floor for several feet, arms and legs spread-eagled.

He would have laughed if it had been a different moment, but now he knew she was further enraged.

Instead, he gulped.

Morgeth slowly stood up, shaking. She turned, face bloody. He suddenly flew high in the air as she raised her arms. He tried instinctively to seize his magic, but a solid, immovable wall blocked him.

She began pulling his arms and legs off. His shoulder and hip joints stretched, and pain flooded his body. Invisible hands of Power held tight to each limb, stretching him in all directions. He felt his left shoulder muscle tear.

"Morgeth!"

A high voice pierced the cacophony of screams. Through blurred vision, he saw the High Witch turn to her mother, her face contorting with rage.

"Release him!" Zara ordered. "His death would only weaken our position. He is harmless now. Control yourself."

Morgeth stared, the ripples in her face finally subsiding. "Know your place, Mother. I am the High Witch." She turned back to Chip and then dropped her arms.

He struck the ground hard, spraining his right ankle, then rolled awkwardly to land on his back. The boy gasped in pain. His limbs didn't seem to work right.

"Very well, I will keep him alive." She came and stood over him, eyes still blazing, then leaned down. "But you will suffer." She straightened. "Bring forth the cage!"

Zara came forward. "Morgeth, that could shatter his mind…"

"Enough, Mother. I will have Dora monitor him. In four millennia, I have never been so…humiliated." She trembled again, this time looking like she might vomit. The affront was apparently too much for her to bear. "No one has dared raise a finger to me. He harboured a shapeshifter. I want that thing captured so I can slowly dissect it and then spill its blood on the altar. The Force will be pleased."

Zara nodded with appreciation. "That's my girl. Yes, it will be a glorious sacrifice."

Morgeth looked down at Chip and smiled. "Let's see what this so-called Chosen One is made of. Enjoy your stay here while we wait for our guests. Don't worry. Whatever I do to you here will pale compared to what you will suffer in the hands of the Demon King. I will sit by his side and watch with glee." She picked him up with two hands and pulled him close. "Did you really think you could come into my home and destroy me? I have lived hundreds of your lifetime, boy. My mother and I have planned this for ages." She let one hand go to pat his cheek. "You are a puppet. The Force controls all."

Chip clenched his teeth as she released him, trying not to put weight on his right ankle. Although his joints felt inflamed, he was able to stand.

"Dora!" the High Witch called, signalling to a smaller young witch who came forward subserviently. "Take him to his room and put him in the cage. Once a day, give him a little food and water."

"Yes, Mother," the girl said, hooded head bowed.

"Bring the cage in." Morgeth signalled to two other witches and then turned to the old woman. "How many Seers did we lose?"

"Four," Zara said sadly, wringing her hands. "The others have been healed."

The High Witch gave her mother a sympathetic look and kissed her warty cheek. "Don't worry. The shapeshifter cannot get through the exit door. They will bring him back shortly. You can get your vengeance then."

Zara looked at her daughter and nodded with pride. "The Force will lap up his blood like the kitten does milk. It will be a glorious spectacle. The Seers have given up their lives to satiate the true

Creator." The High Witch turned to her daughter. "Support him if he cannot walk, but do not heal him. One's pain is magnified in the cage. He needs his mind retrained to understand he is nothing and worthless. For the rest of his life, he will know subservience. Deception and treachery will not be tolerated. Killian and I will be his masters forevermore. Perhaps one day, after a few millennia of suffering, we may even show mercy. When I read his mind, I will know if he still holds deceit. I suspect he will beg me to see his most private memories in a few days, but first we must weaken his defences."

She gave him a sinister smile.

Dora held his arm, and he took a step, nearly stumbling. His ankle was severely twisted. Chip refused to vocalize his pain, not wanting to satisfy the witches. Morgeth's daughter put his arm around her shoulders and guided him towards the cell.

He looked at his companions, surrounded by a circle of witches, and saw their dejected expressions. Yet beneath it, there was still determination. Xander gave him a slight nod, indicating he should stay strong while the twins lifted their chins in defiance. Eleanor's sad face showed concern but also an underlying anger. The troll healer Daria was stone-faced. The Protectors and One Eye were nowhere to be seen.

They all looked different in some way...normal. It was as if a piece of them were missing. Even in himself, he felt much weaker. Lesser. Not whole.

The boy sighed.

For once, he did not feel up to the challenge. His body ached all over, and his shoulder burned fiercely. The journey through Darkwood had been taxing in every respect, depleting his physical, mental, and emotional reserves. And now they would lock him in a cage.

It could always be worse.

The thought popped into his mind from his store of lessons. It usually held true, but now he wasn't so sure. The boy would try and sleep before tackling his mountain of problems. It would also allow his injuries to begin healing.

They passed the melted iron doors and stepped around stone rubble before arriving at the end of the hall. His door was still open. Dora indicated he should go in. The boy limped forward then turned around.

"The cage is coming," she said. He couldn't make out her face against the backdrop of light. She wore a hood with a deep cowl.

Several moments passed, and then two witches appeared carrying a black cage with a folded grey robe on top. Chip's mouth dropped open.

The cage was very small.

He looked up sharply, shaking his head. "You can't be serious."

One of the witches set down her end and backhanded him across the face. He managed to move his head enough out of reflex, but it caught him in the corner of his eye. The boy blinked a few times but remained silent.

"You must ask permission to speak from now on. You are nothing and will always be nothing. Put on this grey robe." She threw the garment at him. "You don't even deserve to wear that colour. Acolytes can choose to serve the witches. You will never get that choice. If it were up to me, you would be naked like a dog." Since her hood was on, Chip could not be sure of the woman's age, but she sounded old and mean. It reminded him of Miss Stern. "Hurry up."

He stared at them. "Right now?"

They both hit him at the same time. His shoulders were too sore to defend as they slapped his face.

"We should get him in the cage," Dora suggested. "His treatment is more important right now. Mother wants to make sure he breaks." The other two witches stopped their attack.

"That shapeshifter killed one of my friends today," the older-sounding witch snarled. "Your suffering is just beginning, boy. Now put on the robe."

Chip undressed to his small clothes, trying not to grimace. Using his shoulder in the slightest motion was painful. He picked up the grey robe with his good hand.

"I said, undress. All of it." The older witch raised her hand again. "You have no rights anymore. Get used to it."

He sighed, took the rest off, and pulled the grey robe over his head. It was a simple garment made of coarse cloth. The two witches picked up his old clothes and the unicorn horn. The older witch turned it over in her hand and grunted. "The High Witch will want to see this. Do you need help putting him in the cage?"

"No," Dora said. "I will be fine."

They nodded and left. She went over to the cage and opened a small door in the side, removing the key from the lock. It looked about two feet by three feet by two feet high. She turned to him and lowered her hood. Now, he could see her face in the light through the open door.

His breath caught. She was stunningly beautiful like her mother but younger, around his age. Something about the way she looked at him was mesmerizing.

"I am sorry they treated you like that," she said. "You did not know the rules."

"Are you Morgeth's daughter?"

He stepped back, realizing he did not ask for permission to speak.

She smiled. "I am not going to hit you. Yes, many of us are Morgeth's children." He gave her a puzzled look. "She selects certain acolytes for breeding. It keeps the bloodline strong. Some female acolytes barred from the Guild become lesser Witches, but many are born here. They in turn have children with the male acolytes, so my mother is a grandmother many times over."

"Are you my age or much older? Magic wielders tend not to look their age, especially if you are at a Higher Level."

Her eyes flared blue momentarily, and he blinked at the intense colour. "I am seventeen summers. I broke through my Wall last year."

"Have you lived your whole life here?"

"Yes, I have accompanied my mother to the edge of Darkwood to meet the Triumvirate several times but have never gone any further."

"But isn't it dangerous going through Darkwood?" he asked.

She looked at him and laughed. It was a pleasing sound. "No, silly. We use the tunnel."

He stared at her and then slapped his forehead. "There's a tunnel! Of course, it makes sense. I wish we had used it to get here. It seems obvious now."

"The tunnel can be collapsed. We have known of your arrival for a long time. It would not have worked."

"I suppose you were watching us through the Seeing Stone the whole time."

Dora gave him an odd look. "We have not used the stone in a very long time. It has almost no power left. I have only seen it once, in the cavern below my mother's chambers. We are saving it for our Master."

"What is he going to do with it?" Chip asked.

"The same thing you were going to use it for. To find the missing Light Elves."

His eyes widened. "Why didn't you use it to find them?"

"My understanding is we are not strong enough to defeat the elves. If we locate them and they move, it is for naught. As I said, there is little power left in the stone."

He stepped back, staring at her. She was not like the others. He could feel it. "Why did she select you to watch over me."

Dora looked down shyly for a moment, choosing her words. "It is rare to be a Blue Level here. She says I have much potential. My mother wants to give me greater responsibility so that one day I can replace her." Dora was going to say something else but changed her mind. She stared into his eyes, moving closer. "I cannot stay any longer. We will talk when I bathe and feed you tomorrow."

The boy blinked. "Uh, I can bathe myself."

She shook her head. "You don't understand. The cage will lock your muscles in place. It is a slow way of breaking you but the most powerful. You will need assistance when you crawl out." She paused. I am sorry this is being done to you. I never liked watching people suffer. Morgeth wants me to develop a thicker skin. I will try to make it easier. Once she breaks your mind, I will ask that you be removed from the cage."

Chip felt a ripple of fear as he looked down at the small metal structure.

"I'm sorry, but you have to get in now. You will not be able to lie down or stand up. The best you can do is crouch. It was built that way on purpose. Sleep will be almost impossible. The pain of that position will grow in intensity over the hours. Most can only last a day before they break."

The full enormity of what was happening sunk in. He groaned inwardly, then sucked in several deep breaths. She reached down and opened the small door. Chip got down on his hands and knees. It did not even seem possible that his body could squeeze through. He crawled in, his shoulder aching as he tried to manoeuvre into the small space.

The only way to do it was to angle left, pull his knees up to his chest, and turn into a crouched position. From there, he tried to stretch out, but his spine immediately touched the bars above him, and his feet hit the back.

A feeling of overwhelming panic engulfed him, and he wanted to cry out. Chip heard the cage door close and the key turn.

"I will be back tomorrow."

He craned his neck to see Dora leave the room and shut the door.

Everything went pitch-black.

15

The orphan was all alone.

Chip Oathbinder crouched in the silent darkness, stuck in a cage deep underground in the Secret Caves in the middle of Darkwood Forest. He was bereft of his Power, his sight, and his companions.

He was truly, utterly alone.

The pain slowly escalated. His shoulder and ankle already throbbed, but his knees, hands, and elbows kept pressing into the bars. He readjusted every few moments, but then something else would hurt. Chip tried to calm himself by taking deep breaths, but he couldn't in his hunched position.

Then, the back pain started. It was mellow at first but increased in intensity, becoming a stabbing sensation that a shift in position could not alleviate. It began in his lower back and then progressed to his neck.

A feeling of claustrophobia settled in, which increased his heart rate. At least he could put his fingers through the closely spaced bars, trying to convince himself that he was not fully boxed in. All the negative emotions of fear, anxiety, hopelessness, and depression began to dominate.

He frantically sought a solution to his predicament, but everything was a dead end. Finally, his anger turned to a deep, bitter rage, and he shouted, smashing at his Wall to seize his Power.

The Wall would not budge.

The boy tried again and again. It was to no avail. It was like a part of him had been cut off. He did not feel whole anymore. His magic was a part of him now.

It was him.

It had defined who he was, what he did, and who he was to become. The Power had shaped his beliefs, confidence, hopes, limitations, and friends. People had sworn an oath to the red-eyed boy who could challenge the Demon King, not the green-eyed one with no magic. He felt like a shade of his former glory.

He felt human.

The orphan realized how silly that sounded, but it rang true. He felt like a normal person again and didn't like it. The boy immediately realized he was acting like a spoiled brat, but that was how he felt. He had been given a great gift, and now it was gone.

He felt robbed.

Chip's anger flared again, and he lashed out. His thrashing was pathetic, stopped by the bars after a minuscule movement. His left shoulder throbbed anew.

The pain began to intensify. It felt like he had been in there for hours, yet somehow in his mind he knew it was much less. He wondered how many assigned to the cage had died or gone mad over the millennia. A great sadness took over as he realized the atrocities humans could inflict on each other.

Why? How did people get so evil?

He thought of the Force of Death and its desire to take over the world of humans. It wanted to become sentient and aware, part of life. It was an outside evil that corrupted the minds of its victims. But there was more to someone becoming evil than the influence of Death. It was power, corruption, greed, indoctrination of views over generations, desensitization, and a host of other things. The boy had seen much evil, corruption, and madness throughout his journeys.

Yet there was goodness too. There was love, kindness, and empathy. There was joy, fulfillment, peace and hope. He wanted to believe that good would prevail. It was what he stood for.

But now, surrounded by great evil in this darkest of places, he began to doubt. A sudden memory of the Leader of the Lost Ones surfaced. Kylo had said the evil in the Secret Caves changed him, made him hate and lust for revenge until he had forgotten his former self. Chip had thought Barko's well was the source of Death gaining a foothold in the world. After all, it had created Morgo and made the Demon King immensely powerful through the Dark Arts. But now he realized the Secret Caves were the source. He could feel it in his bones.

Time passed. The pain intensified. He started clawing at the bars.

It felt like a day had easily passed, if not two or three. Perhaps they had forgotten about him. The pain was becoming suffocating, and low groans began to escape his lips. He tried to formulate coherent thoughts, but the pain always came through, bringing with it a flood of negative emotions.

He realized that was the trick of dark thoughts. They came out when someone faced problems or was overcome with emotions. They remained insidiously hidden, waiting for the opportunity to arise and take over. The weapons master once said they were safety mechanisms, having their place in survival. They were valid in life-or-death situations but stayed rooted in the consciousness, appearing when stressed.

Again, he realized the importance of changing those negative thoughts and beliefs, knowing that recognizing their power was enough to limit their control. He had learned to identify them, but now they sought control in this lowest of lows.

He fought against the pain and negativity, pulling up all his weapons of defence, then latched on to an image that seemed to come out of nowhere.

The man with the silver hair.

To Chip, he represented all the good in the world. All the hope, joy, and peace. He was the embodiment of love. The orphan remembered Garth saying once that you shouldn't expect to find the Creator on a bright, sunny day when all was good. No, you would find the Creator in the deepest, darkest hole when hope was lost and you had nothing left. Then you might see him. Well, he saw him now in his mind, and it gave him a measure of hope.

Chip's eyes filled with tears as he fixated on the image.

But the darkness came back, attacking the edges of the picture, trying to wrench it from his mind. He struggled valiantly, focusing with all his strength, willing the image to stay. Yet the pain and darkness were strong, and slowly he succumbed.

His thoughts turned dark once again.

Time passed.

It felt like an eternity before the door opened, and a bright light shone into the room.

The Creator had answered his prayers.

Then reality crashed down. The pain was so intense he was barely coherent. Chip tried to speak, but his mouth was parched.

"I'm here for your daily bath and feeding," Dora said, pulling in a wooden tub on wheels and a basket. She knelt before him with a sympathetic look and put her fingers through the bar to touch his.

"Why did you not come the first day?" he asked with a croak. "Has it been a week?"

"Oh, it hasn't even been a day. I convinced Mother to let me come at lunchtime instead of waiting for dinner to ensure you are still alive. I'm surprised she agreed." Dora smiled.

Chip stared in shock. "That's not...possible."

"Time feels different in the cage. Here, let's get you out of there." He heard the door unlock, and then she turned his body so his feet would come out first.

He screamed in pain. "Stop, please!"

"It is alright. The pain will lessen once the muscles move a bit."

Chip nodded, gritting his teeth. It took a while, but she managed to extricate him from the cage. As he spilled onto the ground, his back straightened, and the boy almost passed out. He gasped and then realized he could finally take deep breaths. He filled his lungs with air, basking in the brief freedom. "Thank you."

"You're welcome. Now let's get you into the bath."

He tried to sit up but cried out, his back going into spasms.

"I will help you," she said. "Here, lift your arms." He did so, his shoulder screaming in pain. She pulled the grey robe off. Dora's eyes blazed bright blue, and he felt his naked body rise horizontally and then descend into the warm water. A feeling of bliss enveloped him, made more potent by his recent struggles.

Warm water infused his aching muscles and soothed his shoulder. Dora pulled him into a sitting position and rested his head on the ledge. She let him lie there for several long moments, letting his muscles become limber and then asked him to stand. It took effort, but he was able to do it.

She soaped him down and washed off all the grime he had accumulated from days of travelling. He closed his eyes, not caring about modesty or anything but the feeling of being able to stretch out.

When finished, she told him to open his mouth and proceeded to brush his teeth with an herbal mixture. He rinsed and stepped out of the tub. The pain was becoming more bearable.

Chip realized how incredibly precious some of the most basic things could be. Only after going through immense pain and suffering was he able to appreciate something as mundane as a hot bath. The boy realized he had been ungrateful for many things he took for granted. It was good to realize this and be thankful for them.

Dora patted him down with a small towel then put his grey robe on over his head. He stood there looking at her, again stunned by her beauty.

"Thank you," he breathed.

She stood in front of him and stared into his eyes.

Then she leaned forward and kissed him.

Chip froze with inaction for a moment, then stepped back, eyes wide. "I'm sorry, Dora, but I can't."

"Why not?" She seemed confused. "Do I not...interest you?"

"No, it's not that. You are very interesting, but I'm with another person."

Dora shook her head. "No, you don't have anyone anymore. You are with no one. The queen is gone."

"What do you mean?" he asked, feeling a chill.

"I mean, your former life is gone. She is not yours anymore. She will be my mother's pet."

Chip shook his head. "No, I refuse to believe that. We are together. Always."

Morgeth's daughter looked at him with a mixture of frustration and something else. "Chip, that life is gone. It is over."

"There is always hope." He stood there, and unbidden tears welled in his eyes. "I love her."

She looked at him strangely, seeing his tears. The girl rubbed a thumb under each of his eyes. "How can you still hold on to hope?"

He gave her a haunted look. "There is always hope. There is always a way. I must...believe that."

"Why?"

Fresh tears rolled down his cheeks. "Because I gave my word. I must fight for good, for life, for hope...for her...and for everybody."

The High Witch's daughter stared at him, and something buried deep inside sprung forth. Chip recognized it as a desperate need for love. He couldn't imagine what Dora had endured growing up in the Secret Caves.

Tears filled her eyes, and she reached out with her arms tentatively, expression fearful. It was unlikely she had ever held anyone.

He stepped forward and embraced her. "It's alright. Don't be afraid. Everyone needs love. It beats hate any day." She began sobbing into his shoulder.

"I'm so sorry. My mother made me do it."

"Do what?"

"Seduce you."

He held her at arm's length and broke into a smile. "Really, why?"

Dora looked startled at his response, then laughed, wiping away the tears. "She wants me to be like her. She has seduced many men, even the High Wizard."

Chip's mouth fell open. He replayed Balor's story about receiving the staff from Morgeth millennia ago. He remembered the High Wizard being hesitant to tell the tale in the first place.

"I believe you. Balor did say she was bewitching." He tried not to smile.

The girl smirked. "The truth is I don't want to be like my mother. I have seen her do unspeakable things. She told me yesterday that seducing you would be a necessary test in my progression. I have heard many negative stories about you and your companions, so I did not want to be with you. Then you grew on me. There's something... about you."

"The stories about us are untrue," he said.

"You don't even know what they are," she countered.

"I have an idea. Most people in power spread the same yarn. If I survive until tomorrow, I will tell you about it."

Dora laughed and bent down to lift up the basket. "You must be hungry."

"And thirsty."

At this point, the boy didn't care what he ate or drank, such was his appetite. She produced a large bottle of water and a piece of bread.

He grimaced. "Really?"

"Trust me, you are lucky to have bread. People in the cage usually get no food. The bath was only allowed so I could seduce you."

He stared at her with such shock that they laughed, covering their mouths so no one could hear.

"I can't stay any longer. Tomorrow, we can talk during your food and bath. I will tell her I have kissed you and am still working on the rest."

"What do you mean the rest?"

"She wants me to take your seed so I can have your child."

Chip almost fell into the bathtub.

She gave him an amused look. "What do you think seducing

means? Anyways, I respect your love for the queen, and I certainly don't want to become pregnant."

"Why would she want you to have my child?"

"Not too bright, are you? Do you have any idea how powerful you are? You are the only human in Amrika at the Red Level. Your child may have red magic too. My mother is hedging her bets if things don't work out with the Demon King. She wants to ensure her bloodline lasts forever. I am her only daughter around your age, and I happen to be the most powerful. She believes it is a perfect match."

"I already have the perfect match."

Dora's face turned sad again. "You must understand the cage will break you. I don't see how you will ever be with her again."

"We will see."

A sudden fear crossed her face. "If Morgeth reads your mind, she will know I have lied to her."

"She won't read my mind."

"How can you be so sure? She is very powerful."

Chip gave the daughter of the High Witch a serious look. "So am I."

Dora took a deep breath and nodded. "Hurry now, back into the cage. We will talk more tomorrow."

The boy prayed to the Creator and crawled back in. She locked it, picked up the basket, and pulled the tub out the iron door, which clanged shut.

Darkness surrounded him once again.

The second day was worse than the first.

The pain was immediate, magnified by the sensory deprivation. His short, panting breaths were the only thing breaking the immutable silence. The dark thoughts started weaving through his defences, strengthened by the resident evil that infested the Secret Caves.

Chip clung to the glimmer of hope that Dora provided. She proved that even under the worst conditions, where evil and darkness dominated, there was still the ability to change. The daughter of the High Witch had been raised in a cult that practiced ritual sacrifice and followed a text inspired by Death. Dora showed him that redemption and salvation were possible despite indoctrination and desensitization. He clung to that hope, which sustained him for the better part of the day.

But the cage was unyielding.

Cracks began to show in his mental faculties as he valiantly tried to use the torch of hope to banish the darkness.

The torch finally sputtered out.

Anger surfaced, then fear and anxiety. The inability to move in the suffocating blackness weighed on him. He struggled, clutching at the lessons he had learned, trying to shield himself from the dark thoughts. Eventually, he out-reasoned all his truths, finding holes in their logic, realizing that none of them were strong enough to sustain him.

Chip reached the brink, knowing the next step was madness.

He desperately wracked his brain to find something to sustain him, praying to the Creator for any trickle of wisdom. Then he realized there was a solution.

The Calm.

It was best to dispel his thoughts if he could not use them. If thinking was not working, then he wouldn't think. The Calm provided a respite from all thought, allowing the habits to take over. It worked countless times in physical combat, relaxing his mind so he could react without thinking.

The boy took as deep a breath as the cage would allow, soothing his mind. He had used the technique a thousand times in training, dispelling fear and anxiety. It wasn't easy at first. The implacable evil that resided with him tried to puncture his defences, insinuating fragments of dark thoughts and tendrils of negativity. He broke them apart, using the experience of his death to soothe him. He remembered being a spirit floating towards the Divide, feeling a peace he had never known. He floated in that peace, thinking about nothing. It soothed him, and the pain diminished.

He felt calm.

The door opened, illuminating the room with a beam of light. His senses jarred back into reality, and the pain returned in full force. Despite its weight, he felt a surge of hope and an insatiable need to move.

Dora entered the room with the tub and basket.

"It's the end of day two. They made me wait until dinnertime, so you have been locked up for over a day this time. Are you alright?"

He squinted up at her beautiful face. "I think so. Please open the door. The pain…"

Chip heard the lock click, and then she pulled his feet out. He screamed involuntarily as his locked muscles spasmed. His ankle had swollen up, resisting any movement. She got him out, and he settled down gingerly, gritting his teeth.

She pulled his robe off and lifted him into the water with magic. Chip gasped, feeling his muscles loosen. He began to stretch his limbs, basking in the freedom of movement. Dora bathed him again and, when he was clothed, handed him the bread and water.

She leaned against the tub while he sat on the cage, chewing the small morsel slowly, savouring every bite. Even a piece of stale bread tasted like the most delicious food in his current state. He was grateful.

Dora smiled. "I will tell Morgeth the task is completed. She will try to read your mind tomorrow. Are you sure you can keep her out?"

"Yes, even better, I will read her mind instead."

She looked surprised. "You can do that?"

"Yes, I can't fully explain it other than to say I wrap her in the Calm, lulling her into thinking I'm not there. I used the technique to good effect today to relax my mind when nothing else seemed to work."

"Who taught you how to do that?" she asked.

"My teacher, the weapons master, Garth Stone."

Dora tried to keep a straight face. "Ah, is he the one dressed in black?" The boy nodded. "I see. Morgeth has been…taking him to her quarters each night."

Chip's eyes widened. "Really?"

She broke into a laugh. "Yes. What Morgeth wants, she gets. He is a fine Protector."

"He is the best." Chip's face turned serious. "How are the others? Are they safe? Is Eleanor alright?"

She gave him a reassuring smile. "They are all locked in separate rooms. Don't worry. None of them are in a cage. The Protectors are kept together in a larger room except for the one in black and the tall boy. They have their own."

"The tall one is Chase, my best friend. Why has he been isolated?" he asked.

"My mother says he's dangerous, requiring special treatment. She says the Demon King will be interested in studying him. Two powerful witches guard his door in case he tries to break out."

"Makes sense. He has a bit of my magic in him. Nobody knows how. I wanted to ask you a few questions." She indicated he should continue. "Why does your mother want to align herself with the Demon King?"

"To answer that, you need some background. *The Book of Seeing* was created after the Great Forget. It started as a few pages written by my grandmother, Zara. She gained the gift of Telling with her Power. She has a connection with the Force like no other. It whispered in her dreams and gives her visions."

"Why do you call it the Force instead of Death?"

She gave him an odd look. "Death is a simplification. He or she is an integral part of our universe, a Force more powerful than we can imagine. There is an equal but opposite Force to it that proclaims to be good, but it is a trickster. It is the false one, the true evil." She saw his mouth drop open. "At least, that is what we are taught. Your coming makes me doubt many things."

"What would you say if I told you I have met them both?"

Now, it was her turn to stare at him with mouth agape. "I'm not sure I would believe you." Dora wrung her hands. "I have been trained since birth to believe *The Book of Seeing*. I can recite every word. Yet...it has never felt right. My mother's actions are despicable."

"Admitting one has been wrong about something their entire life is extremely difficult," he said. "It requires great courage. Nobody wants to admit they've wasted years professing a lie. I will show you the truth, and then you decide if you want to believe it, but first, carry on."

Dora took a breath and continued, "Zara learned that symbols and runes made it easier for the Force to come through. For hundreds of years, she studied what you call the Dark Arts, birthing her followers. The gift of youth was passed on to my mother so she could seduce men and increase our numbers. An adept student named Morgo came to us early on, searching for a way to increase his magic."

Chip blinked in surprise. "Morgo came to the Secret Caves?"

"Yes. Zara was going to kill him, for he was weak in Power, though cunning. Even as he was forced onto the altar of sacrifice, a vision told her not to. It was the only time such a thing ever happened. She told Morgo to seek a cave troll named Barko, who was also learning the Dark Arts. He had built a well in a mountain with intricate runes and symbols, summoning the Force and allowing him to make bargains. My mother recently received a report from the Triumvirate that you killed him. Is it true?"

"Yes." He sighed. "If only Zara had killed Morgo, then the world would be different. That evil man became a dead thing that controlled kingdoms and shaped the rise of the Demon King. He was given almost limitless Power."

"Then it is true that you killed Morgo?"

"Yes, I even saw his memories."

She stared at him in awe. "We are taught that you are the great evil in this world. Only the Demon King can stand against you. Death tells us through prophecy that the Force will manifest through the Lord of the Dark Elves and defeat anyone who defends the Light, the greatest trickster of all time. He will cast this so-called Force of Light from the world and give us unimaginable power."

"Why would you need unimaginable power?" Chip leaned forward. "Do you not see it? The real trickster is the one who offers you something based on your greed. With power comes duty. Those who get it should serve and help others. I am the strongest human magic wielder in Amrika. It is a heavy burden because I know I must do my part in fighting for what is good and what is right. I also gave my word." He stood up. "I cannot erase a lifetime of lies in one sitting, but I can show you the truth. My memories are yours."

The daughter of the High Witch rose. He could see the fear in her eyes, but something else. It was a long-buried hope. She had said her beliefs didn't feel right. Now, he would show her.

Dora's presence entered his mind, and he wrapped it in the Calm, not to see her memories but to allow her to see his.

Time slowed.

He showed her the loneliness of his youth, the tribulations, and the lessons. He followed it with his encounters with the demons on his Manhood Quest, then revealed Morgo's private memories and his first meeting with the man with the silver hair. He went on to the threat of the Dim and the torture chambers in Cave Mountain. Dora's presence responded to each of the memories. The truth about the cults in Banfar and the kidnapping of Eleanor caused another jolt. He brought out the vivid memory of Death and Life meeting in his spirit essence in the Wizard's Guild. The boy was about to show her Barko's cave, but it was too much.

She wrenched her presence out of his and vomited in the bathtub.

Chip waited patiently, giving her as much time as she needed. The shattering of a falsehood of such magnitude had shocked the core of her being. It was all she had ever known. Living her whole life surrounded by the presence of Death had put her on a dark path. He regretted having to break it to her in such an abrupt manner, but he was running out of time.

Dora finally wiped her mouth and faced him. "I see it now. I have been so blind."

"It is not your fault, but now is your chance to make a difference and do what's right."

"How?" she asked.

He held her hands. "Do you know how to break through the

Permanent Wall?" He had been waiting to ask her this, but only when he could trust her.

"Yes. It's quite simple. You only have to know which..."

"Are you almost finished, Dora?" Morgeth's voice called from down the hall. It cut through the air like a knife.

Her eyes widened. "Yes, Mother. Almost done." She turned to Chip, quickly hugging him. "Hurry, get back in the cage. We can talk more tomorrow."

Dora ushered him in then shut and locked the door.

"Wait," Chip whispered through the bars. "How do you break through the Wall? Do you focus on the weakest spot?"

She started moving towards the door, then turned back. "Yes, but you won't know where that is unless—"

"Why do I hear whispering, Daughter?" The voice was much closer now. "Has he gone mad?"

"No, Mother." Dora pulled out the basket and tub.

"Did you do what I asked?" the High Witch asked quietly.

The door started closing. He saw Dora smile, feigning satisfaction. "Yes, it was..." The door shut.

16

Chip's mind raced in the darkness. Dora's explanation about finding the weak spot in the Permanent Wall was cut off by the inopportune interruption from her mother. The boy knew where his weak spot was due to the revelations in the Wizard's Guild. Back then, he had lost all hope, thinking Eleanor and Chase were dead, so he attempted the shameful feat of walling himself off. With the last brick of Power twirling in his fingers, he realized that every Wall had a weak point.

He knew where his last brick was going, but the others likely didn't. Yet, there must be a way to find it. Maybe pushing on it with magic would reveal its weakness. But that sounded too easy.

Before he could muse more, the pain returned with a vengeance. He had scarcely slept for two days and nights, wracked with dark thoughts and increasing discomfort. The lack of rest was making his mind weaker. He could feel it. But he only had to last one more day.

The boy closed his eyes, immersing himself in the Calm. He banished all the dark thoughts that were racing towards him. A burgeoning hope had sprung in him with Dora's realization that he was not the enemy. Having an ally in this darkest of places was crucial if he was ever going to escape. He let those thoughts go until he floated in a sea of black space. Nothing existed but the emptiness.

Time passed.

Then things began to push in on his sanctuary. It was an evil presence, and it wanted to break him. Snippets of thoughts broke through.

...not good enough...

...never escape...

...no hope...

He breathed in, trying to dispel them, but they were insistent. How much longer did he have? The pain began returning in excruciating waves. His back hurt terribly. He let out a whimper.

The Calm vanished, and the pain struck him full force. Dark thoughts raced through his mind. Why was he even bothering to try? He couldn't win? He had no Power, no freedom, and no chance of escape.

"You are mine now."

Chip gasped. He could hear the voice as clear as day. It was somewhere with him in the darkness. Was he going mad? Was he hallucinating? The pain increased to such an intensity that he had no choice but to scream.

An evil laugh sounded in front of his face. He could swear someone or something was breathing on him outside the cage. Fear fell over the boy like a blanket. The voice was familiar. Rich but cold. A voice only one thing could make.

He was locked in a cage in the blackness with Death.

"Come to me now."

The pain was unbearable. He screamed again.

"Bash your head against the bars. Be with me."

Rage ignited, and he lashed out, his head hitting the bars, and immediately a warm liquid ran down his cheeks. This enraged him further, and he pushed against the cage out of pure anger. The bars dug in deep, causing more blood to pour down.

"Good boy," an evil laugh sounded.

Chip's mind reeled. Was this what it felt like to be mad? Was this how the Lost Ones felt?

Despite everything, he began to laugh at the irony of it all. The pain was so intense that it jumbled his thoughts, and he laughed harder, maniacally.

The evil voice joined in. He hit his head on the bars again, not even caring. It made him laugh harder. If he could break through, he could choke whatever was in the room. He struck the bars again. Chip heard droplets of blood landing on the floor like dark bells in a melancholy tune. He felt light-headed, but why did it matter? As the pain became utterly unbearable, he began to welcome the icy embrace of Death. The feeling of floating towards the Divide in bliss was too tempting. After all, what did he have to live for?

Eleanor.

The thought was an automatic response. Yet its power sliced through the darkness like a knife. That was what he had to live for. He also had to live for himself. That was why he couldn't embrace the darkness.

The darkness?

Han's telling rang through his mind. "Two darknesses will descend on you. One you cannot defeat. The other you will lose yourself in unless you see life."

The first darkness had been Death in Barko's cave. This prison was the second darkness.

He could not tell if Death was with him again or his imagination. Regardless, the boy knew he would lose himself and go mad unless he saw life.

Eleanor.

She was the beacon of life for him. Amidst a sea of pain and darkness, he emblazoned her image in his mind. He would live for her. He would live for himself. He would live for life.

Chip immersed himself in his memories, reliving his first encounter with Eleanor in the schoolyard all those years ago. He put himself back there, forcing his senses to imagine every last detail. He remembered her laugh, her smell, and the wind blowing through his hair. He remembered everything.

The pain began to subside. Something sighed in the blackness, and a weight lifted off his body. Such was the power of the image that a smile formed on his bloody lips.

The door opened.

A shaft of glorious light lit up the dark room, chasing away the shadows.

Morgeth entered in her black dress, staff in hand. Behind her stood Dora, looking frightened. The girl covered her mouth as the light illuminated his face.

"Have you gone mad, boy?" The High Witch peered at him. "Open the cage."

Dora produced a key with trembling hands and unlocked the door. She slowly pulled him out. Chip gasped at the pain.

"Hurry up. I want it to hurt. This is only a taste of the endless pain he will suffer." The High Witch's beautiful face broke into a broad smile. "Now, stand him up. Never mind, I will do it." Morgeth's eyes blazed bright blue, and she straightened the boy out.

Chip screamed, feeling his locked muscles tear through contracted tissue. He let out low whimpers but stood tall before the High Witch, gritting his teeth. He felt the blood run down his cheeks from the gashes in his mangled forehead. Despite it all, he stared into her dark eyes with defiance.

Morgeth let out a rich laugh. "Impressive. You are not mad yet, but your mind is weak after three days in the cage. Your memories are ripe for the plucking. Let's see what secrets you are hiding in there."

Chip seized the Calm, immersing himself in its soothing embrace. It surprised him how quickly he could bring it forth. He had strengthened his dexterity with the technique while in the cage. Usually, he would wrap someone in the Calm, but there was a risk of detection by strong minds. Now, he enveloped himself in it first so she would think it was his normal state of being. The pain diminished to a distant throb.

A strong presence entered his mind, probing for his memories.

Chip let her slide in then lightly wrapped her in it. He felt her presence pause for a moment before it continued searching. An array of memories appeared before him.

Time slowed.

He saw Morgeth as a little girl staring up at the sky. "What is it, Mummy?" she asked, pointing to the east. Multi-coloured lights shot across the heavens in a dazzling display.

"I don't know, dear." The woman glanced at her daughter with a worried look. She was strikingly beautiful. They stood on a low hill surrounded by a small village with thatched houses. Other inhabitants were staring up as well, pointing. A forest of towering trees ringed the open space. "Perhaps we should hide in the caves until it passes."

The woman looked up as the colours intensified, and suddenly, her body arched backwards, hands clenched in agony.

"Mummy, what's happening?" The little girl's voice rose in alarm.

The woman dropped to all fours, head bowed. The other villagers looked over, faces etched with concern. A low, deep laugh bubbled out of the hunched form. Then she snapped her head up.

Morgeth screamed. Her mother's eyes had gone milky white. The woman stood slowly, her neck cocked at an unnatural angle, staring at her daughter.

"I can See," she intoned in a voice higher than it should be. The woman cackled as the lights in the sky began to dissipate. "Bring me parchment and ink. Our new home is in the caves."

The little girl stared at her mother in terror, and then her face went blank. "Mummy, I can't remember what happened before. The world... What was it like? I feel lost."

"It matters not. Only the future is important. I am now Zara, the Seer. I have been chosen to lead our people." She paused, "What is this? It is a...Wall." Her eyes suddenly blazed bright blue. "Ahhh, the Power. It's glorious."

A man rushed up to her. "Zara, what happened? I know our names but nought else. What is going on? Why are your eyes like that?"

The beautiful woman stared at her hands and then looked at him, eyes blazing. She pointed one finger and sent a stream of blue fire into his chest. He screamed as his skin melted, and then his clothes went up in flames. The other villagers backed up.

Zara let out a boisterous laugh as the man slumped to the ground in a pile of melted skin and burning clothes. She turned to the other villagers.

"I am now your leader. What happened before matters not. I have been given a gift from a powerful...Force. We will make our new home in the caves. We have much to do." She turned to her daughter. "You, my dear, will be very special."

Chip flew through her memories, watching *The Book of Seeing* go from a few pages to a bound manuscript. Zara taught her daughter the lore of runes and symbols. She built an altar in the caves and began sacrificing villagers to the Force, slitting their necks on the stone while a circle of women chanted. The caves were excavated using forced labour to create an upside-down star. Creatures were brought in from far-off lands to inhabit the forest, which became known as Darkwood. Runes and symbols were carved into the twisted trees to keep the monsters in.

Morgeth broke through her Wall at sixteen summers, becoming a powerful Blue. Zara grew old unnaturally quickly, passing her youth and beauty on to her daughter in a macabre ritual. The Force would sustain her, but she would become a hag living on the strange fungus in the caves. All Seers became like her, sustained by a dark energy. Their bodies grew hunched and warped, sprouting odd lesions. They tattooed themselves with runes and symbols, learning the ways of the Dark Arts.

Hundreds of years passed. An elf in his underclothes appeared. A see-through stone lay on the altar, surrounded by white-eyed Seers.

"What is it?" the elf asked.

Zara stepped forward. "It used to be something else, but now it is a Seeing Stone. It sees everything. Say a person's name, and it will show you what they are doing. Pick up the stone, and it will lead you to them."

"How do you know all this?" the elf breathed in wonder.

Her milky eyes seemed to stare right through him. "*The Book of Seeing* prophesied your arrival. Only someone in dire need can pick up the stone. We have waited centuries for you. With the stone, we can see our enemies, who worship a false Force. They call it the Creator. We will bide our time while the trolls and elves dwindle in their foolish war. The book speaks of a man of great Power who will unite the humans. He will seek us out one day, but we will not be strong enough to fight him, so he shall only find empty caves. I am not concerned, for one day he will cease to exist. We will wait for our true Master, an elf of unimaginable Power. The witches will pave the way for his coming, creating sects who worship the true Force. One day, his Power will be married to us through my daughter, and the Force will manifest into life through him. Then the world will be ours."

She cackled shrilly, the repulsive sound echoing around the cavern.

The elf stepped closer to examine the see-through stone, only visible due to the reflection from the green fungus growing on the walls. "It sustained me for several days. I never tired or knew hunger. I sense it once held unimaginable Power." The elf stared at it in awe.

"There is no harm in telling you what it is." Zara smiled. "You know too much, so your fate is already sealed. The stone is the source of the Great Forget. It is an Orb of Power. There is one other on Earth, though its location is shielded, even from me. I do know that the holder of it is not of this world. One day, our future Master will find it and become unstoppable."

"Do you know what happened before the Great Forget?"

The High Seer stared at him with her milky eyes.

"Our Master will be the one to share that knowledge. There is a Balance in the world that makes up the very fabric of this universe. It is formed of Laws and constants. Think of a spiderweb. You can cut a few threads, and the web will hold. If you cut a major one, the whole thing will unravel and collapse. Certain knowledge given before its time can set off a ripple effect that can have life-altering consequences. Prophecy fits in the small spaces between these constants. Any knowledge I receive can be balanced by the knowledge given by the false Force. For now, I have not received this information, for it may upset the Balance. I do know that one day my future Master will find the answers to the Great Forget. It is all but certain. One will come to challenge him, but the witches will be ready. It is ordained that we will offer this challenger up to our Master and ensure a place by his side. This stone will allow us to monitor our enemies, though its power dwindles. We will use it sparingly. I want to thank you for playing your part. What is your name?"

"Galador."

Her eyes blazed a bright blue. "Your sacrifice will now appease the thirst of the true Force, Galador." The elf suddenly levitated towards the altar.

"No!" cried Morgeth. "He did nothing wrong."

Zara did not even look at her. "He knows too much. He will die for our just cause."

"Mother, stop. Please. At least allow him one night. I...fancy him."

The High Seer stopped and allowed herself an indulgent smile. "I suppose it won't hurt for you to hone your craft." She set the elf down and turned to her daughter, face becoming stern. "Make sure he does not impregnate you. Our Master will be the only elf to do that once you are betrothed. A new mixed race will come into being, half-human, half-elf. The others will be annihilated. It will be a glorious union. You may keep him for one day. Tomorrow evening, his blood will spill on this altar and be done by your hand."

Another memory appeared showing Morgeth fleeing through the forest with the elf in tow. At the edge of Darkwood, the beautiful woman handed him a pack with supplies. He wore a black robe.

"Take these, Galador. Go and never return." She leaned up and kissed him deeply.

He smiled. "I knew you would save me. It came to me in a vision. Ever since I touched the Seeing Stone, I have felt...different. I will become a Teller. I will write down what I see."

Morgeth stepped back, eyes widening. "What have I done? Go now before I change my mind."

He gave her a confused look then nodded. "It is meant to be. We are but pawns of prophecy."

"Go!"

He turned and headed southeast. She watched until he had disappeared behind a low hill. Morgeth returned to the Secret Caves only to be locked in a cage by her mother for three days as punishment for helping the elf escape. She never saw Galador again but heard he had become the most revered Seer of the elves, writing the Galad Prophecy.

Hundreds of years passed, and *The Book of Seeing* warned again of Arkan's coming. The witches had gleaned his name when he rose to prominence, uniting the human settlements. He also began to train magic wielders, creating a powerful army of wizards. The witches used the Seeing Stone to monitor his whereabouts, but its power was diminishing.

Arkan's strength was unmatched, so the witches emptied the caves before his arrival, hiding in the newly excavated tunnel below Darkwood. They vowed to strengthen the forest by experimenting and interbreeding certain creatures through the Dark Arts to create heinous oddities like the four-armed apes with glowing green eyes. They brought others from various parts of Amrika, such as the great serpents from the southern marshlands around Flod. The eventual incarnation of the Darkwood king came about from a sinister ritual using large Yagrs taken from the barbarian forests.

A millennium passed, and Chip saw Morgeth prostrating herself before the Demon King on his diamond throne in Cave Mountain. Morgo stood to the side, his reptilian face exposed. Intricate runes and symbols covered his skin.

"Rise, witch," the Lord of the Dark Elves intoned.

Morgeth rose gracefully, radiant in a finely embroidered low-cut black dress displaying ample cleavage. She calmly folded her hands, waiting.

The Demon King nodded in appreciation. His blazing red eyes

burned bright behind a black horned helmet. "You are the only human to dare seek an audience with me. Your life hangs by a thread. I am known for patience, but I do not like to be disturbed. State your request."

"My request is to be allowed to serve you, Master, may we grovel at your leisure. My mother, the High Seer, extends her deepest apologies for not making the journey, but her communication with the true Force takes a toll on her body. I am the High Witch and stand for the sect. We have developed a network of informants throughout the lands and wish to provide you with some valuable information to help your just cause."

"What do you seek in return?"

Morgeth pushed her folded hands up higher, emphasizing her bosom. "We seek an alliance. *The Book of Seeing* has ordained your coming, Master. The Force we worship speaks to your rise and domination of the world. We would stand by your side to see our common enemies destroyed."

"I need no help."

"Of course not, Master. Your victory is a foregone conclusion, but we have a way to expedite the end of the Elf Wars so your eminence can bathe in Luminor's blood sooner."

The Lord of the Dark Elves let out a deep chuckle. The demon guards to the sides mewled with joy at his pleasure. "I like you, witch. Your interests align with mine. Why have you not sought me sooner?"

Morgeth fawned at the compliment. "We feared you would not value our worth if we came earlier, but our strength has grown since then. *The Book of Seeing* recently gave us valuable knowledge to make us a worthy ally."

The Unnamed One turned to Morgo, who stood silent, appraising the witch with slitted eyes. "What say you, General? Is she worthy of my ear?"

Morgo emanated darkness. The light around him seemed to bend to his will as he fed off its energy. "I travelled to the Secret Caves long ago, seeking knowledge and increased Power," he hissed. "The High Seer, Zara, sought to sacrifice me to the Force, for I had little magic then. A

Telling stopped her, and she sent me to the Magic Man to seek answers. I made bargains with Barko and learned what humans call the Dark Arts. I was going to return to the caves and skin Zara alive for treating me as a sacrificial lamb, but she Sees true." He turned to the Demon King. "You are the Master of this world, but Death is the Lord of the Dark Realms and sustains me. Through its power, I have learned ways to make you stronger. I am close to perfecting a ritual that will make you supreme in the mortal realm. The white-eyed demons are the key." He turned back to Morgeth. "The witches are a conduit for Death. An alliance is wise. I would hear her proclamations at your leisure, Master."

"Very well. You have my ear, witch. Few have been granted such an honour." Red coils of Power flickered across the Demon King's body as he leaned back. "Speak."

The High Witch prostrated herself. "I am humbled by the honour." She rose and took a step forward. "I can give you dragons, Master."

"The dragons are extinct. The last ones died out a century ago."

Morgeth took another step. "Not so, Master. *The Book of Seeing* provided us with the location. King Jaggar still holds three eggs. They are the Originals."

The Demon King clenched a gloved hand, trembling with rage. "They were considered lost over a millennia ago when Malkor fell. Jaggar will bow before me while I take back my birthright. He will swear allegiance to aid us in the Great Battle or fall by my hand." He turned to Morgo. "Set up a meeting with the Troll King. A private one." His eyes flared brighter. "I yearn to soar the skies again." He unclenched his hand. "Your information is of value, witch, so I will spare your life."

"There is more, Master." She took another step forward.

"Speak, Servant of Death."

Morgeth smiled, craning her neck as a cat would when scratched. "There is a talisman buried under an ancient city. Arkan attempted to retrieve it but failed. A creature of great power guards the entrance."

The Demon King leaned forward. "A guardian powerful enough

to defeat Arkan would not protect something of little value. Where is this city?"

"I know not, but the wizard council does. I'm sure a member would reveal the information if...persuaded." She folded her hands again under her breasts and waited demurely.

"There is also the Dim, Master," Morgo hissed.

Morgeth's eyes widened as fear crossed her beautiful features. "Master, that creature's touch is death to all. May I humbly suggest that it remain buried."

"You may not suggest anything." The Demon King stood up, red coils of Power rippling across his body. "Normally, an affront such as this would meet with instant death, but you have proven your value. The Dim has almost escaped its mountain prison of its own accord. With this talisman and Morgo's aid, we will unleash it upon our enemies." He walked up to the High Witch, black cape flaring.

The Lord of the Dark Elves reached out and stroked her cheek, then ran a long gloved finger down her cleavage. "Serve me, and you will have your desires."

Chip flew forward in time, sensing her becoming aware.

A recent memory surfaced. Morgeth stood with Zara, facing the Seeing Stone. It was on a stone table in a small cavern.

"If only it contained more power," the High Witch mused, "we could have seen the world's events unfold instead of relying on our informants and the Triumvirate.

Zara scoffed. "Saying if is a fool's thought. We must be wary of the Balance and work with what the true Force provides."

Morgeth smiled. "Don't worry, Mother. I have planned for all eventualities."

Zara shook her head. "Have you? Asking Dora to take the boy's seed is risky. Killian will destroy the child if he finds out."

"If things go according to plan, we will not need Dora or her child. Despite her Power, she seems unwilling to engage in the dark practices. The Demon King's victory is now assured with the capture of the red-eyed boy, but I always keep my options open. It's how we have survived this long. Besides, she needs to learn the art of seduction."

The High Seer conceded. "*The Book of Seeing* will provide. We must keep faith. If the child's true identity is exposed, we will blame Dora and sacrifice them both."

The High Witch nodded. "The Force will be pleased."

Morgeth wrenched her presence from Chip's mind. Shock and horror crossed her features. "You are walled off. How could you...do that?"

"It does not require magic, only a strong mind. The cage made me strengthen the technique." Chip turned to Dora. "Your mother and grandmother will sacrifice you and your baby to the Force of Death if need be."

Morgeth's eyes flared a bright blue. "Do not lie to her. You have been seduced. We have no further use for you other than to keep you alive. Yet, even your dead body will be a sufficient gift. It matters not anymore."

He grinned at her through his bloody lips. "Do your worst, witch."

Her magic flared out, surrounding and pushing him roughly into the cage. His shoulder struck the bar, but she shoved him in anyway. Chip screamed as it popped out of its socket. Once inside, the High Witch pointed both hands and crushed the sides and top of the cage until he was fully compressed.

She bent her head back and chuckled evilly.

"Three more days in the cage."

17

Ethrang barreled through the witches as the Darkwood King. Zara's shield had scorched his shoulder, but he ignored the pain. Once through the throng, he shapeshifted into a sparrow, speeding down the arm of the star that led to the tunnels. Multi-coloured fireballs flew past him, and then the corner appeared. As he turned to safety, a ball of magic glanced off his wing, and he lost control, nearly colliding straight into the tunnel wall, which would have ended his life. He managed to veer right before his wing failed. He should have thrown up a shield, but his intent had only been to escape.

The boy shifted into a wasp demon, and his armoured skin protected him as he somersaulted across the stone ground. His right arm was badly damaged, and he knew that without some healing, he would not be able to fly. Ethrang shifted into Furiosa and ran head-long down the tunnel. His fear had subsided, so he used his magic to mend his elbow somewhat. He was not a great healer, but he did his best.

The sounds of pursuit intensified.

A large number of witches were chasing him, screaming fanatically. The boy came to a fork in the tunnel and stopped, wracking his brain, trying to remember the way out. As the fly, he had tried to memorize the left and rights, but insects constantly focused on other threats. He became part of each form he took, losing some of his humanity and assuming their idiosyncrasies. Otherwise, he wouldn't be able to react like they did.

Worse, the longer he took a form, the more he lost his humanity until he shifted out of it. An ever-present fear of becoming lost forever in one of his forms was always at the back of his mind. From his understanding, he was the only human shapeshifter in the world, so he did not know how long he could stay in one shape. There was no rulebook on such a thing.

Left. He was supposed to turn left. Furiosa lunged down the tunnel, running full speed. Her long legs ate the ground, but his pursuers were not far behind. He took several more turns, repeating the path in his head. He came to another fork and cursed. He knew the last turn was left, but the stone exit door wasn't there when he looked in that direction.

Screams sounded behind him, increasing in volume. He could hear dozens of feet pounding on the stone, getting closer. He began to panic and guessed right. After several long strides, he came up against a stone wall.

It was a dead end.

Frantic, he ran back and went the other way. The witches were almost upon him. Flickering torchlight cast their long shadows down the tunnel behind him as he darted down the last passage. He reached the final fork as several fireballs whizzed towards him. The orphan rolled through the opening and sprang to his feet.

The door was up ahead.

Wrapping himself in a green shield, he charged down the hall. The older witch on guard stared in shock, then her face grew hard and cold, and her eyes blazed with magic. Thankfully, she was a Green. He had never met a Green he couldn't beat.

Furiosa flew towards her, surrounding the witch with green magic, rendering her Power impotent. He only had moments to convince her to open the door before the pursuing witches turned the corner. Coming from Banfar, he knew how to strong-arm people.

"Open the door," Furiosa snarled.

The witch shook her head. He put both hands on her left leg and broke it in half. She screamed.

"Open the door."

Her refusal this time was much weaker, so he grabbed her neck and lifted the witch off her feet. Furiosa pulled a dagger quick as thought and held the point up to the old woman's eye.

"Last chance. You refuse, and I pluck out your eyeball."

She chose to keep her eyesight and made the intricate symbol in front of the stone wall. It slid back into a recessed alcove as the witches rounded the corner.

Shrieks erupted as they realized he was escaping. Ethrang ran up the final tunnel to freedom, throwing the old witch across his back for protection. Fireballs streaked down the tunnel. He shielded the old woman as best he could but then felt several fireballs connect. She went limp, and he flung the melted witch aside before shifting into a sparrow. He was too big a target as Furiosa.

It was a gamble turning into the bird, for his wing was still damaged. It took all his skill to keep the sparrow from careening into a wall, but then he saw the opening. He strengthened his shield as a brown fireball exploded into it. The impact sent him hurtling through the cave entrance.

Cold night air greeted him as he tumbled, shifting into the wasp demon before he crashed into the rocks that covered the opening.

His shield disappeared as a wave of dizziness engulfed him. Ethrang staggered to his feet, feeling the melted skin on his back, even in the wasp form. Clenching his teeth to fight against the nausea, he shifted into Silvermane and darted around the rock as more fireballs crashed into the stone. Now, he had a brief barrier between himself and his pursuers. His foreleg was still injured, and the fur singed off his back, but he forced Silvermane to run down the hill. If he could reach the forest, he would be safe.

As soon as the thought entered his head, he saw a dozen Rakshas standing with glowing green eyes at the fringe. The boy groaned. Were they waiting there the whole time? Screams behind him indicated the witches had reached the cave entrance. He reached the bottom of the hill and loped across the meadow.

A fireball whizzed by his shoulder. He wasn't going to make it. The orphan from Banfar swivelled his wolf head back to see more witches emerge from behind the rocks. They all began raising their hands. He only had one option.

After all, he was a gambler.

Silvermane leapt into the air and shapeshifted into the giant eagle, throwing green magic into his wing to stabilize it. He was about to find out if he could fly. At first, it didn't work, and he almost crashed into the ground, but the magic gave him enough stability that he was able to flap the monstrous wings and rise.

A flurry of fireballs sped towards him, but he was the giant eagle, an expert flier. He wrapped himself in a green shield and relied on the shape's unique talents. He did not have the height to make it over the ancient, towering trees, so he circled the meadow, veering left and right to avoid the dangerous projectiles. The great bird weaved through the air, dodging the condensed magic, all the time gaining height. The witches had stopped in the middle of the meadow, tiny figures in black cloaks with hands raised. He felt them link, and then a swath of fire raced towards him, blanketing the sky. The eagle thrust twice more with his mighty wings, and then he was over the treeline, flying across the top of Darkwood Forest. The enormous swath of fire missed his back as it sailed harmlessly into the night sky.

To the east, the sun was beginning to break the horizon, and he realized it was dawn. Ethrang had little sense of time in the Secret Caves but thought he had been inside for much longer. A fly felt time differently, he supposed.

The giant eagle beat its great wings as he soared over the forest out of danger, feeling an immense rush of freedom after the confines of the caves. He rode the wind currents, letting out an eagle's piercing cry, knowing he had escaped the clutches of the evil witches.

Yet his friends hadn't.

The thought sobered him up. He needed to find a way to rescue them. First, he had to make it across Darkwood.

He was in rough shape. The feathers on his back were gone, replaced by melted skin and scar tissue. The eagle's head hurt, and its wing throbbed. His magic could not sustain it forever. Not to mention, he was completely exhausted. Yet the Banfar orphan was resilient. The Guardian and his street kid upbringing had taught him to never give up.

Ethrang focused on flying, pushing the feelings of hunger, pain, and exhaustion to the side. He did his best to heal the wing and then withdrew his magic. The last thing he wanted to do was land anywhere in Darkwood. He'd had enough of the cursed forest.

The hours dragged by, and dizziness overcame him. The boy felt a rising panic that he might crash into the forest.

But then he saw the end of it.

Letting out an cry of joy, he sailed away from Darkwood, gliding on the air currents. He considered finding the Triumvirate for aid but suspected their allegiance might shift once they heard the wizards had been captured and walled off. They might even hand him over, such was their fear of the High Witch. He had learned long ago to trust few people. Once they had shown betrayal, they would do so again. If he were ever an army general and an enemy soldier switched sides to give him information, Ethrang would use it to his advantage but banish the man. What stopped the traitor from switching sides again? The same went for those who told him secrets about others. He would use the information but never trust them. They were as apt to share his secrets. Banfar was rife with rats and oathbreakers. The orphan was surrounded by them growing up. He learned to guard his tongue and never break another's confidence. It allowed him to rise in rank on the streets, and respect was everything there.

The blond boy thought of going to the Wizard's Guild, but it was too far and help would arrive too late. That was assuming they could make it through Darkwood. No, he needed a place to think and plan. He needed to go to Banfar.

He needed to go home.

The giant eagle continued flying, heading southwest. A short while later, he spied the trade city of Yucan nestled on the shore of the Lumber River. He flew on, gliding over the Great Plains. By midday, hunger got the better of him, and the eagle's eyes spied a white rabbit trying to blend in with the snow. He swooped and snatched it unawares, ripping it to shreds with his large beak. The eagle landed, wolfing down the stringy morsels of muscle. It was a small meal, but it would satiate his hunger for now. He decided to rest before continuing.

The boy heard a low growl behind him.

A memory surfaced of Chip telling him a story about the Brown Tigers on the Great Plains. Such was their prowess that they would growl to give their enemies a chance to escape.

He leapt into the air with all his might.

Yet he was not fast enough. A claw raked down his leg, and he crashed back onto the ground. Ethrang turned to see a large Brown Tiger bound through the snow towards him. The orphan shapeshifted out of pure instinct, knowing his death was a moment away.

As the tiger lunged, a massive Yagr appeared in the eagle's spot.

The Darkwood King lashed its paw out with blinding speed, knocking the beast off course. The tiger was on its feet instantly, and the two great cats circled.

Ethrang let the feral nature of the Yagr take over. The black cat's insatiable desire to kill set it apart from other shapes. The creature was always on the brink of madness. The boy could not risk shifting into the eagle again to try and fly away, for the tiger would catch him in a single bound. Besides, the Darkwood King relished the challenge. The black cat was much larger than the Brown Tiger but wounded.

He felt the blood run down his hind leg.

The tiger attacked first, darting in with impressive speed, trying to slash his shoulder. The Yagr pivoted and countered faster than the attacker could withdraw its paw, creating deep rents in its foreleg. The tiger stumbled, allowing the larger cat to move in and wrap both forelegs around the brown cat's neck. Ethrang snapped his massive jaws on its face and wrenched violently. The tiger's neck snapped, and the beast sank to the ground.

Ethrang was amazed by the Yagr's ferocity. He submitted to its need to feast. Besides, he was hungry. He slit the tiger's belly open with one claw and devoured the organs first, savouring the heart and liver. He would not desire to eat such things in his human form, but as the Yagr, it was the greatest delicacy. He tore into its flesh, instinctively knowing which parts were the softest until his hunger appeased. Blood covered the snow in a wide swath, and crimson droplets ran from his muzzle.

The Yagr shifted into the giant eagle and leapt into the air, heading southwest. He flew the better part of the day along the western edge of the Great Plains. The winter air was brisk, but the parts of his body with feathers remained warm. Snow covered everything, and ominous clouds developed in the west. Before sundown, he spied the walled town of Banfar in the distance.

The orphan sensed something in the sky before he saw it.

Tiny black specks appeared above the city, growing larger at an alarming rate. They materialized into three black shapes winging towards him. He veered west against the backdrop of the setting sun, but they altered course to intercept him. As they neared, he realized they were wasp demons, but their white eyes were more frightening.

They had magic.

Suddenly, their eyes blazed yellow, green, and brown. The brown-eyed one could be trouble. The eagle lifted higher into the air, wrapping himself in a green shield, and dove straight down on the lead yellow-eyed one.

The wasp's armour was thick, but it seemed weak at the neck, so he landed on its head, wrapping his massive talons over its face and twisted. As the demon's head came off, he felt two arcs of fire strike his shield, knocking him sideways. Some of the brown fire got through, singing his back, adding more burns. The boy grimaced and dove straight down as their jaws snapped at him. They followed clumsily, seemingly unused to their large bodies, and he took advantage.

The giant eagle levelled out and flew straight up, so they went under him. He hung in midair momentarily then dove onto the back of the green-eyed wasp. He tore at its neck with his sharp beak, taking out chunks of flesh. It screamed in pain, trying to bring its magic to bear, but it was facing the wrong way. He bit two more times savagely and felt its spine break.

The Brown Level wasp turned and formed a fireball with its forelegs. Ethrang pushed off the back of the dead wasp to avoid the fire. The demon with the severed spine fell helplessly to Earth, creating a huge plume of snow on impact.

He turned to face the brown-eyed one, both hovering in the air. It reminded him of the Wizard's Duel tournament. They both unleashed their magic at the same time. Since he had wings instead of hands, he controlled his Power through his taloned feet, directing his magic at the demon's face. Yet it was a strong Brown, and had little in reserve. Some of his magic had replenished during the day, leaving him with enough to hold the creature at bay but too little to overpower it. He also needed to save some to shift back into his human form.

The boy broke off the stalemate and veered to his right, maintaining a green shield. The wasp demon followed, sending arrows of magic at his fleeing form. He avoided most, but a few struck the shield, weakening it.

He decided to fly straight for the city.

Ethrang altered the giant eagle's path, but the wasp adjusted. He was much faster but still within range of the demon. More magic struck his shield until it began to sputter. He dove like an arrow at the town walls, clearing them, then beat his wings furiously to land out of sight. His shield was almost non-existent, so he shifted to a form he had never used.

As the wasp demon flew over the walls to get him, a grey four-armed ape with armour-like skin leapt straight up and smashed into the winged creature. Both fell to the ground in a tangled mess of limbs and wings. Ethrang disengaged himself then repeatedly slammed all four fists down on the wasp, pounding its back and head. The blue fire in its eyes flickered. He heard the satisfying crunch of its head caving in as it hit the cobblestones, then sat back, panting. The boy shifted into human form, looking at his hands. He was burned everywhere, and his arm and leg throbbed. He used his remaining magic to heal part of his wounds, but it ran out.

He was stuck as a Banfar orphan for a while.

Ethrang fell on his back to catch his breath. The last three days had taken a steep toll on him, and he could not remember feeling so tired.

Something nudged his foot.

"You alright, boy? What the heck is that thing?"

He looked up to see an old man in a dirty overcoat with a bottle of booze in one hand, peering at the dead wasp.

"It's a demon," Ethrang said, getting to his feet.

"He must have done Wack for a long time," the man muttered, walking away. "Stay away from that stuff. It will kill you." The boy stared at him and laughed.

He realized he had landed on the north side of town in an alley leading to the Lower District. The sun had set, making the alley dim and unsafe. Strangely, he felt at home. Pulling his green cloak tight, he limped past the old man onto the main street. He expected to see a whole throng of drunken revellers, gamblers, prostitutes, and addicts, but the main thoroughfare was subdued. The taverns had occupants, but most wore soldiers' uniforms. The stores with runes and symbols on their signs, previous havens for the cults, were now filled with various people, including families. He supposed making them homeless shelters made the most sense.

He did spy a few recessed alcoves containing shadowy figures, but far less than there used to be. A few were smoking from a pipe, which meant they were on the deadly drug Wack, but it was rare.

He decided to get some answers and a good night's rest before finding out who was in charge. At the Wizard's Guild, Chip had mentioned Captain Melvin, and he knew his friend Rabbit had enlisted. First, he wanted to see the man who would know everything that was going on in the city. Ethrang turned right down an alley near the end of the Lower District, lit weakly by the torchlight coming from the street.

A half-dozen street kids lounged against the wall, but surprisingly he did not recognize them. Two older, burly boys stepped in front of him. Ethrang was about to shapeshift but knew he was out of Power. He would have to resort to old-school techniques.

"Pay the toll to get through our alley," the largest boy said. He had a few scraggly chin whiskers and a scarred forehead.

"This is actually my alley. You must have arrived recently. Where are you from?"

"Calgar. Isn't it obvious? Where have you been? We fought demons while the scummy people of Banfar ate wheat. Now it's our city." He spat on Ethrang's shoe. "Now pay the toll."

"Where are your parents?"

"Huh, dead. We are orphans. Why do you think we're here?" He came closer, smiling crookedly. His breath smelled of tobacco smoke. "We can always beat it out of you."

Ethrang stepped back with his right foot when the large boy moved, knowing how dangerous it was to be flat-footed before an adversary. He pulled a dagger smoothly and held it under the apparent leader's chin.

"Listen to me carefully, scumbag. I had a rough day. I killed three white-eyed wasp demons circling the city...not to mention a Brown Tiger and some witches before that...but the point is the demons are going to attack Banfar next, and you should all be helping with the war effort."

There was a long moment of complete silence.

The leader leaned his head back and bellowed in laughter. The others joined in, some doubling over. Ethrang sighed, admitting it might sound a little farfetched.

Finally, the burly boy straightened. "You must be on Wack. If you buy some, we will let you pass." His face turned mean. "Otherwise, pay up or get a beating."

Ethrang did not wait any longer. The element of surprise was imperative against six people, children or not. He kicked the leader hard in the groin, causing his eyes to roll back, then struck his burly friend between the eyes with the base of his dagger. The other four jumped in from the side, pummelling the back of his head and shoulders. He darted around them and spun with his knife in hand.

The remaining four were younger, between twelve and fourteen summers. They looked dirty with unkempt hair and torn clothes. Their eyes held the numb look of children who had seen too much and didn't care anymore, mixed with the wild need that orphans shared.

The need to survive.

Ethrang sheathed his dagger. The code of thieves was clear, even in Banfar. Weapons were not to be used on anyone under sixteen summers. Instead, he raised his fists and waited. Being in an alley was an advantage, for it was difficult for them to surround him. In the open, they would have had a much better chance. Plus, the toughest one usually made the mistake of jumping in first, giving him an opportunity for one-on-one.

True to form, the largest of the bunch leapt in with a wild swinging right. Ethrang ducked and gave him a vicious uppercut to his solar plexus. He would have liked to finish him off, but with multiple combatants, he knew to dart in and out in anticipation of the next attack. It came swiftly from the next two, smart enough to lunge from both sides. He kicked one in the stomach but landed wrong on his torn leg. A fist rocked him on the side of the head. The blond orphan felt a wave of dizziness, his signal to lash out like a maniac. He spun around with a back fist, feeling it connect with the side of a cheek then sent a wild flurry into the face of the first one, hearing the street kid's nose break. The two went down.

He turned too late as the youngest attacker planted a fist square into his mouth. Ethrang staggered back, his vision blurring. Two more fists struck his chin, and he stumbled. Everyone was down except for this last attacker, who looked barely twelve summers old. He had dirty blond hair and a smudged face.

He looked like Spider.

Memories of his dead friend surfaced. He had taken Spider under his wing, desperately trying to set him on the right path. But the cults had recruited him, poisoning his mind with their lies. Then Bashan had arrived, the Depraved Elf, turning him from a thief to a murderer.

Ethrang stared at the small orphan as he approached, his vision clearing. The boy pulled out a knife.

The shapeshifter backed up. "I had a friend like you once. He was an orphan like us. He started as a thief but ended up kidnapping and killing people. Now he's dead. If you use that knife, you will regret it for the rest of your life." Ethrang spat out a mouthful of blood and stopped moving back. "You realize you have a choice, right? No matter what anyone tells you, even your mind, you always have a choice."

The boy stepped closer.

Ethrang lowered his hands and faced him, flat-footed. "I'm sorry about your parents. The demons took them, but don't let them take your humanity. You may not care now, but you will." The orphan stopped before him, his small face working through his next decision.

"Why do you care about me?" he asked in a high voice.

"Because I was you. I am you. And my friend died because he made the wrong decisions. If he were here, he would be screaming at you to put down the knife and choose a different life. But he's not here anymore, because he's dead, forever. All I can say is that no matter how bad life looks, it is precious beyond words. It's everything. Don't throw it away."

The boy stared at him, and Ethrang finally saw the fear show through, followed by the devastating sadness. The small orphan lowered his knife.

Then his friends stood up, clutching various parts of their bodies. The burly leader stumbled forward with the others.

"Don't worry, Ollie. We are coming."

Ethrang swayed. His injuries and exhaustion were undeniable. He looked once more at the small orphan, his eyes wet. "You don't have to join them. You always have a choice." The boy nodded and stepped back.

The shapeshifter raised his fists as the others approached. He would never give up.

"That's enough!" called a high voice behind him. "Bagan will cuff your ears for this!"

The shapeshifter turned around.

"Ethrang! It's you!"

A girl with long red hair ran up and hugged him. He swayed unsteadily. "Good grief, what happened to you?"

"You know this guy?" asked the leader. He stood with the others, still holding his crotch.

"Of course, he's a legend. Bagan's favourite. Well, after Spider left." She turned to the group. "You know the rules. No attacking other orphans. I'm surprised he didn't kick your asses."

"Well…he kind of did," another boy said, rubbing his jaw.

"You leave him be. Ask for the toll, and if they refuse, let them pass. Go pickpocket or something. No violence. The last thing we need is the soldiers coming by again. If they arrest Bagan, we will have nowhere to live."

The boys grumbled, nodded, and began walking away.

"Nice to meet you, Ethrang," Ollie said, sheathing his knife. He looked embarrassed. "Uh, thanks." He put his hands in his pockets, looking down.

"Come with me," Ethrang said. "I will have my friend Rabbit find you something to do in the army."

"Hey, are you coming or what, Ollie?" the leader called from the alley entrance.

The small boy looked at him. "No," he shouted. "I'm not." He turned back to Ethrang. "How do you know Trixie?"

The shapeshifter smiled at the red-haired girl. She was a couple of years older than him, living on the streets of Banfar her whole life. He grinned through his bloody lips. "We grew up under Bagan's wing. I've known her since we were little."

"We got into all sorts of trouble." Trixie winked with a mischievous grin.

Ethrang put his hand on Ollie's shoulder. "Can you do me a favour?" The small orphan nodded. "Get a soldier named Rabbit and ask him to bring a healer to Bagan's place."

"Rabbit is a captain now," Trixie said. "He was promoted after General Morris got killed a week ago."

The green-robed boy blinked. "How did the general die?"

"He was assassinated. Witnesses saw a creature with white eyes leaving the administrative building."

Ethrang swore. "It's a demon. Some were flying over the city earlier. They have magic and don't feel the winter's cold. More will be coming. Get Captain Rabbit, please."

Ollie grimaced. "Alright, but he doesn't like me. He's tried to clear us from the alley a few times now."

"That's because he's doing his job. Banfar is a lot better than it used to be, trust me. Tell him it's me, and he will come. Don't forget the...healer." Ethrang suddenly fell forward as a wave of dizziness washed over him. Ollie caught him, and Trixie draped one of his arms over her shoulder.

"Go quickly," the shapeshifter mumbled. The boy ran off.

"We need to get you to a bed," Trixie urged, leading him down the alley.

Ethrang tried to answer but felt like vomiting. His leg burned fiercely, likely infected. In fact, everything hurt. He always prided himself on his energy, but now it was gone. The orphan gritted his teeth and trudged forward. At least he did not have to walk far.

Bagan's residence was a large three-story rectangular building one street over in the seedy district of town. It was plain, and he liked it that way. No lights lit up the front entrance. Trixie knocked on the door.

"Who is it?" A voice answered almost immediately.

"Trixie, open up."

"What's the passphrase?"

"You only get in trouble if you get caught," she said impatiently.

Several locks clicked, and a beefy boy with rolled-up sleeves opened it. "Bagan's in there," he said, jerking his thumb behind him.

Trixie nodded, dragging Ethrang inside. "Captain Rabbit and a healer will be coming soon. Let them in."

The boy shook his head. "Bagan's not going to like that."

"It's alright. We will talk to him." They entered a huge common room with orphans lounging on couches and chairs. A man sat at a large wooden desk facing them. He had a pinched face and frizzy grey hair. Several orphans started clamouring.

"Look, it's Ethrang!"

"Where have you been?"

"Why are you wearing a green robe?"

Ethrang recognized several orphans, but most were new, likely Calgar refugees."

"Ha, my favourite orphan!" Bagan said in a nasal voice. He clapped his hands together and hurried over. He put a palm on Ethrang's forehead, peering at him with beady eyes. "You have a fever, boy. Come here." The old man reached over and swatted several orphans off a nearby couch. A bigger one didn't react fast enough, so he cuffed him behind the ear. "Move it." The boy grumbled and slouched off. "Put him here."

Ethrang turned and fell on his back, groaning.

Bagan unbuttoned his long coat and pulled up a chair. "What have you gotten yourself into now?"

"Rabbit is coming with a healer... let them in," he gasped.

Bagan shook his head. "Rabbit has switched sides. I don't like him snooping around..."

The shapeshifter grabbed his hand. "Just do it. I will explain later. Trust me."

"Hmmm. Trust is a word I don't use much, but I suppose you have earned it. Very well." Bagan stood up, clapping his hands. "All of you, get to your rooms. The new captain is coming, and some of you are wanted. Stay out of sight." The orphans jumped to their feet and scurried up the stairs. It was obvious Rabbit was having a significant impact on the city.

They did not have to wait long before there was a knock at the door. Bagan opened it and pointed to the couch. Rabbit gave the man a curt nod before hurrying over with an older yellow-robed woman and Ollie. The brown-haired captain wore an impeccable uniform with a wool coat.

"Ethrang! It's good to see you." Rabbit clasped his hand with a look of concern. "You don't look so good, but I would hate to see the other guy."

The shapeshifter gave him a tired smile. "Not 'guy,' demons, and they're dead, but more will come. We have to talk about—" Blood bubbled out of his mouth.

Rabbit ushered the healer over. "This is Miss Owl. She arrived from Calgar before it fell to assist the war effort."

Ethrang blinked through his bleary eyes. "I've heard of you."

"Nice to meet you, dear." She pushed her glasses higher before placing both hands on his chest. Miss Owl's eyes blazed a bright yellow. "Oh dear, your wounds are infected. You would not have survived the night. What's this? Oh my!" She stared at him in wonder. "I've never met anyone like you."

Ethrang put a finger to his bloody lips, and she nodded. Only Rabbit and Spider knew he was a shapeshifter. The boy felt healing energy flow through his body as she repaired his leg and arm. For a moment, all his veins felt afire as she cleared the infection. The woman's healing skills were incredible. He could barely follow what she was doing. The skin on his back reformed as the scar tissue dissolved. He had not realized how much pain he was in until it disappeared.

Miss Owl lifted her hands and brushed the sweat that had formed on her brow. "There, that should do it. I cannot fix your exhaustion. Only sleep will do that. I recommend two days of bed rest."

Ethrang looked at her tiredly and smiled. "Thank you. I'm sorry to put you in such discomfort, but I've been through a lot."

"If you were with who I think you were with, then you have been through a lot indeed. Trouble always finds that boy."

"Who roughed you up?" Rabbit asked.

Ethrang glanced at Ollie, who was pretending to study his fingernails. "I fell coming over the wall into town," he lied. Trixie smiled from a couch across the room. Telling on someone, or "ratting," could get you killed in Banfar, especially to the authorities. He was close with Rabbit, but his older friend was working on the other side. Ollie breathed a sigh of relief.

Miss Owl coughed delicately. "That's quite a fall."

"What were you saying about demons?" Rabbit asked. "We have seen some flying around the city."

"Those are the white-eyed ones. Demons can't survive long in winter, but a new breed with magic can. I am worried they will attack Banfar."

The captain nodded. "A white-eyed one killed General Morris a week ago. Witnesses saw it slinking away."

"Who's the new general?"

"The army promoted Captain Melvin, who is well-liked and respected. He is the one who accompanied the Guardian to the Guild. He was the only one who survived."

Ethrang nodded. "I arrived at the Guild the same day. The Guardian made quite an impression. Since then, I have had a part in saving Queen Eleanor, ending the troll war, securing their allegiance, killing a nasty bugger named Barko, making it through Darkwood Forest, and escaping the Secret Caves full of psychotic witches who worship Death. Otherwise, I haven't done too much."

Everyone stared at him. Ollie giggled.

"Oh dear." Miss Owl sat back.

"Are you pulling a fast one?" Rabbit gave his friend a sly look.

"Nope. I wish I were. There's more, but for now it's important to find out what the demons are up to. To be honest, I'm surprised Banfar is still standing. It's only a two-day journey from Cave Mountain. The Demon King could easily take it with a small number of

Dark Elves and white-eyed demons. Maybe he has been busy doing something else. I would like to know what."

"And how are you going to find that out?" The captain gave him a suspicious look.

"I used to be a thief, trained by the best, remember." He gave Bagan a wink. "I have certain...talents."

"Ha!" the old man chortled, rubbing his hands together. "You were the best." He gave the skinny blond boy a mischievous look. "Don't think Bagan doesn't know about your...talents." He tapped the side of his long nose. "Bagan knows all."

Ethrang's eyes widened, and then he laughed. "You sly fox."

"What are you two talking about?" Trixie asked, twirling her red hair with one finger as she lounged on a worn couch.

"Never you mind, girl." Bagan waved his hand. "Our good friend here knows what he's doing."

"Where are the others, dear?" Miss Owl asked in a concerned voice.

Ethrang pushed down his mounting anxiety. "Imprisoned in the Secret Caves by the witches." She gasped and covered her mouth. "That's another reason I need to go to Cave Mountain." He took a steadying breath.

"What are you going to do?"

The boy's face hardened. "I'm going to find a weapon."

She stared at him. "There's only a few magic wielders in the city, but we could gather them and..."

"There's no time for that. You would slow me down, no offence. Some emissaries are arriving from the Demon King to see the High Witch, so I need to return soon. I have a plan, I think. Besides, no one travels as fast as me."

She nodded. "Very well. May the Creator shine on you. In the meantime, you need to rest. You will need all your energy for this."

"I know," he said wearily.

"He can stay in my room," Trixie piped up. "Have some of the cleaners wheel in a hot bath. He's not sleeping in my bed with those filthy clothes. I will launder them while he rests."

"A hot bath would be real nice." Ethrang stretched, yawning. He looked at Rabbit. "We will speak again in a couple of days when I return with news. If I don't come back, evacuate the city."

"We have a scout patrol a day's ride west, but they haven't reported in. See what you can find out."

He nodded sleepily. "Will do."

"It's settled then," Bagan said. "Thank you for stopping by, Captain."

Rabbit gave the old man a neutral look. "You think I'm out to get you, Bagan, but I'm the reason they haven't shut you down. I did not forget that you sheltered me. Stick to pickpocketing without violence, and they will look the other way. Banfar is a different city now since the Guardian cleared the cults. Nobody wants it to return to the old ways."

"I agree," the old man said. "The recruits from Calgar are a little feisty sometimes but will settle down."

"Good. That's all I ask." He turned to Ethrang. "Good luck, my friend. One day, you will have to tell me the whole story."

Miss Owl patted his hand. "Rest now."

Bagan showed them out, then turned several locks, including a chain. "Have the cleaners fix up a bath, Ollie. Have them take it to Trixie's room." He gave the girl a stern look. "Don't keep him up."

She feigned a look of surprise. "I would never think to do such a thing." Bagan grunted.

The girl grabbed Ethrang's hand and pulled him off the couch, herding the orphan up the stairs. Ollie followed them. They walked to the second floor, a long hall lined with equally spaced doors. Orphans of various ages ran to and from different rooms, creating a din of talk and laughter. Bagan's orphanage contained three levels, with new arrivals housed on the top floor. Over the years, one could work down to the lower levels, which meant fewer stairs.

"I'm on the third," Ollie said. "I'll tell the cleaners to fix you a bath."

"Remember what I said." Ethrang gripped his arm. "Who you

hang out with matters. Find friends who lift you up, not bring you down. Ask Rabbit if he can find something for you to do."

The small boy looked at him, raising his chin. "I remember. Life is precious. There is always a choice."

Ethrang gave him a quick hug, hoping he had made a difference. "Be grateful too. We orphans don't have much, but it's enough. Bagan is a crabby old con artist, but he does care about us. Stay out of trouble." The boy nodded and continued up the stairs.

"Aw, he likes you," Trixie said.

"Keep an eye on him," Ethrang responded then turned to the hall. "Looks pretty full."

Trixie nodded. "There were a lot of Calgar refugees. Most went to Toron, but many fled north since Banfar was much closer. The cult shops are now homeless shelters for families and adults. The orphans were sent here. We have to keep them in line." Even as she said it, Trixie swatted a young boy's head. "Keep it down, Gopher. If you want to be loud, go to the common room." He looked at her and giggled before running off.

Trixie's room was at the end of the hall. Ethrang entered to find a single unmade bed and a heap of clothes in the corner. The tub arrived soon after with a bar of coarse soap and a towel. He waited for Trixie to leave, but she didn't. Instead, she sat on her bed, twirling her red curls.

"Want help?" she asked.

He smiled. "No, I can manage." She gave him a disappointed look. "You used to want help."

"I'm with another, and...I've changed. Trixie, you are a beautiful girl. Find someone who will treat you the right way."

He disrobed and slipped into the steamy water, exhaling in pure bliss. The heat made his eyes droop, and he realized it would be so easy to close them right there. He imagined how silly it would be to survive Darkwood Forest but drown in a tub.

"Fine, be that way." She came over and kissed him on the cheek. "Everyone missed you when you were gone." She picked up his clothes and left.

He relaxed for a few more minutes but realized he was getting dangerously close to drowning. He forced himself to his feet then soaped down, rinsed, and dried off.

The orphan stood there, realizing he had no clothes, then shrugged and slipped under the blankets.

His eyes closed themselves, and he surrendered to sleep.

18

"Want dinner?" Ethrang opened his eyes. "Huh." He leapt out of bed. It took him a few moments to realize he was naked. Trixie giggled, holding a plate of food. "Awkward. Where are my clothes."

She pointed to a folded pile in the corner. He grinned and then got dressed. "Thanks. How long have I been sleeping."

"A full day." She set the plate of food on the small table next to the bed.

"What!"

"It's dinnertime."

"I've got to go." He looked at the plate of chicken, boiled potatoes, and a hunk of whole wheat bread. "I am hungry though." He sat and wolfed down the food. She gave him a mug of water. "Thanks."

"When will you be back?" she said, sitting beside him.

"By tomorrow morning, I hope."

"How is that possible? It's two days to Cave Mountain. What are you going to do, fly or something?" she laughed.

He looked startled then smiled. "Something like that. The point is if I'm not back tomorrow, something went wrong. I suggest you get ready to flee the city. If the demons surround it, you won't be able to get out. Watch out for Ollie and the other orphans. It will be hard for Bagan to leave this place. It's all he knows."

Ethrang turned and hugged her. "You are a good friend, Trixie. I will be back soon."

"You better. Why are you wearing green robes? Are you a wizard or something?" She gave him a strange look.

"Something like that." He laughed and left the room, dodging orphans as he traversed the hall.

Bagan was in the common room scolding some youngsters.

"You off?" the old man said as he came down the stairs. "Good luck, boy."

He nodded. "I'm going to need it."

Ethrang exited the large brown building, pulling his cloak tight against the cold wind. It was evening again. He had slept a whole day, but the boy felt refreshed and energized. He was impatient, knowing his friends were trapped in the Secret Caves.

The boy crossed two streets then entered the alley where the orphans had demanded a toll. They were hanging out in the same spot. With relief, he saw that Ollie was not with them. He did not feel a need for vengeance. Most of the friends he had made growing up in Banfar were ones he had fought first on the streets.

"You back for more? The girl won't save you this time," the burly leader called.

"I won't need her help. This time, I brought my pet. Wait there. I'll be right back." He turned around and left the alley, darting around the corner.

A moment later, the Darkwood King appeared, charging into the alley with fangs bared. Its massive fifteen-foot-long body was a living projectile of muscles and talons. The Yagr roared, bounding at them like a thing possessed, wild eyes bulging with madness.

The burly boy turned in horror and let out a high-pitched scream. The other orphans stared in shock, first at the massive cat charging at them and then at the tone of their leader's scream.

They all ran for their lives.

Ethrang had to slow down to avoid colliding with them, such was his velocity. He allowed the boys to flee onto the main street then shifted back into himself and sauntered around the corner. They looked back in terror, then stopped. He walked up to them with a wide grin.

"Did you like my pet? I can call him back if you want?" Ethrang turned and whistled. The orphans dashed off without waiting.

The shapeshifter laughed. He proceeded through the Lower District, realizing how much had changed. Banfar looked much more civil now. There weren't many drug users in sight, few drunken revellers, no cult members, and only a couple of prostitutes. He had to admit there was a part of his wild upbringing that would miss the parties, violence, and mayhem. It had never been boring in Banfar. However, he would not miss the cults.

He had left Bagan's residence with Spider to join the cult of the horned helmet. At first, they seemed caring and concerned, providing them with food and shelter. He had even learned to read. But then they introduced them to bizarre rituals, the sacrificing of animals, and the art of luring new recruits. He had come into his Power then and could survive easily on his own.

As a shapeshifter, he could take anything he wanted and become anyone he wanted. At first, it was intoxicating, even addictive. He left the cult and returned to Bagan's residence, but Spider remained. The small boy was enamoured with their teachings and became more brazen, turning into a bully. The older orphans became afraid, knowing the cult backed him. Spider began enjoying the violence and eventually the torture. His sense of empathy vanished.

And then the Guardian arrived.

Ethrang sighed. The only person he could truly change was himself. It did not mean he couldn't advise others or lead by example, but he was not in control of their thoughts and behaviours. He only had control over his. The realization was freeing. Trying to control others often led to frustration and conflict despite good intentions.

Yet he could change himself, which would have a powerful ripple effect. People were likelier to listen to someone who set a good example anyway. With this realization, he felt a burden lift. The

Guardian, Garth Stone, and the others had powerful effects on him. He learned many things by watching or listening to them. They were forces of change by their very nature. He had done many bad things in his life, but it was never too late to change.

The boy looked at the city of Banfar in a new light, seeing the hope and promise. The citizens had been the downtrodden, the outcasts, and the shunned, yet they were changing.

But something was coming for them.

He felt it in every fibre of his being. He needed to find out when the demons would attack. The white-eyed ones added a new level of danger. They could come at any time. Rabbit said the scouting patrol had not reported in. He was going to find out why.

The orphan turned right down an alley to the north wall, and then a giant eagle flew out of the city, riding the cold night wind. He arced westward, extending his great wings. Before him were the Great Plains and the foothills leading to Cave Mountain. He flew low to the ground, knowing his eyesight was poorer at night. Yet the eagle's speed was unmatched. The low foothills, a dark smudge on the horizon, grew as he neared the edge of the plains.

Then he felt the peculiar crackle of magic. The source was distant, but the use could only mean one thing. The eagle slowed and shifted into a great owl. The bird's night vision was without peer and still a formidable opponent. He saw a flurry of movement a few leagues in the distance. Even from here, he could see white eyes. The demons would unlikely sense his shift to the owl from that distance as it required little Power. That meant he had the element of surprise.

The boy flew soundlessly, gaining altitude. Soon, he was close enough to see individual bodies and their exact movements. Four white-eyed demons of various shapes surrounded eight dead men on the snow-covered wheat fields. The moonlight painted a garish picture. Body parts were strewn in a bloody circle. Charred remains indicated the white-eyed demons had used their magic. The men never had a chance.

But now they were up against him, and he was at full strength.

The giant owl dove soundlessly. No predator possessed the ability to be silent like an owl. He aimed for the largest demon, a spider-like creature busy tearing the fingers off a human hand. As he approached, the boy heard them chortle with ecstasy as they tore into tender flesh, blood dripping from their fangs.

Upon impact, Ethrang seized the spider's head with his massive talons and tore it clean off. Then he disappeared.

The other demons looked around, sensing something but seeing no one. They stared at the headless spider demon, watching it topple over, mouths frozen in mid-chew. A sparrow swooped around behind two man-like creatures and a massive Yagr appeared, swinging one giant claw with blinding speed, shredding both heads. Then it disappeared.

The lone remaining demon's eyes blazed yellow as it leapt to its feet. It was a short, pig-like creature with tusks. Ethrang appeared behind it in human form, tapped its shoulder, then sent green fire through the back of its head. It died instantly.

He turned, peering into the night, scanning the snow in the moonlight. He was alone. A mournful wind blew across the plains. The boy looked at the dismembered bodies, knowing they were once living, breathing men. Blood stained the once-white snow, shimmering crimson in the light of the stars. Some likely had families they would never see again.

Despite the horror before him, the boy felt a simmering rage. They intended to do this to the entire city. The white-eyed demons would have killed the scouting party only if an attack was imminent.

He stared at the headless demon bodies with revulsion. The Dark Elves' constant use of the Power had created these monstrosities. Yet the white-eyed ones were novices in magic. Their minimal training was evident. They did not shield themselves when attacked, and their mental faculties seemed slow. Perhaps the Balance was at work, levelling the playing field. He imagined a world full of slow-witted, white-eyed demons and shuddered. These abominations must be destroyed.

Two eyes suddenly opened a short distance away, and he noticed a brown shape slunk low in the snow. Ethrang leapt into the air as he heard the warning growl from the Brown Tiger. This one didn't leap for him, likely more content to feast on the bloody remains.

The giant eagle resumed its flight, scanning for the enemy. The foothills were before him, and he soared higher, riding the currents. The shape of Cave Mountain appeared in the distance, a dark monolith blotting out the stars, yet it did not look like a bent old man or a witch's hat. Instead, a perfect circular top reached for the clouds. Only great magic could have restored its shape. The enormity of the undertaking struck him, and a shiver of fear raced through his body as he sped towards evil.

He was flying to the lair of the Demon King.

Ethrang reached the eastern base and shifted into a sparrow. He had to be careful when using magic. Someone might sense it.

He flew around the base, heading west. An icy wind sprung up, and dark clouds blotted out the stars. A storm was brewing. The boy rounded the southern part of the mountain, and the caves appeared.

A long line of white-eyed demons were trudging up the mountain carrying various objects. Dark Elves walked up and down the line. Ethrang flew into the forest and then hovered in the canopy. A last group of white-eyed ones were about to leave the trees. Several larger demons carried a large wolf carcass. Seeing an opportunity, he swooped down and appeared at the back of the group, shifting into the pig demon he had killed on the Great Plains.

"Who used magic?" a voice called from up ahead. Some of the demons turned around, so he did too, pretending to look for the source of the infraction.

A Dark Elf's face appeared at the side of the group. "Knock it off. You know the rules. Magic is only used for hunting and training. Our Master, may we grovel at his leisure, wants all magic to be authorized among you lout. Since the hunt is over, there is no need to use it. Do you understand that, you slow-witted fools?"

The demons around him grunted in agreement, so he joined in, sounding eerily similar to a pig. A man-like thing at the back with teeth and claws turned to him. Its white eyes chilled him to the bone.

"Where you...come from?" it croaked.

Ethrang lifted his chubby claws, pointing at the trees behind him then pointing between his legs. "Ma...mo...me...pee," he finally got out. His voice box was not suited for speech. The demon stared at him for a moment then nodded, giving him a devilish grin. He was a head taller than the pig and heavily muscled.

"You with...other group." He pointed ahead. "You got lost."

Ethrang nodded emphatically with his tusked head. "Yay...yab...yet...yes...lost." He could not believe how difficult it was to speak. He felt like he was in school again, though he had only gone once. Bagan would rather have them work.

The demon looked at him and chortled then threw a heavy, clawed hand over his shoulders. The boy nearly gagged from the stench. He suspected the pig form he was in didn't smell much better.

They continued up Cave Mountain. Occasionally, the large demon to his right would say something, but he only nodded and grunted. They arrived at a plateau with three caves, and several Dark Elves ushered them in. "Leave your kills here!" barked one of them. "White eyes to the throne room."

The demons in front tossed the wolf carcass on a mound of dead bodies. There were wild boars, frog-like creatures with red eyes, brown hairy spiders, giant foxes, bears, mountain wolves, and other creatures he couldn't recognize in a tangled heap. Countless dead eyes stared at him. Demons emerged from the cave on the right to pick up the corpses. They shivered and carried the bodies back.

"Cook the good stuff for us," one of the elves said with a grin. The Dark Elves looked primarily human except for their black, almond-shaped eyes and pointed ears.

They entered the cave in the middle and proceeded down a long tunnel lit by torches. Depictions of humans fighting demons lined the walls. They reached a set of gold doors opened by two muscular black-eyed demons. Ethrang noticed the last image on the right showed the Demon King standing victorious on a hill of human skulls, holding a sword in one hand and a round orb in the other.

The boy did not have time to stare before a Dark Elf following the procession pushed him through. "Hurry up, pig. Our Master, may we grovel at his leisure, does not wish to wait."

The tunnel continued, but now the corners were perfectly chiselled, and gorgeous paintings adorned the walls. Depictions of ancient battle scenes lined the ceilings, and the polished floor shone with a waxy substance. The passage sloped downward, deep into the mountain, and they arrived in a large foyer. The white-eyed demons congregated in front of two ornate silver doors. Dark Elves were stationed around the circular room.

"Enter," a deep voice commanded, exuding power. The hairs on the back of Ethrang's pig neck stood up.

"Bow or die," a Dark Elf intoned at the front and signalled for two massive demons to open the doors. The white-eyed ones filed in.

The orphan grunted as he took in the throne room. It was the pig's version of a gasp. A few demons gave him an odd look.

The room was enormous, rising high to stalactites. It reminded him eerily of the cavern in the Secret Caves, but that was where the similarity ended. The floor was inlaid with shimmering gemstones, giving the impression of walking on multi-coloured stars. Bronze pillars supported a lower silver ceiling that ran the room's length, ending at a raised dais. Ethrang lifted his eyes.

The Demon King sat on a diamond throne, eyes blazing red through his horned helmet. His black, gloved hands rested on the armrests as he looked unmoving at the procession before him.

Ethrang stared at him in awe.

As one, the white-eyed demons dropped to their chests, grovelling at their master's leisure. For a moment, he stood then dove forward, prostrating himself, pretending to mewl and fawn like the others.

"Master, may we grovel at your leisure," they said as one. Those who could not speak well garbled the phrase. He was one of them. His snout could only say a couple of the words. The rest sounded like gibberish to his pig ears.

"Rise, my children," the Demon King commanded, then stood up, black cape fanning out behind him. His presence was palpable.

Everyone rose to their feet. Ethrang noticed a long gold table between the bronze pillars filled with Dark Elves sitting straight-backed. There were at least fifty seats on either side. Empty silverware place settings adorned each spot. They must be the Inner Circle and higher-ranking Dark Elves. Richly coloured paintings covered the walls, framed by plush drapes. Below them were rectangular stone tables.

Naked humans stood on the tables, chained to iron rings in the walls. Many were missing limbs, their faces full of anguish and fear. Ethrang felt sick, remembering Bashan and the cults. His revulsion turned to frustration, knowing there was nothing he could do.

There was dead silence in the room as the Lord of the Dark Elves stepped forward. "The Balance has spoken. Our cause is sanctified. You herald a new era of magic wielders. Every day, more of you are born with white eyes, growing faster than I had thought possible. You are the new generation. I am pleased."

The demons started cooing with joy at their master's pleasure. Some fell, legs weak with ecstasy, basking in the glorious moment. Ethrang stifled a laugh, causing a weak snort. Several white eyes stared oddly at him. He then raised his talons and leaned his head back, imitating some of the others, pretending to bask in the Demon King's glory. The demons around him nodded with appreciation.

"Tomorrow is your first test. It will be an easy one. You will destroy the pathetic human city of Banfar." Ethrang's head snapped back. "Slashar from the Inner Circle will lead you." The Demon King turned to the gold table, and a burly elf leapt up and prostrated before the dais.

"It is an honour, Master, may we grovel at your leisure," Slashar intoned.

The Demon King waved him off. "One hundred Dark Elves will accompany you. A few weeks ago, you were only a couple dozen. Now you number over one hundred. By winter's end, thousands of you will be ready for the Last Battle. We will crush our enemies into dust." The demons chortled and shrieked, raising their talons. "Tonight, we feast on the last of the humans from Calgar and the delicacies brought in from the hunt. I encourage your appetite for human blood. They are a vast food source for the hordes. It is time to replenish our stock. Herd the Banfar humans back here with your magic. They need to last us the rest of the winter." The Dark Elves and demons nodded eagerly, many licking their lips.

The Demon King took a step down the dais. "I had thought of unleashing my pet on the city but reconsidered." His eyes blazed brighter, and he gestured with his hand, using magic to pull forth a triangular diamond structure that had lain hidden in shadow at the back of the room.

Darkness seemed to fall across the hall. Inside the diamond, a black figure with long fingers was clawing at its prison.

It was the Dim.

Ethrang's heart skipped a beat. A sudden hopelessness filled his mind as he stared at the creature. The white-eyed demons in the front shrank back, letting out low moans. Even the Dark Elves at the table looked apprehensive.

The Demon King stared at his minions. "You are wise to show fear. My pet commands it. I have decided Banfar is not a worthy treat for such a creature. I have decided to unleash it on the Wizard's Guild first, then Toron." Ethrang's eyes widened. The Lord of the Dark Elves chuckled deeply then waved, and the diamond prison slid back into the corner. Everyone, including the demons, let out a sigh of relief.

The Unnamed One moved a few more steps down the dais. "Eat well, my children, for tomorrow you march at dusk on Banfar. The day after, you go to war!" His voice boomed throughout the throne room, magnified by his magic. The enormity of his Power floored Ethrang. He had never felt anything like it. Bellows and cheers rang throughout the room. The demons leapt up and down, their eyes frenzied.

"Come, white ones, let me see each of your minds. Show me your Power," the Lord of the Dark Elves commanded. Ethrang felt a streak of fear as the white-eyed demons lined up to meet their Master. He knew that if the Demon King entered his mind, he would recognize him as a shapeshifter.

The boy turned to see a Dark Elf and two black-eyed demons guarding the closed silver doors. He had to think fast.

Yet that was what he was good at.

Ethrang ran up to the Dark Elf, grabbing his own groin.

"What do you think you are doing, Pig?" the elf demanded, not hiding his disgust.

"Poo...Pa...Pee." He pointed between his legs. In any other circumstance, he would have laughed, but the orphan knew how serious this was.

"What?"

The pig demon gestured at the floor. "Na...Ne...No want dirty." He then pointed to his behind as well for added effect.

The Dark Elf wrinkled his nose. "Do your business outside then get back here. Run. Our Master waits on no one." He jerked his finger at the guard, and the demon opened the silver door enough for him to slip through. Ethrang started moving across the foyer and, for a split second, wanted desperately to continue through the tunnel to escape Cave Mountain, but he needed something important.

He needed a weapon.

The pig demon turned right and plodded down the tunnel. He came to a fork and chose left. The hallways were empty, which meant everyone of importance was in the throne room. The lesser demons and elves would be in the lower levels. He came to another fork and heard voices to his right. Rooms ran the length of the hall with iron doors. Judging by the intelligent speech, these were the residences of the Dark Elves. He turned left, seeking a way to the demons' chambers.

A cold, high voice yelled behind him. "Hey, where do you think you're going? You should be in the throne room." The boy turned to see a Dark Elf in a black cloak coming out of a door.

He did the first thing that came to mind. He ran.

"You dare defy me?" Ethrang heard running behind him. He

moved his pig feet quickly, but the design was flawed. He had hooves with talons, which made speed awkward.

The tunnel branched, and he darted right. He took two more turns before the footsteps were too close to ignore. Using a trick he learned in Banfar, the boy waited around the corner. If your pursuers were going to catch you, you might as well use the element of surprise. The Dark Elf rounded the corner and stopped in shock.

"What do you think you're doing, pig?" he demanded. He had dark short hair and a white face with black almond-shaped eyes.

Ethrang slapped him across the face.

The Dark Elf had a moment to gasp before the shapeshifter sent green fire through his eyeballs, ending his life. He then burned his head to ash so no one would recognize him and shifted into his shape.

"Who used magic?" he heard a distant voice call.

The boy took off at a full run, turning left and right. He passed more rooms with Dark Elves in them. Some were coming out to investigate.

"Where are you going?" one asked, poking his head out a door.

"Master has sent me on an errand," he called then added, "May we grovel at his leisure."

The elf did not respond. He raced through several more tunnels, feeling the ground sloping downward.

Then he saw the demons.

Several were standing in a rough-hewn tunnel with rooms to either side. There were no doors. The three in front of him all had black-eyes. One was a nasty-looking spider shape with a bulbous body. The other two were slender with long teeth and claws. They immediately backed up against the wall to allow him passage.

"Greetings...lord," one said haltingly, bowing his bald head.

Ethrang skidded to a stop. "Where is the tunnel with the largest demons?" he asked.

The black-eyed creature looked at him in surprise. "You mean...cavern?" it asked, confused. It started pointing left then right and back again. The boy heard distant shouts behind him.

"Never mind. Show me instead. Run!"

The demon grinned and dashed off with impressive speed. Ethrang followed, doing his best to keep up. They zigzagged left and right, avoiding all manner of demons in the halls. Thankfully, most of them were in their rooms eating, though he knew not what. The stench was unbearable.

They continued moving downwards. He could hear the shouts behind him growing. The tunnels became more primitive as they descended into the mountain's bowels. Ethrang could not believe the number of demons. They seemed endless. A low chorus of shrieks and bellows pursued them as more gave chase. Whoever had found the Dark Elf's body was mustering recruits along the way.

Finally, they entered a large tunnel with no torches. The air was noticeably cooler. The demon pointed left with its long talons to a spot of light at the end.

"Good work. You can leave now," he ordered. The creature nodded and ran back the way it came.

Ethrang hurried down the tunnel towards the light. He realized it was an entrance to a massive cavern. The boy burst forward onto a ledge overlooking a monstrous room that could fit a good chunk of Banfar.

His mouth dropped open.

Wide, steep stairs with no railing ran to the stone floor two hundred feet below. An assortment of creatures such as he had never seen milled about. Each was larger and scarier than the next. Some had immense, fat bodies with dozens of legs. Others were covered in spikes several feet long. An enormous hairy spider, bigger than a house, rested in a deep alcove off to one side, multiple insect-like black eyes staring everywhere at once.

Ethrang looked up at a ceiling of massive stalactites. Wasp demons and other strange creatures were flying between them. Ledges jutted out from the cavern's rocky walls, providing a perch for hundreds of flying demons.

One ledge drew his attention. A giant black-skinned bird stood alone, its raptor's gaze scanning the demons below. The creature's arms and legs were skeletal, attached to absurdly large, folded, leathery wings.

A wasp demon flew too close, and the bird's six-foot-long beak snapped at the flying insect. The wasp circled in anger, taunting it. The bird then opened its enormous wings and dove off the ledge. Its forty-foot wingspan astonished him. The creature launched straight at the wasp then turned at the last moment, making its right wing horizontal, exposing a razor-sharp edge. There was a slicing sound, and the wing effortlessly severed the wasp in two. As the pieces plummeted, the bird dove, snatching up half of the falling body before it hit the ground. The demon brought the prize back to its ledge and tore into the armoured carcass, shredding it with ease. The damage those wings could inflict would be devastating. The boy made a mental note, coining it the razor bird.

His gaze turned back to the milling throng of oversized demons. There were hundreds of them. Most were too large for his purpose, but then he spied a long, muscled creature covered with armoured plates. Its massive head was shaped like a battering ram. Bony ridges jutted out of a square face with deep-set eyes. As he watched, it rammed a much larger demon that came too close, completely knocking it over. The others gave it a wide berth. The boy smiled. It would do nicely.

Ethrang assessed the other creatures, recognizing benefits depending on the situation. There was so much to choose from.

It was a shapeshifter's paradise.

19

The orphan noticed lesser demons pulling cages through the throng. They seized carcasses cut into chunks, feeding them to the larger ones. Several cages held live demons, and he watched as they pulled them out, kicking and screaming, before throwing the creatures into the gaping maw of a monster.

The caged demons had an odd number of legs, two heads, or some other affliction. He guessed these mutants were unworthy of fighting alongside their stronger brethren. They had become food.

The boy scanned the massive cavern full of mewling, grunting beasts, taking in the sheer number of horrors about to be unleashed on the races. Gazing at the abominations the Dark Elves had cultivated over millennia, he felt a rare moment of hopelessness. What chance did they have? How could they win against such odds?

"Kiran, there you are." Ethrang turned quickly to see an older Dark Elf coming down the tunnel to stand on the ledge. Three other elves and several assorted black-eyed demons followed behind.

The boy nodded in greeting.

"We found a dead body back in the tunnels near our quarters," the older elf said quietly. "Someone used magic to kill him. Burnt his head to a crisp. Then the killer used another form of magic that's very rare. It is a talent that only Murk could use but he's dead."

Ethrang feigned surprise.

The elf's black eyes studied him intently. "What's strange is the body wore the same cloak, tunic, and breeches as you." The boy tensed. "I have sent word back to my Master, may we grovel at his leisure. I'm sure he would like to meet you." The other Dark Elves and demons stood at the ready. "This cavern has a rock gate that takes ten large demons to move. You have nowhere to go. Come with us."

The Banfar orphan knew when a situation was about to get explosive. It was usually best to strike first. "That sounds fun, but I'm going to pass."

Ethrang launched himself straight into the elf, carrying them both off the ledge. The stairs whizzed by as they fell two hundred feet. He seized his magic at the same time as the older elf. Above them, he felt the other elves link.

The boy shifted into a sparrow and flew across the cavern floor before landing on the demon that looked like a battering ram. He glanced back to see that the other elves had stopped the older Dark Elf's descent with their combined magic and set him on the ground. His eyes blazed a dark brown, and he started running between the demons, searching for him.

"Find the small bird!" he yelled, magnifying his voice with Power. The large demons looked around, and then several black-eyed heads swivelled to stare at his tiny form perched on the armoured creature's back.

Pandemonium broke out.

Giant jaws and taloned hands reached for him. He launched skyward, escaping. Several demons landed on the armoured monster, and it responded with a bellow, swinging its spiked tail in a wide arc before charging at the nearest attacker. Its bony face struck the side of a six-legged monstrosity, sending it crashing into several others.

They retaliated, leaping onto each other's backs or snapping long jaws around exposed necks. Within moments, a dozen monsters were slashing and biting each other, drawing more into the fray.

Ethrang flew above the throng, using the opportunity to find new shapes. He landed on a massive beast with a dozen legs on either side of its thick-skinned body. It had the head of a crocodile with ten-foot-long jaws. He sprang off it as several nearby demons raced to get him. They crashed into the crocodile demon, causing it to spin around and snap a tall, skinny demon in half. Another melee ensued.

The boy hopped from demon to demon, trying to be selective, but he had already amassed enough shapes that it didn't matter anymore. Each time he landed, more demons would snap at him, attacking the creature he touched. Soon, half the cavern had exploded into a flurry of vicious fighting. Ethrang flew out of reach, pleased with the chaos.

The boy heard a loud skitter behind him and turned to see the house-sized spider demon lurch out of her alcove towards him, windmilling her eight legs in a blur of motion. He beat his wings frantically, gaining altitude, and then she leapt into the air.

The orphan did not expect a spider to be able to jump that high, but then again he had never seen one that big. She blotted out the wall as her bulbous body sailed towards him. The bird could not escape in time, so he shifted into a giant eagle. The spider's head was as big as his body, so he aimed his talons straight at her eight eyes. He pushed off as she struck, taking four of the eyes with him, using her momentum to launch himself higher. She screamed and gnashed her long fangs at the empty air as she fell back down on a dozen other demons. Her rage and pain were uncontrollable, and she slashed at anything in sight with her taloned limbs. Some of the demons fell back, but others tore into her bulbous body. This enraged her further. The mayhem was unstoppable.

Ethrang noticed the older Dark Elf trying to get off the cavern floor as creatures jostled him left and right. A fireball flew out from the other elves, who had stopped halfway down the stairs. He easily dodged it with a swift beat of his wings then watched in horror as the razor bird cocked its raptor's gaze at him and leapt off the ledge.

He did not think any armour would stop the slice of its forty-foot wingspan. He needed to figure out how to avoid the creature and touch it at the same time. Its shape would be most useful.

It glided towards him like the reaper of death. Wasp demons veered out of its way, but one was too late. The razor bird's left wing sheared off its head in a fountain of black blood. Then it was right in front of him, and he was out of time. Ethrang did the one thing he usually did when he was terrified.

He turned into a flea.

He fell through the air as the massive winged body sailed above him. The wind from its passing pushed him down as his tiny body hurtled to the ground. Before he struck, the boy shifted back into the sparrow and beat his wings, realizing he was floating in between the crocodile demon's massive jaws. He arced upwards as they snapped shut, brushing his tail feathers. He aimed straight for the razor bird, dodging wasp demons that had entered the fray.

The massive bird glided in a wide turn, its raptor's gaze searching. He hugged the cavern wall as he raced after it, desperate to touch the deadly creature. It would be a valuable weapon in the battle to come.

Other demons pointed at him as he flitted across the cavern, but most were engaged in life-and-death struggles with their brethren. The razor bird turned, and he swooped behind it, giving chase.

The giant bird fanned out its deadly wings, coming to a stop, searching for its prey. The boy landed on the center of its back, feeling a rush of elation that he now possessed such a shape. It was cut short when the giant head turned around on its long neck and snapped at him. He hopped to his right, avoiding the curved beak, and then shifted into a shape he had wanted to try since it had patted his head when he was the Darkwood king.

The boy became Gruk, the leader of the ogres.

His twenty-foot-tall body was more than a match for the bird, and he seized its neck with two massive hands. The ogre squeezed while the bird flailed its razor-sharp wings. Some demons stopped fighting to watch the mad spectacle as the two giant bodies struggled in the air. The bird's neck felt like iron cords, but the ogre's strength was formidable. He twisted violently to his left, hearing an audible crack.

The razor bird's wings stopped beating, and its head drooped from its broken neck as it fell. He leapt off its back, shifting back into the sparrow. The razor bird's massive body fell into several demons, crushing them.

Ethrang flew to the back of the cavern, looking for a way out. He spied a towering rock gate, which likely opened to the side of the mountain, but it was closed. He chirped in frustration.

Then he felt a magic ignite well behind him in the tunnels, and a presence entered his mind.

"I'm coming for you, shapeshifter."

It was the Demon King.

Ethrang had never felt such Power from such a distance. It terrified him, and he needed to get out.

The orphan watched as a dozen wasp demons fell from the stalactites, aiming for the sparrow. He shifted into the razor bird and felt invincible. The wasps veered off in terror. The boy beat his massive wings and glided across the cavern. He looked down with his raptor's gaze, taking in the carnage in razor-sharp detail.

Over half the demons were dead or grievously injured. Many were still fighting. He uttered a piercing cry of satisfaction and glided towards the ledge leading back into the mountain. The older elf was on the cavern floor with his skull smashed in, likely trampled as the large demons rampaged. The three Dark Elves on the stairs sent a multi-coloured fireball at the giant bird. He dodged the attack, surrounded himself in a green shield, and dove straight at them. At first, they stood strong, raising their hands, but then one bolted, and the others ran frantically up the stairs.

The razor bird dove low then mounted the steps after the fleeing elves. He banked left and swung his right wing in a tight arc, cutting them into pieces. Their body parts flew off the stairs in a spray of blood. He turned back and mounted the steps again, aiming for the tunnel opening.

Several more Dark Elves and lesser demons burst forth onto the ledge. Ethrang did not slow. He shifted into the ram demon at the last moment and smashed through them. The elves tried to seize their magic, but it was too late. He broke bones like straw, sending some flying off the ledge while the others crashed against the walls. He continued down the tunnel, feeling almost nothing from the impact.

More demons began appearing, but he hurtled past. Some were too slow, and he went through them like butter. He reached the original fork in the tunnel but kept running through. He needed to find an iron door.

Chip said there was a door with stairs leading to the center of the mountain when he recounted the story during their travels. Dark Elves appeared behind them, so Ethrang shielded himself, not bothering to hide his magic anymore.

Then he sensed the immense Power coming closer from his right. He knew the Demon King was racing down the tunnels to get the shapeshifter. Something struck his shield, but it held. Ahead, the tunnel ended, and he turned left. The sounds of pursuit increased.

As he rounded the corner, the orphan shifted into the Darkwood King to increase speed. It was a wise move. Now, he could navigate by smell.

He picked up on a musty dampness and followed the trail. He needed to find the entrance to the lake and island in the middle of the mountain. He heard screams from the rooms on either side and glanced to see humans chained to walls being tortured by small, evil-looking demons holding various tools. A few peeked out the doors to investigate the growing shouts of alarm, so he swiped their heads off without slowing.

He desperately wanted to rescue the tortured humans, but if he stopped, they would have him. Growing up on the streets had hardened him to life's suffering, and he learned that sometimes you couldn't rescue someone in need or else you would suffer the same fate.

The Yagr bounded down the tunnel, deciding which forks to take by following his nose. The air became mustier as the tunnel sloped downward. He was getting close.

"Your suffering will have no equal."

The voice screamed inside his head as he felt the Power behind him grow stronger. Somehow, the Demon King was catching up to him.

The tunnel ended, and the only option was to turn right. He glanced around to see a horde of demons and Dark Elves turning the corner at the other end. Immense Power grew behind them.

He dashed forward to a dead end.

Thankfully, there was a heavy metal door. He shapeshifted into the ram and struck it with everything he had. Metal hinges tore off, and the door bent in half, partially blocking the stairs. He switched back to the Yagr and leapt over the twisted metal, but the stairs wound down in a circular fashion, which was difficult for his large body. He turned into a Banfar street dog and descended at breakneck speed.

"I am coming."

The voice was louder in his mind, and the immense magic grew closer. He knew it would be his end if the Demon King had him in his line of sight.

Ethrang tore down the stairs, strengthening his shield to light the way. The steps seemed endless. He spiralled down and heard a distant sound of metal flying through a wall. The Power was now above him, and he knew with a sickening lurch of his stomach that the Demon King was now on the stairs, coming at a terrifying speed.

He continued spiralling downward, his heart racing. He could hear footsteps growing louder behind him, moving insanely fast.

Suddenly, the stairs ended, and he burst onto a rocky beach. Without slowing, the dog turned into the razor bird and sailed above still water to an island.

The shapeshifter came face to face with a black dragon.

It reared up and leapt in the air, spreading its wings. He veered in terror before realizing it was still a baby. It couldn't get airborne yet. He sensed a strange magic in it as he soared upwards. The razor bird beat his enormous wings, gaining altitude.

"I will feast on your flesh soon, shapeshifter." A malevolent voice sounded in his head. It was the dragon. Its cadence and tone dripped

with malice. *"When I grow into my Power, my Master will find you. No shape can stand against mine."*

Ethrang beat his wings with everything he had, nearing the open crater at the top of the mountain. He could see the stars in the night sky.

Then the Demon King burst forth onto the beach.

With one last thrust of his wings, Ethrang sailed to the top of the edge and glanced down. The Demon King raised his hands and sent forth two streams of red Power the likes of which he had never seen.

The razor bird disappeared over the rim, but the fire struck the tip of his right wing, shrivelling it into a black husk. The orphan cried out in pain as he flew over the top.

The boy looked back to see a column of red fire bursting forth from the top of the crater like a live volcano. The display of magic was breathtaking. He banked to the right as the lip of the mountain exploded. The boy strengthened his shield as chunks of rock rained down. The Demon King was sending his magic through the top of the mountain itself.

For a moment, he flew through a shower of flaming rock, his shield holding, and then it subsided. A distant scream of rage rang through the night, and a voice exploded in his head.

"You will die by my hand, shapeshifter."

The presence pulled out of his mind as the razor bird left the vicinity. He looked back to see that a huge chunk of the cratered peak had broken off. Cave Mountain looked different once again.

Ethrang exhaled, realizing how close he had come to a torturous death. His hand hurt terribly, but he was alive. He let out a piercing cry of triumph as boys do when they narrowly escape death. He had learned the enemy's plan, destroyed many terrifying creatures, and escaped with several weapons.

Yet even as he tallied his successes, the orphan knew there was still so much more to do. The races were up against a vast army of demons and Dark Elves led by a being so powerful it almost defied imagination. Not to mention the Dim.

The boy sighed. One step at a time. Now he had to warn Banfar.

The razor bird sailed over the foothills towards the Great Plains. His body started getting colder, and he remembered that the black-eyed demons froze in winter. Ethrang could use his magic to stay warm, but he shifted into the giant eagle and continued his flight. Its feathers would give him ample warmth. His wing tip was black and twisted, but he could still fly.

Ahead of him, the sun broke the horizon, and he let the light bathe his face after the darkness of the demon caves. He looked back to see a ridge of black clouds over the Grey Mountains. A storm was coming in more ways than one.

He flew across the Great Plains, watching the morning sun glint off the pristine snow. Soon, the walls of Banfar appeared, and he landed in the same alley as last time. The dead wasp demon was still lying there, frozen in the snow. The same homeless person sat with his back against the wall. He shifted into his human form, smiling at the man's gaping face. Who would believe him?

Ethrang looked at his right hand, which was black and withered. The man stared at him for a moment more then shrugged and took a drink out of his flask.

The orphan crossed the Lower District and entered the alley, but no one was there. Likely too early in the morning. He arrived at Bagan's residence, knocking loudly.

"What's the passphrase?" A muffled voice called through the door.

"Uh, you only get in trouble if you get caught," he said.

"No, that was yesterday's."

The shapeshifter cursed. "Tell Bagan that Ethrang is here."

The old man opened the door. "Come in, boy."

He entered the common room to see a dozen orphans lounging about.

Trixie leapt to her feet. "Ethrang! You're back." She gave him a tight hug.

"Ow, watch my hand."

The red-haired girl looked down. "Oh my, what happened?"

"Long story, but first I must tell you something very important."

Bagan made room for him on one of the couches by swatting several orphans away. One of them was Ollie, who grinned and came back to sit beside him. The old man pulled up a chair, leaning forward with trepidation. "How bad is it?"

Ethrang gave him a sad look. "It's over, Bagan. Banfar will fall. The demons march tonight."

The old man slowly sat back with a deep sigh and looked around the room. He stared at each orphan in turn with sad eyes. Everyone stopped talking. They looked at their caretaker, sensing the gravity of the moment. He smiled at them, eyes growing wet, showing a deep compassion he rarely displayed.

"This is all I have ever known. I grew up in this very orphanage and stole enough to buy it. I may not have been a model citizen, the Creator knows, but I have raised thousands of you." He studied his hands as a tear slid down his cheek. "I remember all your names. Now I will have no one."

Trixie walked over and put her hand on the old man's shoulder. "Cheer up, Bagan. We are still with you."

He looked up and smiled, patting her hand. "Thank you, dear one." He smoothed his wispy hair and took a deep breath. "Very well, no time to waste. Let's pack up our things. I will purchase some wagons and horses before they run out. Perhaps it's time for old Bagan to see the world."

The orphans crowded around him.

"We won't leave you."

"You're all we've got."

"Orphans stick together."

Ethrang stood up. "Head to Toron. Find a way to help with the war effort. We must prepare for the Last Battle." He turned to Trixie. "Can you take me to Miss Owl and General Melvin?"

She nodded happily. "I will be back to pack up later, Bagan." She grabbed Ethrang's good hand. "A lot of citizens won't leave. You know that, right?"

The blond boy nodded and looked at the old man. "Once the orphans pack up, have them scour the city, announcing that the town needs to be evacuated. The demons will arrive within two days. Anyone who stays will be enslaved, tortured, and eaten. The same thing was done to the people of Calgar. I witnessed it firsthand. Questions can be addressed to General Melvin."

"What happened to your hand?" Ollie asked.

"The Demon King burnt me with his magic."

Everyone stared at him.

Ollie was the first to react. "Cool. Can I come?"

"Sure, but don't fall behind."

The small orphan beamed and followed them out. The trio proceeded through the Lower District to the other end of the city. Trixie took shortcuts through alleys and laneways until they arrived at a large park facing a brown administrative building. Wooden barracks had been erected to house the new soldiers. Several regiments were doing drills in the open.

"Rabbit will know how to find Miss Owl. He's over there." Trixie pointed to the young captain training a group of recruits.

Ethrang marvelled at the changes in such a short period. The Guardian's influence on Banfar had been profound. Rabbit had changed from an orphan thief to a captain, reinforcing the belief that everyone could change. They walked across the snow-covered grass and waited to the side.

Rabbit issued orders, and the recruits started jogging around the park's perimeter. He hurried up to Ethrang and embraced him. The captain looked at Ollie suspiciously.

"I hope this little rascal is not up to no good. How was your trip? Did you find our patrol?"

Ethrang's face grew grim. "Bad news, I'm afraid. They were set upon by white-eyed demons with magic. All are dead." Rabbit's face sank.

"I knew those men," he said quietly. "Did you get those responsible?"

"They will never attack anyone again."

The captain nodded. "Any other news?"

"The demons march on Banfar. They will be here in two days."

Rabbit blinked. "We must prepare at once."

"No," Ethrang warned. "The city must be evacuated. This is a foe you cannot beat. Two hundred Dark Elves and white-eyed demons, all magic wielders, will attack at the same time. Common soldiers would be decimated. Take me to General Melvin. He must order the evacuation."

Rabbit seemed about to protest but looked into his friend's eyes, then nodded. "Come with me."

The captain led them between several barracks before ascending the steps of the administrative building. The day was relatively mild for mid-winter, but dark clouds were pushing towards the city from the west.

They entered a large foyer supported by decorative stone columns. A gleaming marble floor led to a soldier sitting behind a large wooden desk.

"Captain Rabbit, you should be in the yard training your regiment." The man had grey hair at his temples and three stripes on the shoulder of his impeccable uniform.

"I understand, Colonel, but something of great importance has arisen," the brown-haired boy responded. "I need to speak with General Melvin on a matter of the highest urgency."

"Why do three street orphans accompany you?"

"They have the message."

"General Melvin is in a meeting, Captain."

Ethrang's impatience got the better of him. He hated bureaucracy. The boy held up his blackened hand. "The Demon King did this to my hand. I was in Cave Mountain. Get me the general now, or I will find him myself. Tell him I am with the Guardian."

The colonel's eyes widened. Chip's influence over the city was transformative. "Watch your tone, orphan. I will ask him, but there are no guarantees."

"You do that."

The man was about to retort then shook his head. "If this is some game, you will lose your captaincy, Rabbit." He stood up and slipped through a large wooden door at the back of the room.

Moments later, General Melvin came out, moving with hurried footsteps. He looked young but had the eyes of someone who had seen much. He stopped in front of them. The colonel trailed behind with a sour expression.

"Who claims to represent the Guardian?" the general asked.

"I do. I am Ethrang. I met Chip at the Wizard's Guild after you dropped them off in the Ancient Forest." Melvin's eyes widened. "Since then, we have travelled the lands seeking allies in the war to come. We are in a dire predicament up north, so I came south to find a weapon in Cave Mountain." The general looked perplexed. "I'm afraid the news is grave. Your patrol is dead, and the demons are leaving tonight to march on Banfar."

"Dear Creator," the general breathed, then his face hardened. "We all knew this day would come. If what you say is true, we must ready the city. It is time to show these creatures what the people of Banfar are made of."

"No, General, with all due respect. One hundred white-eyed demons and an equal number of Dark Elves are coming. They are all magic wielders. You will not stand a chance. Your purpose in training and readying the men have been served. Do not throw their lives away needlessly. Evacuate the city and head to Toron. You have one day. I will hold the demons off for as long as I can." Captain Melvin blinked.

The colonel let out a raucous laugh. "I warned you, Rabbit. Consider your captaincy dissolved. Take this rabble out of here before I throw them in jail."

The general turned to the man with an icy look. "I make that decision, not you." He looked back at Ethrang. "No offence, but your story is hard to believe. However, I have learned not to make rash judgments after what I have witnessed, most in the accompaniment of the Guardian. I would hear more before deciding to relinquish the city."

Ethrang studied him, mind racing, then nodded to himself. "I've learned that most people hide from the truth because they are unwilling or unable to hear it. I think a demonstration is the best way to show everyone how dire the situation has become. All I ask from you, General, is an audience with your men to show them what they are up against. I ask this in the name of the Guardian, Chip Oathbinder."

The colonel's jaw dropped, and he was about to retort, but General Melvin raised his hand. "Do you vouch for him, Captain Rabbit?"

The former street orphan made a salute. "I will stake my honour, title, and reputation on it."

"Very well." He turned to the colonel. "Assemble everyone in the yard." The man looked like he was about to object. "Now!" The general's voice exuded authority. The man saluted and hurried out.

Melvin's face softened. "How are the Guardian and the others?"

"In trouble," Ethrang answered. "There is nothing you can do about it, so I will not put that burden on your shoulders. First, we need to save the citizens of our city."

The general nodded. "Let's wait on the steps while the troops gather."

Everyone turned and exited the administrative building. Shouts rang out as the troops of Banfar formed up before them. In short order, over two thousand men in clean uniforms and a dozen high-ranking officers assembled in the park between the barracks. Miss Owl came out of the administrative building to join them. She gave him a reassuring smile.

Ethrang stood on the steps in his green robes and wool cloak. Trixie and Ollie looked on with wide eyes. They were not used to so many people staring at them. Melvin stood beside the skinny blond boy and cleared his throat.

"Soldiers of Banfar, this is Ethrang, a citizen of our great city and a friend to the Guardian. I'm afraid he has grave news. I have granted him an audience to hear him out."

The orphan of Banfar surveyed the army.

Over two thousand eyes looked at him silently, but he felt no fear. He had never been a shy person. Embarrassment or judgment didn't bother him. Truth be told, he rather liked the attention.

"I grew up in our city, a street orphan, an outcast, like most of you.

When the Guardian arrived and gave his speech in the Lower District, I felt something I had lost long ago. It was hope. It was meaning. It was a way out of a life I am not proud of. Yet despite our failures, addictions, criminal behaviour, and low self-esteem, we are survivors. The Banfar people are resilient. The Guardian told me challenges make you stronger. Well, I'm here to tell you it's true. I am also here as living proof that we can change. Our lives are precious. We matter. If we work together, anything is possible. You have proven it already by enlisting." The men nodded, faces serious.

"What I'm about to tell you may be hard to believe, yet you must. The lives of everyone in this city depend on it. Yesterday, I went to Cave Mountain, the lair of the Demon King. I sought a weapon to help the Guardian and, in doing so, uncovered the enemy's plans." He paused, letting the significance take effect. "Our scouting patrol on the Great Plains is dead, murdered by a new breed of demon with white eyes. They carry magic. Tonight at dusk, two hundred magic-wielding demons and Dark Elves march to take over our city."

The men shifted, muttering amongst themselves. A few cried out.

"We will be ready."

"Two hundred is nothing."

"Let's bathe in their black blood."

The general held up his hand. "Hear him out."

Ethrang turned to Miss Owl. "How many magic wielders are in the city?"

She pushed her glasses up. "Only a dozen, but all are Lower Level."

The boy nodded, scanning the crowd. "Two hundred may not seem like much, but they will run through you like a scythe through wheat." Grumbles sounded, and some faces turned angry. "I know what magic can do. You have been trained to fight black-eyed demons, not magic wielders. You must abandon the city."

Shouts rang out. The general held up his hand again, but this time it took longer to quiet them down.

"How do you know all this?"

"How could you go into Cave Mountain and survive?"

"Are you in the cult?"

Ethrang's eyes suddenly flared a bright green with a silver tinge. He magnified his voice with Power. "I know this because I am a wizard. Well, technically, I haven't passed all the Tests, but you know what I mean." Trixie and Ollie gasped. He took a step down. "I also have a special talent that no other human has. You ask how I know all this. It's because I can do things nobody else can." He paused, taking a deep breath, then raised his blazing eyes. "I am a shapeshifter."

Everyone went dead silent. Most had puzzled looks on their faces. The general stared at him wide-eyed.

The colonel finally broke the silence. "I have heard enough of…"

Ethrang leapt into the air, transforming into the giant eagle, beating his wings to hover above the audience. The colonel's mouth fell open.

Ollie cried out behind him. "Cool!"

Ethrang landed and shifted back into human form to speak. "These were my old weapons. Now, I will show you the new shapes I have taken." Suddenly, the Darkwood King leapt to the bottom of the steps, snarling savagely. Then Furiosa stood eight feet tall, flexing her large fists before a Brown Tiger appeared, then Silvermane, and other shapes. He stopped with Gruk, the twenty foot ogre. The reaction was nothing short of amazement.

Ethrang reappeared. "I used these skills to fly across the Great Plains. I found the dead patrol and killed the three demons that dismembered them. I assumed this shape to get into Cave Mountain." The boy turned into the white-eyed pig demon and then shifted back. "I stood in the throne room of the Demon King with the other white-eyed demons and listened to his plans. I saw humans from Calgar being tortured along the stone walls. The Unnamed One has run out of food and now wants to come here and enslave the citizens. Whoever stays will be tortured and eaten. They especially like women and children."

Fear finally showed on the men's faces.

"In my escape, I found a cavern in the mountain that holds the largest demons. He is saving those for the Last Battle. I was able to touch many of them, which allowed me to assume their shape. These are my new weapons." He stepped into the open and beat his wings as the razor bird, causing the soldiers in front to step back in terror. Then a giant spider sat before them, big as a house. The boy shifted into massive multi-legged creatures including tall ones with long claws, the crocodile demon, and the armoured battering ram.

Ethrang turned into himself and climbed back onto the steps, facing them with blazing eyes. "I will slow down the enemy, but even I cannot defeat two hundred, though I will do my best. My goal is to give you time to escape." He held up his blackened hand. "The Demon King did this to me as I flew out of the mountain. I am lucky to be here. Our goal in Banfar was to provide wheat and supplies to Toron, train men to join the Last Battle, and provide a warning when the enemy marches. We have fulfilled all our goals. Don't throw your lives away. We need to evacuate the city in one day. And I need your help."

Everyone stared at the skinny orphan in green robes. Most were still in shock. Then the faces turned to ones of resilience, and shouts of support rang out, turning into wild cheers.

General Melvin looked at the shapeshifter. "You have our full support," he said loudly. "We will save the good people of Banfar. All ranking officers are to meet in the foyer behind me immediately to plan the evacuation. Men, stand ready for your orders. What we do now will matter for the rest of our lives." He turned and saluted Ethrang. "It is an honour. Thank you."

The orphan from Banfar experienced a moment of vulnerability. The general of an entire city had thanked him, and he felt joy and gratitude. He never dreamed he could make such a difference in people's lives. It felt really good, even better than picking a wealthy man's pocket.

The skinny blond boy grinned. "People in Banfar stick together."

Melvin nodded and waved the officers into the administrative building.

Trixie spun him around. "You could have told me."

"It was a secret before. Now that the Demon King knows, I figured it doesn't matter anymore, plus I had to prove my point."

Ollie was grinning from ear to ear. "That was the coolest thing I ever saw."

Ethrang put his good hand on the small boy's shoulder. "Do you see why we must help each other out? It feels good, and it's the right thing to do. It's never too late to change." The orphan nodded eagerly.

"Let me see that hand," Miss Owl said with concern.

Ethrang gladly held it up. "I wanted to show them what the Demon King could do before healing. I have to tell you it really hurts."

She nodded as her eyes blazed an intense yellow. "I can still use some of it, making my work easier. Growing a hand from scratch is more complicated." She sent magic into his hand, restrengthening the charred bones and salvaging some fried muscle. She worked with incredible dexterity, and he watched in wonder as his hand turned pink, expanding back to its normal size. "There, that should do it."

He flexed his new hand. "Thank you again."

She looked at him as an owl would, cocking her head. "I suspect you will need me again before this is over."

"Oh, probably," he laughed. "I'm sure I will find a way to get into more trouble." He turned to Rabbit, who indicated he needed to attend the meeting. "Thanks, Captain. I will have the orphans spread the word, which the soldiers will reinforce. I can provide physical proof for those who need the visuals. Our goal now is to save as many lives as possible."

"Good work, Ethrang. We will stay in touch." Rabbit took leave, and then the three stood alone on the steps.

The shapeshifter stared at his two fellow orphans. "Let's get something to eat. I'm starving. After that, we will pack up and spread the word. Let's save the people of Banfar."

The trio hurried back through the soldiers, bustling about in preparation. Many clapped the boy on the back and expressed their gratitude. They spent the remainder of the morning helping Bagan and the orphans pack up and load the wagon. When finished, the children ran through the town, crying out the message to the population. They gave each group of orphans a section of the city to cover so that all could be informed.

By then, the soldiers had fanned out, emphasizing the message. Surprisingly, few people protested. The Calgar refugees had seen the demons and knew what was coming. They assisted in the effort to reinforce the severity of the situation.

By nightfall, Ethrang felt exhausted and collapsed on Trixie's bed, falling asleep in moments.

Morning dawned cold and cloudy, but the citizens were already making their way out of the city. The eastern gates remained open to the Great Plains, and a long line of travellers headed out with most of their worldly possessions. Some had wagons and horses, while others trudged on foot, dressed warmly.

Groups of soldiers went with them for protection, but the main army remained until the end, defending the rear in case of attack. Ethrang stood at the gates with Bagan and the rest of the orphans, seeing them off.

"Can't you come with us?" Ollie pleaded. "I feel safe with you."

"It won't be the same without you," Trixie said, pouting.

"No, I must stay here. I am worried the demons will try to follow you. I'm going to make sure that doesn't happen. I will see you again soon. Take care of each other."

They grudgingly acknowledged the logic and embraced him at the same time. Ollie's lip was quivering, but he maintained a stoic face.

Bagan looked down from the wagon he had purchased, which was now full of supplies. "Don't let them destroy the city. This is our home."

Ethrang nodded. "I will do my best. Safe travels, old man."

Bagan winked and flicked his reigns. The wagon lurched forwards, surrounded by the children. He watched as the orphans of Banfar left the city most had known their whole life. He stood there until they had shrunk to a tiny dot, feeling nostalgic. Then he turned.

The orphan knew what he had to do.

Miss Owl approached from the side. Her yellow robes swirled in the wind. A storm was coming. "Do you wish me to stay in the city with you?" Her grey-black hair was done in a severe bun, but her face exuded kindness.

"No, I must do this alone. It's safer that way."

She nodded. "I will leave with the last regiment. Seek me out if you need me."

"I will. Thank you."

"May the Creator shine on you, dear." She turned and walked away, pulling her cloak tighter against the growing wind.

General Melvin waved him over, and he complied, stopping before the young man. "When are you leaving?"

The boy glanced around. "Last."

Melvin looked at him, and his face softened. "I remember you, by the way. When I was a soldier before becoming a captain, there was talk of a blond orphan who nobody could catch. He stole, pickpocketed, and was seen hanging around the cults. Was it you by chance?"

Ethrang feigned disbelief. "I don't know what you are talking about."

The general grinned. "I must be mistaken." He looked at his soldiers ushering the citizens out the eastern gate. "All I know is people can change. I did. The Guardian has that effect on people."

The blond boy's face turned serious. "He has changed my life. I would die for him."

General Melvin nodded. "Aye, my friend." They stood for several moments in silence. "Is he in serious trouble?"

"Yes, but I have a plan. A lot has to go right, but I'm going to do it one step at a time. The impossible is achievable if one focuses on each step. There is always a way."

"Very wise, my young friend. How long will you stay in the city?"

"As long as it takes. I will do everything in my power to slow them down. If I fail and they catch up to you, ambush them. Use the element of surprise. You will lose many men and even your life, but it is the only way. Surprise is your friend. The citizens must be protected at all costs."

The general looked off into the dark clouds. "My wife and son have already left. I will give anything to make sure they are safe."

"If I don't survive, look out for Trixie and Ollie. Give them some errand work, at least. And keep your eye on Rabbit. He is going places."

"Consider it done. Fare you well. May the Creator shine on you."

"As you, General."

20

Ethrang decided to walk the streets, looking for anyone refusing to leave. He found several homeless people but jostled them out, telling them they had no choice. A couple of times, he had to shift into a demon to scare them off. The afternoon waned, and the streets became more deserted. He decided to make sure no one was trying to remain in the more affluent section, the Upper District.

When he arrived, he found a few last families heading towards the eastern gate. Their wagons sagged with supplies and valuables. These folk were the few wealthy ones in Banfar.

A clanging sounded to his right, and he noticed the front door open in one of the mansions. He walked in without hesitation, finding several men inside with arms full of silver and expensive items. They froze then realized he was a lad.

"Get out of here, boy," one man grunted. He had a long scar running down his cheek. "This is our find."

Ethrang did not move. "I won't ask you to drop what you've stolen. I was a thief once too, but get out of the city now."

The man looked at his two accomplices and laughed. "How about you leave before we make you, runt."

The boy stared at him, unmoving.

The man placed the items on the ground and walked up to him, reeking of booze. "Some people learn the hard way." He swung hard at the orphan's face. The air seemed to warble, and then Furiosa caught his hand and squeezed it, breaking his bones. The man shrieked.

Ethrang reappeared. "I asked you to leave. If I see you again, I will kill you."

"That's the boy who shapeshifts," one of the accomplices said, eyes going wide. "He can even become a demon."

"And much more," the orphan said calmly. "Leave the city now and enlist. Spend your energy doing something good for once. Got it?"

"Yes."

"Right away."

"Don't hurt us."

They scrambled out with their items and ran down the street. Ethrang continued his search, looking for signs of life. A silence began to settle over the city. He found one family holed up at the end of the street, refusing to budge. He turned into several demons, which gave them a change of heart. It did not take them long to grab what they could and run for the gates.

He would not take no for an answer.

The boy knew what was in store for anyone who stayed. No one deserved that.

The sun began to set, so he returned to the eastern gates. Nobody was there. He looked in time to see the general's regiment in the distance. He watched as they became a speck on the horizon. Everyone was gone.

Then night fell.

Ethrang turned around to look at the city. It was dark and silent, save for a strong wind portending an oncoming storm. Clouds blocked out most of the emerging stars. He looked over at the administrative building in the distance. It was a dark silhouette overlooking the park. He walked over and traversed the street between the barracks. It felt strange that everyone had gone, but he sighed in relief. They would now have a chance.

The orphan proceeded down the empty streets of Banfar. A few oil lamps were burning in windows, but they would die out. He walked down to the Lower District. It was deserted. For the first time in his life, he heard no sounds of revelry, shouting, clinking of glasses, people hawking wares, prostitutes asking for a trick, fighting, or anything. There was only silence.

A wave of sadness swept over him.

The orphan of Banfar stood alone in the middle of the street. Ethrang never knew his parents. He had been left at the steps of the orphanage one night. Bagan had taken him in, for he never refused to shelter a child despite his flaws. One of the pregnant, older girls had taken the boy in. He had shared their milk for the first year and then stayed with whoever would care for him. He grew up wild, but that was the way it was.

At an early age, Bagan showed him how to pickpocket, and he became the best at it. Spider entered the orphanage at five after his parents were killed in an alley. Ethrang felt sorry for him and took the child under his wing. They were a few years apart, so he treated him like a younger brother. Life became a wild blur of running, stealing, carousing with the other orphans, and caring for Spider.

Then the cults drew them in, promising riches and knowledge. The boys fell for it. Ethrang saw through the ruse, but his young friend got in too deep. Once Bashan came along, Spider's fate was sealed, despite all his efforts.

Ethrang sighed, staring at the desolate, empty city, imagining running through the Lower District with Spider at his side. For a rare moment, he thought of who his parents could be. Bagan always said he never knew, but something about the devious man's beady eyes made him doubt. Call it a street kid's intuition that he learned the hard way by reading people's underlying intentions. It nagged at him, but he let it go. What did it matter anyway? They never wanted him.

The blond boy stared at the vacant storefronts. The main tavern was dark and silent. The food shops had nothing on their shelves, and the night wind carried no mouthwatering aromas.

The orphan felt lonely.

He realized at that moment how important it was to be around other people. Humans were social creatures. He had grown up surrounded by other orphans. There was always laughing, screaming, and fighting. Every day was a new adventure. Banfar was never boring. He got into all sorts of binds but always found a way out. And then he had discovered his Power at fourteen summers. He left the cults and returned to the orphanage. Stealing became ridiculously easy. He kept it a secret from everyone except Spider and Rabbit.

The boy developed guilt for taking precious things from other people. Sometimes, he would watch as a fly on the wall and see the repercussions of his thievery. Families would cry at losing sentimental heirlooms, and children would become afraid that someone had been in their home. Others mourned the loss of their life savings. He vowed only to take what he needed to survive. Spider tried to pressure him to steal more, but he resisted.

And then the Guardian came. His life changed.

The orphan stared at the lifeless city, reliving countless memories. Life was meaningless if you couldn't share it. When things got hard, some people talked about moving away and living alone.

Then they would be happy. No one would bother them.

He shook his head. They didn't fully understand what being alone meant. Now he was all alone and didn't like it.

The boy thought of Chip and the others, imprisoned in tiny cells in the middle of Darkwood Forest, held by a coven of evil witches, walled off from their Power. He needed to save them. He also needed to protect the people of Banfar.

Yet he was only one person.

The skinny orphan stood alone in the middle of the Lower District, feeling the weight of the world on his shoulders. Tears formed in his eyes. He had not cried in a very long time. People saw it as a weakness. He needed to be strong for the others. He wiped away the tears, but more came. The dark city felt dead, lifeless. He looked around, but there was no one else.

It was him against the world.

More tears came. Why had his parents abandoned him? How come they didn't love him? He sat down in the middle of the empty, dark street. He usually had a quip to get him through things like this. Yet now, he could think of nothing. He felt weak and vulnerable. His shapes were really illusions. They weren't him. The truth was nobody liked orphans. He was a skinny kid who nobody cared about. He wiped away more tears. The boy was lucky to have made it this far. Lucky to have escaped the witches. Lucky to have escaped Cave Mountain. He knew luck would eventually run out.

The truth was that he was scared.

A street kid should never admit such a thing, but here, all alone, he could not ignore it. Ethrang was scared.

The Demon King terrified him. He felt like a feather in the wind against such Power. Who did he think he was to challenge such a foe? Did they really think they were going to win? Did he think he had enough to make a difference? Ethrang hung his head, the weight of the dark, lonely city pressing in from all sides. Was he enough?

I am enough.

The Guardian's voice rang in his head. His loneliness diminished.

There is always a way.

He smiled, picturing his friend.

Don't give up.

The orphan raised his head.

He did have people who loved him. He had people who were relying on him. He would not give up. The boy smiled, wiping away the last of his tears. He was not a feather in the wind. He was a shapeshifter.

And there was no one like him.

The boy stood up and leapt into the air, becoming the giant eagle. He soared over the front gates of Banfar across the Great Plains, needing to find the enemy. The bird rode the air currents, relishing the freedom and joy of flight. Dark clouds raced overhead, but he welcomed them. He would blend in with the night sky.

Halfway to the foothills, he spotted three white-eyed demon scouts trekking across the snow. The boy did not hesitate. He circled the figures and then came in low, becoming the ram demon at the last instant, slamming into their backs at the same time. They never stood a chance.

Ethrang slid to a stop, looking at the broken, lifeless bodies. He turned back into the giant eagle and picked them up one at a time, burying them far away in the snow. He hoped the Dark Elves would think they had gotten lost on the Great Plains. After all, they weren't too bright.

He continued on and spied the rest of the enemy camped at the edge of the foothills. He thought of attacking them but wanted to keep the element of surprise. The orphan turned around and returned to Banfar. They would take another day to arrive. It would allow the fleeing citizens to put more distance between themselves and the city.

Ethrang landed in front of Bagan's residence. He could take his pick of any mansion or house he desired, but the orphanage felt like home to him. The boy went inside and stood for a moment in the dark, empty common room. It was eerily quiet, bereft of the sounds of life. He sighed and took one of the empty bedrooms on the second floor.

In the dark, the boy listened to the wind outside and the creak of the old house. He vowed to bring the orphans back one day and make it like the place he remembered. It took him a while to fall asleep, but he regulated his breathing and thought of better days.

In the morning, he awoke refreshed and decided to take a final run-through of the city. He had nothing else to do. The orphan stopped at the Reindeer Inn and helped himself to some leftover scraps in the cold room. Satiated, he wandered through the city, taking a tour of places he had never seen before.

He walked into old man Benson's grand mansion and sat in his upstairs leather armchair, pretending he was a noble. The orphan went into the administrative building, looking through all the rooms, finding it quite boring. He snuck into a few places of ill repute and laughed at some of the toys and equipment.

When afternoon arrived, he lit the torches on the walls to make it appear the city was still inhabited. For added effect, he put burning oil lamps in the windows of some homes that lined the Lower District. Light snow began to fall as the dark clouds released their burden.

Then he waited.

Night fell, and he breathed a sigh of relief. The cover of darkness would allow him to work. Even as the thought crossed his mind, he saw distant lights crossing the Great Plains.

They were here.

He climbed down from the watchtower beside the gates and started running as he shifted into the enormous razor bird. The boy flew south first, then looped around in a wide circle, coming up behind the enemy in the darkness. His raptor gaze was incredibly keen, and the boy spied over two hundred demons and Dark Elves. He kept his distance, allowing them to get near the city.

When they were almost at the walls, Ethrang made his move. Beating his twenty-foot wings, the boy increased his speed and dove straight down, gliding across the plain close to the ground. His wings splayed like giant scythes, and the orphan pretended he was a farmer clearing the wheat fields.

Everything depended on the element of surprise.

As he swooped in, a blue fireball exploded from the lead Dark Elf's hands and slammed into the front gates, knocking them off their hinges. He recognized the stout Inner Circle elf from the throne room in Cave Mountain. His name was Slashar. Everyone faced forward, watching the spectacle.

His timing was perfect.

A white-eyed demon turned around at the last instant, but it was too late. He flew across the enemy's center like a black missile of death. The razor bird's wings sliced through the necks and bodies of white-eyed demons and Dark Elves. Limbs and heads flew everywhere. His velocity and momentum reached Slashar at the front, but the Dark Elf shielded himself and dove out of the way.

Ethrang tilted his wings and arced over the city's wall as a fireball exploded into the stone behind him. Chunks of rock rained down but did no damage. The boy shifted into the Darkwood King and raced down an alley.

This was his city, and he knew every inch of it.

The orphan circled back to peer around a corner from higher up the street. The enormity of what he had done sank in. The enemy now numbered less than half. His forty-foot wingspan had decimated them, timed perfectly while they were bunched in the darkness before the front gates. Some of the smaller white-eyed ones, especially the spider demons, had survived due to their height. The Dark Elves suffered the most losses, for their exposed necks were at the same level.

He watched with cat eyes as they searched each storefront and residence. He would be patient. Slashar began cursing, realizing the city was empty. He assembled several groups of demons and then ordered them to fan out.

"Bring me fresh blood," he screamed, eyes blazing a bright blue.

Ethrank slunk back down the alley and moved deeper into the city. Snow was beginning to build up on the ground, making his footprints visible yet also allowing him to track them. He hunkered down beside the Reindeer Inn and waited. A while later, he spied movement and felt the peculiar crackle of magic. They were using their Power to illuminate darkened homes. None of them seemed to be shielding themselves, though their eyes blazed. A shield could only last so long anyway. Their use of magic made the tracking easier. Now he knew exactly where they were. The giant cat crept forward, a black wraith of death.

It was time for the Darkwood King to hunt.

His slitted yellow eyes picked up light from old man Benson's mansion. He padded stealthily through the open front door to find three white-eyed demons searching the rooms. The Yagr lunged, tearing out one throat before crashing into the other two. He shredded them in a frenzy, black blood spraying everywhere. The cat froze, making sure there was no one else, then left quietly, slipping back into the night.

He felt sporadic magic use throughout the city but focused on the ones closest to continue his grisly work. Several buildings over, a pair of Dark Elves levitated a ball of green magic to illuminate a restaurant. He crashed into their backs, seizing a throat in his massive jaws and decapitating the other. The cat paused, letting the elf's dead body dangle in his jaws, listening. Satisfied, he tossed the crumpled form aside and exited to find his next victim.

The amount of magic he used to shift would not garner much attention, given the constant flares of Power throughout Banfar. He decided to speed things up, shifting into the sparrow to enter a dwelling before changing back into the giant cat to attack. His speed and efficiency increased. The boy cleared out several more buildings before spying a group of six demons and elves coming down the street.

Ethrang flew into the dark sky as the sparrow before crashing into them as the ram demon, sending bodies scattering in all directions. He didn't bother to check if everyone was dead. He did not want to be caught in the open. The boy flew away as the sparrow and immediately saw two spider demons crawling over adjoining roofs. Their white eyes and bulbous bodies made his skin crawl, so he used the wasp demon form to land on one, crushing its black body flat before sending a thick stream of green fire into the other's face.

Then the sparrow disappeared into the night.

Ethrang began experimenting with different shapes, honing his craft. Gruk, the twenty-foot ogre, appeared from around a corner, swinging a wooden bench into a group of Dark Elves, killing them instantly. A Brown Tiger rampaged in a smaller house, killing its trespassers. Furiosa emerged a couple of times, smashing heads in with her fists. He utilized the razor bird in the park before the administrative building, taking out another dozen. A blue fireball arced from a top-floor window, indicating Slashar was inside. The orphan left the area to pick on easier targets, continuing his path of destruction. He killed another score of them before shouts rang throughout the city. The enemy regrouped at the east gates, wisely deciding to stick together.

By then they were down to fifty.

Yet fifty could still wreak havoc on the fleeing Banfar citizens, especially with an Inner Circle leading them. He wanted to find a way to kill them all, but his magic was failing. A night of shapeshifting and fighting had drained him.

He watched with bated breath and sighed in relief when they all entered the administrative building. They would be spending the night in Banfar. He moved farther away before shifting into the sparrow and flying across the city to the Lower District. He was careful to shift back into himself in the alley before walking to Bagan's residence. The orphan stayed on the third floor at the end of the hall. That way, he could hear if anyone approached.

Ethrang flopped onto an uncovered mattress, wholly exhausted. He had wounded the enemy, but not mortally. There was still more work to do to ensure the safety of the citizens. He drifted off into a restless sleep.

Creak.

The sound was out of place. Ethrang opened his eyes. He did not know how long he had drifted off but suspected it was the middle of the night. The orphan knew the noise of the old building settling. This sound was someone stepping on the hallway floorboards near the stairs.

Creak.

They were now in the middle of the long hallway. He quietly rose and stepped to the doorway, peering out with heart racing. A row of dark figures moved towards him, one step at a time. Some had white eyes, but most were Dark Elves.

He made a split decision, shifted into the wasp demon, and broke through the window of his room. Suddenly, a blue shield materialized around the building, and he crashed into it, burning his face.

It was a trap.

Slashar had isolated the building he was in, wrapping it with magic. Shouts sounded as elves ran around the side of the building, hands raised. He shot green fire at them, burning their bodies to a crisp. Ethrang thought frantically and then dove back into the room, surrounding himself with a shield. All attempts to maintain secrecy were gone. He flew into the hall and unleashed a blistering stream of green fire at his attackers. The line of dark figures formed a multi-coloured shield, absorbing it. He spun around, turning into the ram demon and charged the other way. He burst apart the locked door to the back stairs as a fireball struck him on his shield.

He could not withstand it. The magic went through and heated his armour, searing him. He crashed down the stairs to the next level and then shifted into the Yagr, bounding down the next two flights to the basement, where Bagan hid his valuables. The fur on his behind was burnt off, and his skin smoked. A flurry of footsteps sounded above him.

A stout, locked wooden door greeted the orphan, so he shifted again, splintering it with his armoured head. The shapeshifter bounded down the long hall to a dead end. He turned right into a storage room and shifted into himself. The boy used his Power to move a heavy wooden chest, revealing an iron door with multiple locks.

Bagan always had an exit plan.

Only a select few knew about it. The building might be shielded, but not the tunnel below. Shouts rang behind him, and he felt a strong magic join them. It was Slashar.

Ethrang sent a thick stream of green fire into all the locks, then wrenched the door open with his Power. The footsteps grew louder as his pursuers entered the basement. A thought struck him, so he grabbed the wooden chest and iron door with his magic and heaved it through the wall, blocking the passage. He staggered from the effort and dove into the dark tunnel, shifting into the sparrow. He had decided not to spend his waning magic on a shield, hoping he would arrive at the end without needing to. Magic erupted behind him as the elves cleared their way through the blockage.

He flew to the end of the long passage as shouts erupted from the tunnel entrance. Ethrang shifted into himself and raised his arms, using compressed air to blow open the square metal trapdoor above. It led through the earthen floor basement of a warehouse that Bagan also owned.

He started climbing the ladder when a powerful magic seized him.

At the other end of the long tunnel, Slashar stood with arms raised, eyes blazing blue, using dense air to freeze his body. He struggled against it, almost strong enough to escape, but it held him in place.

Ethrang knew the game was up. They had caught the orphan of Banfar.

The thought rankled him, so he decided to gamble it all, knowing he would be dead anyway. The boy summoned his reserves of Power and aimed at the tunnel ceiling above him, unleashing a stream of green magic. At the same time, he shifted into the ogre, Gruk, knowing he would not fit into the tunnel but doing it anyway.

He prayed to the Creator.

Several things happened at once. The tunnel collapsed, caving in on him. The interference severed Slashar's link, releasing the dense air. Ethrang grew into Gruk, but the space was too small, and for a moment, it looked like he had attempted his last shift. Yet the ogre was made of something stronger than loose dirt, and he burst through the warehouse floor, fully formed.

The boy gave a ragged shout of joy and climbed out, smashing through the ground with his fists. A thought came to him, and Gruk broke through the front of the warehouse, landing on the street. He looked across to Bagan's residence then the street, calculating exactly where the tunnel was. He felt powerful magic underneath him. They were trying to clear the debris.

Gathering all the Power he had left, Ethrang pointed at the ground and shot a blistering stream of green magic up and down the top of the tunnel.

Then he ran out of magic.

Exhausted but not caring, he ran across the weakened road and stomped his enormous feet down its length with all his strength. The tunnel roof collapsed with each step, but the ogre didn't stop until he reached the orphanage. Muffled screams sounded, but they died off.

There was a dead silence.

The ogre looked around, breathing hard. He had defeated the entire enemy force. Yet even as the thought entered his head, the orphan felt a magic flare up, and then a geyser of dirt exploded into the sky.

The Inner Circle elf, Slashar, crawled out of the hole, looking beyond angry. He must have shielded himself enough to survive. Yet he was the only one.

Throwing caution to the wind, Ethrang ran at him in two strides, kicking the shielded form in the side of his body. The Dark Elf sailed down a dark alley, tumbling end over end.

Slashar rose unsteadily to his feet, head bent down, eyes blazing. He tried to seize Gruk in a cushion of air, but the ogre's strength could not be contained. The boy broke through and watched blue fire streak towards him. He dived behind a building on the right and rolled to his feet. A deep, venomous scream erupted from the alley, and the ogre ran for his life.

He passed the Reindeer Inn and turned down a side street as a massive fireball flew over his shoulder. He made it back to the top end of the Lower District and almost around a corner. A cushion of air struck him hard in the shoulder, sending him careening into several storefronts.

He did not have any Power left to shift into anything else.

The ogre groaned and got up. There were cuts all over his body. Slashar was running full speed at him, hands raised. He leapt out of the rubble, putting the buildings between them and bounded towards the park in front of the administrative building.

"I'm not going to kill you," Slashar screamed in a deep voice, magnified by his Power. "I'm going to bring you back to my Master, may we grovel at his leisure. First, I will do things even Bashan wouldn't do to you."

The Dark Elf laughed maniacally and sent several more hard

cushions of air into his back. Ethrang staggered before toppling over. The impact shook the ground. He scrambled to his feet, but then more air spun him around.

Suddenly, giant fists of compressed air slammed into his face, turning his head side to side. Slashar walked down the street with an evil grin, swinging his clenched hands in front of him, battering Ethrang's face. Blood sprayed on the road, and cuts appeared over his one eye and the bridge of his nose. The boy had been in many fights before and knew he was about to lose consciousness. He needed to get out of the situation.

Using his powerful legs, he weathered one more punch that knocked a tooth out then rolled down an alley. The ogre scrambled to the end as Slasher appeared, and he leapt to his left behind a three-storey house. He was about to run towards the park but stopped.

Ethrang took in heavy, ragged breaths. He was bruised and bleeding, as if a group of orphans had beaten him up. So what? He turned around, his anger rising.

He was an ogre. And he was raged.

The boy looked at the three-storey house next to the alley and, taking a running start, slammed into its side with all the force he could muster. The whole house caved sideways onto the Dark Elf.

Frustratingly, he saw a shield flare up as the rubble covered Slashar. Ethrang waited, his face dripping blood. He grabbed an enormous foundation rock with two hands. The Inner Circle elf pushed through the debris, shield intact as the ogre slammed the heavy stone on Slashar's head with all his strength. The rock broke in half, and the elf disappeared. He knew shields could withstand a lot, but it depended on their roots in the ground and the force of impact. The irony was that magic could be absorbed more easily by a shield than an impact. The ogre was very strong.

His answer came a moment later when the elf rose again, his face bruised. Ethrang delivered the hardest uppercut of his life, sending the Dark Elf across the street to crash into a stone wall. He didn't care that the shield burned his knuckles.

Slashar got up slowly, eyes blazing. Yet they were flickering as well. A hope surged in the boy. The Dark Elf was running out of magic.

"Change of plans, shapeshifter," he said with bloody lips. "I'm going to kill you after all." He raised both hands and sent a blistering stream of magic across the street. The ogre grabbed a piece of metal, using it as a shield, and ran towards him, bellowing in fury. The fire melted the metal and seared his hands.

Then it sputtered.

The Dark Elf disengaged, eyes widening in fear before wrapping himself in a shield, using the last of his magic.

The ogre threw away the burning metal and then hammer-fisted Slashar into the ground. The boy did not let up. His hands burned against the shield, but he saw it weakening. In a spurt of rage, he picked up the Inner Circle Dark Elf and threw him into the park across the street. Slashar landed with a thud, shield flickering, groaning in agony. The ogre, ignoring the pain in his hands, bounded across the street and uprooted a tree.

Slashar sent one last stream of magic at him, striking his shoulder. Ethrang bellowed in pain then slammed the tree trunk on the Dark Elf. He heard a cry and saw the shield go out. The tree caught fire, and he lifted it aloft.

It was like a giant torch illuminating the dark city of Banfar.

Slashar looked at him defenceless, his face bloody and body broken. Ethrang only saw hatred in his eyes.

That meant he must die.

The ogre used both hands to grab the trunk and with a mighty grunt impaled the Dark Elf with the fiery branches. It punctured his body in multiple places as the branches went deep into the ground.

The life went out of the evil elf's black eyes. The tree was upside down through his body, completely engulfed in flames. The ogre collapsed to his knees, staring at the fire, completely spent.

Ethrang had many wounds, burns, and bruises. And a hole in his shoulder.

But he had won.

The boy sucked in ragged gulps of air, then he grinned through bloody lips. The citizens of Banfar were safe.

The ogre stood up on shaky legs and found several small trees. He pulled them out of the ground with his good arm and added them to the fire. Snow fell all around him, disappearing in the flames. Slashar's body turned into black ash. Another great evil was gone from the world.

Yet there were still so many to fight.

He settled down near the fire, hurting everywhere. Yet the flames warmed and soothed him. He rested his great head back and fell into a deep sleep.

The light of the mid-morning sun woke him, along with the cold, for the fire had burned low. He rose with a groan, feeling some magic return. He used it to alleviate some of the burns and repaired the hole in his shoulder, at least on the exterior. With his remaining Power, he shifted back into himself.

The blond boy's face was puffy, burned, and swollen. His body ached, and his hands were still pretty bad. He decided to enter a mansion facing the park and collapsed on a bed, waking up at nightfall.

He felt a little better and healed more of his wounds. The orphan scrounged around for something to eat. A leg of salted ham had been left in the cold room in the basement with some cheese, and he ate heartily. The boy walked around town, ensuring no one else had survived. It was empty. He sent his presence out, finding no Dark Elves or demons.

Nodding to himself, he returned to the orphanage and chose a room on the second floor. He had the choice of any home in Banfar, but again he chose Bagan's residence. It was his home. The boy was able to heal himself to the best of his ability, but he needed Miss Owl to be fully restored. The muscles and ligaments in his shoulder still hurt, for he was not as adept as others.

Regardless, Ethrang thanked the Creator he was still alive. The orphan of Banfar slept through the night.

Awaking refreshed, Ethrang found breakfast in one of the restaurants and then walked through the alley to the First District. He looked around one last time. The boy prayed Banfar would still be standing if they won the Last Battle.

He smiled. When they won, not if.

The orphan looked up to see the clouds had dispersed, and a bright sun shone on the city. The air was cold, but it smelled clean. The wind ruffled his blond hair.

He gave his boyhood home a last look then leapt into the air as the giant eagle. Almost immediately, he landed back on the ground, crying out. His right wing didn't work right. The shoulder injury was worse than he thought.

He needed an upright shape that could cover ground quickly. It was an easy decision. He shifted into Gruk and walked towards the eastern gates. The twenty-foot ogre stopped to glance back, then stepped onto the Great Plains and headed eastward.

Despite his size, catching up with the fleeing citizens took him until the following afternoon. The soldiers noticed him first, growing larger on the horizon. Some remembered he had shifted into that shape and started yelling.

"Ethrang!"

"It's the shapeshifter."

"He's back!"

The boy ran the remaining distance and then turned into himself. He shook General Melvin's hand.

"Are they coming for us?" the man asked. The other soldiers gathered around to hear the answer. Trixie and Ollie ran up, embracing him. He winced, but Miss Owl was there, holding his hands. Her eyes blazed yellow, and then he could smile again without wincing. His shoulder pain went away, and his scar tissue vanished. A tremendous joy enveloped him at being with those he cared about. He had felt so alone.

Ethrang smiled and looked at the eager faces gathered around him. "You are all safe now. The demons and Dark Elves came, and I killed them all."

Everyone stared in amazement, then cheered.

"Wait, does that mean we can go back to Banfar?" Ollie asked hopefully.

"No, more will come. Banfar is lost."

Miss Owl pushed her glasses higher. "I think this deserves some tea. Why don't we make camp here and set up a fire?"

The general agreed and sent messengers to inform the others. In short order, Ethrang was sitting beside a warm fire with hot tea in his hands. Ollie and Trixie sat on either side of him. Rabbit sat with the general. Everyone wanted to hear the story, so he told it in full. When finished, those gathered looked at him in awe.

"You are a legend."

"You saved Banfar."

"You saved us."

Ollie was looking at him in wonder. "You are my hero."

Ethrang felt a lump in his throat. Telling the story brought out the feelings of fear, horror, and anxiety he had experienced, but it was therapeutic. He felt the emotions again then let them go, knowing the experience had made him stronger.

"Thanks, Ollie. That means a lot." He put his arm around the boy and felt a renewed hope.

Miss Owl's face turned serious. "When will you go."

"Tomorrow morning. I must be in peak form for what I need to do."

"Is there a way we can help?"

He shook his head. "You already have." She nodded.

"Why are you leaving so soon?" Ollie asked, face going sad.

"I have to do something very important."

"The Guardian?" the general asked.

"Yes, Sir."

"You got this," Rabbit said.

"Yes, Sir."

Ethrang spent the remainder of the evening on the Great Plains, surrounded by the soldiers and citizens of Banfar. The mood was celebratory, and he welcomed the camaraderie and attention. At the end of the night, he bade everyone farewell before he retired so he wouldn't have to in the morning.

At dawn, the boy wolfed down an unexpected breakfast provided by Miss Owl, hugged her, and then shifted into the giant eagle.

Ethrang soared over the Great Plains, rejuvenated and refreshed. Much time had passed since he had left the Secret Caves, but he knew it was necessary. He faced an even greater challenge, but his experience and successes in Banfar gave him strength and confidence.

It took him all day to cross the Great Plains without stopping before he entered Darkwood Forest. He looked at the twisted trees beneath him and shuddered. It was the last place in the world he wanted to be, other than Cave Mountain.

From high above, Ethrang followed their path through the forest and arrived at the clearing with the stones. He landed in the center, folding his great wings, and shifted into himself. The malevolence of the forest immediately surrounded him. He walked behind the stone to the stairs leading downward and found the cavern empty.

He felt a stab of fear and doubt. He was too late. They were gone.

Then he remembered Kylo saying there was another cavern, and he sent his presence out. He felt life forms in an adjacent clearing not too far away. The shadows lengthened throughout the forest as the sun set, and he pushed down his mounting fear. Walking with purpose, he made his way through the twisted forest with his senses alert.

A voice reached his ears. It was familiar.

He broke through the trees into a second clearing and found the Lost Ones.

Kylo looked at him in surprise. He was standing before a hundred magic wielders seated on the ground before him, next to a roaring fire. Similar stones surrounded this clearing, and he suspected there was a cavern nearby.

"Hello, Ethrang," the young-looking Leader of the Lost Ones said. His little sister Clare waved from the front.

"It's good to see you, Kylo. I need to ask you if the healings have been a success."

"In almost all cases, I can cure the madness. I have improved my technique. My magic only allows me to heal around ten a day, but I'm almost done. Only a few remain, and then we depart Darkwood. We are leaving tomorrow. Where are the others? What happened?"

Ethrang sighed with relief that he had returned in time then stepped forward. "I need to talk to you about something very important. Better yet I will show you."

The Leader of the Lost Ones stared at the shapeshifter curiously then nodded. "Show me."

21

Chip Oathbinder was dying.

He floated in a sea of pain and darkness, losing his sense of time and reality. Disembodied voices taunted him, encouraging the boy to let go. Visions of death and destruction appeared out of nowhere, vividly describing how life was hopeless. It showed him that everyone died, their lives washed away by time until even the myths and legends were forgotten. So what was the point?

His breathing grew tight and ragged, sometimes overshadowed by a persistent scratching noise. It was tantalizingly close. Grotesque, leering faces appeared out of the darkness, coming right up to the slitted bars. At first, he stared at them in fear, then almost welcomed the accompaniment.

He was so lonely.

The cage pushed in from every direction, encasing him in a prison of cold metal. He wondered if anyone appreciated how free they were. How lucky they were to move. The fools even took breathing for granted. He tried to cough but couldn't, wheezing instead.

Scratch.

There it was again. If only he could find the source and choke the life out of it. His heart fluttered in anger, and then he had trouble getting enough air, which caused his heart to beat faster. The anxiety came on wave after wave. He beat it by welcoming death, grinning in its face.

"Kill me," he rasped. "Do your worst."

He started laughing, causing more breathing problems. He realized that the original cage, before it was compressed, at least allowed him to move a little. He wanted the old cage back so badly. It would feel roomy compared to this metal coffin. It struck him that many things in life felt devastating until one realized they could be much worse. People's definition of life's lows seemed absurd from his current point of view. Could it get lower than this? He chuckled through his cracked lips. Sadly, yes. He could be in the Demon King's hands.

Scratch.

There was that confounded noise again. Where was it coming from?

At first, he had weathered the worst of it, replaying memories of his young life, focusing on every detail. It worked for a long while. The pain had subsided to a point where he did not feel the need to scream anymore. He kept the dark thoughts at bay.

But there was something else with him.

He could feel its dark presence all around. It pulled at the threads of his thoughts, unravelling them. He began to lose focus, and the pain increased.

The voices started, whispers at first.

"Die and be free."

"There was never hope."

"Love is an illusion."

He made the mistake of answering them. "Life is freedom. There is always hope. Love is real."

Yet it rang hollow. The voices started screaming at him, getting insistent.

"I will lap up your blood."

"Embrace me forever."

"Eleanor will die."

Eleanor.

When he thought of her again, the voices vanished. The pain subsided. He relived their memories, filling him with a kernel of happiness. It was enough for a while.

Scratch.

The sound angered him, and he lost her image. Where was it coming from? Consumed by rage, he searched for it, trying to move his hands and feet. His body convulsed with fury, hands clenched.

Scratch. Scratch. Scratch.

In utter horror, he realized his finger was doing the scratching. It was the only thing he could move. A wave of panic hit him, sending his finger off again.

Scratch.

It was his body and mind trying to move. Trying to live. It was the only thing he could do. The reality sobered him, and he refocused on his memories.

Yet it was not enough. The darkness returned.

There is always a way.

He was missing something. Han said he would lose himself in darkness unless he saw life. He had already tried reliving his memories, but it was not enough.

Memories. That was the problem. He was reliving them, but not life.

He needed to create new ones.

Scratch.

This time, he laughed at the sound despite the tidal wave of pain. He wasn't mad at it anymore. It was his body experiencing the tiny bit of freedom it could. Moving his finger was all he had.

Life.

He needed to see life. Chip picked a point in his distant memory and started from there. He returned to sitting on Auntie Clare's lap before a roaring fire while she read a story. Yet instead of reliving the memory, he began to change it. He decided to create his own story.

He made life as he would have wanted it. He was not born with red eyes in this new life, and she was not his aunt. Clare was his mother. He grew up in the castle, befriending Chase and the princess. That he would never change. King Barton was a kind ruler and invited them to feasts in the throne room. The boy went to school and trained in the evening with his father, Garth Stone. Xander was a bard, telling stories for the king.

There was no magic in the world or Pass of Death or Demon King. Everyone helped each other, and trade flourished. He ended up marrying the princess, and they ruled with benevolence. Chase voluntarily became their squire, and they spent many nights celebrating their good fortune in life, grateful to the Creator. The people of Vanalon all received an education and employment. Nobody was poor or homeless. Laws were fair, and punishment was meted out with an eye on rehabilitation.

They lived long, fulfilled lives, reaching their full potential through learning and applying internalized moral truths. Their word meant something along with honour and integrity.

Ample time was given for rest and leisure. They treated everyone with dignity. Community games and fairs were routine, and they mingled with all citizens. Chip would visit Ulrich and Anna on their farm outside Banfar, for they were his uncle and aunt. The children were his cousins. The other cities picked up their governing model, and Amrika thrived in peace and prosperity.

Chip sighed, lost in his recreation of life. The pain and darkness had almost vanished during his reverie. He had seen life, created it in his mind, and the darkness retreated. The incredible power of visualization struck him. It was impossible to achieve something without visualizing it first. Visions could be used as goals to show the mind that it was possible. Garth Stone always said what you imagined and focused on would become reality.

He decided to switch the visualization and focus on his future.

First, he vividly created a scenario where he could escape from his cell and defeat the witches. He would kill them all, save Dora. Then he imagined finding the lost Light Elves, convincing them to join his cause. They would stand united in the Last Battle against the Demon King. He would destroy the Dim and the Lord of the Dark Elves and stand victorious on the walls of Toron. Chip would unravel the mystery of the Great Forget. He would also find out who his parents were from King Luminor.

That thought sent him happiness and joy, even in that dark place. Finally, he would once more see the man with the silver hair. The image sent love through him, and the Guardian of the Races learned the true power of the human mind.

Visualizing life sustained him despite his body failing. The witches had not given him water for days, leaving him in darkness, but now he saw life. He saw hope. He would not go mad.

The orphan kept his visualizations going as his breath became shallower. Even the scratching stopped as his body shut down. The pain, once so prominent, dulled. He knew why. His mind was strong, but his body was dying.

It would not be long now.

A shaft of light pierced the darkness. For a moment, he thought the man with the silver hair was coming to greet him in death.

No, it was the door to his cell. Morgeth opened it fully and walked in, followed by a tall woman with white hair in a midnight-black cloak. Next to her was a man wearing a green woodsman's garb. Chip recognized them as Dark Elves.

"How long has he been in there?" the white-haired woman asked.

"Six days," the High Witch answered smugly, expecting approval.

The woman made no expression. "Did you give him food and water?"

"Not the last three days. He didn't deserve it."

The Dark Elf turned to her. "My Master will be displeased if this boy doesn't survive. Take him out."

Morgeth smiled. "With pleasure." Her eyes blazed bright blue, and she pulled the cage apart with her Power. She pulled him out and then straightened him with no warning.

Chip screamed, hearing his muscles tear, feeling a level of pain he did not think possible, and then, strangely, the pain disappeared. His sight began to dim, and a soothing numbness took over.

"You fool, he's dying." The tall woman stepped forward. "Let me." Her eyes flared an even stronger blue than Morgeth's, and she sent her magic into his body. She started repairing his injuries and then gasped. The Dark Elf released her magic and looked at the elf in green. "Heal him. You are designed for this."

"Yes, Mistress." His eyes blazed an insane yellow, and Chip felt powerful magic infuse his body, stopping his sight from dimming further. Everything seemed to be repairing at the same time. Muscles, tendons, and cuts reformed and closed. Scar tissue vanished. The elf's eyes widened slightly, and a drop of sweat appeared on his brow. He made no further face and then stepped back.

The boy looked down at his body in amazement, forgetting how it felt to be healthy and alive.

"Let's see if his mind is still intact," the white-haired woman said shortly.

"Oh, I doubt that..." Morgeth started.

Chip felt a powerful presence enter his mind, but he had already assumed the Calm, forming it easily. He surrounded her with it and probed her memories. For a moment, he got in, recoiling at a memory of her companion dismembering trolls, and then she pushed him away.

"That will not work on me," she said out loud. "I am not controlled by emotion like others. It is a weakness. You slide in unnoticed because those fools are controlled by anger or greed." The elf woman tried to read his memories, but he gritted his teeth and pushed out the powerful presence.

She withdrew from him, her eyes returning to normal, and stared at the High Witch for a long moment. "You...made him stronger. He even pushed me out of his mind. Few can do such a thing. It's what happens when you challenge someone who has been trained." Her tone turned condescending. "You risked much following your emotions. They make you weak. If something had happened to him, you and everyone else would have suffered in his place."

Morgeth looked taken aback but recovered quickly. "Yes, Mistress. My apologies."

The elf woman looked at Chip. "I am Hagatha. This is Blade. We have travelled far to find you. In a few days, when I'm satisfied with our allegiance here, we will take you to see our Master, may we grovel at his leisure. Blade wishes to punish those responsible for attacking us in the village by the river. He will exact vengeance on your Protectors. He cannot change what he is. Know that you are safe from harm until we arrive in Cave Mountain. After that, you will be at my Master's whim. Put him with the others."

"Of course, Hagatha," Morgeth said, bowing her head. She grabbed the boy's elbow and led him into the hall. "Go sit with the others, but no talking."

Chip nodded and walked into the center of the star cavern. He relished being able to move freely. The six days in the cage had felt like a month to him. He saw Eleanor first and smiled, feeling a lump in his throat. She looked visibly relieved. The others were all sitting beside her at a long table except the Protectors, lined up against the wall. Chase was nowhere to be seen.

Hooded witches stood at either end of the table, arms folded in the sleeves of their black robes. The rest of the coven sat at the other tables. Dora was alone at the back, staring at him with sad eyes. Only nine chairs ringed the altar since the actions of the Darkwood King had killed four Seers. Zara sat in the middle, holding her staff, flanked by the other ancient women. The eye symbol stood out prominently on their black dresses. The grey-robed acolytes gathered along the perimeter.

The boy made eye contact with everyone, who gave him slight nods or small smiles. Kristan risked a wink.

Morgeth strode to the center of the room in front of the large stone altar. The green fungi running up the walls illuminated the Secret Caves in an eerie green light.

"I would like to introduce our honoured guests, Inner Circle member Hagatha, and our Master's weapons expert, Blade. They are emissaries from Cave Mountain." The witches stood up as one and bowed low. "We have prepared for this moment for millennia, guided by *The Book of Seeing*. Now, more than ever, the acolytes must profess their allegiance and join the coven as witches or servants. All who do so will be exulted. We will present those who do not as gifts to the one true Force. Hagatha has asked to observe our rituals and training to provide a report to our Master, the Lord of the Dark Elves. We will do a mass sacrifice in three days to celebrate the occasion."

Zara stood up, her hunched form leaning on the staff, and smiled crookedly, black teeth showing. "Thank you, daughter, High Witch of the Secret Caves. As the High Seer, I will lead the ceremony."

The witches chanted as she walked up to the altar, picked up a book, and turned to stand before the great eye carved into the stone.

She waited until they finished then read several passages about sacrifice and the need to give back to the world by killing those who worship the false Force. Chip looked at the twins, who were trying not to grin. The idea that these people believed the Creator was a false Force was absurd. He realized that with enough group pressure, threats, and repetition, people could be indoctrinated into thinking the opposite of what was true.

"Now, let's drink the blood of the enemy." Zara watched with a leer as several witches emerged to freeze the wizards and Protectors with their magic. They cut each of their thumbs one by one with a shiny dagger and held a silver bowl underneath to catch the dripping blood.

The High Seer beckoned the collectors forward, holding a gold bowl covered in runes and symbols. They all poured the blood into it. She smiled greedily and chanted the verses he had heard earlier. The witches joined in, some lifting their arms with ecstatic faces. When finished, Zara took a generous helping and then passed the bowl to the other Seers. The witches lined up, and everyone sipped blood from the golden bowl.

Chip looked at Eleanor, who had a disgusted look on her face.

The others wore similar expressions except the twins, who were more amused than anything else.

The High Seer took the bowl back, lapped up whatever remained, then licked her bloody lips. She watched as everyone returned to their seats. "This whets our appetite for what is to come. We will make a great sacrifice to honour the union with our new friends." She looked at Hagatha and Blade with her milky eyes. "Now, the true Force wishes to see more blood spilled. The weapons expert will provide the entertainment." The witches murmured excitedly to each other, some gushing like young girls.

Hagatha nodded to Blade, who walked gracefully through the gathering to stand before Garth Stone. "I will save you for last." The weapons master stared at the weapons expert with a face of chiselled granite. They were of equal stature, with a touch of grey at their temples.

Blade scanned the other Protectors before settling on Shimko. "I challenge you to a duel, human. Pick a weapon of your choice. I will use the same one. Know that I am best with the sword."

The stocky Protector narrowed his eyes and nodded.

"Bring their weapons," Hagatha commanded. Morgeth sent several witches scurrying to one of the rooms. They returned a few moments later carrying axes, clubs, swords, daggers, and maces.

"I choose daggers," Shimko said quietly.

Blade's lips turned up in a slight smile. "Very well. Take two."

Shimko moved to the pile of weapons and picked up two straight, double-edged daggers. Blade gestured to the open space before the altar, and they both walked over. Zara sat in her oversized chair with the other Seers, unable to hide a wicked grin.

The Protector and the Dark Elf faced each other.

Blade removed his green cloak and pulled two wicked curved daggers with black blades from his belt. They took their stances. Chip watched with bated breath, praying the elf was not as good as he seemed.

Blade turned to Zara, waiting.

"Oh, what an honour," she cackled. "Begin!"

The weapons expert crouched low, then remained still. Shimko approached warily with a higher stance. When they were almost within striking distance, the Protector broke off and circled. The elf turned his feet enough to follow his attacker without wasting excess energy, eyes looking at his opponent's hips.

Shimko leapt in with a thrust to the elf's face followed by another to his midsection. Chip watched as Blade blocked both attacks and darted to the right in a blur of motion, his hands windmilling at a speed that did not seem possible. The curved daggers sliced up and down the Protector's left arm. The knife fell out of his nerveless grip and the limb dangled uselessly. Blade seemed to know exactly where to cut. Shimko grimaced in pain but remained in his stance. Blade calmly waited.

The witches whispered, pointing at the growing puddle of blood on the floor. Chip glanced at Garth, who looked like a piece of stone.

The combatants circled. Shimko switched stances and leapt forward, right hand extended in a full thrust. Chip knew it was a slight overextension, and Blade took advantage, knocking the knife away with his dagger and sliding in close. He then worked on the Protector's midsection, shredding him into ribbons. The elf leapt back and waited with a bored expression. The stocky Protector stumbled but somehow remained upright. He held his remaining dagger in a shaky hand, face going white. Blood poured out of him to the delight of the witches. Many started clapping with glee.

"You chose the wrong weapon," Blade instructed. "In close quarters, with no armour, the curved dagger is superior to the straight." The Dark Elf waited again patiently.

"Enough. Finish him," Hagatha ordered.

"Yes, Mistress." Blade attacked with blinding speed. Shimko attempted to block, but a curved blade cut his hand off at the wrist. The Dark Elf moved smoothly behind him and sliced his throat. Blood sprayed onto the Seers, who joyfully opened their mouths, basking in the crimson droplets. The elf tossed Shimko's body to the side and yawned.

Chip felt sick, and then his anger flared. He reached instinctively for his Power, but the Wall was immovable. Frustration began to mount in him, and a growing apprehension. This elf was like nothing he had seen before. For once in his life, he feared for the weapons master.

"More!" Zara cried. Blood ran down and dripped off the warty lesions on her face.

Blade turned to his mistress. "Can I challenge the Protector with magic?"

Hagatha shook her head. "I do not want you to kill the boy until our Master has studied him, may we grovel at his leisure."

The weapons expert bowed. "As you wish, Mistress." He walked over to the remaining Protectors, eyeing Bulch with an amused look. He stopped in front of Ward, scanning his rippled, muscular physique. "You. Choose a weapon."

Ward did not hesitate. "Axe."

Blade nodded then looked at Carvor. "And you."

The Silver Sword champion stared without flinching. "Sword."

The Dark Elf smiled. "Get your weapons. Try to last long enough to entertain our hosts."

The two Protectors went to the pile while Blade pulled one of the swords off his back and a short axe at his side. They gathered before the altar, holding their weapons at the ready.

"Begin!" the High Seer shrieked, clapping her hands together.

Carvor looked at Ward and nodded slightly. They moved to either side of the weapons expert, who crouched motionless, waiting. The elf looked down so he could see both in his peripheral vision.

The Protectors attacked at the same time. Ward leapt in with a savage overhand strike of his double-sided axe while Carvor stepped forward with a long thrust. Blade blocked both at the same time then spun left, stepping forward to stab Ward's exposed mid-section. He turned immediately and threw his axe into Carvor's thigh. They both retreated, gasping, as blood poured from their wounds.

Blade stepped to the middle and pointed at his axe. "Do you still need that?"

Carvor grunted, tearing it out of his leg. "No, you can have it back." He threw it hard at the Dark Elf, who caught the whirling weapon by the handle before it struck his face. The audience clapped.

Blade resumed his stance. The Protectors decided to jab and feint, readjusting their technique. The elf nodded in approval, parrying their attacks. The opening came when Ward, holding the wound on his stomach with his free hand, overcommitted with a sideways swipe of his axe.

Blade leaned back out of range and then, like a spring, brought his axe down on the man's knee. A sickening crunch sounded as Ward's kneecap shattered. He grunted, face contorting in pain, then hobbled backwards. Carvor took advantage of the distraction and came in with a blistering attack.

The Dark Elf pirouetted and retreated at an angle, parrying every blow. His movement caused the Silver Sword champion to expose his broadside and Blade danced in, jabbing under his left armpit. Carvor made a funny noise, and his left arm went limp, indicating the sword had damaged a major nerve. He stepped back to regroup, his left arm dangling.

Blade yawned and waited.

The Protectors shared a long look, and then both ran at the elf. Carvor lunged with his sword pointed at Blade's chest, overcommitting, while Ward took a long hop on his good leg and raised the axe with both hands, exposing himself. Chip knew they were both intentionally making errors, causing Blade to hesitate, torn over who he should take advantage of. The elf resorted to blocking instead, knocking the sword sideways and raising his axe to stop the two-handed swing.

Yet Ward had gone all in, throwing the axe hard, his corded muscles bulging. The weapon spun through the air, partially striking Blade's axe then deflecting into the left side of the elf's chest.

Blade kicked Carvor away and looked down, a ripple of anger crossing his calm face. His eyes suddenly shone an insane yellow. He levitated the axe out of his body and let it fall to the stone floor with a clang. Dark blood ran from the gash on his chest, then yellow magic infused the area, and his wound was gone. He reformed his shirt, looking like nothing had happened, and released his magic. Chip's mouth hung open, and he glanced at Garth, who arched an eyebrow.

Blade nodded with approval. "Well done. Few can mark me. Yet you made a terrible mistake. You now have no weapons." He ran at Ward and raised his sword. The Protector lifted both arms in defence, but that was what the elf wanted him to do. Blade dropped low and swung the sword sideways, severing Ward's good leg at the knee.

The man landed by instinct on his shattered leg and went down, unable to support himself. The Dark Elf calmly drove his axe into Ward's forehead and left it there. The Protector went limp, eyes vacant.

Carvor charged in to slice Blade's exposed back, but the elf rolled to the right, and his sword met air. The Silver Sword Champion looked down at his dead comrade then turned angry eyes on the elf. With a scream, he attacked, going through his patterns to perfection. Blade countered each move with expert precision, his footwork and speed unparalleled. He made no mistakes.

Carvor's error was tiny, leaving his foot out a moment too long, and the Dark Elf became the attacker. His sword flashed in the green light in glorious arcs, each move perfectly executed. Carvor blocked with grim determination, retreating step by step, waiting for his moment to counter. It never came.

Blade's speed was too much, and his block too slow. The tip of the elf's sword sliced the wrist of his sword arm, then his shoulder and neck. His blocks became partial, and the Dark Elf did not slow, stabbing him repeatedly until his blood flowed. No wound was mortal, but they were adding up.

Carvor finally stumbled, and Blade lifted his sword to finish him off.

"Do you enjoy beating young novices and cheating with magic? Where is your honour?" Garth Stone called out, stepping forward, eyes smouldering. The witches gasped at the affront.

Blade paused in midair. He lowered his weapon and turned, facing Garth Stone. "You dare speak to me that way, human?"

"I dare to challenge you." The weapons master stood with feet shoulder-width apart. There was an eagerness in his eyes that Chip had rarely seen before. He wanted to test himself. The boy realized Garth had trained his whole life for this. He had never met his equal. Now, he relished the chance.

"I accept your challenge, human." He seemed about to lift his sword to end Carvor's life but waved him off, turning his attention back to the weapons master. "What is your weapon of choice?"

"The sword. I am best at it."

Blade smiled. "Retrieve it." Garth moved to the pile and pulled out his sword. Carvor walked past him with eyes down, too ashamed to look at anyone.

The weapons master strode forward and faced the weapons expert in the eerie green light of the Secret Caves.

Garth Stone's face was a piece of chiselled granite. Blade turned to the High Seer, who grinned fiendishly. Chip looked around. Morgeth was watching intently, her face betraying a hint of concern for the human Protector. The other witches leaned forward with anticipation.

Everyone seemed to sense this was an important duel. The way the elf and man walked and moved differed from the others. They held themselves a certain way, exuding confidence and skill, and if that wasn't enough, one only had to look in their eyes.

The weapons expert stared at Garth Stone's unflinching grey eyes.

"Begin!" Zara shrieked, her face still covered in blood.

Both men smoothly circled each other. Their stances were similar, with one foot forward and bodies angled sideways to minimize the striking area. Each held their sword in a relaxed manner with the tip chest high.

Blade waited calmly for the attack, but Garth remained defensive. The other Protectors had leapt in, to their detriment. He would not make that mistake. Chip would have done the same. He knew Garth had already analyzed the elf's moves to create a strategy. The boy had not observed any weakness, and he'd never seen anyone move that fast. His heart rate quickened.

Blade's eyes tightened, and he shimmied forth with a blistering attack of short, crisp thrusts. Garth deftly blocked each one, his face razor-focused, feet moving backwards but always maintaining his stance. The flurry continued, and he angled off to avoid backing into the Seers. By its nature, the movement shortened the distance slightly between the combatants, and the tip of Blade's sword nicked the weapons master's face. A thin red line appeared on his cheek, and his eyes widened slightly.

Blade withdrew and nodded. "You are the fastest human I have ever seen, but not fast enough." Garth attacked without answering, knowing if the elf was speaking, he would not be focused.

He used short thrusts, keeping his body tight and movements controlled. Blade fluidly blocked each attack, moving with stunning grace and agility. When he was forced to angle in front of the altar, Garth cut him off, closing the distance, and footswept him. Blade pulled his leg back, but the impact wobbled him enough that the weapons master's blade slid down the elf's sword and nicked his hand.

Garth retreated with a strange gleam in his eye. "No one is fast enough all the time."

Blade looked at his hand in surprise, then his eyes blazed a stunning yellow, and the scratch was gone. "Well done, human, but know that no one is like me."

The elf launched into a broader attack, sword swinging in wider arcs to increase power and open new angles. Chip knew it was riskier, for it opened an opponent up to a counterattack of the exposed areas.

Garth took advantage, blocking then attacking, and the fight became a blur of back-and-forth fencing. The boy watched in awe as the two fighters executed flawless patterns with superb swordsmanship. Chip looked at Carvor and Bulch, who watched with wonder. Some of the witches gasped, and others applauded. Hagatha seemed bored.

The fight raged for a long time, both combatants moving at speeds the eye could scarcely follow. The swords became blurs punctuated by the sharp ring of steel on steel. Their feet moved in perfect patterns, lunging and retreating with light footfalls, maintaining perfectly centred stances. Their breathing was controlled, but a light sheen of sweat appeared on both foreheads. They continued their dance with death, two of the finest swordsmen the world had likely ever seen.

And then Garth slipped.

It was the blood droplets in front of the Seers. The weapons master's back foot slid sideways as he tried to pivot. Blade leapt with a long thrust, and Garth blocked a hair too late. The tip entered his left shoulder and sliced down, creating a deep gash. New droplets of blood spattered the stone floor. The Seers clapped, some emitting high cackles.

The weapons master grunted and then kicked the elf hard in the stomach, sending him tumbling backwards. Blade regained his feet in time to block a ferocious attack. It was a risky move that almost worked. Chip knew that as time wore on, Garth would bleed out or tire, so the time for defensive swordplay was gone.

The weapons master attacked hard then lifted both arms in a wild overhand strike. Blade seized on the opening, thrusting at Garth's midsection, but that was what the weapons master was expecting. He turned to the right, letting the sword slide past him, then smashed the elf's face with his pommel. The sound of several teeth breaking was audible.

For a moment, Blade's eyes rolled back, and Garth turned his sword around to attack the elf's exposed neck. Somehow, Blade got his hand in the way, and the blade sliced across it, sending several fingers to the stone floor. The elf leapt back in shock, looking at his hand, watching blood spurt out of the severed digits.

"That's...not possible," he looked up at the weapons master with grudging admiration. Garth was about to leap in, but a yellow shield formed around the elf, and his fingers regrew right before their eyes. In mere moments, he had a newly formed hand. Chip had never seen anyone heal that fast save Chase. Blade released his magic and resumed his stance.

"Everything is possible," the weapons master said, sighing. A light sheen of sweat covered his face, and his shoulder continued to bleed. "Let's get this over with."

Blade nodded, and they circled. The opponents attacked and retreated, putting on a show for the ages. Chip watched his trainer in awe, finally seeing him at his peak, using all the tools he preached. His respect and love for the man increased, and he marvelled at what the human mind and body could achieve. Garth Stone was at his full potential.

But it was not enough.

Slowly, the tips of their swords got through as they both tired. More wounds appeared on each of them, but Garth's stayed while Blade healed himself. Many times, the Protector's blade slid off the Dark Elf, for he was made of something different.

As time wore on, Garth slowed, bleeding from many spots. More wounds appeared, and then he stumbled. Blade danced in and drove his sword through the weapons master's stomach, coming out his back. Garth cried out and even while impaled swung his sword across the elf's neck. Blood spurted out of both fighters, each inflicting a mortal wound. Chip stood up in anguish.

Blade staggered back and fell hard, holding the neck wound with his hand. Dark blood spurted between his fingers. Yet despite the force of the strike, the cut only went partially through. The blow would have decapitated any other opponent, but the Dark Elf was unlike anyone else.

Blade's eyes blazed bright yellow as he convulsed, and then his body relaxed. The blood stopped spurting. Within moments, he was whole again and stood up, facing the weapons master.

Garth Stone tottered on his feet, the elf's sword sticking through his body. "You are the best I've ever...seen," the weapons master whispered, spitting up blood. "But you will never have...honour."

Blade stared at him, and a look of sadness briefly crossed his features. He grabbed his sword and pulled it out of the weapons master. Garth groaned and almost fell. The elf spun him around and pushed him to his knees.

The weapons master looked at Chip. "Don't give up," he mouthed through bloody lips. Tears formed in the boy's eyes as he watched the man who had taught him everything give his final lesson.

Blade stood behind him, his face going through different expressions, then took his sword with both hands and swung sideways at Garth Stone's neck. Chip watched in horror as the weapons master closed his eyes, waiting for the end.

22

The sword struck Garth's neck, then stopped. Blood leaked out of the small cut. Blade stood stock still, freezing his weapon, then stepped back. Garth began to fall forward, a look of peace on his face. The Dark Elf's eyes blazed a ferocious yellow and stopped the man's descent. Magic infused Garth's body, and his wounds started closing. The weapons master levitated to his feet, surrounded by yellow magic.

And then he opened his eyes.

Garth took a deep breath and stared at Chip, a rare look of surprise on his chiselled face.

"Why did you do that?" Hagatha asked. Morgeth stood beside her, looking relieved. Even she wanted Garth to live.

Blade turned to her. "He is not like other humans, Mistress. I want to keep him alive and train with him. He is a worthy opponent. In three days, I will kill him."

Hagatha seemed about to object then shrugged instead. "Very well. It matters not." She looked around. "That is all for today. Show us to our quarters."

Morgeth scurried forward. "At once, Mistress. Follow me." She turned to the other witches. "Send everyone back to their rooms."

The black-cloaked women began ushering the prisoners out. Garth Stone walked by Chip and winked. The boy smiled back in relief, overcome with emotion. His tears were now ones of joy. He saw Dora nod to him slightly before turning away. The Seers seemed a little disappointed that no one else had died, but they started talking animatedly and soon were cackling. It had been quite a show.

The mean, older witch grabbed Chip's arm and shoved him towards his wing. He glanced at Eleanor and the others, offering a small smile of encouragement. They looked different without their magic, but he still saw hope in their eyes. The orphan was glad to see that their rooms were in the same arm of the star as his. The old woman steered him to the end of the long hall.

The witch opened the metal door, and his heart clenched. He expected to see the cage, but it was gone. She shoved him in and shut the door with a clang.

The orphan took a deep breath, grateful for the ability to do so. He stretched his arms wide in the darkness, bathing in his freedom. He was stuck in a little cell deep in the Secret Caves in the middle of Darkwood, yet he knew it could be much worse. Everything was relative. The cage taught him how to control his mind and appreciate the smallest things. He breathed blissfully, saying a prayer to the Creator.

Then he realized how tired he was. For the past week, he had slept very little. His body had healed, but his mind needed rest. The boy slumped onto the cold stone floor and fell into a deep sleep.

The door opened, and he awoke refreshed. There was no way to tell the time, but he assumed it was morning. The old witch led him down the hall to the central cavern. The wizards, Protectors, and trolls were each given their own table.

"Don't talk to anyone, or you will be punished," the old witch said, pushing him down in an empty seat near Xander. Everyone waited, and then male servers in grey robes brought plates of eggs, bread, and cheese. The treatment surprised him, but he suspected they wanted to keep them healthy until they arrived at Cave Mountain. The High Witch also likely wanted to please Hagatha after almost killing him.

The Seers arrived, and he watched in disgust as they picked green fungus off the walls and ate it. They took chunks with them and arranged their chairs before the altar. Zara picked up *The Book of Seeing* and began reading to the others.

Hagatha and Blade arrived. Chip watched as the white-haired elf woman walked purposefully over to Xander's table and sat opposite him. The weapons expert stood to the side, motionless.

"Orb Stealer," she said without preamble.

"Ah, Hagatha, it's good to see you," Xander said politely, feigning a smile.

"Many have dreamed of your capture and devised new ways of torture for you alone."

"I'm flattered," the wizard replied, finishing his last egg.

"We were trapped for three thousand years due to your meddling."

Xander's face turned serious. "I fight for my side, and you fight for yours. Mine happens to be righteous and good. You represent evil and death." Blade shifted slightly.

Hagatha stared at him with no expression. "I cannot be swayed by foolish emotions such as revenge, anger, or greed. My Master, may we grovel at his leisure, can be swayed. It is in his nature and has its uses when one has nearly unlimited Power. I feel no empathy for you, but you will wish for death a thousand times over before this is done."

"At least I will die with honour. Your soul will answer for your crimes when you perish."

"Crimes?" She looked genuinely perplexed. "The Light Elves cast out their own people because we embraced the Power. They locked us away for millennia because we tried to evolve. Now, we have white-eyed demons with magic. The Balance has spoken. Our cause is just."

Xander stared at her, then broke out in a long, boisterous laugh. She waited without expression. The old man wiped his eyes. "My goodness, you think that's evolving. You really don't know, do you?" Hagatha looked at him blankly. "Those white-eyed abominations have lost their souls. Barko said as much before we killed him. Why do you think they have white eyes? Their spirit essence has given them magic at the price of their soul. The Demon King's descendants are soulless horrors that will die forever. The Balance has indeed spoken, but not in your favour."

Her eyes narrowed. "You lie."

"Sadly, I do not. Even if you win this war, the Dim will kill you. It will unravel the very fabric of the universe. The Demon King thinks he can control it, but nothing can. Even if the Dim is destroyed, the Force of Death will control your Master and kill everything. Even if you win, you lose." Blade shifted again.

"I will ensure the Dim is destroyed after it serves its purpose. As to the Force of Death, my Master will control the Earth, not it."

The old man leaned forward. "Allying yourself with the witches is a grave mistake. They have found ways to bring Death through. That Force will control Killian and enter the world of life. If you hand us over, it will be the end of everything."

She stared at him for a long time. "As you said. You fight for your side, and I fight for mine. Did you think you were going to win?" This time, she gave herself a tiny smile and rose from the table.

Xander smiled broadly. "Good day." Hagatha started walking away.

"Mistress," Blade said, "may I stay and train?"

She waved without turning. "Do as you must."

He bowed and sought Garth out. Chip couldn't hear what they were saying, but he saw each reach for two daggers, and they squared off. Both executed perfect patterns, yet again, Blade slowly gained the upper hand by using his magic to heal his injuries. After a while, they stopped, and he healed the Protector. The pair picked up another weapon and continued.

The wizards returned to their rooms so the acolytes could take their seats. Chip gave his companions slight nods each time he saw them.

For two more days, they ate their meals in silence. After each one, Blade would train with Garth. Chip noticed the weapons master was adjusting, anticipating the other's move despite his speed. It took longer each time for Blade to defeat him. Both began acknowledging the other with grudging respect, and they even exchanged words, commenting on technique or the meaning of honour. He only caught snippets but found the exchange fascinating. The boy picked up their techniques, seeing moves he did not think possible. Many were tiny movements or a shift in stance that the untrained eye would not catch, but he memorized them, replaying the patterns in his mind using his newfound visualization skill.

If the mind could see it, then it could be done.

The third day came, and he realized it was the day of sacrifice. It was also the day Blade promised to kill Garth Stone. Upon awakening, the orphan felt anxious.

At lunchtime, Zara made an announcement. "Tonight, after dinner, we will be entertained with a duel to the death, followed by a celebratory evening of sacrifice for those unable to see the true Force." She smiled, displaying her black teeth. "We will send our emissaries back with great gifts for our Master, may we grovel at his leisure. It will be a joyous occasion." She looked over at Hagatha, who nodded with approval.

Chip felt his heart flutter, knowing their time was running out. He knew which cell Chase was in. A group of witches fed him meals by seizing their Power and linking before opening the door and sliding his food through. He felt sorry for his friend. It wasn't the cage, but he had been holed up for nine days in the dark.

For someone who cherished freedom and movement, the tall boy would have a hard time. His thoughts turned to Ethrang. The blond orphan would not be returning with help after all. It was a fool's dream anyway. Chip was happy that his friend had made it out alive.

Dinner came and went, and then everyone gathered before the altar. The grey-robed acolytes lined the perimeter while the witches took their seats. The wizards sat at two tables, surrounded by the black-cloaked women. The Protectors and trolls stood to the side.

The High Seer moved to the front, staff in hand. "Welcome. We gather here to honour our alliance with the Dark Elves and our Master, may we grovel at his leisure. We will begin with a passage from *The Book of Seeing* and then reflect on how important it is to make sacrifices to the true Force. He is the real Creator. Without his guidance, we would not be here. We will start with a toast of blood."

As before, the witches cut them and collected their blood before pouring it into the large gold bowl. Zara drank greedily, spilling some down her chin, and then shared it with the others. When all were satiated, she drained what was left, licking her lips grotesquely. The woman's warts shone brightly in the sickly greenish light. She read a long passage from *The Book of Seeing* about the importance of recognizing truth, then spoke of the joy of sacrificing others who couldn't see it."

She cackled and clapped her hands together. "Now, let's whet our appetite further with some entertainment." She turned to Blade and waved him forward.

The weapons expert walked over and faced the crowd. "I challenge Garth Stone to a duel to the death." Everyone clapped excitedly. Some still had blood on their lips. "What is your weapon of choice?"

Garth stepped forward. "All of them."

Blade stared at him and nodded. "Yes, it would be fitting. Retrieve them." The Protector walked over and selected several different weapons. Garth sheathed his daggers, sword, and axe, then picked up a mace and slid it through his belt. Finally, he grabbed One Eye's stout club.

Blade already wore similar items and selected his mace to start.

The two combatants squared off.

Both man and elf stood bristling with weapons.

"In the name of honour, do you agree to duel with no magic?" Garth asked suddenly.

Blade studied him, then nodded. "In the name of honour." Chip noticed Hagatha roll her eyes.

The weapons expert looked at Zara.

"Begin," the High Seer squealed, leaning forward in anticipation.

The combatants closed the distance. Each had a feral gleam in their eyes, knowing that all their training culminated in this moment.

They both lifted their weapons at the same time. The mace arced through the air, the metal ball whistling with stunning speed. Garth swung the club down with both hands.

And let go.

Blade tried to block it but the weapon spun over his arm. The end struck him square in the face, sending a spray of dark blood over the altar. The elf staggered, releasing the mace. It struck Garth a glancing blow on the shoulder, but he ignored it, pulling out his axe, which he also threw with stunning speed. It struck the Dark Elf in the shoulder, the blade going in halfway. The weapons expert looked down in shock as the weapons master pulled out his sword.

Blade savagely wrenched the axe out in time to block Garth's life-ending thrust. The sword deflected sideways and struck the altar stone in the center of the great eye. Sparks flew.

Garth was overbalanced, and Blade struck him hard with the butt of the axe. The weapons master stumbled backwards, a welt forming on his forehead, and Blade chopped down, slicing open his thigh. Garth leapt back, barely hanging on to his sword. The elf threw the axe at him with lightning speed, but Garth, only through a lifetime of training, turned at the last moment, and it sailed harmlessly over his shoulder. The weapon landed squarely in the forehead of one of the Seers, exploding her head open like a rotten melon.

The witches gasped. Zara turned in horror, watching her friend slide off the chair. The combatants froze, waiting.

"Carry on," Hagatha called. The High Seer looked like she would protest then shrugged, waving for them to continue.

Blade pulled the two short swords from his back and advanced. Garth held his longsword at the ready. The elf's shoulder was bleeding, but the wound was not as deep due to his thick, strange skin. His face was a mash of broken teeth and a crushed nose. Garth limped slightly, but his face was chiselled granite.

Blade attacked first, his speed uncanny. Yet even so, Chip noticed his right arm moving slower due to the shoulder wound. Garth retreated as he parried both blades. The sounds of metal on metal echoed throughout the cavern. The weapons master's face was a mask of concentration, eyes flicking about, looking for a weakness. He followed the slower right arm and made his move.

Blocking a right thrust, he slashed down on the elf's retreating wrist with both hands, causing a neat gash. Blood spouted out but Blade ignored it, flicking his left sword to nick Garth's right shoulder. The trade-off was worth it.

Blade's right hand began to droop, and Garth seized the opportunity, coming in with a blistering attack on his bad side. It took several frenzied swings, but finally the Dark Elf's sword slipped out of his fingers, clattering to the ground.

Now, it was the short sword against the long. Garth lunged in repeatedly, using his greater reach, and the tip started getting through. Holes appeared all over Blade's body, staining his green woodsman clothes. They were not deep due to his tough skin, but they were many.

The elf started to slow, realizing with shock that he was losing. Then Blade gambled by leaping in, allowing Garth's sword to go through his right arm, while he drove his into the Protector's midsection. Garth managed to turn enough that it sliced across his ribs then released his sword to grab the elf's wrist. He slammed the man's arm against his knee several times until the short sword dropped to the floor. Blade fumbled for his dagger, but his right hand wasn't working. Garth kicked him hard in the stomach then leapt up as he doubled over with a vicious jumping knee, landing full on the elf's chin.

Blade toppled backwards, the sword still in his arm, and Garth jumped on him, slamming the elf to the floor with both knees. Blade suddenly produced a dagger in his left hand and drove it into Garth's side.

The weapons master grunted, grabbed the elf's wrist, and twisted hard. Blade released his grip, and Garth pulled the dagger from his side. The weapons master yanked another from his belt and then, straddling the elf's body, put both daggers under Blade's chin, drawing blood.

Garth Stone leaned forward so they were face to face. "It is never too late to regain your honour."

Blade's eyes blazed yellow momentarily, breaking the agreement, but then he released his magic. The weapons expert dropped his hands to the stone floor, awaiting death.

Garth Stone held both blades to the elf's neck, staring into his eyes.

Then the weapons master stood up and cast both daggers aside.

Blade sat up slowly, staring at him in shock, then looked down in shame.

Those gathered were dead silent. Some had their hands raised, about to clap, and froze in disbelief.

Garth Stone stood with his hand on his side, breathing heavily. Chip looked on in admiration.

His teacher had given everything and won.

At that moment, Chip thought he heard a distant, dull thud. A few other witches seemed to notice at the back. A few even looked up, then their attention reverted to the scene before the altar.

"What is the meaning of this?" Hagatha asked coldly, looking at Blade in disgust. "You men and your ridiculous code of honour. It's illogical, but I suppose you can't help yourself. If you won't kill him, I will." Her eyes blazed a striking blue as the Dark Inner Circle elf raised her hands and pointed them at Garth Stone.

The weapons master turned to her, standing tall, his face at peace. "Stop."

Hagatha turned to see who spoke with a cold look.

Morgeth stepped forward. "I wish to keep him."

"Keep him for what? He is a human."

The High Witch's eyes narrowed. "So am I. From where I stand, a human beat an elf. He...amuses me."

Hagatha studied her with pursed lips then dropped her hands. "Fine. Blade, heal yourself and the human. Know that I am disappointed. Our master will be most displeased. My loyalty requires me to inform him of this."

Blade stared at her for a moment longer than he should then bowed. "I understand, Mistress. Forgive me."

"I do not forgive. Only the weak do."

The weapons expert bowed again, and then his eyes blazed yellow. He healed himself and Garth at the same time. Both combatants gave each other curt nods. Blade looked down as he moved to stand beside his mistress. The weapons master went back to stand with the other Protectors. Garth Stone looked at Chip, who couldn't hide his pride. The man never ceased to amaze him.

Zara stood up, looking a little flustered. "That…was entertaining." She glanced around, and the witches clapped politely. "But now it's time to see more blood." Her face lit up at the word, and she absently licked her lips. "Bring out the acolytes who refuse to see the truth."

A score of witches went down the arm of the star that held the grey-robed magic wielders who would not join the coven. Chip watched in disbelief as they led more than fifty people to the front. They were going to sacrifice them all.

A fly landed on his neck.

Chip froze. It must be Ethrang. The Banfar orphan wouldn't use his magic to communicate, so they needed to go somewhere else. The Guardian looked at the older, mean witch, clutching his stomach. The fly left his neck.

"What is wrong with you, boy?" she whispered.

"I have to go… My stomach…please."

She rolled her eyes. "Make it quick. I want to be back to watch the bloodshed." The woman turned to another witch, and they escorted him to his room. Morgeth looked over, and the witch pointed down the hall. Chip continued holding his stomach, pretending to walk funny. He saw the High Witch nod out of the corner of his eye.

Before he entered the hall, the boy glanced back to see the acolytes form a line in front of the altar. The witches began their grotesque chant.

For sacrifice of blood on stone,
We seek to rend the flesh from bone.

Water and wind, to Earth and fire,
Give us power, our hearts' desire.

The chant continued as he reached the end of the hall. The older witch shoved him in hard, causing him to trip and land on all fours. His anger ignited, but he ignored it. They both stood in the doorway.

"Hurry up. We aren't taking our eyes off you." He got to his feet and turned to see a fly hovering above them. The Guardian smiled, showing all his teeth.

"What are you laughing at, boy," the mean witch asked coldly.

Suddenly, Ethrang was standing behind them, eyes blazing green. "Duck."

Chip dived to the floor as the blond boy flung the witches with compressed air headfirst into the back wall. Two audible cracks indicated their skulls had fractured. They slid to the floor, unmoving.

The Banfar orphan stepped inside. "Quick, they will be here soon. What do I do?"

Chip's mind raced. "Push against my Wall in the bottom left corner. It's the weakest spot. Ethrang's eyes shone a bright green with a hint of silver and he inserted his presence into the Guardian's mind. Chip felt him locate the spot and push with considerable Power.

Nothing happened.

Shouts erupted down the hall.

"What's going on in there?" A high voice called. "We sensed magic."

Chip's heart rate increased. There was no time. He thought frantically. "Wait. Try pulling it out instead."

Ethrang focused. Footsteps could be heard coming down the hall.

Chip felt him tug on the weak brick. His Wall started to shift. "Use all your strength."

The blond orphan pulled with everything he had, his eyes shining, and a pop sounded.

The brick pulled free.

Three witches appeared in the doorway, staring in shock at the green-robed boy. Ethrang grinned.

Chip Oathbinder pulled his bricks of Power into himself, eyes blazing a ferocious red. The boy's rage ignited as memories of the cage swirled in his mind. The feeling of his magic was indescribable, like finding a large piece of himself that had been missing. It felt like he was truly free.

He felt invincible.

The orphan with red eyes pulled in his Power like a tidal wave, and something snapped in his mind. Another piece of it opened up, and newfound magic appeared. His Power had increased.

"Move," he commanded Ethrang in a voice like thunder.

"Gladly," the blond boy squeaked, pressing against the wall.

The witches seized their magic. One was a Blue, and the other two Green. They linked and formed a shield.

Chip knew nothing would stop his rage. Red coils of Power snaked around his body. The boy raised his arms and released a fireball of such Power that the witches simply vaporized as it smote through their shields and bodies. His magic continued through the bedrock of the Secret Caves. The whole place shuddered, and bits of debris fell from the ceiling.

Ethrang stared in awe. "It's good to see you, Guardian." Screams erupted, and immense magic flared up in the arm of the star leading to the tunnels.

The green-robed boy smiled. "The Lost Ones are here."

Chip nodded and strode forth from his dark cell. A group of witches were running down the hall towards them. Without slowing, he sent a blistering stream of red fire into their bodies. They burst apart and spattered the walls.

What he saw then was pandemonium.

The witches were sending streams of multi-coloured fire towards the cavern entrance. A rumble sounded overhead, and he sensed Kylo's Power explode into the ceiling. Giant stalactites began falling, crashing down on the witches and upending tables and chairs. He saw Xander and the others huddled in the middle. Chip threw out a hand of air and pulled them towards him, surrounding them in a red shield.

They flew down the hall, and he shoved them into an empty cell. "Guard the door, Ethrang." Chip stepped in and entered Xander's mind, probing his Wall. "Where's the weakest part?" he asked quickly.

"The last brick."

"My goodness, boy, I don't remember."

Chip seized on the word.

Remember.

"Show me your memory of putting up your wall!" Explosions sounded in the cavern. People were running down the hall.

Xander pulled his memory of putting up his Permanent Wall after they tortured him mercilessly. Chip's eyes widened, but he remained focused. He watched the wizard put the bricks up and then noted the last one, a little off center. He grabbed the brick of Power and pulled. Magic flooded into the Grand Wizard, and his eyes blazed blue. "Do the same to the others. I will hold them off."

Even as he said it, witches rounded the corner, and Ethrang unleashed green fire into them. A blue shield surrounded the black-cloaked women which repelled the attack.

Chip stepped out into the hall and unleashed.

The knot of witches tried to scramble backwards, but the red fire blasted through their shield, melting their bodies into a gooey mess. The boy turned to the cavern. It looked like the witches were gaining the upper hand against the Lost Ones.

Zara stood at the end of the hall, holding her dark wooden staff. The High Seer's warty face contorted with hatred. The other Seers fanned out behind her, hands raised. More witches turned to face him. Seeing the old hag made Chip's blood boil. He strode forward and sent a wicked fireball into their midst.

It struck the staff and disappeared.

Chip blinked. The Seers released their magic at him as one. He formed a thick shield and repelled it. The boy counterattacked with a stream of deadly red fire, but the staff absorbed his magic. The High Seer cackled with glee. "The shapeshifter created a new Path for you, but I have the power of the one true Force."

Chip was tired of hearing that phrase. He decided to test it out. He sent a thick stream of red magic into the staff, pulling in more Power and concentrating on the piece of wood. Zara continued to cackle, standing triumphant.

And then the staff disintegrated.

"The true Force is the Creator," Chip screamed, sending a massive red fireball into the evil woman.

Her eyes opened wide. "I See...my death..."

It blew through their shield and struck her full in the chest. The High Seer of the Secret Caves wailed as she disintegrated into a fine mist of warty flesh and bone. The witches and Seers retreated to the center of the cavern.

Xander and Eleanor, the twins, and Daria gathered beside him. Their eyes blazed with magic. Chip walked into the cavern, surrounding them all with a red shield.

The coven of witches had regrouped. Chip watched Kylo, and the remaining Lost Ones retreat down the tunnel. A group of witches pursued. They had been overpowered.

"I will get the Protectors," Xander called. "Shield me."

Before Chip could protest, he ran around the altar. The boy threw a shield of red Power around the old man.

Morgeth walked to the fore, staff in hand, her face an ugly mask of fury. Dora stood beside her, looking terrified. "You cannot defeat us all, boy. You will pay for what you did to my mother." The witches raised their hands as one. "Acolytes, join us or die," she screamed.

The grey-robed magic wielders looked at each other. About half ran up.

"Link with me," Chip said.

And then they attacked. The full force of the coven's magic struck his shield, and he gasped. He used the other's Power to strengthen it, holding them at bay. The acolytes' eyes blazed to life. These were the ones who the witches allowed to use magic. They were the most loyal. The grey-robed figures raised their hands and unleashed.

Chip's shield buckled but held. It was all he could do to hold them off. He saw Xander come back with the other Protectors in tow.

He could not maintain the shield around him. He needed everything he had to hold his.

Hagatha stepped out from the throng. Blade stood beside her. The Inner Circle elf's eyes blazed a terrifying blue. "Looks like you will die after all, Orb Stealer." She raised her hands and sent blue fire at the Grand Wizard.

Xander formed a shield around himself and the Protectors. Garth Stone stood at his side. The impact pushed them back against the cavern wall. The wizard groaned, feeding all his Power into the shield.

But she was too strong.

Chip watched in horror, unable to lend aid.

Slowly, Xander's shield thinned, and his robes began to smoke. Beads of sweat formed on his brow. The Protectors began turning red as the heat of her magic worked its way through.

Hagatha laughed evilly, finally giving into her emotion. "I have to say it feels good to watch you burn, old man. Your Protectors will die with you. I will finish the job Blade couldn't. Honour is for fools." The weapons expert looked at her sharply.

She sent more blue magic into the shield. It was almost gone. The Grand Wizard gasped, and Garth's fingers began to melt.

The weapons master turned to the Dark Elf. "Blade, it...is never... too late."

Hagatha laughed shrilly. "It is too late for him. My Master will take what honour he has left. He will learn true loyalty."

Blade looked back and forth between the weapons master and his mistress.

Then his face changed.

A dagger appeared in his hand, and he plunged it into Hagatha's chest. The white-haired elf woman stared at him in complete surprise. "You...of all people." She turned her hands on him, sending blue fire into his body. Blade seized his magic at the same time, healing his melting skin. Various weapons suddenly appeared in his hands. He plunged them into the old woman with blinding speed.

Another blade went into her mid-section, and then his axe found her collarbone. Her magic sputtered out, and she stood for a moment, unable to breathe, turning to stare at Xander.

The emotion of pure hatred contorted her features. Blade pulled both swords off his back and beheaded her.

Chip clenched his teeth, holding on to his shield, watching Blade run over and heal Xander and the Protectors. He let out a sigh of relief. Garth Stone looked at the elf and placed a hand on his shoulder. Blade nodded then turned and ran through the witches' shield, yellow eyes blazing. He started to melt but reformed on the other side.

The the killing began.

The weapons expert slipped through the witches, dealing death at will. They fell around him in droves. Chip felt the shield weaken.

At the same time, the Lost Ones returned, much smaller in number but there nonetheless. Kylo led them with blazing brown eyes. His masterful use of Power shook the ground under the witches, making it unstable. The black-cloaked women stumbled. Morgeth turned in anger, screaming at them to hold.

Chip looked at Dora and nodded. The young girl took a breath then seized her mother's staff and threw it aside. The High Witch turned to her with disbelief then backhanded her across the face. Morgeth pointed both hands at her daughter. Chip, not needing to use his full Power to maintain the shield any longer, threw a wall of red magic between them. It was not necessary since Dora's eyes had blazed a stunning blue, and she shielded herself.

"Everything has been a lie, Mother. It's over." She calmly walked away from the High Witch to stand with the wizards.

Now, it was Chip's turn.

He pulled the metal door off Chase's cell across the cavern. His best friend sprang out, the red chips in his eyes shining wickedly.

"It's about time."

The witches had shrunk to less than half their number, and Chase dashed through the shield to join Blade, unleashing his pent-up ferocity.

Morgeth turned to Chip, seething with rage. Despite her beauty, all he could see was ugliness. "How?" she managed to ask.

He looked at Ethrang, Blade, and the Lost Ones. "With lots of help."

The High Witch of the Secret Caves raised her arms, sending all her magic at him. He maintained his shield and picked her up with his Power, sending the woman high into the air. The Guardian flung her hard against the ceiling, impaling her on a stalactite.

It came out of her stomach, and she held it in disbelief with two bloody hands. Morgeth let out a dying scream and then went limp. Chip brought his hand down and dropped her lifeless body onto the altar with a jarring thud. Blood spread around her to cover the stone.

She would be the last sacrifice.

The other witches wailed and screamed, seeing their leader fall, and released the shield. They attacked individually, mad with grief. Kristan and Thomas broke off the link and moved among them like blond wraiths of death, burning them with blue fire. Ethrang turned into a green-shielded Darkwood King, rending flesh from bone. Eleanor stayed with the Guardian, adding to his Power. The boy turned to the group of grey-robed acolytes. He magnified his voice with magic. "If you still choose to stay and defend this cave of lies and evil, do so. Those who want the real truth, step aside."

The Guardian waited with Eleanor. Sadly, only a few broke off from the fight. He sighed, raised his hands, and sent red fire into those left standing. They erupted into pillars of flame before turning to ash.

The grey-robed acolytes who would have been sacrificed a short while ago stood off to the side, cheering.

Chip turned to finish the rest of the witches, but Blade, Chase, Ethrang, and the Lost Ones had completed the job. Dora stood off to the side. She had removed her black cloak. Morgeth's daughter looked like a lost little girl. Eleanor hugged him tight. He picked up the Queen of Vanalon and swung her around. His joy was indescribable.

He reluctantly set her down. "Morgeth's daughter, Dora, helped me. She is on our side now. I showed her the truth." Eleanor nodded without a word and went off to console the scared girl.

Everyone else gathered in the middle.

Chase stared at Blade. "I'm confused. Aren't you a Dark Elf?"

The weapons expert shook his head. "Not anymore. They have no honour."

"What will you do now?" Garth Stone asked, walking up.

Blade sighed. "I have caused much pain and suffering in the world. Killian made me into a weapon of evil. There is only one way to atone for it." He looked up. "I will attempt to assassinate my Master."

Garth nodded. "What are the chances of success?"

"Slim," Blade answered. "His Power is beyond imagination, but I am one of the few who can get close." He looked at Chip. "He is more powerful than you, but you can take much pain. Your mind is strong. Perhaps there is hope, after all." The Dark Elf smiled, but then it vanished. "There is another named Victor. He is the only other like me, but bigger and better. He will not be persuaded to fight without magic. It may take all of you to defeat him."

Chase nodded. "I was itching for a fight anyway."

Blade looked him over. "You fight well, but not like him." He gave Garth a sly grin. "Who throws a club?"

The weapons master let out a rare laugh. "Who shows their enemy all their moves? I needed to do something you wouldn't expect."

Blade nodded. "Well played."

Ethrang shifted into himself, and Chip hugged him before he could say a word then pushed the blond orphan to arm's length.

"What took you so long?" he asked, trying not to laugh.

"Well, I was a little busy, you see." They all stared at him. "I only had to escape the Secret Caves, go to Cave Mountain and kill half of the greater demons, take a bunch of their shapes, flee the Demon King who chased me into the center of the mountain, get past the baby black dragon, evacuate Banfar before the Dark Elves and white-eyed demons enslaved the city, kill the entire invasion force including an Inner Circle elf named Slashar, and then get Kylo and the Lost Ones to join me in rescuing you."

No one said a word.

Garth arched an eyebrow. Kristan and Thomas started snickering.

"So what did you really do?" Chase finally asked.

Ethrang threw up his hands. "I just told you."

Kylo stepped forward. "He showed me his memories. Ethrang speaks true." Everyone began patting the skinny orphan on the back. The boy tried to maintain his bravado, as if it was nothing, but couldn't help smiling.

"You must give us the full story soon," Chip said. "How did you get through Darkwood and enter the Secret Caves unnoticed?"

"Easy," Ehtrang answered. "We killed everything in our path. It's not that hard with one hundred Lost Ones. The wild boars charged us, but they took off after half of them died. There were only a dozen four-armed apes left alive. Kylo buried them in a deep hole. After that, we didn't use magic to avoid detection. I ran through the stone entrance door as a battering ram demon, killing the witch guard on the other side. I was worried it made too much noise, but no one heard."

Chip slapped his forehead. "That was the thump I heard before the Seers were going to sacrifice the acolytes. A few other witches heard it, but everyone was too focused on Blade and Garth. Then you landed on my neck."

Ethrang nodded. "I told Kylo to give me a bit of time so I could break through your Wall. It worked out rather well."

Kylo's face took on a sad look. "We lost half the Lost Ones." Then his face hardened. "Yet we got our revenge. The witches cannot hurt us anymore."

Chip nodded. "There are still a few lesser witches in the cities and likely a few cults, but we will root them out. The head of the snake is gone."

Daria pushed forward. "I can help heal any who need it," she said to Kylo. "We can also treat any of the acolytes who are not mentally well."

The Leader of the Lost Ones smiled. "I have improved your technique. I would love to show you." She smiled.

One Eye stood next to her, shaking his head. "Too much magic for me. Give me a good fight with soldiers any day."

"Sounds good to me," Chase added. "I've been locked up for nine days in complete darkness. Is there anyone left to fight?"

"Yes," Chip replied. "The Last Battle. But first, we need to find the Light Elves. Morgeth's daughter, Dora, is on our side. She will show us where the Seeing Stone is. Let's free these acolytes from their Permanent Walls. That practice must end for good." He looked down. "I also would like my old robes back. These grey ones are depressing." Everyone nodded.

Chip walked over to Eleanor and Dora, who seemed in better spirits. The girl even smiled.

The queen of Vanalon spun on him. "I heard she saw you naked." His mouth dropped open. "And kissed you."

Chip blushed. "Well...it's not... It wasn't..."

Eleanor laughed and hugged him. "It's alright. She told me what happened." The queen kissed him. "At least now us girls have something to talk about."

He stood there, looking perplexed, then smiled. "Dora, what will you do now?" he asked.

"You are coming with us," Eleanor said firmly.

"I'm ashamed for being a part of such great evil," Dora said sadly.

"It wasn't your fault, and it's never too late to change," the queen said, taking her hands. "Doing good in the world is contagious. Even one person can make a huge difference. The shame will go away once you forgive yourself. What do you say?"

Dora looked up at them with tears in her eyes. "I never had real friends before. I have only known Darkwood and the Secret Caves. I have only known darkness." Her eyes filled with a heart-wrenching yearning. "I want to live and see the world. I want to be free."

Chip smiled. "Now you are free."

They both hugged her, and she latched on, sobbing with joy.

"Can you take us to where my belongings are?" Chip asked.

Dora wiped her eyes. "I saw her take your things into her chambers. There are stairs at the back leading down into a small cavern."

"What's in there?"

The daughter of the dead High Witch of the Secret Caves looked at him. "The Seeing Stone."

23

The next few hours were a flurry of activity. The Permanent Walls were removed from the grey acolytes about to be sacrificed, and the servants were released from bondage. They pledged allegiance to Chip Oathbinder and agreed to join the Lost Ones under Kylo's leadership. Together, they were over one hundred strong. The bodies were cleared and burned in a pit which vented through fissures in the hill.

The witches had created a network of cells, pits, and kitchens over the millennia to sustain their evil coven. The books were burned with the bodies except for a few copies that would go into the Wizard's Guild library for study. Chip asked the servants to erase the runes and symbols throughout the caves. One day, they would cleanse the trees of Darkwood too. Dora and several former servants brought their things from Morgeth's quarters, and they gratefully changed into their old robes.

When finished, the place had a different energy. It felt lighter as the weight of darkness lifted. Everyone gathered before the altar, which had been cleansed of blood and the great eye sanded off. It now looked like a stone table.

Chip gazed upon the survivors and felt a newfound hope. Besides Chase and Garth, only two Protectors remained, Bulch and Carvor. Of the dozen trolls who set off, only One Eye and Daria had survived. After Mary's death, there were six wizards and Dora. Kylo stood in front of the Lost Ones.

Chip leapt onto the stone table and raised his voice.

"We have lost good people in our quest. Many more have died today. May the Creator shine on their souls."

Everyone bowed heads, and the trolls thumped their chests. The Protectors held a hand over their hearts. The boy looked up after a moment of silence.

"We have rid the world of a great evil, yet it still seeks a foothold. It wants to manifest in the Demon King and end life on Earth. A creature called the Dim seeks to destroy all it touches, including existence. We have been victorious today, but the greatest fight is still to come, the Last Battle. Only together do we stand a chance to defeat these ancient evils. We will go through the tunnel under Darkwood and leave this cursed forest. From there, we must part ways, but all of us will stand together in the capital city of Toron to face our enemies. I thank you for your allegiance and uphold you to it. We don't fight for us. We fight for everyone. We choose Life over Death. We choose the true Creator."

Everyone cheered and applauded. Chip saw joy and hope, which had been missing for far too long in this dark place. "Gather supplies. Take any items of value. I for one don't wish to stay a moment longer in this place. We will reconvene here. Dora, take the magic wielders and Protectors to Morgeth's chambers."

The girl nodded and led them down the furthest arm of the star. At the end was a finely detailed metal door that opened into a hallway with plush carpet. It led to a gorgeous living area. Velvet couches and chairs sat next to beautiful wrought iron tables supporting stained glass oil lamps. These were already lit, bathing the room in a soft light. Gold-framed paintings with strange symbols covered the stone walls. Luxurious throw rugs softened their steps as they stared in wonder. Strange artifacts and objects stood in special alcoves. Most looked to be things for rituals. The smell of incense filled the air.

"I see she lived lavishly," Chip noted. "Most people in power do. What about the High Seer? What do her chambers look like."

Dora shook her head. "Not like this. Her chambers are empty. She lived with the other Seers, sleeping on stone beds. Zara got her joy from Seeing and sacrificing, not material things. The dark Force sustained her."

"That is the correct term for it," Chip agreed. "Please take us to the Seeing Stone."

The girl led them into Morgeth's bedroom, which boasted a four-poster bed adorned with luxurious quilted blankets and silk pillows. The ceiling was made of polished glass, which served as a mirror. Chip wondered why someone would put a mirror on the ceiling of their bedroom. He glanced around and saw Garth with a rare look of embarrassment. The boy forgot that Morgeth liked him and stifled a laugh. Ethrang looked at him funny.

Dora picked up an oil lamp and moved to a silver door at the back of the large room. She opened it and led them down carved stone steps. They entered a small, square cavern with a stone table. On it rested his pouch with the dragon egg and the sheathed unicorn dagger.

Chip retrieved his pouch and looked at the perfect oval egg inside. He said a silent prayer of thanks to the Creator and tied it to his belt, doing the same with the horn. The boy looked at Dora, perplexed.

"Where is the Seeing Stone?" He felt a stab of fear. Had it been moved?

Dora laughed. "It's in the center of the table." Chip turned around with a blank look. "Here, let me shine some light on it. She brought the oil lamp closer.

Then he saw it.

The light reflected slightly off a glass sphere. He stared in disbelief. It looked so fragile and beautiful. He could see right through it except for the hint of an outline.

"I see it. Now, what do I do?"

She smiled. "Feed it with your Power and say the name of the person you are searching for."

Chip took a deep breath and nodded. He was finally going to find the missing Light Elves. The boy seized his Power, red eyes flaring to life. He gently sent his magic into the sphere, which immediately glowed. He sensed it had once held a power beyond imagining, but it was almost empty. Only a flicker remained. It felt oddly familiar. He knew in the core of his being that this was the cause of the Great Forget. Someone had released the incredible power of this orb to erase history and make people forget. Why? He brushed his conjectures aside and reached for the Calm.

"Show me King Luminor of the Light Elves."

The glow around the orb suddenly increased until it was several feet across. Chip stepped back but maintained his flow of magic.

An image began to form in the white light. The boy held his breath.

King Luminor appeared dressed in flowing white robes. He had shimmering silver hair fastened back with a gold circlet above his pointed ears. He stroked his long white beard. The old elf sat on a stone bench on top of a hill, gazing at a breathtaking white palace framed by a bright blue sky and perfectly formed clouds. Quaint white houses lined polished stone roads below him, leading to lush green vineyards and fields. The sun bathed his face, and the wind ruffled the ends of his luxurious hair.

"That is Elvar," Xander breathed. "But the weather... It is summer... How is that possible?"

"I do not know, but it is so beautiful," Chip said in awe. "He looks sad. Dora, what do I do?"

"Tell the stone you seek him and pick it up," she instructed.

"I seek King Luminor of the Light Elves." The glow and image vanished from the stone. Chip's heart raced. Did he make a mistake?

The boy picked up the stone, which was incredibly light. Nothing happened, and he looked up in consternation.

Then he felt a pull towards his left. The feeling stayed with him.

"When you release your magic, you won't feel the pull anymore, but it will be there when you connect again." He nodded, and his eyes returned to green. The pull disappeared. He broke through his Wall, and it returned.

Chip turned around, severing his magic. He looked at them with wonder. "It will take me to him. I feel it. Let's go before it runs out of power." He felt a growing excitement.

"I still do not understand how it's summertime there," Xander muttered.

"Neither do I, but I know it will lead me to Luminor."

"So what are we waiting for?" Chase called from the back. "I personally never want to be in a cave again."

"I second that," Ethrang laughed.

Chip put the Seeing Stone in his robe pocket, and they headed back to the main cavern. The servants carried in supplies and food, passing them around. Dora went behind the altar and brought forth her mother's staff.

"What should I do with this?" she asked with disgust.

"Do you want it?" Chip asked.

"No," she said quickly. "It reminds me of her."

"Xander," Chip called. "Do you want a staff to match your brothers? It does contain darkness, but it will provide you with a defence against powerful magic, at least for a short while."

"Yes, why not. It will help an old man walk. I can handle the darkness." He winked. "After all, I'm not my brother."

Dora passed him the staff, and his eyes flared blue. "It does hold great Power. Sometimes, you have to use the enemy's weapons against them."

"Indeed," Chip said in a gravelly voice, trying to imitate the wizard.

"Good show. Let's be on our way."

In short order, everyone was ready to go. Chip felt a growing need to find the Light Elves without further delay. He started walking and then realized he had no idea where to go. "Uh, where is the tunnel under Darkwood?"

Dora laughed. "Follow me." She took one last look at the Secret Caves and led them out the exit tunnel. Instead of turning left at the first fork, which would have led to the entrance out of the hill, she continued straight. The tunnel hit an end, and she turned left without slowing. A large metal door appeared before them.

"Only my mother knows the symbol to open it, but we don't need to bother with that anymore."

Dora seized her magic and shot a blue fireball into the door, sending it whirling down the tunnel. Everyone's eyes widened.

It was clear the daughter of the High Witch was done with the Secret Caves. She smiled and waved them on. They lit torches pulled from sconces on the walls and walked down a passage carved through stone.

They walked through the night, stopping every few hours to rest and eat. The deafening silence in the tunnel felt too similar to the cells. People talked in whispers as if afraid the denizens of Darkwood above might hear. Garth and Blade discussed battle tactics while Eleanor described the outside world to Dora. Ethrang relayed the details of his adventures while everyone listened in amazement. No one knew the exact time of day, but the trek was shorter than going through the forest.

Nothing impeded them in the straight tunnel. Nobody wanted to sleep in that environment, so they continued. Xander guessed they would get out by late afternoon. Despite being enclosed with little visual stimulation, the time passed quickly compared to the cells.

"The end is up ahead," Dora said. The light revealed another metal door. She seized her magic and destroyed it. They walked around the twisted metal to climb stone steps. These led up to a large trapdoor she pushed open with a cushion of air.

They were near the edge of the forest between three stunted trees. The late afternoon sun shone weakly. Everyone piled out, and Dora closed the door. It had rocks attached to the top, making it look like part of the forest floor.

"Blade, is this where you entered?" Chip asked.

The Dark Elf nodded. He had put his hood on now that they were almost out of Darkwood. "We arranged a meeting with a witch from the Hill People village a week's ride east."

Chip grimaced. "How many attacked you in the village of the Hill People?"

"I think all of them."

"Uh, what happened?"

Blade gave him a look but said nothing.

"Alright then."

They did not have to walk far before they were at the edge of Darkwood, looking at the black stone outside the perimeter.

"We were this close to the tunnel entrance the whole time?" Chase complained.

"The witches would have collapsed it on you." Dora said.

"Oh, nevermind."

Chip breathed in the fresh air in the late afternoon sun. Xander had been correct in his timing. A feeling of freedom washed over him despite his exhaustion. The boy stared at the black rock, sensing its evil presence. He broke through his Wall and surrounded it with red Power. The symbols and runes on the rock melted away. A black shadow seemed to move away from it and dissipate in the sunlight.

Everyone stared at him.

"Sorry. I really didn't like that rock."

He held on to his magic and pulled out the Seeing Stone. Immediately, he felt a pull to his right. His eyes widened in surprise.

Chip released his magic and looked at the others. "It wants me to go west."

Xander blinked. "West is the Dwarf Kingdom. It is certainly not summer there. I assumed it would be somewhere far to the south, perhaps past the Swamplands, though no one has ever made it through."

"I have to trust it. Let's follow and find out."

"Very well," the wizard agreed. "It is called the Seeing Stone, after all. Let's walk south a few leagues first to see if our friend, the tracker Rake, is in the area. It's been ten days, but you never know."

"The unicorns may be there too." Chip felt a rush of joy run through him at the thought of being reunited with the elegant animals. It would also shorten their journey considerably.

"I'm afraid Hagatha attacked the unicorns on our way to Darkwood," Blade said quietly. "She has a particular hate for them, despite the claim that she feels no emotion."

Chip felt a stab of fear run through him.

The Dark Elf noticed his discomfort. "They shielded themselves, so she only managed to kill two white ones. I'm sorry."

The boy felt relief and sadness. He nodded. "Let's go."

They did not have to travel far. Two leagues further on, they found Rake camping by a fire. Horses were tied to a small cluster of trees, munching contentedly.

The tracker from Yucan stood up in surprise, taking in all the people. "Well, I'll be. Good day to you, Sirs and Madams." He bowed low.

"I'm surprised you are still here," Chip said with a wide smile, shaking his hand. "You know the wizards, but the group behind me are the Lost Ones. They were enslaved by the witches and released into the forest."

Rake looked frightened. The scars on his thin cheeks stood out in the setting sun. "What about the witches? Are they coming?"

"The witches are dead. We killed them all." The man stared in disbelief. "Can we join you by the fire? It's been a long day."

Rake finally found his voice. "Of course. I don't have enough to feed them all…"

"No need," Chip said. "We brought food and tents. We will sleep here tonight. Do you know, by chance, if the unicorns are still around?" The boy held his breath.

"Of course, they are always close by."

Chip couldn't wait any longer. The boy seized his magic and sent his presence out. A league to the south, he felt a connection.

It was Redmane.

The unicorn exploded with joy, and a short while later galloping hooves sounded. The herd crested the rise, and Redmane appeared with the white ones in spear formation. The horse skidded to a stop before the boy, and Chip hugged his neck, feeling him shiver with excitement. The unicorn nuzzled him.

Chip instinctively leapt on his back, feeling a rush of pure joy. Ethrang and the twins did the same, shouting wildly. Chase landed on one in a single bound, which prompted Kylo to join them, showing great agility as he mounted a white one. The others looked on wide-eyed.

"Let's go for a run," Chip yelled, and they took off across the meadow. The wind whipped through his hair as they ate up the snow. He felt one with the horse, wild and free. Memories of the cage made him feel grateful, and he raised his arms to the sky, laughing uncontrollably. The others joined in.

Ethrang climbed to his feet on the back of his horse, holding his arms out. The white unicorn dipped into a hole, and the blond orphan flew off its back. He shifted into a sparrow and was suddenly back on his horse, laughing hysterically. The twins raced each other, whooping with joy. Chase was pumping his fists, screaming at the heavens. Kylo grinned from ear to ear.

They turned around and raced back, seeing who could get there first. Redmane won easily.

The riders pulled up in front of the others. Everyone was mesmerized by the sight. Garth Stone arched an eyebrow while Eleanor and Dora rolled their eyes.

The Lost Ones started cheering and came up to pat the unicorns.

Kylo leapt off. "Simply amazing."

"Fastest way to travel," Kristan laughed.

"Then why couldn't you beat me?" Thomas asked, giving him a light punch.

"I have to let you beat me in something," the stronger twin tried to say with a straight face.

Chase sprang off, landing like a cat. "I miss that."

Chip patted Redmane before lowering himself to the ground. He held the horse's muzzle and explained they would leave in the morning. The red unicorn made a musical whinny and dashed off into the field.

Without asking, the servants bustled about, preparing dinner. More fires were lit using wood from a nearby thicket of trees and in short order the companions were eating various meats, vegetables, and stews.

The wizards, Protectors, and trolls sat with Rake along with Blade.

"Let the Triumvirate know the witches are dead," Xander said between bites. "Have them root out any remaining cults in all cities and disband them. The Lost Ones will travel with you. Make sure they are not sent to the Wizard's Guild. That's how this trouble started in the first place. They were originally going to go to Northbane, but since we are heading west for a while, they should be housed in Yucan. We can pick them up on the way back. At that time, we will meet the Triumvirate once more. Tell them to beware of the white-eyed demons. The Demon King may send them north before winter's end to take the city, though Ethrang may have killed most of them for now. He told us quite a tale in the tunnel. They multiply rapidly and may be used for assassinations. I'm afraid Banfar is lost, but the citizens are safe, thanks to our wily friend. They are enroute to Toron. Come winter's end, all able fighters will meet in the capital for the Last Battle."

Rake nodded after each instruction then took another bite of stew. "Yes, Sir. Did you know a group of ogres came through here a week ago? They were each as big as a house. One wanted to eat me, but the leader said no."

"Yes, we know them," Chip laughed. "We are the ones who told them to leave Darkwood. They should come in handy in the Last Battle."

"They are very strong," Ethrang added. "I would know."

Rake looked at him quizzically, then turned back to Chip. "I wouldn't want to fight them. They gave me your message, and I escorted them to the Triumvirate. That caused quite a stir in Yucan. I understand they will travel by ship to the Wizard's Guild." He paused. "Can I ask what you found in Darkwood? I've been studying the forest for years, Sir."

"It's everything you thought and worse. Monkeys, snakes, poisonous spiders, a Yagr, two-headed wolves, four-armed apes, ogres, and more. The witches put every nasty thing they could find in there."

"I'm happy you made it out," Rake said. "To be honest, I was going to leave tomorrow. Then again, I've been saying that every day, Sir."

"We are grateful you stayed." The boy stood up. "We walked through the night, so I am going to sleep. At dawn, we set off to continue our quest...Sir."

"Good night, Sirs and Madams."

Everyone retired early in the tents provided. Chip slept like the dead with Chase and Ethrang in a tent provided by the former servants.

The morning dawned cold but clear, and they bid farewell to Kylo and the Lost Ones. Xander repeated his instructions to Rake, and then everyone thanked the tracker and rode west on the unicorns. Chip felt a growing sense of urgency he couldn't explain. He used his magic again and confirmed the pull still wanted him to go west.

They took two days to reach the road running parallel to the Lumber River, sleeping in the tents provided. The river had iced over, so the traders used the road, their wagons loaded with all manner of goods, but otherwise, there were few travellers.

"This is where I head south," Blade said without preamble.

They all looked at him. "You should join us in Toron. We need someone like you," Garth said.

The weapons expert shook his head. "I cannot go closer to the Light Elves. My betrayal is unforgivable. I have killed countless of my kin. There is no redemption for me. I can only do good deeds to help you. My life is forfeit."

"The Creator will decide that, not you. Good luck in your task... my friend. It has been an honour." Garth Stone extended his hand, and the Dark Elf clasped it, looking into his eyes.

"The honour is mine, my friend."

The others said farewell and watched as he walked across the ice-covered river on foot. He reached the Great Plains and started jogging towards the southern horizon. The Dark Elf shrunk into a speck, and Blade was gone.

Garth Stone stared after him.

Chip used his magic and pulled out the orb. "It's pulling me slightly northwest, which is the exact direction of the road."

"It looks like we are headed to Northguard, the capital of the Dwarf Kingdom," Xander stated. "Maybe it wants us to pass through, yet there is nothing beyond but snowy mountains and the Western Ocean."

"Let's find out," Chip said, spurring the unicorns on at a faster pace, feeling his sense of urgency growing. He felt the pull weakening, which meant they were getting close, or the orb was running out of power. He hoped it was the former.

The companions spent the next three days making good speed. At night, they stayed in village inns along the road, which were mostly empty. They were down to six wizards, two trolls, four Protectors, and Dora. Everyone had their own unicorn, with two more used for supplies.

Chip marvelled at the comfort of a bed and enjoyed a nice warm bath with Eleanor. Dora decided to hang out with Chase, who initially appeared shy, but she set him at ease, and soon they were making silly jokes. The daughter of the former High Witch constantly pointed out and commented on the new things she saw. Nobody could blame her. It was how Chip felt when he first left Vanalon. The boy chuckled to himself. It was how he felt when he first left the kitchens, the city, and finally, the valley. Garth always said to try something new. It was the spice of life.

As the sun set on the third day, they spied the dwarf capital, Northguard. The road ran straight into it. He confirmed with the Seeing Stone, which pointed towards the sturdy wood walls.

The gates were closed.

"That is odd," Xander remarked. "The gates are usually open in

Northguard. The dwarves are friendly, hospitable people who welcome traders and travellers. Then again, these are dark times."

The unicorns stopped a short distance from the gates, unwilling to travel further. The companions dismounted and removed their packs. Chip admitted he did not know how long he would be. Redmane made it clear the herd would stay nearby, however long it took. He touched his forehead to the unicorn's muzzle, and they reared once then departed.

The group approached the gate with Xander in the lead.

"Who goes there, kind folk?" A bearded dwarf raised his head over the wall.

"Grand Wizard Xander from the Guild and his friends. Is that you, Oaken?"

"Ha, it is indeed. It's been a long time, old friend. What brings you to our neck of the woods?"

The wizard paused a moment. "It's a long story, but one your king would like to hear."

Oaken's face turned sour. "Things here have changed of late, I'm afraid, but far be it from me to refuse the Grand Wizard. Open the gates!" he boomed.

There was a squeaking sound, and then the massive gates rolled open. The party walked through, and the road turned into wooden planks.

Oaken met them inside, vigorously shaking the wizard's hand. He was short but stout, with a rich red beard, and wore a checkered shirt tucked into his trousers. A short sword was sheathed at his waist. The dwarf had a jovial face with a gleam in his brown eyes. Xander made introductions. For Chip, he called him his apprentice. The boy knew he was being careful.

"Why the closed gates?" the wizard queried.

The dwarf's face turned downcast. "Orders from the new Regent, I'm afraid. As I said, things have changed."

"My goodness. When did this come about?"

"A couple of weeks ago."

"Who's the Regent? And what happened to King Lumbar?"

The dwarf's lips pursed. "Lumbar is very sick. The Regent's name is Scar, nephew to the king. He will succeed him."

"Scar? My goodness." Xander turned to the others. "Sometimes acts of kindness work against you. We showed mercy to Scar in Banfar, and now he has taken root here. I had no idea he was Lumbar's nephew. What illness does the king have? He's old but not that old."

Oaken shrugged. "Nobody knows, but he can't get out of bed. The dwarf council heard him name Scar Regent."

Xander's eyes narrowed. "Take me to this Regent."

"I have already been demoted from captain to gatekeeper. I'm only supposed to let tradespeople in. I will probably be banished for this. I don't even care. I will move to Yucan. Northguard is not the same."

"We will see about that." The wizard's face turned dark. "Lead the way."

Chip knew the dwarves were master craftspeople specializing in wood, but the city was a sight to behold. They travelled down a plank road between large wooden buildings. Many were carpentry shops, but some were dance or beer halls. The sounds of violin music and boisterous laughter floated on the night air. Dwarves bustled about wearing plaid clothes while the females accompanied them in beautiful dresses. The workmanship on the log cabins and timber frame structures was of the highest quality. Many had elaborate wood decks, railings, and overhangs.

Oaken walked down the road, exchanging greetings with various people, all in a jolly manner. It looked like dwarves, even when depressed, appeared happy. They turned to a large square with a gorgeous frozen fountain and headed for a monstrous wood structure at the end of the road. It was a wooden palace covered with exquisite carvings of forest animals and visages of dwarf kings. Stairs led to two massive doors with large brass knobs. They were made of logs expertly fitted together.

Two guards stood at either end of the entrance. One stepped in their way.

"State your business."

"I'm bringing guests to see the Regent," Oaken said.

"The Regent sees no guests. Only tradespeople may enter the city. Nobody enters the palace."

Xander took a step. "I am the Grand Wizard and will see the Regent."

The other guard moved forward. "He said no one enters. We don't care who..."

Chip pushed between them, seizing his magic. He was tired of the games foolish rulers played. The boy flicked his hand, and both guards flew to the sides, where he froze them in place.

The Guardian removed the Seeing Stone and felt a weak pull towards the palace. He turned to the others. "I don't know how it's possible, but it says to go inside."

"Then let's do that," Xander said, giving him a nod. "You first."

Chip grabbed both brass knobs with his Power and pulled the great doors open. The others fanned out behind him. He strode forward into a massive hall. The woodwork was beyond anything he had ever seen. Two balconies with finely wrought balustrades encircled the cavernous room. They were attached to soaring pillars comprised of large tree trunks. Animal carvings covered them from top to bottom. Seamless wide-plank hardwood flooring led up to an elaborate dais. The stained-glass windows shone light onto a detailed throne of breathtaking beauty made from what appeared to be a solid piece of wood.

The dwarf Scar sat on it.

"What is the meaning of this?" he boomed in a loud, deep voice. The dwarf's red hair stuck out in all directions, and he looked tiny on the absurdly large throne. A long scar ran from his ear to the corner of his mouth. "Guards! Get the High Mages." A dwarf soldier standing to the side in silver armour ran behind the throne.

Chip did not bother answering. He pulled out the orb and felt a very weak pull downwards. Then it vanished.

The orb that created the Great Forget was out of power.

He stared in disbelief, looking at the empty Seeing Stone. To the dwarf Regent, it must have looked like he was holding nothing.

The boy turned to the others. "Its power is gone. The last signal was to go down. They are somehow beneath us."

"How is that possible?" Eleanor said.

"What are you doing here?" Scar screamed. "I am the Regent. You will answer me!"

The Guardian turned to the dwarf. "I do not answer to you. Where is the king of the dwarves?" He magnified his voice with Power.

A flurry of footsteps sounded, and a dozen mages in blue robes spread out on the first balcony.

"Grand Wizard Xander, it has been a long time," one of the mages said, looking over the short balcony. He looked to be the oldest with a long white beard.

"Ah, Treewood, it is good to see you. Where is King Lumbar? We wish to speak with him."

The dwarf mage's face took on a sad look. "I'm afraid he is gravely ill. He cannot speak. The Regent rules in his place."

"That's right," Scar shouted. His feet could not touch the ground, so he hopped off the throne, wagging a finger.

"I am the next Dwarf King."

Guards in armour ran into the room and lined up on either side, weapons drawn. "You made a mistake coming here, wizard. You will now pay for the numerous crimes you committed in Banfar." The veins throbbed in the dwarf's head, and his face turned bright red.

"I banished you from Banfar for treason," Xander said calmly. "You allowed the cults to flourish, turned a blind eye to thievery and murder, and padded your pockets with bribes. I stripped you of your title of Keeper, and now I renounce your title as Regent."

The dwarf sputtered, bits of phlegm dripping onto his red beard. "How...dare you! You have no authority in the Dwarf Kingdom. I sentence you to death for the murder of Banfar citizens. This red-eyed boy won't save you this time."

Chip stepped forward, eyes blazing. "I am the Guardian of the

Races, second only to High King Dominor and High Wizard Balor. I uphold Grand Wizard Xander's proclamation. I strip you of your title as Regent. Now, take me to King Lumbar."

Scar stood on the dais, face red. He looked at the guards and mages. "I command you to seize them!" His eyes blazed a weak blue.

The old mage with the white beard looked at Xander. "I'm sorry." The High Mages lifted their hands, eyes flaring to life. All were Blues.

Chip threw a red shield around everyone as they broke through their Walls and linked with him. The dwarves unleashed at the same time. Ropes of blue fire struck the shield, but it held. Chip pulled in more Power and advanced upon the Regent.

Scar stared in shock. "How is that possible?"

"I have grown stronger," Chip said simply. He reached out and squeezed the dwarf with a hand of air. Scar's feet left the ground as he sailed across the room to hover before the boy. Red coils of Power swirled across Chip's body. The dwarf sent his weak blue magic into the Guardian, but it had no effect. Then his Power sputtered out, replaced by sheer terror.

"Tell them to stop!" Chip commanded in a thunderous voice.

Scar nodded, and a wet stain appeared on his breeches. "Please don't hurt me." He looked up at the balcony. "I command you to stop."

Treewood lowered his hands, followed by the others. The old dwarf stared at Chip with wonder and then relief. It was clear he did not want to hurt them.

"Take me to the king of the dwarves." He dropped Scar to the floor.

The Regent righted himself and turned around. "Follow me." He scurried forward, casting fearful looks over his shoulder.

Chip released the shield but not his magic. The guards let them pass, faces white. Scar went to an ornate wooden door behind the throne and led them down a short hall to another door with a carved emblem of two crossed double-sided axes. Two guards stood on either side, staring in wonder.

The Regent opened the door to reveal a bedroom with rich wainscotting running from floor to coffered ceiling. A fire burned brightly in the hearth. At the side of the room stood a four-poster bed holding an old dwarf with a thin face. The sound of his raspy breathing was audible.

Scar pointed. "There lies King Lumbar, but he cannot speak. He has named me Regent."

Chip waved him out of the way and stood beside the bed. It was clear the old dwarf did not have long to live. He sent his magic gently into the king, searching for his ailment. Not even he could cure someone of old age. He sensed a degradation of the organs and brain. Even as he probed, the king's breath rattled in his throat. He was about to withdraw his Power, but something about his blood gave the boy pause. It was something that shouldn't be there. He ran his magic up and down the dwarf's veins, sensing a foreign substance.

Chip's eyes widened. "Daria, come here please." The troll mage walked forward, her yellow eyes blazing. "Look at his blood."

She sent her magic into the king's body and turned to him in surprise. "He has been poisoned."

Scar looked around nervously then edged towards the door.

"Keep him here," Chip said to the others, glancing at the Regent. He turned back to Daria. "Can you heal him?"

For once she looked uncertain. "I do not know. He is on the cusp of death. I will try."

Chip watched as she pulled the poison out of his veins, burning it away with her magic. The king gasped and started to choke. She immediately began healing his organs, strengthening the weakened tissues. The old dwarf started to shake.

"His body is so used to the poison that it is going into shock," she said with concern. She sent soothing Power into his brain, pulling out the heat and inflammation. He fought her, making jerking motions.

And then his heart stopped.

The king's eyes stared unseeing at his beautiful wooden ceiling.

"Keep his heart beating while I repair his veins," she ordered.

Chip felt a flutter of anxiety, knowing how high the stakes were, and made the dwarf's heart beat with his magic. He had trained for this in the Wizard's Guild and real life. He pumped air into the old dwarf's lungs. The king's heart was fragile, so Chip strengthened its fibres and tissues, improving its function. Beads of sweat appeared on his forehead.

Daria delved deep into the old man's brain, increasing blow flow into the weak areas and repairing blood vessels. It was similar to how she had cured Kylo's sister of mental illness. Her dexterity and knowledge were something to behold.

She healed his skin and bones, restoring him to his health before the illness. "Release your magic. He must breathe on his own." Chip withdrew.

Lumbar now looked like a vibrant older man, yet he remained still, not breathing.

The king of the dwarves was dead.

Chip sent a last burst of magic into his heart, a desperate measure to make it beat one more time.

King Lumbar gasped, drawing in life, heart beating on its own. His eyes opened in shock. Colour returned to his skin. He drew in full, deep breaths.

The dwarf looked at his hands, opening and closing them. He swiveled his head to stare at everyone, his bright eyes narrowing in confusion.

"What happened? Who are you?"

Chip smiled, wiping his brow. "I am the Guardian of the Races. I have come to seek the aid of the dwarves in the Last Battle. I also have some questions."

King Lumbar sat up and noticed Scar. Recognition crossed his features. "You!" He pointed. "I remember now. You poisoned me!" His face contorted with rage.

Scar backed up, but Oaken blocked his way. "No, I would never. I tried to help..."

"Your teas made me sick. I couldn't think straight. Then I became addicted. You withheld them until I named you Regent."

Ethrang raised his hand. "The drug Wack from Banfar can be

altered to have those effects. You get addicted to it until it kills you. People think you died from drug use, but really it's poison."

"You came from Banfar," the king accused. "You are a disgrace to your people. I sentence you to death for treason."

"I didn't do it," Scar protested. "You are my uncle. I would never do such a thing."

"Then show me your memories, now!" he commanded.

The former Regent looked like a cornered rat. "I..." Then, his face twisted evilly. "I will kill you!" he screamed, and his eyes flared a weak blue. Scar started to raise his hands, but a short sword arced through his neck, decapitating him.

Oaken stood behind him, bloody sword in hand. The headless body slumped to the ground. "I've wanted to do that for a long time."

The king nodded in approval. "So ends the reign of Regent Scar. I am embarrassed he is of my bloodline." He turned to the others. "Thank you. Ah, Xander, well met, old friend. What brings you to my kingdom?"

"King Lumbar." The wizard bowed. He made introductions for those gathered in the room. The old dwarf's eyes widened at Chip's titles. "We need your assistance on a matter of the utmost importance."

"I am all ears."

"We are here to find the missing Light Elves."

A look passed across the king's face, but he covered it quickly. "How could I possibly help with that?" The old dwarf looked down at his hands.

Chip had learned to read the signs of someone covering up. He went to one knee and stared into the king's eyes, releasing his magic. "Please, we need your help. The Seeing Stone led us here to find the Light Elves."

The Dwarf King looked into the boy's green eyes, and his face grew haunted. "I...I cannot...break oath."

"Oaths are sacred, I understand, but everyone's lives are at stake. Here, let me show you." Chip's eyes flared, and he inserted his presence into the dwarf's mind, revealing his memories. He instinctually trusted the old man and showed him the entire quest, culminating in the Seeing Stone leading them to the Dwarf Kingdom. The orphan withdrew his presence and magic. Lumbar stared at him with mixed emotions.

Chip held the king's hand. "We must find the Light Elves to have any chance in the Last Battle." He paused. "King Luminor found me as a babe and left me at the gates of Vanalon." The boy looked at him earnestly. "He did it for a reason. I need to know why. I yearn to know where I came from." Chip's eyes grew wet as he released a flood of emotions that had been pent up for so long. "Please, tell me where the Light Elves are."

King Lumbar sat quietly, staring at the boy. Tears formed in his rich brown eyes. "My father, Lumber, was good friends with Luminor. They would trade goods and send delegations of mages to train with each other." The old dwarf chuckled, eyes distant. "He even developed a palette for wine. It was the finest in the world." His face grew sad. "My father was only a Brown Level and died two millennia ago. I outlive him." The king's eyes flashed a powerful blue, and then he released his magic. "After the Great Battle, Luminor made him swear an oath, one that each generation must carry. That oath binds me." He looked at the orphan's anxious face. "Dwarves don't break oaths, so I cannot tell you where they are, even given the gravity of the situation."

Chip Oathbinder hung his head.

"But I can show you."

The Guardian's head snapped up, eyes full of hope.

King Lumbar leapt off the bed, looking at his limbs. "I feel great. Come, I will show you what you seek." He threw on a plush robe and slippers then ushered them out of the room.

The High Mages and guards had gathered in the hall.

"King Lumber!" cried Treewood. "I cannot believe it!" Relief flooded the old mage as he embraced his king.

"Believe it, old friend," Lumbar laughed. "The traitor Scar is dead. Do something with the body, will you? I don't want his filth to stain my chambers a moment longer." The mage signalled for the guards to remove the corpse. "I am back, and we have much to do. These are my honoured guests. Give them whatever they need for as long as they need. First, I must show them something."

Treewood put his hand on Xander's shoulder. "No hard feelings?"

"None," the wizard replied with a genuine smile.

"Come, my new guests," Lumbar urged. "The rest of you stay here."

He led the visitors down the hall between the guards and mages, who patted him on the back and let out boisterous cheers. It was clear he was a well-loved king. Their jolly faces made Chip smile amidst his growing anticipation.

They turned down several flights of wood stairs, running their hands in awe over the beautifully sculpted railings. Finely carved wood statues sat on pedestals or in recessed alcoves as they descended.

The stairs finally ended in a long hall with a plain hardwood floor. He waved his hand over a locked door at the end, his eyes briefly flashing blue. From there, the palace became stone, and they went down three more flights before coming to an iron door. The king paused again, waving his hand, and they entered a dusty stone hall. He lit a torch with his magic and moved to a point midway down the hall.

The king faced the wall of stone and stopped. "You are the only ones ever to see this." He passed the torch to Garth and crossed his arms, making Chip think of the double axe symbol. Lumbar's eyes shone a bright blue, and he separated them. A line of blue fire appeared in the wall, tracing out two stone doors. They swivelled inward, revealing steps. The king sent a blue ball of light into the room, then stepped aside, looking at the Guardian.

"Enter, Light Seeker."

Chip nodded, his face full of wonder. He walked down seven stone steps into a small room and caught his breath.

Before him, on an ancient stone table, rested the Orb of Power.

It pulsated with a rich, white light.

The dragon egg at his waist began to hum.

The boy moved closer, mesmerized. He knew it was the orb that Killian had stolen from the Red-Eyed King. It was the orb that Xander had stolen back and his father, Arkan, had used to erect the barrier. It was the orb that disappeared with the Light Elves.

Chip Oathbinder spun around, the dragon egg humming louder.

"The Light Elves are inside the Orb of Power."

King Lumbar smiled, saying nothing.

The others crowded into the room.

"How is that possible?" Chase asked, completely confused.

Xander stared at the orb with a look of recognition and sadness. "The orb contains a power none of us understand. It is possible." His eyes grew wet. "My father used this object to erect the barrier. That feat likely pales in comparison to the Great Forget. This orb still has much power, and the Light Elves used it to hide themselves from the world."

"So what are we going to do?" Chase asked.

Chip stared at his best friend. "Now, I garner the allegiance of the Light Elves and bring them back into the world. Now, I go inside and birth a dragon. Now, I find out who my parents are."

"And then?" Chase asked. Chip paused, and his face hardened.

"And then I meet the Red-Eyed King."

The egg at his waist started vibrating.

The tall boy's eyes widened. "And after that?"

"Then, my friend, we fight the Last Battle." Chip's eyes blazed red.

"Now you're talking!"

The boy looked at the king of the dwarves. "Will you swear allegiance and join us?"

King Lumbar stared at the Guardian of the Races. "The dwarves stand with the Light Elves. If you acquire their allegiance, you have ours."

Chip nodded and turned back to the orb. He touched the sphere with his magic. The boy gasped in wonder and then fear.

He spun around. "They know I am here. I sense resistance. I can only take some of you." He looked at Xander. "The Light Elves all have magic, so I believe I can bring all the magic wielders, but we must hurry."

"The elves have no love of trolls. I will stay here," Daria said. One Eye nodded in agreement.

"I will also stay and keep an eye on the Protectors," Dora added, glancing at Chase, who blushed.

Garth Stone looked at the king. "May I help ready the dwarven army in case they are needed, King Lumbar?"

"Gladly, the dwarves have softened since the Great Battle three millennia ago." The king smiled.

"It's settled then," Xander said.

"Stay here for as long as it takes," Chip said, suddenly feeling emotional. The wizards quickly embraced those remaining behind and faced the Orb of Power. Xander handed off his wooden staff to Garth Stone.

"May the creator shine on you," King Lumbar intoned. The Protectors, Dora, and the trolls repeated the phrase.

The dragon egg hummed louder.

The Queen of Vanalon, the Grand Wizard, the shapeshifter, and the twins turned to Chip.

The boy smoothed his red cloak and took a deep breath.

The Guardian of the Races sent his magic into the orb. He felt a strong resistance and pushed back hard, gritting his teeth. "They are trying to keep us out. Link with me."

The wizards did so, and he forced the talisman to open.

He would not be denied.

The Orb of Power expanded into a sphere wide enough for them to enter side by side.

Chip Oathbinder and the five wizards walked into the light.

END OF VOLUME SEVEN.

. . .

IF YOU ENJOYED READING THIS, please leave a review on Amazon. It would be greatly appreciated.

Please visit my website: www.terryironwood.com

Type your email address at the bottom of the page to be notified of my next book launch and other important news. I do not send a regular newsletter.

I have added a free short story prequel called "Weapons Master" in the upper right corner of my website. It is Garth Stone's backstory.

The Orphan's Quest audiobook with special effects by the renowned narrator Nigel Peever is available on Audible.

Volume Eight: Last Battle – May 2025.

I hope you enjoyed Volume 7: Light Seeker. Be sure to look out for the epic conclusion in Volume 8: Last Battle.

The Great Forget Fantasy Series:

Volume 1: Orphan's Quest

Volume 2: Defenders of Hope

Volume 3: A Dim World

Volume 4: Guardian

Volume 5: Wizard's Guild

Volume 6: Stone Kingdom

Volume 7: Light Seeker

Volume 8: Last Battle (Coming May 2025)

Acknowledgements

I offer my heartfelt thanks to my family and friends, who provided invaluable support, wisdom, and encouragement. You know who you are. I especially want to mention Kevin C., Steve S., and Ward C., who went above and beyond.

I am delighted to work with my editor, Jason Letts from Imbue Editing, who continues to improve my writing.

Last, and certainly not least, I wish to thank an orphan, Chip, for taking me on his quest.

Many thanks,

Terry Ironwood

ABOUT THE AUTHOR

Terry Ironwood resides with his family. He holds multiple university degrees and is interested in the science of self-improvement. He is equally fascinated with physics and spirituality. Terry believes in an 'attitude of gratitude' and is grateful he can write full-time. His dream is to help others reach their full potential.